THE
RECKONING

CLÁR NÍ CHONGHAILE

Legend Press Ltd, 107-111 Fleet Street, London, EC4A 2AB
info@legend-paperbooks.co.uk | www.legendpress.co.uk

Contents © Clár Ní Chonghaile 2018
The right of the above author to be identified as the author of this work has
been asserted in accordance with the Copyright, Designs and Patents Act
1988. British Library Cataloguing in Publication Data available.

Print ISBN 978-1-78719814-2
Ebook ISBN 978-1-78719813-5
Set in Times. Printing managed by Jellyfish Solutions Ltd
Cover design by Anna Green | www.siulendesign.com

Clár Ní Chonghaile was born in London but grew up in An Spidéal, County Galway. She left Ireland aged 19 to join Reuters in London as a graduate trainee journalist. Clár has been a reporter and editor for over 20 years, living and working in Spain, France, the Ivory Coast, Senegal and Kenya.

She now lives in St Albans, England, with her husband and two daughters. Her debut novel, *Fractured*, was published by Legend Press in 2016 and her second novel, *Rain Falls on Everyone*, was published in 2017.

Visit Clár at
clarnichonghaile.wordpress.com
or on Twitter
@clarnic

To David, Lucy and Rachel

CHAPTER 1

It does not feel quite right to be sipping wine as I try to figure out if I killed a man. Or, perhaps more accurately, if I drove two men to their deaths. I fear wine is not up to the task. After a lifetime of loyalty to Sauvignon Blanc, I have opted for a 'ripe and bold' South African red. I bought it partly because I liked the description on the label – this wine sounds like me, although I am, now, more ripe than bold – but mostly to annoy the sweaty, limp-haired lady in the wine shop in Caen. *Quelle horreur! L'Anglaise is not buying French wine. In France!* But however bold, even this wine does not, in my opinion, have the gravitas needed for what I am trying to do. I forgot to buy whiskey from the scowling crone and so wine will have to do.

In any case, at my age, whiskey might finally prove my equal. I've always won our battles before, still standing as the bottle spun off the table and onto the floor, empty, exhausted, submissive at last. I was proud of my prowess as a drinker. It was something I worked hard at, a professional badge of honour. But nowadays, I'm not sure I wouldn't end up on the floor myself, my old carcass rattling noisily onto the flagstones like bones cast down by wrinkle-stitched shamans predicting the future. Of all the indignities of old age, not being able to hold my drink bothers me most. Not least because of the pure maliciousness of it. Old age is precisely when one has the greatest need to be a functioning drunk all the livelong day. The irony distresses and delights me in equal measure.

You know where I am because I wrote to you the day before I left, asking you to join me. But I do not really believe you will come, Diane. To be crude, what's in it for you? I know why *I* am here. You might say it's an odd fancy, the product of an age-addled mind that's beginning to misfire, but I think I might be able to unearth the beginning, the end and most importantly the middle of my story in this place. Even though this is the first time I have set foot in Lion-sur-Mer.

I could have chosen another town. This coast is pimpled with human acne – bars, restaurants, nondescript apartments with bright towels hanging over the balcony rails like flags of convenience. But Lion-sur-Mer is *his* beach and I liked the absurdity of the name. Lion on the sea. The king of the savannah, adrift and lost in the waves. An aptly fantastical Narnia name for a place that wears the horror of its past so lightly. The welcome booklet on the hall table of this pastel-primped cottage tells me the name may have come from some lion-shaped rocks or reefs. That is too mundane for my liking. I want to imagine a real lion striding down the beach with that peculiarly slow motion, flip-footed grace that all felines have. Where did he come from, this regal sea lion? Who knows? There are more things in heaven and earth, as my mother used to sigh, when she did not know what else to say. If such a thing is true anywhere, it must be true here, where the unthinkable was thought, the undoable done and where the ground still bears the scars of a war that did not know it was not supposed to be. Pockmarked and gutted, the grass and wildflowers do their best to blur the edges, but like wreaths on a coffin, they only draw the eye to the truth.

Enough of fantasies. Shall I tell you what I see before me right now? Shall I fool myself into believing you will read this letter, be transported beyond anger by my masterful prose and pack your bags to come and join me? Why not? I have all the time in the world now to indulge the wildest, most unfounded dreams. At least until the wine, bread and cheese run out and the sand stops trickling through the hourglass of my brain. I've never set much store by fad diets with their restrictions, deadlines and unreal expectations but I may have finally found the perfect diet for me: eat this food and then be done. I like its simplicity. I will dream my fantasies as long as I can, as long as there is some cerebral activity to spark these visions into life.

I have dragged a chair and table to the hawthorn hedge that marks the boundary between this sun-freckled garden and the bedazzling beach. The chair is upholstered in white with stripes in the same shade of peppermint green as the wooden shutters on the house: more evidence of the primly perfectionist hand that has made this cottage so insufferably flawless. I am sitting behind the low, wooden gate, a wine glass in my hand and sunglasses protecting my watery eyes from the glare of the sun setting to my left. The beach is nearly empty, just a few families packing up buckets, spades, deckchairs, parasols and all the accoutrements that illustrate just why that word has to be French, even in English. Do you really need a wine bucket on a beach? I fancy I am observing without being observed. It is what I do best.

The sand still bears the day's imprint – a deep hole hacked into being by querulous, bronze-limbed children, a shallow valley where an achingly beautiful boy and a long-limbed girl lay wrapped around each other like amorous snakes for the best part of the afternoon, a moonscape of craters where brash, sure-footed men played bombastic volleyball. But the sea is coming now to make everything smooth and fresh once again, as it did, no doubt, over 50 years ago, after Robert and all the others staggered through the waves and onto the sand. The sea is the ultimate pardoner. Given time, it will remove all traces of our spilt blood, broken limbs, shattered brains and deflated bodies. If only all relics of our lives could be washed away so easily.

The received wisdom is that people like me, writers and artists, all of us dreamers, are on a quest for immortality, desperate to leave an eternal mark on the world so that when we die, our names and ideas will live on. Maybe I did subscribe to that particular vanity once. But now, I can honestly say that I would rather my footprints be kissed into oblivion by the white-flecked lips of the sea. I crave obliteration. There has been too much pain and it delights me to know that when I am gone, at least some of it will stop. There is a selfishness to this too, of course. Me, me, me. What *I* want. Still, it will amuse you, Diane, to know that I have fallen foul of that age-old axiom: be careful what you wish for. You'd think I'd have learnt that lesson over the years. I didn't think obliteration could be partial. I, the ultimate creative, lacked imagination.

I know you'll find it hard to believe but I haven't always been so self-obsessed. There was a time, when your father was still here in body and mind, that I felt part of something bigger. We three were a story that I believed was everlasting and irrefutable. Our lives mattered because they slotted into all the other lives to form part of the train track of endlessly improving humanity. In essence, I believed that love conferred immortality. Today, I struggle to fathom such naiveté. What was I thinking? I do not believe in time as a healer but it has certainly cured me of *that* bullshit.

Sorry, I shouldn't be profane. I shouldn't be cynical. I shouldn't be *here* and I certainly shouldn't be speaking to you – albeit through a letter – after what I did. I shouldn't be alive when he isn't. And the others, all the others, lurking like restless, can-kicking teens on the wasteland between this world and its reflections. Where is the justice, you might wonder? And I would have to agree. Why has the universe kept me around given what I have done and failed to do? But justice is another of the many things I no longer believe in. Justice and time or rather, to be precise, linear time. I don't believe in redemption and causality either. I am not even sure

I believe in myself in any substantial, meaningful way. Do I believe in you? As an existence, certainly. I know you exist. And then what?

After I arrived here today in a steaming, sun-baked coach, I dumped my suitcase and typewriter and took a stroll around town before heading along a lane inland. I might come across as cold-hearted and cynical, and that's probably the best you could say, but I can still, somewhat to my own surprise, fall prey to a touch of the whimsy. I thought I might feel something if I walked into France from the coast, the way Robert and the other soldiers did more than half a century ago.

The air was alive with the crackling, end-of-day heat that throbs sullenly along silent countryside roads. I moved slowly, as I imagined they did, weighed down by their soaked kit – the water bottles, ammunition pouches, spades and all the other tools needed to sustain life and dole out death. The hedgerows extended haughtily above me, as they must have towered above your father. They loom out of built-up earth banks; dense lattices of hawthorn, bramble, hazel and blackthorn, shading the labyrinthine paths where I imagine soldiers' souls still roam. Do you believe in parallel universes, Diane? I do. Call it my opium.

What do the men of Britain's Second Army make of us all now in the final years of a century that at one point seemed intent on imploding well before reaching a gentle old age? Are they still squatting here, smoking cigarettes and discussing how the world has moved on without them? As I walked along the hedgerows, I imagined what they might be saying on the other side of the looking glass, in that place where the only time is the present. Humour me, Diane. You may not believe it but I am at my most truthful when I am making things up.

So here, I present to you, your father, Private Robert Stirling, in conversation.

Private D. Myers: It's like we never existed. Or maybe what I'm trying to say is, what was the point?

Private R. Stirling: Good God, Dan. Are you still going on about a point? How many times do I have to tell you? There was no point. The war started, the war was fought, the war ended. We were unlucky. End of.

Private D. Myers: *You* weren't unlucky. *You* survived. You coulda seen all the rest, all the things that happened so fast and that made what went on here seem so… out of place. Like we was dinosaurs, or something.

Private R. Stirling: I'm dead, aren't I? Isn't that enough for you? What does it matter how or where? I didn't see much more than you, remember? Okay, I saw that life could go back to normal or something like normal. It was all still there: hot dinners, clean sheets, living to be happy instead of just trying not to die, thinking your own thoughts. It was all still there like a giant slap in the face. I didn't think it could be possible. And perhaps it shouldn't have been. Perhaps that was my whole problem in the end. So, yes, I stuck around a bit longer. But it's not like I got to see Elvis, the Beatles, the moon landing, any of that. I'm here with you, dammit. The war killed me, same as the rest of you.

Private D. Myers: Fair enough, keep your knickers on. Still, d'you get what I mean? All those things you just said and all happening just a few years later. It's like a big two-fingers-up to us.

Private R. Stirling: Have you been hitting the Calva too hard again, Dan? You're all over the place this afternoon.

Private D. Myers: I'm just saying it's like we fought on a different planet. Or in the Dark Ages or something. If all those things were around the corner, how'd we get beaten by hedges? Blown up on beaches? What the hell made us think crossing the sea and running up the bloody sand into the arms of the waiting Nazis was a good idea?

Private R. Stirling: To be fair, Dan, *we* never thought that. We were just doing what we were told. Very little thinking involved at all. But all the same you might have a point, Danny boy. And speaking of planets let me tell you something else that'll fry that brandy-soaked brain of yours. They've discovered these black holes in space now. Albert Einstein imagined them first but they only named them in the 60s. They are literally nothing, a vacuum where all matter has collapsed in on itself, like that bridge we blew up near Caen, right? The pull of gravity inside these black holes is so damn strong even light can't escape. They're like huge magnets, sucking everything in. They come in different sizes, see, and are found in loads of galaxies but the biggest ones are called supermassive black holes. It got me thinking. Maybe the war was a kind of supermassive black hole? It destroyed everything and then became invisible because not even light could escape. Sure, we laughed and joked because nothing can ever be totally, utterly awful. Not for six years anyhow. But underneath and at its core, it was all horror, running deep and sticky through all the days. Maybe the war didn't end. Maybe it collapsed or caved in so that everything was sucked away. From one day to the next, it was gone.

Private D. Myers: Jesus, mate. I was just saying ain't time strange. What d'you have to go on about outer space for? You know I ain't got your smarts. Fuck's sake.

There's a fresh piece of writing, Diane, just for you. Your father *was* something of a science buff. He was endlessly and sometimes annoyingly curious; he couldn't see a beautiful night sky for the individual stars and he couldn't see those without trying to name the constellations. I sometimes think it was that desire to put a name to everything that was his undoing. Some things can't and shouldn't be named. Naming confers legitimacy and that's not always wise. Robert fell apart when he realised there was no name for what he'd seen. No name for what he'd done. Even if there had been, he wouldn't have been allowed to use it.

I suppose I'm picking up where he left off. I want to find

the perfect words to describe what happened to him and to us. I've come here to find those words and to look for the pieces of your father that were missing when he came back at the end of those six sodden years when time broke its leash and ran wild across the world, while simultaneously standing still like smoke in the air. Time was the bullet speeding towards you as you hid behind a hedge. You didn't know the end was coming until that infinite moment between your realisation and the bullet's impact. The infinite and finite twisted around each other like yin and yang. That nanoscopic moment was all and everything, and time was standing very still and very small for you, but also running out very fast.

I imagine you are already rolling your eyes. You know only too well that I am using your father to lure you to this place where, of course, you will not find him, only me. And why should you do that when I gave up my right to see you? It doesn't matter that I thought I was saving my life and yours. And is that even true? They say hindsight is 20/20 but memory is not. When we look back through time, our mind's eye is neither clear nor honest. Our gaze is refracted through so many bitter thoughts, so many regrets, both past and present, so many red-faced justifications that it bends and warps until the memory it uncovers bears as much resemblance to what happened as our reflections in crazy mirrors at funfairs. Do they still have those? I used to like them.

All too often, we speak of our powers of recall as if they were independent and neutral. But memory is as much about selection as recollection. We create our perfect selves through the stories we tell every day and we use our memories to embellish this ideal image. The very act of remembrance has motive, as does everything we do. Memories are not static – we recreate them every time we revisit them. We remake them, using fresh information on behalf of the person we have become.

For years, I believed I gave you up to save you and to save my sanity. I am not so brazen that I would entirely deny my own interest. I am self-aware enough to know that I did it partly for myself. Maybe even mostly for myself. But not solely. I have told myself this version of what happened so often, in those measureless hours before dawn, that it feels real. But what if the original memory was false? What if what I told myself on the day I gave you up was false? I am perfectly capable of lying to myself. And I am perfectly capable of believing my own lies, if I want to. I might've been a journalist for years but I am also a writer of fiction and if there is one thing I have learned through practicing both disciplines, it is that all facts are subjective. Especially the ones we believe are empirically true.

The woman I am now does not, or cannot, believe she is guilty of callous abandonment. But maybe even in that I am not being honest. If I don't feel guilty, why am I reaching out to you? There is a thread worth teasing there. Whatever guilt I may or may not feel I am woman enough to recognise that I *do* want your forgiveness. How crass, you will think. How very common to look for redemption as the door opens to that long night. How very crude to use pity as a lever to pry open your heart. Rest assured, Diane. I am not dying. At least, I am not dying any faster today than I was yesterday. Death is a constant presence at this point. I am 77 after all and just as the century is nearly done, so am I. We have both almost run our course. There will be no place for us in the new millennium and that is as it should be. But I do not have an immediate expiry date. Not yet.

I am not sure how my stay here ends. Part of me wants to slit my wrists and run wild through this tasteful cottage, spurting blood all over the cream sofas, rattan rugs and pale green walls like a balloon pirouetting wildly as the air screams out. I have a visceral, rage-filled desire to obliterate *l'ambiance rustique* so painstakingly created by the house-proud owner of this cottage. But that seems a bit overblown, even for me.

I'm going to pretend you're sitting here beside me. It's a tough assignment even for someone as well versed in the imaginary as me. Ten books under my belt but summoning up *your* image is almost too much for my powers of imagination. The last picture I saw was from Millie's wedding two years ago. It was a photograph in your local paper, the *Ham and High*. I'll tell you one of my secrets, Diane, but this is just a naughty peccadillo compared to others I will reveal later. Sometimes, I take the train into London and stop in West Hampstead. I wander slowly up to your neck of the woods, puffing my way past the gaudy money transfer outlets and stifling corner shops, up the hill until I get to the rarefied air of Hampstead. I always wonder if I will see you. To be honest, I'm not sure what I would do if I did. Duck into a doorway, probably.

The newspaper photograph was a little blurry but you looked good for almost 50. You wear your years lightly, as I have been told I do though past 70 there is a certain degree of inevitable decay no matter what you do. I'm going to assume nothing much has changed since then. I remember my early 50s, cruising along the flat of life, beyond the peaks and valleys of youth and not yet dodging the precipices of old age. Yours is a tranquil landscape.

You've not given in to grey hair and I am glad about that. When we met that one time, back in the 60s, I felt an irrational delight to see you had my fine, blonde hair. You wear glasses – you must've inherited your weak eyes from your father's side. Robert's parents both needed glasses though he said his mother was too vain to wear them. I'm sure he needed them too in his last year but by then, I don't think he wanted to see the world too clearly any more. I have my own pair now but I don't always wear them either. One doesn't always need to see everything.

I was delighted to see that photo – payback for years of anonymous snooping – but the image was disappointingly static and formal. A wedding pose. Your eyes are squinting, your smile is tight and fake as though you are fed up now with this mother-of-the-bride stuff. Even as a baby, you had a no-bullshit glare. It used to frighten me a little – I was thinner-skinned then – but the woman I am now rejoices in its memory. The photo, however, gives me no sense of fluidity. I cannot imagine your face in motion. What would you look like if you were here, staring at me through the shadow-shimmering rays of the dying sun? Would you have hate in your eyes and what would that even look like on you now? Do you hate me, Diane? I am genuinely curious. I have always been so quick to hate, so quick to condemn, so quick to deny love, at least since that awful September day 50 years ago. Are you like me? Or did you manage to preserve the optimism I felt back when I still believed that life could be perfect, that all things being equal life would, in fact, be perfect? Did the scales fall off your eyes too? Or is the final, fabulous irony the fact that I, Lina Rose, the acclaimed writer who 'wields her pen like a scalpel as she probes false prophets of naïve idealism and unfounded optimism', have a daughter who still believes in a benign universe despite everything?

When I said earlier that I was wondering if I had killed a man, or men, you probably thought I was being facetious. I was not. How can we possibly estimate our individual responsibility for any event that involves us? We would need the omniscience of a deity to know how our actions are seen by those they affect. Then we would need the calculus skills of a Leibniz to make sense of the infinite sequences and series that bring us to our defined limits. And then, on top of all that, we would need a Caroll-ian imagination. It's a tall order for any human, even the most rational and clear-sighted. I am neither of those things.

I was, of course, referring to your father. Primarily. I will tell you of the other man too but later. For now, the question is did I kill your father? Having dodged the bullets bending around these hedges, having survived the road to Paris and the push into Belgium and all the rest, did my big-eyed incompetence as a wife and my inexcusable inability to hear him bring about his end? Or was it 'just' the war? But that seems too pat. The war killed millions in its time and afterwards when overloaded brains exploded behind drawn curtains in poky bedrooms or on lonely moors where curlews carved the skies with their spiralling cries. Your father *was* among these casualties of war but that is not the whole story. And what a daft concept the whole story is anyway. As if our messy lives could be stitched together with a single thread.

The sun has gone now and it is getting chilly. Northern Europe will disappoint like that. This continent has no consistency. I am going inside to sit on one of those pristine cream sofas, under the faintly sinister eyes of the fake Degas ballerinas, bowing and arabesque-ing across the walls. I know that's not a word but I am a writer and a rebel and I will make up my own words if I damn well please. I might very well have to soon.

I have a story to tell you, Diane. It is my story and your story and the story of a century that remade the world like a supermassive black hole. When we reach the end, you will be the ultimate arbiter of whether it was worth your time. You will also sit in judgment on me and on the memories I reveal. I do not expect absolution but I must conclude that I yearn for forgiveness.

I will walk up to the main street to post this tomorrow morning. Finding your address was too easy for an ex-journalist like me. It begs the question: did you always want to be found? The next chapter will follow in a few days. I shall imagine myself as Dickens and you as my reader, agog for the next instalment of this fascinating serial. Modesty has never been my strongest quality and besides, I need to feel the heavy hand of time on my shoulder because it is there and it is not moving.

CHAPTER 2

You already know the bare bones of who I am despite… what shall I call it? Our estrangement? That will do although you are right: it does not lay enough of the blame at my door but I can think of nothing better. You might choose other words but since I am telling this tale, I get to choose. You would narrate another story and both versions would be true. That is the beauty and tragedy of the human condition.

When I started as a journalist, I thought there was a definitive truth that could be unearthed by thoroughly researching a topic and tirelessly interviewing witnesses. But over the years, I have realised that no two people see the same event in the same way. What we believe shapes what we see as though there is a secret passageway from the frontal lobe with its reasoning capacities to the occipital lobe, which governs sight. Just as dogs only see blue, grey and yellow, it appears our vision is more limited than we would like to believe: we only see what we want to see or what we can bear to see. With any two versions of an event, neither is totally wrong and neither is necessarily right. What we know of life is a synthesis of multiple viewpoints.

The basic 'facts' of my life are public property, laid out in black and white on the dust jackets of my books. No mention of you, of course. I forfeited my right to claim you when I decided in 1947 to reinvent myself as a single woman. A woman without a past who no longer believed in the future but who could not bring herself to say the ultimate goodbye. That woman eventually wrote my novels, taking a naughty delight in wrong-footing readers. I am known for my plot twists and that tendency to obfuscate extends even to the short biography I have allowed my publishers to print: *Lina Rose was born in St Albans in 1920. After her husband died in 1947, she worked as a journalist for two decades before turning to fiction. Her first book,* Under the Canopy, *was published in 1976 and was translated into 15 languages. She has since written 10 novels. She lives in St Albans with her golden retriever, Sam.*

I don't have a golden retriever or any kind of dog. It just seemed like the natural end to that sentence. I could hardly write: *She lives in St Albans with her regrets and her rage, wondering if the daughter she gave up will ever forgive her and whether her husband killed himself because she didn't know how to hear his screams.*

Although, I suppose that might have lifted sales.

I know I shouldn't lie about my life. It is not only mine to lie about. Apart from betraying you, I am giving a bum steer to anyone who studies my work. That might sound arrogant. It is not. I am unapologetically clear-sighted when it comes to my professional achievements. Whatever you may think of me as your mother, you cannot deny my talent. I am proud of the essays, reportage and fiction I have produced and I am comfortable with the accolades bestowed on me. False modesty offends me enormously. It is another example of the destructive myopia that sees most of us drift through our lives without ever appreciating the import of our actions and inaction. I have no patience with that, not least because that is how I lived until your father died. No, let me be precise, at least here: until he killed himself.

Sometimes even I get caught up in my own fabrications. It has been a long time since I described Robert's death as a suicide. Those who knew us then are all dead and I've never felt anybody else needed to know the details. In truth, few care to ask. The isolating bubble of grief is remarkably indestructible. Even after many years have passed, few people will ask a widow to explain how her husband died. It must be an atavistic fear of contagion. I too was reluctant to speak the truth out loud. I told myself I was hiding his shame but I wonder if it was just mine.

My work has already been dissected many times and Lina Rose, the woman, is always brought into it. Of course, all fiction springs from the author's own experience – a moment, a glance, a random thought, the mystery of the counterfactual – but that does not mean it is true to that person's life. At best, the author's life adds authenticity but the work is by no means a mirror. It must not be, for if it were, the truth would never appear. It stuns me how few people understand this. They say they do but really, they are always looking for you inside the pages of your book.

Let's imagine it now: an earnest 20-year-old, a girl probably, sits in one of those dreadful circles that they favour in college tutorials. Maybe she's squeezed awkwardly into one of those old-fashioned wraparound single desks. Let's call her Brenda. It's her turn to speak. Maybe she's chosen to look at *Under the Canopy*. Let's say she has. I imagine she will call me Lina because she thinks she knows me. She's asked a question. She shifts in her uncomfortable seat, trying unsuccessfully to seem authoritative despite her absurd posture, and says:

"I read this as a novel of redemption. Gary's admission of his complicity in the Bình Hòa massacre, even though he was not physically present, Bao's realisation that his avowed neutrality was another form of cowardice and Sheila's acknowledgement that the horror of war gave her the emotional kick she needed to deal with a world that denied her very nature. I think these themes must have resonated for Lina when she wrote it in the mid-70s because she had returned to St Albans and was living a quiet life of reflection – a redemption of a sort, I suppose – after decades

of being on the frontlines of some of the most horrendous global events."

Brenda will think those things because that is what I said in the few interviews I gave before I retreated even further from the world. I said I came back to St Albans in 1973 to be near my husband's grave and to dedicate myself to writing as a way of exorcising the demons that had come to haunt me as I bore witness to the dark side of the post-war era.

It's all lies, or if you prefer, fiction inspired by real events. I started *Under the Canopy* on Stijn's veranda in the late 60s as I watched cloud-shadows ripple across Kenya's Rift Valley. I was not seeking any kind of redemption. I was in love with Kenya, with Stijn, and with my life. I was full of sizzling energy, like the static-filled highland air before the afternoon rains. The end of that era sent me into a spiral, and yes, here's the kernel of truth: I ended up back in England and the book was finished during a period of reflection and mourning and to stop me from losing my mind. *Under the Canopy* was written in delight and published in a kind of despair. A literary cry for help. I had lost everyone and I could no longer live alone with my ghosts. I sought solace and hope among strangers – my new readers – and I did not want them to know too much about the woman, Lina Rose. I wanted to be someone they could love. I had disappointed too often before.

In any case, *Under the Canopy* is what it is regardless of what Brenda says. She will take from it what she needs. Just as you will take from these words what you need and what you can bear. I have no control after the keys have been struck and the last full stop placed. That is the beauty of this métier. Everything is always a work in progress; the story is perpetually in motion, a lump of dough refashioned by every reader's hands.

To her credit, Brenda has a point. I *did* fall into a kind of reverie when I returned from Kenya to St Albans in 1973. I had failed in my attempts to break free from my past. My career as a journalist was over and I was not yet a published author. Home again in the land of my youth, my ghosts came calling and death was on my mind constantly. Has the panic caught up with you yet, Diane? Can you hear the sibilance of the sand's remorseless slide through the timer? Do you know definitively that you will never read all the books you've bought, never use that pretty letter-writing set you picked up in a village market five years ago, never dance in public again? Never, never, never.

For me, the fear came calling in my mid-50s. Of course, there were particular circumstances but even without what happened to Stijn, I think I would have succumbed to its torments. Fifty is a monumental number. It refuses obfuscation. It will not be massaged into something more palatable. The new 30 or the new 40? Heavens, no. It is irreducibly itself. I was able to ignore it while I was in Kenya but when I found myself back in England, there could be no denying its significance. And so the fear found me.

At first, it made me wake gasping for breath in the middle of the night. Or I would lose my bearings at odd moments during the day when I couldn't see the point of whatever I was doing. I laugh now to think how weak I was, especially from this vantage point where the oblivion that terrified me then is so much closer. Eventually I pulled myself together – we always do, we children of the wars. I realised the fear was unravelling my moorings and so I decided to walk myself back to some kind of sanity, to stride out and say, "Watch me be. Watch me walk, you darkling ghoul." I trekked for miles, tunnelling back to my past and my parents' past through rutted lanes overhung with honeysuckle and echoing with the strangled yelping of startled pheasants.

I discovered I could drown out death's insistent whining with my memories. As we age, the past becomes so much more engaging than the future and so I started revisiting all the places that once made up my world: Folly Lane, Hatfield Road, the Bernards Heath park, my schools and the war memorial on St Peter's Street. Retracing these paths calmed me, restored my balance so that I could face the fear.

Something else has also helped me these past years but I have not yet decided whether to tell you that part of my story. I'm not sure I can bear your judgment on this particular betrayal. I beg your patience, Diane. I don't mean to be a tease, not really. This letter is my personal twelve-step programme to unearth the truth or, at the very least, to set down as honest an account of what happened as I can. We have a long way to go.

As I walked myself out of my shrinking, unreliable future and into my rich and solid past, I began to dream up snippets of stories, barely-there plot ideas, curious nuggets of name and nature. The rest, as they say, is history. Now, with all these books to my name, I find that the only story left for me to tell is mine, and yours.

Let me explain why I think you should read on. We did not have the luxury of time that would have allowed me to slowly unveil your family history so that your sense of self expanded organically as you grew. Other mothers might have said: "What a beautiful drawing, darling. Your grandmother loved painting. That picture of the canal in the hallway is hers. Her name was Lily too." Or it might be the grandparents themselves who stitched a child into the family fabric. "Ooh, you're a right mucky pup. I remember your uncle when he was your age. Just the same. Into everything."

That was not to be for us. Among the many things I denied you was any real sense of where you came from. That was some theft, my dear Diane, and I apologise. I did not think of it then but now that the past has become so important to me, I see my crime more completely. I suppose I must have shared some family history with you during your first year. But you will not remember those night-time whispers and daytime pre-language chats and once you were gone, you had to be truly gone.

Society abhors mothers who give up their children. It

is an unconscionable act and so the punishment must be unthinkable: permanent exile. I do not dispute my punishment but I find now that I yearn for a kind of understanding from you. I want to tell you why. It is presumptuous beyond belief but that is the truth. You deserve to know our story because it is also yours. I want to give you back your history. This is the debt I owe you and only I can pay it.

When I gave you up, Diane, I did so because I was scared I could not care for you, that I could not love you or love anyone. I could barely care for myself after everything that had happened. I could blame the war, of course, but that is not excuse enough. So many people lost so much but they found the strength to count their blessings. I couldn't. In a kind of defiant madness, I threw your love onto the pyre as well. I was paralysed by despair and loneliness but I was also hungrier than ever for life. We used to speak of war aphrodisia. I had a kind of grief aphrodisia. My anguish co-existed with a frenzied desire to escape. When I gave you up, I was irrational, incoherent and utterly exhausted. They have words for this today – post-traumatic stress disorder. But what of it? We were all PTSD sufferers in the late 1940s. During the war, we did what we were told. We got on with things. Made the most of it. Snapped out and buttoned up and moved on. But there was a price to pay.

When I gave you up, I was like a spiderling: I needed to move to survive. And so I climbed high, stood on my toes and released silky silvery threads into the wind, so that I could be borne away. I knew you could not come with me into the clouds. You would weigh me down. So I let you go. Let me say it straight. There was relief as well as anguish when I gave you up. It is terrible but all truths are.

As I said earlier, Diane, perception is everything. Did I sin against motherhood if I alone know the relief I felt at breaking free? From that day until now, I have curated my story with care, removing the details that tarnish my image. I have shaped what people think they know of my life. This is the one advantage of being the sole survivor. But now, I need your wide, no-nonsense eyes on me. I have fibbed and fabricated for too long. I need to tell the truth, for once. You are the only one I can imagine doing this for. So you shall have my final story, Diane, and it will be as true as I can make it. Do with it what you will.

Let us begin. We have a lot to cover. I will, of course, take some liberties but not with the facts. I will honour them and the people they concern but I cannot help myself from embroidering a little. There is a certain truth in such fripperies too.

Chapter 3

We will start with my mother for that is where all great stories – whether tragedy or farce, from *Goodnight Mister Tom* to *Pride and Prejudice* – start. What can I say that will not diminish Charlotte Baker in the telling? Born in 1896, she was in some ways a typically fin-de-siècle child. She grew up in a country finding its feet in a new century even as the ground shifted underneath and trembled with the dull rumble of an approaching war. It must have been a frighteningly heady time for people pinging between the elastics of tradition and modernity. Queen Victoria had been a beacon of stability but her time was nearly up and Britain was tentatively stepping into a new era that would redefine what it meant to be human.

Charlotte was not a revolutionary – she would never rock the boat – but I believe she always knew which boat she wanted to be in. She was outwardly respectful and modest, as women had to be then, but she generally got her way. It was an admirably lady-like form of insurrection.

As a young woman she loved those penny novels that were so popular at the time, especially romances. She kept the books under her mattress to avoid having to endure a lecture from her mother on the dangers of 'trashy' stories designed to tempt women away from their God-given duties.

She was delicately pretty rather than beautiful – the fine blonde hair we all share above a broad forehead and brown, feline eyes. She was profoundly loving. This may sound banal but as you and I know, this quality should never be taken as a given. She sang beautifully, her clear voice soaring like a lark's from the garden or skipping along before her as she walked down the street. This kind of singing doesn't seem to happen much any more. As I remember it, people used to sing all the time. Snatches of melody shimmied over fences along Hatfield Road or played hide-and-seek between the market stalls in St Albans town on Saturdays. Charlotte also loved Busy Lizzies. Just like spontaneous, public singing, they are not so popular these days. I suppose there is something unfashionably modest about the flowers. A little too pastel for our Technicolor world. Charlotte herself would undoubtedly be deemed too pastel today.

Charlotte had phenomenal restraint when necessary and it was always necessary after my father returned from the Great War. When I was a young child, she drank consistently and methodically, marshalling all her self-discipline to control the visible results of her alcoholism, although we would not have called it that then. Those who lived through the Great War had little use for judgmental labels because it was almost impossible to determine what a normal baseline for behaviour should be after such a trauma. Charlotte's addiction was nothing out-of-the-ordinary and she bore it with such gentility.

What else? I never called her 'mother'. She was always Charlotte to me, and Lottie to her husband and friends. I can't remember who decided I should forgo tradition and call her by her first name. I like to think it was her wish. She had a great respect for the individual and a concomitant horror for nebulous masses. Maybe that extended to nomenclature too. This is pure speculation, as I never asked her. By the time I was old enough, my reference to her, as Charlotte, no longer seemed eccentric. It was just the way things were. We always assume we have all the time in the world to quiz our parents about the people they really are but we forget that time does not stand still. We turn a deaf ear to the ticking of the clocks. That's the danger with clocks. They become part of the furniture and we forget what they are doing. I am keenly aware of the irony of saying this to you but it is no less true for that.

When war broke out in 1914, Charlotte was using her typing skills to help out at the *Herts Advertiser*, where her father was a sub-editor. It was not really a full-time job, just enough to keep her in clothes and shoes.

What else can I say about her? I'm finding it fiendishly difficult to paint an accurate picture of her despite this being my job, so to speak. The details I am giving you seem so random; they do not add up to the whole person. Adjectives appear too flimsy. They hang loose and baggy on the real woman I knew. It's as though they have been stretched too much by my use of them over the ages. But I *will* fall back on my craft. I must show not tell and so I will become Charlotte's ghostwriter and gift you this family fable, Diane. Her low, mesmerising voice will soothe me as I write. To this day, I find it hard to believe that her voice is no longer part of the world. The constancy of my grief over Charlotte's death has been one of the few things to surprise me as I have aged.

Let me recreate the moment she met my father, Henry Rose. Or rather I will let her recreate it. Charlotte loved to recount this tale and she would do it often, sometimes sitting by the fire sipping brandy after supper, holding court before her guests. It was, I suppose, her party trick but it bored me in the way parents' tales bore all children. Now, I understand why she retold it so often. It was the defining moment of her life and she delighted in reliving it because she genuinely believed she was lifting the veil on the mysterious workings of Fate. Maybe she was; who knows and does it really matter if she was right? Remember what I said about perception, Diane? She believed this story encapsulated destiny and so it must.

***

Charlotte Baker felt a blush spread across her cheeks. She lowered her eyes because that was what a girl should do, but curiosity got the better of her and she dared to peek again at the soldiers marching up the main street, their fresh, sharp steps propelling untested broad shoulders. They all faced up the hill except for the naughty blighter who had winked at her seconds before. As she raised her eyes, she saw that he was still looking back. He winked again. She tossed her head and deliberately looked away but not before she had seen the start of his slow smile. Maybe it was true then what her mother had muttered when Father said thousands of young army lads were to be stationed in St Albans before shipping out to France.

"That's the last thing this town needs," her mother said, frowning at the teapot in her hand as though there might be a rogue soldier hidden among the tea leaves. "There's not enough trouble already without throwing a bunch of fresh young lads with their foul language and drinking into the mix."

Father grunted but said nothing, pursing his lips under a brow that had been permanently furrowed since war was declared on August 4th. Charlotte made no comment but secretly she was delighted, first with the news and then with her mother's characterisation of the men who would soon be flooding the streets. St Albans could do with a bit of a shake-up and the soldiers might be just the ticket. The cheeky so-and-so who had just winked at her seemed to prove her mother delightfully right.

She stared at his back until he turned the corner onto the main street but he didn't turn around again. She had only glimpsed his face but the word now echoing in her head was 'sultry'. They were always using 'sultry' in the novels she kept hidden under her mattress. If she was honest with herself, she had only the vaguest idea of what 'sultry' actually meant – she assumed it was something to do with exotic sultans – but whatever the exact meaning, that soldier with the laughing eyes and the pencil-thin moustache probably embodied it. In any case, she wouldn't be wearing the word out for any of the boys from St Albans, she thought.

When the procession had passed, she joined the rest of the gossiping people as they straggled up the hill, stepping carefully between piles of steaming horse dung. That's all we need in this heat, Charlotte thought. More bloody horse poo. The stench made her throat itch. She opened her bag, reaching for her handkerchief, but then remembered she'd given it to her father before she left the office. He'd appeared in the corridor, sweat pouring down his forehead, and said he'd left his own handkerchief at home. She gave him hers, meeting his wink with her own as he told her not to inform her mother of his lapse. That was Father all over. So lost in his work that he wouldn't remember to mop his brow even in this hellish heat.

Since war was declared last week, he'd become even worse. He even left the house without his hat the other day, sending Mother rushing into the street after him, the hat held aloft like a battle flag. Mother had been mortified by her own unseemly haste in the street but not as mortified as she would have been if she'd had to think of her husband being in public all day with no hat on his head.

Charlotte was thankful now for her own straw hat. How in heaven's name had the soldiers managed to march all the way from London to St Albans in this heat? She was wearing her lightest summer dress but she could feel the sweat running down her back, pooling where the lavender ribbon she'd sewn on herself pulled the soft cotton tight above her waist. She glanced up but the sky above the clock tower was as blue and empty as it had been every day for the past two weeks. Surely, it would rain soon. The weather in St Albans certainly didn't give a fig for what the papers called 'the clouds of war gathering over Europe'. The last few weeks had unfurled like the longest, most wonderful summer ever. A summer to end all summers. As Charlotte reached the top of the street and turned the corner, she saw the soldiers had already passed through and she felt an unreasonable pang.

The next day, Charlotte was walking down Hatfield Road, heading to the newspaper's offices, when Sally Betts shouted to her from the other side of the road.

"Lottie, Lottie. Wait for me," Sally yelled, dashing across the road and nearly colliding with the milk truck. She giggled madly as the milkman shouted after her, tossed her head at him and linked her arm through Charlotte's.

"I've some big news. Bigger even than the war, if that ever really starts. Lord knows, it seems to be all talk for now."

Charlotte smiled at her best friend, even though her own feelings about what was coming were darker, shaped by her father's subdued comments and anxious eyes.

"Go on, then. I can see you are genuinely on the point of expiring. What's this big news then, Sally?"

"Well, it's only that one of the soldiers, the ones that arrived yesterday, has been billeted at our house. Imagine, we have a male lodger. Mother wasn't one bit happy but what can she do? There's no arguing with the army. When the captain brought the young man to the door, he told Father it was his patriotic duty to support our brave fighting men. Those are the very words he used. Of course, Father was furious, you know how tight he is, but he could do nothing and now we have a man living in the house!"

Sally ended on a note so high and triumphant, Charlotte had to shush her, pointing to the hard-faced women squinting at them from the steps of the squat red-brick homes lining the road. If there was one thing her mother hated, it was making a show in front of what she insisted on calling 'the common people'. Charlotte once made the mistake of repeating what her father had told her after he'd had a few too many glasses of port one evening.

"Weren't you one of the common people too, Mother, before you married Father? Didn't Grandad work in the

Kershaw hat factory and didn't you live in one of those small houses when you were a girl?"

Her mother had turned on her, her clenched fist rising as if to box Charlotte's ears.

"Never speak of my family in that way again," she hissed before turning on her heel and walking out of the kitchen, her arm still raised as though it didn't know where to go now that its purpose had been thwarted. Charlotte had learned two things that day: class warfare is most acute between those closest together on the ladder; and her mother had quite the temper as well as impressive control. She never mentioned her mother's past again.

"You'll have to come over later," Sally gushed. "I'll be home around five. Come and have a gander at our own brave fighting man."

She rushed across the road again, a whirlwind of waving hands and trailing ribbons.

"This might be the one," she shouted back. "This could be Fate at last, Lottie!"

Sally was everything Charlotte wanted to be. Her thick brown hair could be twisted into the most elaborate styles, she was loud and confident and men's eyes followed her down the street like dogs after the butcher's delivery boy. But Sally was such an incurable romantic that Charlotte couldn't imagine any man ever meeting her lofty standards for love. Unless, perhaps, a brave fighting man from out of town.

When Charlotte arrived at Sally's elegant, ivy-draped house in Marshalswick just after five, she was ushered into the garden by a harried-looking Mrs Betts.

"Sally is upstairs, dear. She'll be down in a minute but I thought you could wait in the garden. This heat is beginning to turn my head. What with the weather and the war, food riots and banks not opening, I don't know whether I'm coming or going."

Charlotte had known Mrs Betts since she and Sally were placed next to each other on their first day in primary school.

Even in the coolest, most temperate weather, with no war on the horizon, she was a bundle of nerves. Charlotte thought Sally was Mrs Betts through a prism: what was ceaseless anxiety in the mother had refracted into effervescent enthusiasm in the daughter.

Mrs Betts disappeared back into the house, plucking at her sleeves and muttering to herself. Charlotte sat on a wicker chair under the willow tree, watching goldfinches pecking at the seeds on the bird table under the branches of the cherry blossom. Even the birds seemed uncharacteristically sluggish in the unrelenting heat.

"He's out. Oh, Charlotte, he's out!"

Sally's words galloped before her as she sped across the lawn, carrying a tray with two glasses of lemonade.

"What a shame. He'll have to come back for his supper but I don't know when."

Sally dropped heavily into the sagging wicker chair beside Charlotte and put the tray on the low, wooden table between them.

"Mother insists you drink this. She's convinced we're all going to die of heat stroke. As if that's our biggest worry right now."

Sally paused to catch her breath and sip her drink.

"You know, we get food for our brave fighting man: meat, bread, potatoes. They deliver it in a wheelbarrow every day. Not a bad deal, I say. A dreamy soldier and better meals too. Food for the soul and the stomach."

She giggled.

"So exactly how handsome is he?" Charlotte said.

"I thought you'd never ask," Sally said, leaning closer. "He's tall, taller than Father by a good foot. He has dark hair, an ever so tidy moustache and a rather too-pretty face. But it does sit well on him, I must say. His name is Henry Rose and he's in the second London Division. At least, I think that's what he said. It was hard to concentrate when he was telling us. I was drowning in his eyes, Lottie. Such beautiful, dark

34

eyes. And he has a lovely voice. All London but warm. It's like having treacle poured into your ears only not so messy."

She blushed and Charlotte burst out laughing. Sally never did anything by halves. She always fell head-over-heels in love and when the object of her affection inevitably proved unworthy, she was invariably beside herself.

"Oh, and he's an orphan. His mother died when he was three from some kind of illness, I think, and his father didn't last much longer. His aunt took him in and so he grew up with her in Ealing. He was just starting an apprenticeship at an accounting house when all this started."

Sally paused, wrinkling her forehead.

"I think that's it. It's all I can remember in any case."

"It's a real pity but I can't stay to meet him," Charlotte said, putting her glass of lemonade down and standing up. "I told Father I'd play chess with him before supper. But you certainly paint a pretty picture."

"Speaking of pretty pictures, I don't think I've seen one as stunning as this for some time."

The voice came from behind Charlotte and she spun around too quickly, snagging her low heel on the grass. And so it came to pass that Private Henry Rose darted forward to place a steadying hand under her arm. And, of course, he was the very same soldier who had so cheekily winked at her the day before.

Those are the exact words Charlotte used, Diane. Every time she told that story, she would conclude with "And, of course, he was the very same soldier…" Her personalised version of 'happily ever after'.

I can see her now, coming to the end of her tale and leaning back in her chair like a self-satisfied preacher, her long fingers wrapped around her glass. Her melodious voice and unshakeable conviction always enraptured her audience, even if they'd heard the story before. My father never joined her in retelling her favourite fairy tale. He just sat, smiling in that quizzical way he had, as if he wasn't sure whether to be flattered or embarrassed by the whole thing. As if, in fact, he wasn't really sure the story concerned him. But every now and then you might catch him inclining his head ever so slightly. Without those slow, silent nods, I would have struggled to believe a word of Charlotte's story. It was too beautiful even for my beautiful, broken parents.

Maybe that's another reason why Charlotte loved to retell that tale. It was not just an ode to kismet. It was also an act of mourning, a nostalgic elegy for something more terrible than death: living absence.

Nobody survives war intact, Diane. It is no accident that spelt backwards it is 'raw'. War strips the skin off society, leaving the muscles, sinews, tendons and organs exposed. Its effects are irreversible because all who live through it are changed forever. Our story, Diane, yours and mine, is the story of war. We owe our existence to a wave of euphoria that swept the land because the guns had fallen silent at last. But we grew up to learn that a war never ends. The guns echo in the chamber of the mind forever.

Charlotte's war was, on the surface at least, easier than Henry's. She did not end up questioning her God, her country and her everything under a bleeding dawn sky in France. She continued to help out on the *Herts Advertiser*, even writing some articles after the male journalists left to fight. I found one after she died. It was among a handful of papers she kept in a tin biscuit box on the top of a cupboard in the kitchen. I imagine she kept it because it had her byline – a rarity then – and also because the subject intrigued her. The article told how a young man was approached by three ladies outside St Albans town hall on a Saturday morning. They stuck a white feather into his lapel and the ringleader shouted: "You coward! Why won't you enlist?" A crowd gathered and the young man was within a whisker of being beaten when someone recognised him as a medical volunteer. He had been unable to join the regular army because he was short-sighted and although he was a volunteer, he did not wear a uniform. Apparently, he was regularly taken to task by *"upstanding women of the community, fired with a passionate, if occasionally over-enthusiastic, determination to support the war effort"*. The words in italics are Charlotte's and I like to think she meant them critically. As I said, she had a horror of what we would now call 'mob mentality'.

I hope I have breathed some life into Charlotte Baker for you, Diane. What can I tell you about my father? Henry Rose was not much of a talker by the time I came into his life. The man who steadied Charlotte's elbow in Sally Betts' garden in 1914 was not the man who became my father in 1920. We can never be who we were, even yesterday, but war speeds up this natural metamorphosis.

Charlotte used to say that when Henry made it back from the war in mid-1919, he had 'lost his sparkle'. It was perhaps the only way she could describe the cataclysmic change without bursting into tears. But it fell far short. A diligent application of Brasso would not make Henry new again. He was entirely diminished.

I always thought my father was like a man living underwater: he moved through the days like those early divers with their oversized metal helmets and deadweight shoes. It wasn't just his ponderous motions but also the fact that he seemed to be constantly rediscovering a new world. Despite it all, he was not a grim man: he smiled, he laughed with me and later, much later, with you. You won't remember this but he used to tickle your stomach with the wiry, unkempt beard that replaced his pencil-thin moustache after the war. I can still see him kneeling on the soft, cream rug that I used to lay you on, pushing his head slowly towards your tummy until you were writhing with delight. You must have been about 10 months old. The June sun was pouring through the windows and Charlotte was sitting on the sofa, a cup of the rancid brew we jokingly called coffee in her hand. Robert was there as well, of course, sitting in a rocking chair by the fire, smiling that empty smile of his, eyes fixed in the middle distance, scanning a perilous horizon that existed only in his mind. It was the summer of 1947 and we were all survivors, but by the end of that year, that same room was quiet, the chairs were empty and nobody was tickling your face any more, or if they were, I could not know it. Fifty years ago now. Imagine that, Diane. I remember it like yesterday but it was the ancient past, wasn't it?

CHAPTER 4

I'm sorry. I have digressed. That will happen at my age. But insofar as anything can have a beginning, there you have it: a beginning to my story and your story and everything that leads us here to this moment.

After that first meeting in Sally Betts' garden, Charlotte and Henry saw each other regularly and their love grew as steadily as anything could grow in the unsettling paralysis that marked the end of 1914. Britain was at war, but still mostly in name only. Henry knew his days in St Albans were numbered, and maybe he feared a more definitive ending than that, but he did not know exactly when he would be ordered overseas. After the searing heat of summer, autumn brought heavy rainstorms. As the days shortened and the mud thickened in the training fields at Bernards Heath, where soldiers jabbed their bayonets into sacks of straw, Charlotte and Henry did their best to disregard the dull detonations drifting across the Channel. What a feat. To imagine a future when all around you the world is imploding. I thought I knew what that was like, given my own wartime experience, but it was not the same. By the time our war came, we had fewer illusions about what man could be asked to endure and what cruelty he could bring himself to inflict. I believe we were in some ways resigned to what was coming but also reassured that we would survive. We had seen our parents come through and so we had faith that the war would end, eventually. I'm not sure Charlotte and Henry had that luxury. The scale of suffering was unimaginable. The possibility of an end equally so. The idea of survival must have seemed like a ludicrous fancy. The first time is always different.

Henry was finally sent to France in March 1915 and he stayed in the parallel universe that was Western Europe until after the war ended in 1918. Neither he nor Charlotte ever said a word about their reunion. I only know she went to meet him off the ship – I think it was in Portsmouth – because the moment was captured by a photographer and that print sits on a bookshelf in my home today. It is not a typical image of victory. None of the flag-waving fugue, none of the hysterical euphoria I was to experience in 1945. Just two young people with the haunted eyes and hunched shoulders of the middle-aged, facing the camera solemnly. They do not ask for the viewer's pity and they will not accept questions. They will not shrink from your gaze but they will give no more than what you see. Whatever was left of their hope and joy was concentrated in their interlocked fingers, half-hidden by Charlotte's long tweed coat. That white-knuckled naked need is almost too painful to look upon. It is worse than the emptiness in their faces. Or maybe it breaks *my* heart because my man came back like that too and his trembling fingers with broken, dirty nails held on too tightly to my own. The man in that photo of my parents had been stripped of the cockiness that first caught Charlotte's eye. You can read neither relief nor despair in his face. It is as though he left the top layer – the moving, malleable surface – in the mud by the Somme as he lay there, beseeching the sky for one more minute, dreading each unbearable second, until a minute was gone and then he needed one more. As though *his* Shroud of Turin was a layer of mud where he left not only the imprint of his features, but something of their acuity so that now his face was just another war mask, identical to all the others flowing back across the Channel to an England that didn't know what to do with all these broken men.

Of what Henry endured, Diane, you will have read. There are no secrets now but I believe neither poetry nor prose captured the reality. Henry fought at the Somme, if you can call what happened there fighting. He laid mines and then scurried back to take cover at Vimy Ridge, he pushed through Belgium and at some point ended up back in France, before one day making his way home.

It's a cliché as all truths, especially uncomfortable ones, are but Henry rarely spoke of the war. Very few of the men who came back did. It was as though they believed that if they refused to bear witness, the horror could not live. Through their silence, they denied it oxygen. How else to deal with a period that exposed all that was base and cruel and savage in our psyche? The only answer for many of these men was silence. There was another reason too for your grandfather's quietude but I will get to that later.

Life carried on, as it must. Charlotte and Henry married in 1919 and I was born on a June day in 1920 in St Albans. At first we lived in Charlotte's parents' house but after Henry got a job in a solicitors' office, we moved into a cosy two-bedroom house a little further along Hatfield Road. That is where I grew up.

So there you go, Diane, we are both post-war children. That is something we have in common. Both born from our species' incongruous, indestructible hope. What funny beasts we humans are. No matter how many times we disappoint ourselves, we persist in peddling the notion of 'happily ever after'. We persist in our quest for happiness. We insist on believing it is possible.

From the fairy tales we tell our children through to the notion that when we die we are going somewhere better, we nurture these fantasies despite all evidence to the contrary. It is as though hope is engraved into our DNA, like a pattern through a stick of Brighton rock. We cannot separate it from our souls no matter how many times we fall, no matter how many villages we bomb, how many babies we slaughter, how many innocents we incinerate, no matter how many hatreds big and small we allow to colour our lives. It's not even that we are bad and constantly striving to be better. We know we can never change but we persist in believing that one day, miraculously, we will be better. That hope is our salvation and its eternal disappointment lies at the root of all our agonies.

To this day, Diane, I have been blessed with a meticulous memory. Or maybe blessed is the wrong word. I like my words to be precise and 'blessed' only tells half the story. It is also an unusual choice for an agnostic but for my personal lexicon, I have remade such words in my own image, stripping them of their religious import so that only their secular meaning remains. In any case, my memories are a blessing and a curse. When I wake now at 4 a.m., which I do almost every day, I am soothed and haunted by the past. These are not vague recollections. No shady figures, unexplained lacunae or forgotten sequences for me. I remember who did and said what and when. I remember whole conversations and more importantly, I remember what was not said. That is the worst kind of clarity but I am used to it now and wonder what it will be like when the fog descends. We shall see, I suppose.

I remember exactly how you looked on our last day together, the way your eyes widened as I held you out, how you twisted towards me as the lady from the adoption agency took you.

My earliest memory from our home in Hatfield Road is being in Charlotte's arms, aged around three, looking out into the back garden where my father was on his knees, weeding our tiny vegetable patch. His head was bent and his back was to us so that with the sun beyond him, his truncated silhouette looked like a headless Roman statue, a former hero who had fallen out of favour and had his stone head removed. That image has stayed with me perhaps because I always knew my father was not whole.

Charlotte was whispering in my ear.

"Look, darling. Daddy is planting carrots so that we can

eat our own carrots. We love carrots, don't we? Won't that be wonderful? We can pick them together when they are ready. Would you like that, darling?"

I said I would. Charlotte's face was radiant in the sunshine; she had filled out again after the war, her cheeks were round, her eyes sparkling and I remember she was wearing the cream eye-shadow that always drew admiring looks. But at the corners of her mouth, there was a brittleness. That fragile determination was etched into the features of many of the women I knew as a child. The faces of the men who had fought were also friable but in a different way: broken vases glued back together. The women's faces were cracked vases, hairline fractures holding together. Just.

We walked out to my father. I was wearing red Mary Janes and Charlotte told me to be careful not to walk in the mud. I held onto her brown felt skirt so I wouldn't be tempted off the narrow path. I still respected the rules then and, as young as I was, I had already learned to be careful around my father. He would start at the slightest noise, his whole body expanding and then contracting into a hunched rigid shell. Charlotte spoke loudly to me as we walked. She was talking to signal our arrival but my father's head still whipped up and around too quickly and his heels came down and dug into the ground, his legs braced to run.

"Henry, it's just us," Charlotte said in the almost-whisper she reserved for her husband and a few of his battalion friends. I thought of it as her librarian voice. I never heard her shout when Henry was in the house. When he was at work, safe in the cluttered, dim office where he took refuge in piddling by-laws that were stable and unbreakable, she would sometimes roar at me, like a pressure cooker venting steam. Her outbursts were rare and short-lived. She was not a saint but she came damn close. I always loved her but as I grew older, I understood just how much that restraint must have cost her.

"We didn't mean to startle you," she said now as his eyes slowly refocused on us.

A robin fluttered onto the top of the fence and punctured the silence with a volley of staccato trills. Henry leapt to his feet and then burst out laughing as the terrified bird darted into the bushes next door.

"Daddy, you scared the pretty bird away. Why, Daddy?"

Henry bent down and picked me up, smoothing my hair with his mud-caked hands.

"Lina, sweetie, I'm so sorry. The robin startled me but it's all fine now. Let's sit here quietly and wait for him to come back. I'm sure he will. He'll want to look for worms for his supper."

We sat on the grass by the furrowed soil while Charlotte went back inside to get some bread crusts. Sure enough, the robin hopped back onto the fence and then down onto the ground, not three feet from us. It pecked the damp soil frantically, twisting its head quizzically between each bout of poking. I held my breath. The robin stayed for a few minutes and then flew away with half a worm in its beak.

"Did you see that?" Henry said, pulling me onto his knees. "Wasn't that beautiful?"

I twisted around to smile at him and he kissed my cheek. His eyes were too full and my smile was too bright but that is what the Great War did to people, Diane. It filled us brimful with too much emotion. Even after 1918, the war was still being fought in every home. We sat together on the grass until Charlotte came back, the heels of her boots clacking deliberately on the paving stones as she made her way towards us.

When I was about 13, and hungry as all teenagers are for the macabre, I asked Charlotte what she knew about Henry's war. It turned out to be not very much.

"He thought letters would worry me," she said. "Can you believe it? What worried me most, of course, was his silence. Despite the censors and their ridiculous communiqués, we still knew some of what was happening over there. They could not shroud everything in the fog of war, as my father used to say. But it was just like Henry to try to protect me, at least just like the old Henry. He's never really understood how much I can bear. I also think he didn't write because really, what good would it do? We just wanted it all to be over. We were desperate to start our lives. And I suppose we hadn't had enough time together to know how to tell each other about what we were seeing and feeling. Old married couples can do that with a glance. But we were so young and new. What words could Henry use to describe what he had seen, to try to make sense of it all? In the end, he preferred not to try. I do understand. After 1916, I stopped reading the papers and went back to my silly romances. I just couldn't bear the lies any more, the way words were being used to remake history. I don't know what I expected to find in those love stories though. They didn't work for me any more but I kept reading."

She was sitting on the couch, a cup of tea in her hand and whiskey on her breath. I don't know how much she drank but drink she did all day, every day. Slowly and carefully and very consistently. She must've been doing it for years by the time I was old enough to understand. I noticed the smell first and then the way her eyes glittered above flushed cheeks from about 5pm. Despite this, she was a woman of absolute control. She had to be. Nothing had turned out as it should have and the only way she could manage the brutal disappointment of her life and love was to keep herself on the tightest possible leash.

"What I know about Henry's war, I know despite him," she continued. "I would never dare ask him. There are some women who need their men to talk but that's not really my way. I got my Henry back and I am content with that. There was a time when I thought even that simple thing was the most impossible of dreams. Yes, he's changed and silent, his hands shake and sometimes he is too scared to sleep so he goes out walking and maybe part of him *did* die in a way, but I still have him. He's still in there. I did not choose these terms but I do accept them. What choice do I have? And together we made you. That's more than enough for a life in these times."

I do believe Charlotte went to her grave respecting Henry's need to shroud the war in silence and so she never truly understood what happened to him. That scalds my soul. Secrets are often best left untold but in this case, there would have been healing in the telling. My father underestimated Charlotte's love and so he carried his shame alone. Her error was to believe that silence could cure. And so, for the rest of their lives, they circled around the truth, loving each other too much to share their pain.

Do you know how Charlotte and Henry died, Diane? I didn't have time to tell you that one time we met in Brighton. When was it? 1967? You stomped away from me too quickly, your feet slipping awkwardly over the pebbles in your haste to be gone. I too was taken aback by our resemblance but I saw more of Robert in you. The mirror did not frighten me as much. Only you were driven to flee. But then, I did not believe I was meeting a monster. I had less reason to be afraid.

Charlotte and Henry were killed in a train crash in October 1947. Robert had just died, you were 14 months old and I was adrift even before the knock on the door. When I saw the police officers' silhouettes through the glass, I felt the strongest urge to run away. I didn't want to open that door. I was already at breaking point. I must have squeezed you too hard because I remember you started squealing in my arms. Your wriggling pulled me back. There were two officers, a woman and a man. They took me to the front room, made me sit down and then the lady took you from me and sat you on the carpet at her feet. She found one of your teddies and gave it to you and so when I remember being told that my parents had been killed in a train crash, all I see is your face, wide-eyed, smiling and staring at me above the button eyes of that grey woollen teddy we gave you for your first Christmas.

I couldn't breathe. The lady officer rose swiftly from her chair and stepped carefully over you, reaching her hand towards me. I must have fainted then. I woke up hours later in my bed. My first thought was for you and I half-rose to come and find you but then I remembered the rest. I fell back onto the pillows, unable to breathe again. I couldn't think what to do. I was utterly lost.

My poor parents, who had seen so much, died because a young signalman didn't see enough on a foggy day in South Croydon. They were travelling to the funeral of one of the men who had served with Henry. The signalman, who was new to the job, forgot there was a train already in that section of the line. Normally, a safety system should have prevented him from letting another train in but he thought the system was broken and overrode it. The two trains crashed into each other and 32 people were killed. Such a small number given the two dreadful wars that had dominated the past three decades, but for me this tiny tragedy was the straw that broke the camel's back.

The Great War stole my father's spark before I could really know him. Barely 20 years later, another war took my husband but what really reconfigured my soul was the death of my parents because of one young man's miscalculation. Henry was 57. It was considered a long life then but my goodness, how I regret his young death from where I stand now. Many of the men who survived the war with him had already passed on, some succumbing to illnesses that could be traced back to those sinister yellow clouds that drifted over their trenches, while others were smothered by unutterable burdens of grief or guilt. They carried these leaden loads for decades, as Henry had, while they raised their families and tried to get on with their lives. But the day came when they were no longer needed, or so they thought, and then many quietly checked out. Henry might have been tempted to do the same but I think he sensed that Charlotte would always need him. She seemed the stronger of the two but if there is one thing I have learned in my 70-odd years here, Diane, it is that what lies beneath is what counts. Charlotte needed Henry as much as he needed her. Her strength came from his need.

You're probably wondering if I am projecting my own relationship with your father onto my parents. There were, of course, similarities – war, damage, fractured souls and lives. But just as no two people see a robin in the same way, no two people experience war in the same way. It is not a static, unitary object or state. It is shaped by those who live it, by their strengths and weaknesses, by what they can and cannot bear.

Charlotte was 50 when she died. The last time I saw her she was reaching for Henry's hand as they walked down the path from our home. They had come for tea and to tell me they were going to London for a few days to attend the funeral. She was wearing her brown coat and a maroon hat. I watched as Henry let her take his hand just before they reached the gate. His fingers curled around hers. I can see it as though it was yesterday. I like to think they were still holding hands when the end came. I realise this is an unforgivably maudlin thought but even an old cynic like myself needs fairy tales sometimes.

Chapter 5

It is time to let Henry speak for himself. Only he can bear true witness to his experience. I have seen my share of war. I endured the Second World War and I will tell you of that. I have seen war in Korea and Vietnam and other smaller conflicts. I have spoken to people on all sides and then I have relived the pain and the absurdities, through a glass darkly, in my writing. But I have never been a soldier and although I am willing to undertake any feat of imagination if I think I can pull it off, in this case I neither think I can, nor is it necessary.

As I sorted, tight-throated and scratchy-eyed, through my parents' things just days after they died, I found a letter Henry had written in 1916 but never sent. It was in the breast pocket of the khaki wool tunic he was wearing when he returned to Britain. The tunic had never been cleaned. What would have been the point? There was still dried mud on the collar and around the hem. One of the brass buttons was missing. The tunic must have hung silently in that mildewed wardrobe in my parents' house for decades, a deflated reminder of absent bodies.

I took the tunic down into the kitchen, wondering what I should do with it. Would it be appropriate to wash it and give it to a charity? It seemed wrong somehow to treat it as just another item of clothing. Could I bear to keep it knowing that this uniform and all it stood for had destroyed my father's life, and indeed my own? Then I found the letter – a tightly folded square of unlined white paper. It had the rigidity of something long unopened and that's why I believe Charlotte never saw it. She would certainly not have left it in the jacket for fear Henry might stumble on it again.

I sat down slowly at the kitchen table, taking my usual chair although I could have had my choice of any. My back was to the window and I was facing Charlotte's empty seat. I closed my eyes to better imagine her sitting there, calmly sipping her tea, her cat's eyes warming my face like an embrace. I knew what was coming would hurt, as you know in the millisecond between your foot hitting an uneven paving stone and the fall that it will hurt. Even today, there is a composite kitchen smell – a hint of chicken dinner, hot milk and the lingering trace of Charlotte's lavender-scented hand soap – that catapults me back to that moment. I was still utterly discombobulated by grief. At night, lying beside you in our double bed, I could hear my soul splintering, like a giant iceberg wailing its disintegration into an empty Arctic sky. But we don't die from blistered souls or broken hearts. More's the pity. There was nothing actually wrong with me and so I went on. I could do nothing else. I did not have the courage then to act against myself. I never have.

I knew the letter would deepen my anguish but I knew too that it had to be read. It was not very long but it took me some time to get to the end. Each word flayed my exhausted brain.

I am sharing this letter with you, Diane, because you deserve to know and Henry deserves to be heard. I have never shown this letter to anyone. Now, it is yours.

October 4, 1916

Dearest Lottie,
What does it mean to live? I am lying here in this stinking hole, my back to the wall, my knees to my chest and I can't work it out. Maybe there is no answer. Maybe the very idea

that there should be an answer just shows how arrogant we are. We dare to assume our lives mean something. Why should they? Because we are human? But what does that mean? I don't know any more. Who is it that said: "To err is human, to forgive divine"? I can't remember but all I see now are our errors. Is that it? Is that all being human means? There is no shortage of errors out here but there is nothing divine as far as the eye can see. The idea of a God makes me laugh when it doesn't make me cry.

Something terrible happened, Lottie. It has taken me three days to be able to even write about it. You know me. I don't have your gift for words but someone needs to bear witness to what we did. What we were made to do. No, that's not fair. What we did. We always have a choice.

Sally Betts' brother showed up here in the middle of August. I don't know if you knew that? He was assigned to our unit, or rather flung into the muck alongside the rest of us.

When I first saw him, I couldn't for the life of me figure out who he was. I recognised his blue eyes and the sandy lashes, that funny upturned nose and the way dimples appeared when he smiled. I knew the face but it was in the wrong place. When I finally got it, I yelled out "Bettsy! Daniel Betts! What are you doing here, you blighter?"

It wasn't just that he was out of place. He was too young to be on the frontline. He told me he'd lied to the recruiter, saying he was 19 instead of 16. He was always tall for his age and I'm sure the recruiter was happy to turn a blind eye and squirrel away a few more bob for signing up another one. Bettsy had done a few weeks of basic training and here he was on the Somme, full of laughs and larks the way the new boys always are. The laughs didn't last long though. None of us are laughing any more. You'll know I suppose that we've been fighting here since July and all of us have lost friends to the bombs and the diseases and the Great Fuck Up as we call it. I'm sorry to use such language but it's the truth. Some men simply passed away in the mud at night and I honestly believe it was nothing but downright misery that killed them. They were the really strong ones, the ones who could will themselves out of it, who refused to go on. I envied every one of them. I know that sounds terrible but it's true.

I was beside Bettsy when he copped his first big barrage. When the guns kicked off, he flinched – we all do, every time, no matter how long we've been here – but he said nothing at first. His jaw just tightened and he pulled his helmet lower and crouched into himself. It's the sound, Lottie. The sheer scale of it. It's like the world is breaking. It'd turn you to jelly even if you weren't stuck in a trench, waiting to die. That sounds like I'm over-egging it but I promise you, I'm not. We're just waiting to die. Every day, men are blasted to bits where they crouch, reading, carving pretty flowers into shell cases, playing cards, smoking or making tea. One minute, they're beside you, talking away, and the next minute, you're wiping bits of them out of your hair. Over here, we're like ants. Our lives, our deaths mean just as little. We disappear without a trace. But I suppose the Huns feel the same so the question is, whose boots are crushing us all?

"It's the sound, isn't it? I didn't know it would be so bloody loud," Bettsy shouted. After that he went quiet until the guns fell silent and then he asked me for a smoke. His hands were trembling but so were mine. You don't pay any attention to things like that here. If it's not the cold making you shake, it's the fear.

Bettsy stayed with us for a few weeks but then he was sent off to another section after they lost a lot of men when the Germans tried to break through the lines. To be honest, I didn't think about him much after that. You can't let yourself worry about the other ants. You'd go mad. Thinking about Bettsy would bring me back to those months in St Albans, when I lodged with his family and met you, and I try not to think of that other world. It'd be like imagining a slap-up meal when you're starving. I've stopped that too. Sometimes I don't even dare think of you, Lottie. It's too painful and

I'm scared that if I remember too much, I'll get lost inside my head. If I think of how you looked that day in Sally's garden, if I remember how your skin smells of lavender, or how your hair curls into little ringlets by your ears when the air is damp, I might never be able to find my way back to this bloody grey world where the only smell is death and the only colour the red of spilt blood and guts and those bleeding poppies. I've seen enough men get lost in their heads to know that that is no way to survive either. You can't even be safe inside your head here.

I saw Bettsy again a few days ago. Me and some of the boys were told to move back to a village about two miles behind the frontline. We didn't know why and we didn't ask. That's what war has done to us, Lottie: killed our curiosity. Better not to know what's coming. It's never something good and there's nothing we can do anyway.

We were ordered to stop at a farm on the north side of the village. There were purple and crimson roses climbing around the door of the farmhouse and I sat on the brown grass staring at them while we waited for the brass. I hadn't seen anything so beautiful for months. They must've been those winter roses to be blooming so late. I was just getting up to run my fingers over the petals when the Captain came over and we all stood to attention. Not as fast as we used to but we stood nonetheless. He told us we were going to form an execution squad at dawn the next day. Nobody moved, nobody said anything and he dismissed us to prepare our sleeping area. When he was halfway across the garden, heading for his car, another lad, you don't know him and I might not for long so his name doesn't matter, called out: "What did he do, Sir? The lad we're going to shoot?"

The Captain slowed his march but he didn't stop or turn around.

"Cowardice," he shouted back. "He abandoned his sentry post and not for the first time. Damn fool, but there's nothing anyone can do for him now."

That night we bunked down among the mildewed, scratchy bales of hay in the barn. I should've slept like a baby in all that luxury even if I'd brought my old friends, the lice, with me. But I couldn't. It's hard to explain, Lottie, but death can still shock even after all these months. What I mean is: we're here to kill and we do kill some days although most days we just try not to die but I couldn't get my head around shooting one of our own. I'd heard about these executions all right. There was another lad, who was shot in March when we were near Wipers. Everyone knew he was a thief and there was even talk he'd done something to one of the French girls in the village. I didn't see the execution anyway. I just heard about it and shook it off. Otherwise you'd go mad. But this was different, Lottie. I didn't want to do it. It didn't feel right.

We were woken before dawn and told to go behind the barn. Someone had stuck a pole into a small hill midway between the barn and the back wall of the property. We heard a car drive up and the Captain and another soldier appeared around the side of the barn, supporting a young lad between them. His feet dragged behind him. He looked drunk. I hoped for his sake he was drunk, poor devil. It wasn't until they started to tie him to the pole that I realised it was Bettsy. His eyes were half-closed and he seemed to be singing or humming, though it was hard to be sure. As they twisted the ropes around his wrists and ankles, a flock of crows exploded from the trees that rose above the boundary wall, cawing and flapping and making us all jump and squeeze our guns tighter.

A lad beside me whispered: "They sometimes get them drunk to make it easier. If it ever happens to me, that's how I'd like to go. Drunk as a lord."

He tried to laugh but it didn't come out right.

They fixed a white piece of cloth over Bettsy's heart and then went to tie the blindfold round his eyes but he suddenly raised his head and roared.

"No, no, I don't want that. I want to see you and I want you all to see me, to know exactly what you're doing. You don't get to do this the easy way."

He looked straight at us then, Lottie, but I don't think he could make out our faces. We were several yards away and we'd all pulled our scarves around our mouths. I can't be sure though. I'll never be sure.

I looked away, up at the sky where a thin line of red was bleeding across the horizon. What would be the point of staring at his young, swollen face? Better not to see what could do no good, I thought. I could do nothing. I might as well have been someone else, someone who didn't know him. This is what war does, Lottie. It makes us look away, from ourselves, from each other, from what we do, from what we don't do. We might as well be those ants I was talking about for all the mind we pay to each other out here.

When I dared to look over at him again, Bettsy was slumped, chin on his chest. I hoped he'd fallen asleep. But when the first command rang out, he lifted his head and stared straight ahead, eyes suddenly wide. I swear, Lottie, I was sure he was looking straight at me. That fierce look from a dead man threw me off so that my shot went into the sky above his head. No one hit the white cloth although I saw him jerk when two bullets went into his right arm and right leg. I'd heard tell from other lads that this happened a lot. In the end, men just couldn't bring themselves to deliberately kill one of their own, not after all we went through every day to stay alive.

The Captain stormed to the post where Bettsy was groaning. He pulled out his pistol and for the longest second, they just stared at each other. Then the Captain put his pistol to Bettsy's temple and fired. When he stomped back past us, his breathing was fast and his eyes were tiny.

"Two days leave for all of you, you useless bastards," he said.

So we got two days leave, Lottie. For killing Bettsy. Or

rather for not even having the guts to kill him but hurting him instead and leaving him to be shot in the head so that he had all the time in the world to feel the terror we all feel every day, but this time knowing there was no curve on the shell that was coming.

I didn't know what to do after that. I spent most of my two days in the town's only bar, drinking and brawling until I was kicked out into the street where I looked for a few more fights, found them and then walked four miles back to the front, joining my unit a good five hours before my leave was up so that I was hunkered by the trench wall when the first shells came over the next morning.

I wanted to die. For that first hour, I closed my eyes and waited for the end. I was sure it was time. How could it not be after what we'd done? All Bettsy was guilty of was trying to survive. Why aren't we allowed to do that any more? Until this war, this madness we all thought would be a jolly adventure, our whole lives were about surviving. We were not raised to walk towards death, placid and uncomplaining like obedient cows. Nothing we did before prepared us for sitting in a hole waiting to die. Lottie, I have seen men walk deliberately into the bullets because each second lived is just another second to fear death.

Whatever made Bettsy do what he did, whether it was the ringing that some men have in their ears, the cries from no man's land that can last for days, growing fainter and fainter, or the confusion that smothers us all but that some men can't shake off with a brew and a smoke, whatever it was, he was braver than all of us because he did not walk quietly towards the guns. He made a run for it and we shot him down. We said no to that most basic human instinct, the will to survive. So how can we call ourselves human? All this talk of bravery, nobility, sacrifice. It's all bloody lies. I've no idea what I'm here for, but worse, I don't even think it matters.

I have to go now, Lottie. Do you know what really scares me, more than anything else? The thought that even if I make it through, if it ever ends, there won't be anything left of the man you loved. How could there possibly be?

I love you. I don't know what else to say. The sound of those crows exploding from that tree rings in my head, their wings beating the light out of everything.

Yours forever,
Henry

Chapter 6

That was the sound at the heart of your grandfather's silence, Diane. It was his secret, or at least one of them. Who knows what else he carried with him from his war? We all have secrets and the best place for most of them is the grave. Why should we share the many tiny treacheries and deceptions that make up a life? Who would benefit apart from the teller, who might gain some solace from sharing? You're right, of course. I have caught myself again like a fly in a sticky web of words. Isn't that what I am doing, after all? Sharing my terrible secrets to make myself feel better?

In this case, I promise you I am not sharing Henry's secret to make it easier for me to bear. It is too late for that. It was already too late when I found that letter. I just want you to understand how the man who was my father and your grandfather was reshaped by war. Do I secretly hope this will help you understand me? Hand on heart, that is not my aim. Or at least not for this part of the story. What I do want is for you to understand the world as it was then. I believe that is fundamentally important.

As I watch my contemporaries pass on – I cannot in all honesty say friends, not since my dearest Evelyn died last year – I feel like a hoarse-throated oracle with one foot in the grave and still too much to tell. I have a duty to bear witness even though we all swear blindly, blithely, uselessly, falsely, that these things will never happen again. Never again. The most over-used, trite phrase in the English language. We blasted that phrase into oblivion in 1939. If there is another world war, I will not be here but you, my darling, might be and your children, Millie and Jacob, might be. I feel it is my duty to pass on what I know about what happens when we let the dogs of war slip their chains. I worry that the only real deterrent is memory and those of us who bear that crippling burden are dying off. We have a duty, before we go, to tell our tales to those who will carry on, to show the true cost on the human spirit.

I have never been able to write about the Great War or the Second World War in my novels. These conflicts are too personal, too bleak and too incomprehensible to fictionalise. Writing about them would endow them with a kind of reason and logic and I will not, I cannot, do that.

And yet that is the role of the writer, Diane. We sculpt figures from sand. We take human lives in all their fragmentation and we turn them into narratives. We give our transitory flit across this earth structure and, through structure, a false meaning. We turn wars into epics, soldiers into heroes, disasters into destinies. That is the real reason why reading fiction is escapism. It is not that it allows us to break free from the actuality of life not if you eschew science fiction and fantasy, those tawdry baubles that have never interested me. Fiction allows us to escape the pointlessness, the arbitrary and the random. Writers are the real gods because we are the only ones who can confer sense on the senseless and order on chaos. We are the sole purveyors of immortality but like all the stories we spin, it is a fiction.

When I was a child, Charlotte told me that Sally's brother had disappeared in the war, whispering the story to me one night. War stories were often whispered. It was as though the whole world had become a church full of traumatised worshippers, fearful of speaking of evil out loud in case that very deed would bring it to life again.

She said the Betts family never discovered Daniel's Fate. (You see, Diane, I did it there. I described his paltry, degrading death as Fate. I've turned it into a destiny. I've told a lie, a fiction). They were told he was killed in action, the body never found. He just disappeared.

Sally never married. Like many women at that time, she didn't find her Prince Charming before the war and afterwards, both men and motivation were lacking. Of course, she had a crush on Henry at first but when she saw how smitten he was with Charlotte, she graciously backed away and I truly believe she never felt jealous. In reality, she fancied the notion of Henry more than the man himself – she was in love with the idea of the brave and bold soldier with the pretty face. Such a slight caprice was not enough to damage her most enduring friendship. And then when Henry came back from the war, he was not the same man. The myth of the hero-soldier had been obliterated, leaving Sally with no one to worship. I have read that marriage rates were already decreasing before the war and that after 1918 the change wasn't that great. But I am sure those statistics did nothing to comfort Sally.

When I was a child, Sally visited our house regularly. She would turn up around 4pm, before Henry returned from work and sit with Charlotte, drinking tea and eating biscuits. I say drinking tea but there was often a bottle of Gordon's gin on the table as well. Despite her still-young face, Sally always seemed sad and somehow aged to me. She was alone in the world by then. Her parents had survived the war and their son's vanishing only to die of Spanish flu in that kick-in-the-teeth year of 1919.

"They got up, had breakfast, said they felt shivery, their skin turned purple and they were dead by supper time," she told me once, her eyes wide with the unfathomability of it all. I was only six and I shivered at the exquisite horror of it, imagining purple faces and hands. Charlotte's own parents were also gone by then. Her father died of a heart attack in 1922 and her mother followed just nine months later, ostensibly of pneumonia but Charlotte said it was because she could find nothing good to do in the world once the man she doted on and cared for like a pampered son was gone.

One April day, when I was about 10 years old, I stood at the kitchen door and watched Sally sobbing loudly at the table, her head in her hands, shoulders shaking as though waves were rippling along her spine. Charlotte stretched her hand across the pink-and-white cotton tablecloth to rub Sally's arm.

"He would have been 30 today, Lottie. Same age as the century. He's been gone so long but he would only have been 30. Can you believe it? He'd so much living to do. So much growing up. I didn't even get to see what kind of man he would be," Sally said, raising her head.

Her brown curls were flattened across her forehead, her eyes were red and her nose was running. I remember I felt a little disgusted by her streaming, snotty face. That is how we are. We are always disgusted by the wrong things.

"He would've made a fine man, don't you think?"

Charlotte nodded, picked up the bottle of gin and poured a generous amount into two glasses.

"We'll drink to him," she said. They clinked and raised their glasses "to Daniel". Charlotte took a genteel sip while Sally gulped the gin but then this wasn't Charlotte's first drink of the day. Eyes locked on each other, they didn't notice me standing near the door. I have always been good at becoming invisible when it suits me. A trick of the trade.

"He's been dead almost half my life," Sally said and her voice was a bitter wind through the bare branches of a winter tree. "All day I've been thinking, what have I done in that time? I've done nothing except bury my parents. I can't even find a husband. Daniel was so bright, so alive. He would have done something with his life. He would have travelled and made things and seen things. I don't know but it would've amounted to something special. He would have laughed so much and made so many people happy. It's so unfair."

Charlotte had both hands wrapped around her glass, holding it tightly just below her lips so that her knuckles gleamed white.

"Don't think like that, Sally. It doesn't work that way. You don't have to justify your life just because you didn't die. You don't have to prove your right to exist. That's what I keep telling Henry. We mustn't make more of life or death than they merit. All we can do is try to go on happily. We owe the others that."

She smiled as she spoke and I could see Sally's shoulders drop an inch or two as Charlotte's low voice filled the kitchen with a comfort blanket of sound. Charlotte rarely seemed overwhelmed by anything. As a child, I thought it was because she was my mother and mothers were always calm and measured. I learned the hard way that this is not the case. I now believe her equanimity was a curious by-product of the trauma of that age. She had pushed through pain and fear to the other side and she would never again, and could never again, feel the same degree of terror as she had when Henry was fighting in France. That was why our home was a place of utmost reserve. During the war, the guns roared so loudly that the individual's voice could barely be heard. When they fell silent, Charlotte and Henry and all the others found their voices again but they used them so very carefully, imbued with new reverence for the delicate fragility of individual speech. But all the words she didn't say, all the screams she didn't scream, could be seen in Charlotte's white knuckles.

"Do you remember, Sally?" Charlotte said now, her eyes illuminated by the sunlight pouring in the window so that she looked like a seer. "Those romances we used to read before the war? The ones where the handsome man always got the pretty girl at the end?"

Sally nodded as she reached into her purse for a clean handkerchief.

"I can't believe we ever liked them." Charlotte shook her head. "I feel so stupid now. As though we didn't understand anything. We were worse than the stupidest girls around. And the thing is we weren't dunces, we were both smart. But we believed in fairy tales. We should have seen all this coming. Or at least not have thought it was impossible. Why was it so unforeseeable for us? We never believed seriously in the monsters and we took the fairy tales at face value."

"I don't think it was just us," said Sally, sniffing and shaking her head. "No one could have imagined what was going to happen. Look at poor Daniel. He thought the war would be a lark, an adventure. That's why he was in such a hurry to sign up. He was scared it would be over before he got a chance to fight. He wouldn't believe the stories coming from France. We all knew it wasn't going well. You'd have to have been blind and stupid not to, but Daniel wasn't stupid. He was just... just too young to see beyond the posters. He could have been safe, Charlotte. He slipped out that day in April, signed up and that was it. He didn't even come home to say goodbye. If he'd waited until he was 18, it would have been over. I sometimes think that's what really killed my mother. Knowing he could have missed it all. She just didn't want to live in a world where such an absurdity was possible."

She took another sip of gin and for a moment, the only sound in the kitchen was the ticking of the Bakelite clock that looked like an old lady with a brown hood round her white face.

"We were fooled by those stupid romances, Lottie, and Daniel was hoodwinked by tall tales of derring-do. He used to read those scouting books and all those stories of adventure in foreign places. He loved Rider Haggard's novels. There was one in particular, I can't remember the name, I think it was set in Africa, something about mines. For a while, he used to carry that book around with him, stuffing it in the inside pocket of his jacket. Oh, he did make me laugh but I also thought he was special because not many boys liked to read. Now I wish he'd never learned his letters. He might be here now if he hadn't believed all that tosh. Pretty words made fools of us all."

Charlotte sipped her tea and sighed.

"We're all smarter now, Sally. Fat lot of good it seems to be doing though, knowing what we know and watching what's happening over there."

She tilted her head towards the window, towards London and the Channel and the continent where a despot was already hatching plans that would derail our lives again.

The front door clicked. Sally jumped from her chair, pulling her hat onto her head and her purse to her breast, as though my father was the kind of man who would come marching stoutly into the kitchen. I could've told her she had time. Henry always stopped to hang his coat in the hall. I'd caught him a few times, immobile beside the coat stand, staring into the mirror as though wondering who was looking back at him. He saw me hovering at the kitchen door and I ran to hug him. Every hug from Henry was what I secretly called a goodbye embrace – tight and desperate, his fingers fluttering like butterflies on my shoulder blades. He never took anything for granted. As we stood there, Sally rushed past me, eyes down, edging past my father and out the door. I remember thinking she could have at least said hello.

At that time, I thought Sally hated my father. It's a strong word, I know, but that's how 10-year-olds see the world. I guess it's how 16-year-olds, like Daniel, do too. Love and hate, black and white, good and evil, war and freedom, death and life. Old men and their complex, grey grudges spark conflicts but the fighting is done by idealistic teenagers. I assumed Sally had grown to hate my father because he survived and Daniel didn't. I was angry with her for it but even a 10-year-old could understand her pain.

After my parents died and I found Henry's letter, I had to re-evaluate all my memories. Did I impute feelings to Sally when really it was my father who could not bear to see her? I started to question everything. Did it all really happen as I recalled so unshakably for years? Maybe Sally didn't rush out of the house that day. Maybe she did say hello. Maybe she even smiled.

I sifted through my memories of other occasions when Henry and Sally were forced to be together – Charlotte's birthdays, or my birthdays, or the street party we had for the King's Silver Jubilee. I realised I had rarely seen them speak directly to each other but this distance wasn't just Sally's doing. Forcing myself to dig deeper, I remembered seeing my father moving away from Sally at a church fete, inch by deliberate inch so that he ended up on the opposite side of the draughty hall where he stayed, facing the bare stone wall, pretending to read a newspaper. I remembered him turning away from Sally during a dinner at home and deliberately placing himself at the opposite end of tables over the years. Unearthing these memories was like discovering a new dimension that warped the space-time continuum.

One time, we were in our garden, there was bunting and a table of cakes and sweets and it was my 13th birthday. It was one of those soft English summer days, not warm enough for short sleeves but pleasant. What a perfect moniker for this country; a green and pleasant land. I used to think Blake's faint praise was belittling. I realise the value of pleasant now, having spent most of my life chasing the extreme. I can see how such banality might come to seem like paradise.

It was 1933 and we were drawing close to the end of what we called the post-war era because we had not yet allowed ourselves to accept what was coming. In six years, I would meet Robert and fall in love and war would start again. If the summer of 1914 was my parents' last hurrah, then the summer of 1933 was mine. I found out later that 1933 was also the year Dachau opened. Even as I sat in our garden, an unspeakable horror was being birthed on the ground of a munitions factory outside a medieval town none of us had yet heard of.

I was sitting on an upturned crate, one of several that Charlotte had covered with pink-and-white fabric left over

65

from when she made our curtains. I was picking at the fibres and thinking how much I hated pink when I looked up and caught my father staring at Sally, who was standing at the food table with my mother. They were ooh-ing and aah-ing over the birthday cake, a three-layer sponge made by a lady down the road. I was behind the table and so I could see my father clearly, though the ladies could not, and he could not see me. The pain and regret in his face hit me like a physical blow. It was so raw, so unfiltered. Suddenly, he lurched forward, just a few steps but with such energy that it seemed as though he was about to rush over to them. I held my breath: at last, I thought, we would know everything that had been going on behind those dark eyes. He was about to break his silence and it would be as satisfying and definitive as the crash of cymbals at the end of an orchestral piece. But suddenly he froze, swaying with the force of repressed motion, his arms falling to his sides. From behind the table, where Charlotte and Sally were still laughing, I saw the shades come down over Henry's eyes, like net curtains being tugged shut on nosy neighbours. His face gradually returned to normal and he turned on his heel and headed into the house, shaking his arms out to the sides as though they alone had held him back and were now exhausted and trembling.

What gobsmacks me, Diane, is that for well over a decade I remembered that event, and several others, completely differently. When I used to recall that party, conjuring up the image of Charlotte and Sally laughing at the table, I thought the two friends were somehow excluding my father. In my mind, he hovered on the edge of their laughter, like a dog tied to a stake, unable to move closer. I felt sorry for him and I viewed Sally as an interloper, depriving my father of Charlotte's attention. It angered me because I knew Henry needed Charlotte's eyes on him at all times. Her gaze tethered him to the world. But after I read Henry's letter, when it was too late to forgive those involved, I thought back to that day and I saw my father's face again and this time my brain gave up its secret. What I had thought was isolation or loneliness or even jealousy was really the most crushing pity and guilt, the kind of despair that should turn a beholder to stone. Maybe that is what happened to my heart, Diane.

And so I conclude that we see what we want to see even when we don't consciously know what that is. Is there such a thing as a pure memory? I doubt it. And what does that mean for our understanding of history? Is there even such a thing as pure history or is that another illusion that we have created to make sense of the senseless?

I'm afraid I cannot give you the end of Sally's story. Just before the war – it must have been 1938 – she left England for Australia, sailing from Liverpool on a damp June day. Charlotte and I said we would see her off and, to our surprise, Henry insisted on joining us. We sat silently in an otherwise empty compartment on the train. We had little to say, beyond commenting on the wind-swept countryside sprinting past the window as though trying to outrun its own destiny. Sally had left a few days before to pick up her ticket and sort out her trunk.

We met her on the docks and she appeared to be in an almost indecent haste to get going, to start the new life she had been talking about for months. Who could blame her? We all knew war was coming and for Sally, that was the last straw. She would not endure it again, she said. Standing in her best red coat and a tight red hat, she seemed unsettled by Henry's presence. Her conversation with Charlotte was stilted, unnatural. I remember thinking it was a shame and then blushing at my disloyalty to the broken man standing stiffly on the edge of our sorrowful bubble.

Charlotte cried as she hugged her friend but Sally remained dry-eyed. She held Charlotte's hand for a long time though. When she embraced me, she whispered: "Take care of your mother, Lina. She is strong but only because she has to be."

I nodded but could not speak. I had grown up with Sally

and at the time, going to Australia was a kind of death. I knew I would never see her again. It's hard for you to imagine, I know, but there were still geographical impossibilities then, Diane.

Sally nodded to Henry and he nodded back. She turned and started up the gangway, a middle-aged woman with slumped shoulders and a bowed head. She cut an isolated, lonely figure among the helter-skelter of young emigrants, all shiny shoes, sharply cocked hats and new world enthusiasm. I wondered if she would seem as out-of-place when her new black boots touched land in Sydney.

Suddenly, my father darted into the crowd, heading for the gangplank. Charlotte gasped, her hand coming to her mouth, her eyes darting to me and beyond, looking for help should she need it. You never knew with these men who'd come back from over there when you might need assistance.

"Where is he going?" I heard her whisper. "Where is he going now?"

At nearly 18, I was a head taller than Charlotte and by standing on my tiptoes, I could just glimpse my father's head as he pushed through the crowd. He caught up with Sally, grabbed her arm and she whirled around, her eyes wide. Henry leant in and whispered in her ear. He had her hands clasped in his and I remember being shocked by this familiarity. I turned quickly to see if my mother was watching but Charlotte was darting her eyes left and right, scanning the crowd for answers. I turned back to the gangplank, just in time to see Sally shake her arm free of Henry, shout something that was lost in the hullaballoo of new lives starting, and then storm up the ramp. She was swallowed by the people milling around on the deck. We stood there until the gangplank was raised, the ship's horn bellowed its melancholy goodbye and the tugs began to haul the great beast out into the channel.

Henry returned to Charlotte's side. She opened her mouth, as though to ask him something, but stopped when she read the bleak anguish on his face. She turned back to the ship.

"I thought she would wave," she said quietly. "I imagined we'd see her again."

Henry, eyes red in a red face, said nothing but he took Charlotte's hand in his and they stood for a few minutes more, watching people they did not know sail off to a place they would never see. We never saw Sally again.

CHAPTER 7

I turned 18 three weeks after Sally left. You remember the fizzing potential of 18, Diane? Of course, your own 18th birthday is less distant than mine and your children's birthdays must seem like yesterday. I think they are both in their 20s now? You see, I have kept an eye on your family, from afar. Information is, after all, what I have long traded in.

From my vantage point, a human life seems a mere blip – an echoless clap in an infinite space. But then I think of how much changed between my 18th and yours and I wonder at the brazen speed of the world's transformation. Our linear measurement of time is inadequate. It falls short because it cannot convey depth and arguably that is more important than duration. The Great War only lasted four years but that cannot be the truth. How to measure the endless stretch of a day in a flooded, rat-infested trench? The eternity of that last minute ticking down for an exhausted, lice-ridden, black-fingered soldier waiting to go over the top into the void? The hours it took for the screaming to stop in no man's land? Time should be graded in some way, like coffee perhaps. One measurement for the day-to-day tick-and-tock, and another for time that devastates and defines. For me, 1938 was a year that defined.

I won a place to study literature at Somerville College in Oxford and one drizzly day in early September, my parents drove my leather trunk and me the 40-odd miles from St

Albans to the women's college. It was a good hour-and-a-half trundle through the kind of honeysuckle-stippled, velveteen landscape that poets celebrated and men who fought with my father died to preserve, or so they said.

Charlotte and Henry were mostly silent. There was little to say. We had worn our excitement out in the weeks since I had been accepted and there was no question of talking about current affairs. What could not be helped, must surely be ignored. I felt jittery, as though my blood was fizzing through my veins. We drove past fat-haunched cows and vacant-faced sheep, grazing peaceably as though their time would never end even as our car and my life raced forward. I had declared age 12 that I would go to university and it had been a given in our household since then even though neither Charlotte nor Henry had gone. We chose Somerville because it was relatively close and Charlotte's father had also gone to Oxford. A tenuous enough reason for a decision that would change my life.

Who was the almost-woman, all big eyes and fidgety fingers, sitting in the back of the car that Saturday morning? If you had asked Charlotte, she would have said: "Lina is headstrong, smart and a little too forward for her own good. She is the girl I might have been if I had been born in this century." She might also have mentioned my oft-noted tendency to blame others when I myself fell short of expectations. She was fond of gently pointing out this unseemly trait.

If you had asked Henry, he would have said: "Lina is delightful, always smiling. She brings light into my day."

Both descriptions were true and both were incomplete. I did always smile when my father was around. Charlotte had schooled me in this perpetual cheerfulness since childhood. I felt it was my duty, the only thing I could do that might in some way make up for what he had suffered. Henry and I could never have a truly honest relationship. He was too damaged for that. We could never lift our masks but maybe that is the case to some degree with all parents and their children, with all people, in fact. Who among us has the courage to reveal all, except to themselves, in the slightest of whispers, in the darkest of dead hours?

With Charlotte, I was more relaxed. She was the one I railed against when things didn't go my way, when homework was too hard, dresses too frumpy, hair too unruly, teachers too mean, life too unfair. But there were things I could not show her. I admired her control so much that I felt unable to honestly reveal all my own weaknesses. Especially not when I was cleaving both away from and towards her, as all teenagers must. But what would I know, you say. I never was a mother to a teenager. Perhaps, but one doesn't need to be a painter to appreciate art.

We were winding our way through Worminghall when Henry spoke.

"I knew a lad from here. His name was Dick but damned if I can remember his surname. Funnily enough no one called him anything except Dick though we usually called lads by their last names. Maybe it was because he looked so young. Lovely looking boy, dark curly hair, big brown eyes like a puppy and he'd one of those wide smiles that'd set everybody off. He bought it on the Somme, first day in fact."

I could sense a new tension in Charlotte's back but she said not a word. I wondered what was coming. Henry so rarely spoke of the war.

"He was a little ahead of me when he took a bullet to his right leg and fell, but very softly, like he was kneeling down. I saw him and I was about to run over because I thought I could pull him back to the trench – we'd only gone about 40 steps. But then I saw him jerk again and there was red all over his chest and a bullet whizzed past my cheek so I dodged the other way. And then it was already too late to go back. That's how it was. One second, and one second, and one second, and something terrible happening in each one, and nothing to do about any of it."

Charlotte and I didn't say anything. I tried to catch her eye in the rear view mirror but she was looking out at the fields and her face was as closed as a tomb.

"Yes, that's what it was like then. Just like that," Henry said and then he fell silent again.

Later, when we were alone in my new quarters, I asked Charlotte why he had suddenly decided to speak of the war. She shook her head slowly and said, "I don't know why, Lina. Maybe because you were going away or maybe it's this new war coming. It's preying on his mind a lot. But I couldn't say for sure. Only Henry really knows."

When we arrived at the college, Henry carried my trunk up the stairs of the student hall and into a cramped room with chaste twin beds in matching pale blue covers. He kissed me once on the top of my head, wished me luck and said he would wait in the car. He left the room, his slow steps echoing dully in the hall. He never was one for wordy displays of emotion. At least not when I knew him.

Charlotte sat on the bed, pulling me down beside her.

"Now listen, Lina. Your father and I will miss you terribly but this is your new life and I don't want you to be moping around, thinking of us. Make the most of every opportunity. This is the start of something wonderful for you. No matter what happens. This is where your dreams can begin to take flight. Let them. Don't allow what is happening out there to distract you because there will be an after. There is always an after."

I hugged her, mainly so I could discreetly rub the tears from my eyes. I wish I could say I was worried about the possibility of war but I wasn't. Sitting there in that tiny room, so clean, so bare and so foreign, I was terrified of not fitting in, of not making friends, of failing. But I couldn't let the side down by crying over such piffling concerns. Not in front of Charlotte, not after what she had been through.

I dried my tears and forced myself to smile.

"I just wish Evelyn was here. If she was, I would be so much happier," I said. I nearly said braver but that would just have drawn attention to my cowardice. I was ever the great dissembler.

Remember I mentioned Evelyn earlier, Diane? She was my best friend and she died last year. Evelyn, who never gave a fig for danger or risk, was finally defeated by her own body, losing herself to the ovarian cancer that ate away at her from the inside. Nothing else could have bested her, that's for sure.

In 1938, she had decided to enrol in a secretarial college near St Albans to be closer to home. Her mother's health was failing and although Evelyn would have scoffed at the idea, she was too loyal a daughter to walk out on a sick parent.

Evelyn arrived at my school aged nine after her father took a job in the town. That first day in the playground, we slotted into each other like pieces of a puzzle. By the end of the hour, we were walking arm-in-arm and laughing at nothing, secure enough already in our world-of-two to disregard the other children. Soulmates seems such a trite word, the kind of thing one might see in a lonely hearts column. But Evelyn and I *were* soulmates. Perhaps that is why this past year has unsettled me so. With Evelyn gone, how can I be complete? How can the world be complete? I feel, sometimes, as though Evelyn took gravity with her when she passed. I hope you have a friend like Evelyn, Diane, but I wish I could spare you the grief of their passing. Love demands such a high price.

I always envied Evelyn her relationship with her father, particularly as we got older. On summer evenings, Evelyn and Mr Watts would sit together playing cards in the garden, he with his pipe and she with a look of perfect contentment. I envied her that ease. I desperately wanted a father who was whole and I hated myself for it.

Mr Watts was a little older than Henry and he'd been disqualified from fighting because of his poor eyesight and bronchial chest.

"Blind as a bat and with puny lungs to boot," Evelyn said with a rueful laugh. "But he did his bit. He was living down in Devon then, a place called Dawlish Warren, and his job as part of the Home Guard was to patrol the coast in case of invasion. Mind you, I'm not sure what they were thinking letting him do that with his dodgy eyes. He spent most of his time trying to shoot rabbits on the golf course. Never hit a thing, obviously."

She laughed and then glanced nervously at me as if in silent apology. We were sitting in the branches of the beech tree at the bottom of her garden and I had just told her Henry's story. We were probably about 12, that age of awakening when the world comes into focus and one's eyes begin to turn outwards.

There were many things I felt jealous about when I was with Evelyn, an only child with straightforward parents, living in a sprawling, creeper-covered house on one of St Albans' poshest streets. She was wealthy, pretty and there were no gloomy shadows that I could see hanging over her perfect life. Of course, that was not true. If it really had been, I doubt she would have remained my friend through all these years. I am petty enough to dislike perfection in others and anyone truly uncomplicated could never have condoned all my many sins, big and small. I never concealed anything I did from Evelyn and although at times she stopped speaking to me for months on end, she never gave up on me entirely. And I never gave up on her.

Without Evelyn's sardonic voice in my ear, I was lonely and overwhelmed in Oxford. To combat the dizziness of displacement, I steeped myself in Somerville's history, hoping to ground my ephemeral new life in something solid and immutable. I had always been obsessed with the Great War, reading everything I could about it, and when I discovered that the college had been converted into a military hospital during that time, my passion was reawakened. I walked around the buildings, imagining injured soldiers in all the places now reclaimed by us girls. I stood on the terrace of the library, wondering what the men who lay there, convalescing, had thought as they looked out at the luscious green lawns. It must have seemed so surreal after what they'd experienced. Did they wake in the middle of the night, sweat-covered and gasping, terrified they were back at the front, fearing that this retreat was the real fantasy? I was quite the daydreamer then, Diane. I suppose I still am, although now I deliberately spin fantasies to turn a buck, as the saying goes. Back then, my daydreaming was less mercenary.

I met Robert Stirling on September 30, 1938. I am not naturally given to remembering romantic anniversaries, despite my otherwise muscular memory, but in this case I remember the date because of something else entirely. It was the day Neville Chamberlain returned from Munich waving that little piece of paper that we thought could hold the line, if you'll forgive the pun.

I was in a teahouse near Balliol, a bright, airy room where I used to go regularly because I liked the bustle of that quarter and because the middle-aged waitress had something of Charlotte around her delicate lips. I was sitting in the window, with a copy of Edward Thomas' *Collected Poems* open in front of me. I had taken to carrying that book in my bag, believing naively that its physical presence brought me closer to my father – like a literary bridge stretching back to St Albans. At that moment though, I was not reading. I was staring out the window, idly observing the Darwinesque struggle between cyclists and cars over the cobbled junction in front of me. It was, as I remember, a grey day, remarkable only for the fact that the heavy rain that had plagued my first term had briefly abated. But the cobbles were still damp, vastly increasing my amusement as I watched cyclists skid into the kerb or each other.

The wireless was on in the background, tinting the air with a soft jazzy melody. The bell over the door jingled and I looked up.

He was wearing a tweed suit without a tie and the first word that leapt to my mind was 'entitled'. It was in his long thin nose and ice-blue eyes, in the angularity of his face under brown hair that was fashionably parted in the centre, rising like little waves to the sides. He marched straight to a table in the back, sat down, asked for a black coffee and pulled a folded newspaper from his pocket, shaking it out with the air of a man who does not mind ruffling the atmosphere around him. I studied his reflection in the window, naughtily thrilled that I could observe him secretly. Economics, Balliol, second year, I thought. Plays rugby well, middling at tennis and supports the Tories, of course. Came up from a sprawling family estate in Wiltshire although his father had to sell off a few cottages and fields to make ends meet after the war. Father an army man, but most likely an officer and spared the trenches.

I played this guessing game a lot in those early weeks at Oxford as I sought to find my feet. I invented backgrounds for interesting, by which I usually meant beautiful, people. I was pretty enough myself back then to be exhilarated by true beauty. These were the people who caught my critical eye. I was superficial, yes, but I will not apologise for this weakness. It is the mildest of crimes. You could, I suppose, call these guessing games my earliest efforts at fiction. I was creating characters and yes, some of them did pop up in my books years later, nuanced by the passage of time.

You would not be wrong, Diane, if you detected some class prickliness in those first impressions of Robert Stirling. I never doubted my right to be at Somerville – I had worked hard and deserved my scholarship – but I did often feel inferior and I abhorred this weakness in myself, seeing it as a betrayal of my own background. I told myself crossly that the fact that I felt out of place was as much my fault as the fault of the place itself. The wealthier students did not care one jot whether I was studying at Oxford or not. They literally did not see me. I wanted to be that oblivious to others' opinions, to others' existences. The Great War had blasted chunks out of the walls dividing classes but they were never destroyed. Our uniquely English sensitivity about class continues to mark us out from the rest of the world. And for all the recent talk about creating a classless society, I doubt we could survive as a race without the ability to pigeonhole people definitively within seconds of meeting them on the basis on their accent, table manners or tea etiquette. To preserve such things did brave men die.

As the daughter of a solicitor and a secretary-turned-housewife, I felt I was barely tolerated in Oxford. And by that I mean I could barely tolerate my own sense of inadequacy. I wanted to walk through the streets with the swagger that only years of breeding and, if I'm honest, an appendage between the legs could confer. All of us women students were still, to some degree, out of place among the hallowed halls of learning but within our own group, we also built walls.

"Could you please turn up the wireless?"

It was the young man, speaking to the waitress.

My fake-mother smiled and leaned up to the shelf above the counter to twist the dial. Sombre male tones filled the room. Chamberlain was back from his meeting with Hitler and had been greeted by cheering crowds at Heston airport, we were told. The young man rose from his seat and went to the counter, the better to make out Chamberlain's words over the scritch and scratch of the broadcast.

"We are determined to continue our efforts to remove possible sources of difference and thus to contribute to assure the peace of Europe."

I thought I heard a stifled groan. I dared to look at the young man directly. At that moment, before I even knew his name, I found something heartbreaking in his stance; the way his head was tilted down, gazing at the wooden counter the better to concentrate on the words squeaking out of the wireless. I felt as though I was looking at one of the beautiful doomed 'lads' who peopled my treasured Great War poems; a perfectly tragic symbol of youthful sacrifice.

Despite Chamberlain's protestations, there was no doubt in my mind that we were heading for war. I never believed for a single second that a piece of paper could make any difference to a man like Hitler, a man Churchill described later as a "bloodthirsty guttersnipe". As I listened to the wireless report, I wondered if the rapturous reception the prime minister had received when he returned with that flimsy paper flag was less relief and more a kind of mass hysteria, a fake joy from people who knew this was their last hurrah for a very long time. The last deception they would be able to permit themselves.

Chamberlain was speaking again: *"We regard the agreement signed last night and the Anglo-German naval agreement as symbolic of the desire of our two peoples never to go to war with one another again."*

Robert looked up and I caught his eye.

"Do you believe that?" he asked, unfolding his long body elegantly and walking over to my table.

"I'd like to," I said. "But I'm not sure that the people's desires have very much to do with things at this stage."

He smiled broadly, sat down in the free chair and extended his hand.

"Robert Stirling. May I join you? Very forward of me, I know, but these are exceptional times and if the threat of war has any upside for cannon fodder like myself, it must be gifting one the temerity to approach a beautiful woman."

He was quite the charmer, Diane. We lost sight of that later.

"You *are* fresh, aren't you?" I replied. "But does that mean you don't believe our good man Chamberlain's words?"

"I believe he believes them, which is something, I suppose. But I can't say the same for Herr Hitler. From all I've read, he wants to expand and expand he will. You know, he fought in the Great War and some say that's what's driving him. But what about you? What do you think?"

He leaned in and fixed those clear eyes on my face. His intensity took my breath away so that I had to bow my head to break the spell. I traced a pattern on the red tablecloth with my finger. I felt ridiculous but it was not an unpleasant sensation.

"Oh, I'm sure I don't know," I said, my touchy shyness returning.

"Somehow I don't believe that for a second," he said and when I looked up, he was smiling again.

"You never told me your name."

"You're right. I didn't," I said but I immediately regretted my archness. Of course, I wanted to tell him my name.

"Lina Rose," I said quickly. "And please don't say it's beautiful because I've heard it all before."

"Very well, I won't," he said. "It's a stinker of a name. I can't imagine what your parents were thinking. I shall just call you Gertrude."

We spent the rest of the afternoon in that near-deserted café as the clouds gathered outside and the rain came down again. My initial assessment was, of course, entirely wrong. He was studying law at Corpus Christi. He was from Suffolk, his father had been a doctor but had died from a heart attack in 1936. His mother's family were in the steel industry and had done well from the Great War.

"It might not have been great for everyone but it was wonderful for the Pritchards," he said. "I owe my place here to the war. What do you think about that? Silver lining or ultimate irony, given what's about to happen? Finally able to afford Oxford but I'll most likely have to fight instead. If only to expunge our family's guilt."

His tone was light but there was something forced about his thin smile.

"I think you'd have to ask someone who's been through war, maybe someone like Edward Thomas," I said, nodding at my book. "He would be a valid arbiter, don't you think?"

Robert nodded and intoned:

"This is no case of petty right or wrong
That politicians or philosophers
Can judge."

"Indeed," I said sharply to cover my surprise and my urge to giggle at his ridiculous arms akimbo pose and ostentatiously sombre tone. I should not have been surprised. We were all steeped in war poetry then. But I had not expected this tall, worldly student to quote Thomas with such ease. That was the first of many epiphanies during my relationship with your father, Diane.

He was clearly delighted to have caught me off-guard.

"Things are not always what they seem, Gertrude. You'd think we'd all know that by now."

I realised he was holding my hand. My fingers curled around his and that was it.

Chapter 8

For the next year, Robert and I took a break from the world, floating above the ground in our own little bubble. It wasn't that we were stupid, although I do now shake my head at our guileless, simplistic faith in love. We knew what was coming – everyone did by late 1938 – but we made a conscious decision not to engage with this knowledge. Our universe-of-two was all we needed and vastly superior to the fear-ridden world around us where, like crockery on a sinking ship's top table, everyone was sliding towards the abyss. The newspapers were full of doom: there was the seizure of Prague in March, the distribution of gas masks, including tiny masks for babies, the delivery of free air raid shelters to quizzical families on narrow London streets, the mass production of boots and uniforms for men to die in and talk that thousands of pets would have to be slaughtered to prepare for the expected bombing of London. Pamphlets were dropped into letterboxes telling people how to evacuate their children, how to erect Anderson shelters correctly so they didn't flood and how to put up blackout material and secure their windows with brown tape. Butlins was offering 'crisis cures' to help people forget the mounting tension. But we didn't need to go away to find escape.

We didn't have time for a traditionally tentative courtship. There was a breathlessness to life then; it was as if we were all, always, rushing for the last train. It was exhausting but since I am being totally honest here, it was also exhilarating. We were young and youth has a ridiculous ability to conflate danger and delight. We were also in love and, as they say, love is blind. Or perhaps it would be more accurate to say our love was wilfully short-sighted.

We spent as much time as we could together, meeting at least once every day. If you had asked 19-year-old Lina what was going on, she would have grabbed your hands in her hot ones, bent towards you as if sharing an earth-shattering secret, and whispered: "It's love at first sight, Diane. We were made for each other. I cannot imagine life without him. Isn't it wonderful?"

Then, she would have hugged you to her and you would have felt the exquisite pulse of her happiness vibrating through her shoulders, down her back and into her arms. She was charming and happy and I do miss her sometimes. Though I would have to tell her, be careful what you wish for, my dear.

We couldn't live together, of course, but we managed to spend many nights wrapped in each other's arms. After suffering some nasty scratches and colourful bruises, Robert became adept at scaling the trellis outside my dorm and slipping into the corridor through a window that I left ajar. There was an empty room at the end of the hall where I had concealed sheets and a thin blanket. We would lie on the damp floor surrounded by the detritus of student life – battered trunks, a broken bicycle, a violin case and slack-stringed tennis rackets. We called it our Shangri-La. If that room still exists, our strangled cries and soft sighs must still be floating in the musty air and echoing behind the walls. Even today, with everything I know, I sometimes feel the most sorrowful yearning when I remember those pitch-black, sweat-filled nights, when I no longer knew where I ended and Robert began.

Robert had his own tiny room in a boarding house near the Grove. His landlady, Mrs Danton, was a plump, fierce widower, who took a shine to me after an animated conversation about poetry. It turned out she "dabbled in verse". I read some of her poems, lyrical nothings full of suns setting on lost loves with an undertone of moralism. I pretended to like them and perhaps I even did back then and in turn Mrs Danton made herself scarce when I crept downstairs in the mornings. She always left the side door to the lane on the latch. I believe she was both deliciously titillated by my scandalous ways and simultaneously breathlessly hoping for my downfall. What a poem she would write then! Oh there would be stanzas depicting sensual joy in flower-studded fields but then the thunderous storm of retribution would pass overhead and smite the sinners. She was not a bad woman; we all enjoy a dramatic downfall.

For several months, I held back from telling Charlotte and Henry about Robert. I wanted to keep him all to myself, as though only isolation from the rest of the world could ensure our love would thrive. But, of course, they had to meet and one damp February day, we had tea and cakes together in the teahouse where we first met. Robert was at his charming best and although Henry did not say much, his eyes were soft as he looked on the younger man. Soft and sad, as they always were. Charlotte clearly adored him, although I do not think she understood the depth of my feelings. She would have been much more concerned if she had.

The end of this blissful era came in late May 1939. It was just after 6am as I scampered barefoot along the lane beside Mrs Danton's house. The sky was beginning to pale, silvering the cobblestones and the rooftops like spilt mercury. As I reached the main road, I slipped on my shoes and tiptoed along, glancing nervously up at the houses across the street. It might be hard to believe now but back then I did actually care what people thought. As a woman, albeit an ostensibly emancipated and educated one, you couldn't afford not to care in 1930s Britain. The Great War had eroded some of the barricades erected around the fairer sex and what was to come would continue the attrition, but the image of the fallen woman has proved remarkably immune to most modernising influences. She lingers to this day – look at Princess Diana, the judgments and the almost indecent glee at the breakup of her marriage. We are all Eves and the world will never let us forget our original sin.

I ran along the street, my body still buzzing from our morning lovemaking. I am not going to go into details – no one wants that from their parents, no matter how lyrically described – but every nerve-end in my body was tingling. I adored sex with Robert. It sounds like a silly thing to say but I do not believe it is always a given in marriage, or indeed in love affairs.

Of course, I was dreadful at it at first. There was no *Cosmopolitan* to tell you what to do in those days and, to be honest, most men did not know very much either. I'd had a few affairs before Oxford but no one we need to bother ourselves with here. Spotty youths fumbling with my bra behind haystacks while crows cawed their sympathy above me and magpies cackled at our clumsiness. At that time, many women still had no idea what an orgasm was. Sex was purely functional for most. There were other voices but they were most definitely in the social wilderness. We did not really expect a great deal of pleasure. Our romantic notions, fuelled by the clean-cut movies and our trashy novels, were so otherworldly that sex often seemed too crude to consider seriously.

I know now that Robert was unusually thoughtful and generous. We never talked about it – one wouldn't have dreamed of such indelicacy – but I have since wondered where he learned to do the things he did. It saddens me deeply that I will never know. Not because I am, or indeed was, jealous, but because I wish I had known more about my husband. We never got to the comfortable phase of marriage where such riddles might have been unravelled gently over a late-night glass of wine. But perhaps that is as it should be. The modern mania for total transparency is overrated.

Secrets, even and perhaps especially between lovers, are no bad thing. One should always retain some distance.

I remember my first orgasm as I remember your birth, Diane. I knew then that everything about me had changed. The knowledge was as sharp and monumental as the waves of pleasure rushing from some hitherto unknown core. It was as though I had discovered a third eye that could see everything in brighter, prismatic detail.

That May morning, I could still feel that exquisite tension between my legs as I ran along the edge of the park, rushing to get back to my dorm to wash and prepare for my lectures. It had rained overnight and the faint perfume of budding flowers and trees wafted over the silent backstreets. It would be years before I would notice those delicate scents again. I must have closed my mind to all sweet fragrances during the war years. Or maybe they just weren't there. All I remember are the gagging odours of damp shelters and sweating bodies, clouds of dust and the stomach-turning, ferrous smell of the dead. But there must have been flowers, of course. Nature gives not a jot for our crises. Flowers did grow and I must have seen them. I just couldn't smell them any more.

That morning, I felt ridiculously happy and carefree. A blackbird was trilling in a bush near the road. I spied a flock of geese flying in a V-shape above me, their wings swishing a soft lullaby above the sleeping town. I noticed raindrops like tears on crimson roses in the front garden of one of the terraced houses. I was tingling with awareness, humming with a sensuous appreciation for the quick of life. As I walked along Holywell Street, I passed a newspaper kiosk and was pulled up short by a headline: *Military Training Act becomes law*. I stood there like a puppet whose strings have been cut. Just like that, my incandescent vigour was gone. That is what war does, Diane. It cuts our strings.

I knew Robert would enlist even though he was entitled to an exemption as a student. When the bill was proposed in April, he had brought it up as we lay in his bed, even though we usually avoided discussing Britain's slow drift to another war. His reasoning was bleakly practical: if war came, all men would eventually be called up so he might as well maintain some control, volunteer early, get whatever training was on offer and prepare himself as best he could.

"I have even more reason now to take my Fate into my own hands," he said, running his finger up and down the hollow between my breasts. "I have to survive for you. For us. Whatever about the rest, we are worth fighting and living for."

It pains me to admit it but when he spoke those sombre words, I smiled, wrapping my legs even tighter around him. I was enchanted by the romance of his declaration. I did not, or would not, understand what the words meant, what he must be feeling as he said them. This is how we fail to hear each other, even when we are listening, eyes locked on a loved one's face.

I took a copy of the *Times*, my hands shaking as I fumbled for coins. This was the end of our idyll. An end foreshadowed but no less painful for that. I was terrified by what I knew and what I could not yet know. I had seen what a war could do but what would this war do to us?

Robert decided to enlist at the employment office in Felixstowe where his mother still lived and so a week later, we put his trunk in the back seat of his black Morris Minor and set off on the journey to the seaside town where I would meet his mother and then, most probably, say goodbye to the man I loved. We did not make a fuss over the departure from Mrs Danton's but we both knew our Oxford era was over. Mrs Danton pulled Robert to her, wishing him luck as if that was the only thing that could help him, as if the luck she wished for would somehow prove more potent than all the other luck being invoked across the country.

"I never had a son to send to war and Mr Danton passed on in 1913, Lord have mercy on him," she said, pulling a handkerchief from her pocket and dabbing her eyes.

"I always thought that was a mercy. He would not have

understood the Great War. Such a gentle man. I declare I am beside myself just thinking about all you young men and what you will endure. I am sure there must be no other way but it does make you wonder."

Robert took her hands in his and beamed down at her.

"Mrs Danton, you mustn't worry. There is nothing people like you and me can do now except try to get through what is coming. Each generation must pay its dues. Our time is now. That's all it is. It isn't more complicated than that. And by all accounts, we have some truly modern weapons now like bigger tanks and faster fighter planes and enormous guns. It won't be like the last time. Maybe it will be more civilised, in some ways."

He released her hands and stepped back. But she was still sniffling and there was something so archetypically moving in the sight that I felt compelled to speak.

"Will you write us a poem, Mrs Danton? Will you write something about Robert and me and send it to my parents? I will make sure to copy it and send it to Robert wherever he is and when he comes back, we will come and tell you whether we liked it or not."

Her face brightened and she wagged a finger at me.

"Aren't you the cheeky one? You ask for a work of art and then have the gall to say you might not like it."

But her smile was wide and her shoulders pulled back again. She narrowed her eyes.

"Of course, if the portrait of you is not to your liking, Miss Rose, that might have less to do with the quality of the poet and more to do with your own inner qualities."

We all laughed and so at least that first goodbye ended happily. You might be surprised to know, Diane, that I truly cared about Mrs Danton. I was nicer back then. By 1945, my ability to feel compassion was greatly diminished. Every bomb whistling its doleful dirge as it descended, every flattened home, every reported death of one of those spotty youths I spoke of before tore a strip from my heart until I could feel no emotion for anyone outside my immediate circle. I would recover, we all would, but some of the damage was, I fear, irreversible.

I hugged Mrs Danton, thinking I would probably never see her again. I'd already decided that if Robert volunteered, I would not continue my studies. It would make no sense to cling onto dreams that belonged to the past while the man I loved fought to protect our place in a new world order. It would be too incongruous to be borne, no matter what Charlotte had advised. I was very idealistic then, Diane. I wanted and needed to share as much of Robert's life as I could.

In those weeks before he enlisted, I used to daydream about how I might follow him to the battlefield, imagining myself as a modern-day, better equipped, less dissolute version of the women who followed their men during the Crimean War. There was something decadently appealing about these ladies who made their way to the Black Sea to peer at the fighting through opera glasses from the decks of private yachts.

In the library at Somerville, I found an original copy of Fanny Duberly's journal, described inexplicably as a classic travel book. I thrilled to the idea of this redoubtable woman riding side-saddle to watch her husband go into battle during the Charge of the Light Brigade. She would rise before dawn with the troops, pack up and glug a mouthful of brandy before setting off on her horse.

I was aware that not all women who joined their men on the journey to the Crimea fared so well — some took to alcohol and some became prostitutes in the narrow alleys of Scutari when they realised the army could not or would not provide for them. Despite this and despite what I knew at second hand of the horrors of war, there was a part of me that wanted in on what was coming. I'd like to say it was a feminist urge to be equal, to be a player not a bystander. But my motives were not purely feminist – did we even really know the word then? In truth, I was gripped by a teenager's lust for adventure. Nothing more complex than that. Empires have been built and wars sustained by this kind of foolish thinking for centuries and our generation was no different.

I did not imagine myself on horseback, of course. I have always hated those beasts, ever since one lunged at my fingers when I was trying to feed it when I was about three. Charlotte and Henry laughed so hard the pain was almost worth it. No, I saw myself – I almost blush to admit this – bringing tea to Robert, as he stood erect and defiant on the fire step, peering with a gaze of steel over the sandbagged parapet into no man's land. You see how naïve I was, Diane. My only reference was the Great War. I thought it would be like that again. I was so wrong. The loss and horror and misery were similar but everything else was so different. Twenty years is a long time for those tasked with improving the killing machines and they had used the inter-war years well, as Robert pointed out to Mrs Danton. He was just wrong about the effect.

Robert's mother lived just outside Felixstowe in an elegant house she had bought with her 'war loot', as Robert called it. She herself had little to do with the steel industry – her brothers ran a clutch of factories in Sheffield – but when her father died in 1914, he left her a percentage of future profits as well as a generous lump sum. When her husband died, leaving her another substantial legacy, she moved from the family's modest townhouse to this grandiose, colonnaded two-storey residence on a couple of acres, just north of the town.

"She loved my father, of course," Robert said as we sped through the countryside around Colchester, hooting madly at any pedestrians, cyclists or animals that had the temerity to step into our path. Robert was an enthusiastic and reckless driver, like most men at that time.

"But she felt he held her back, socially I mean. He was a very plain-spoken, humble man. He hated the fact he had married into what he took to calling 'the industry of death'. When I was younger I thought he was being a bit harsh – after all before the war, steel companies including Pritchards were making railways and ships and cars. But my father found fault with that too. I remember one time when Uncle Toby came to stay and he held forth after dinner about how the Pritchards were an integral part…"

Robert took both hands from the wheel to mimic his uncle's gestures so that the car swerved wildly towards the ditch. When I stopped screaming and he stopped laughing, he continued.

"Sorry about that. I guess you *do* need to keep your hands on the wheel, as they keep telling us. Anyway, Uncle Toby said the Pritchards were an integral part of the Empire-building machine. He's always been a pompous ass but my father was having none of it.

He said: 'You would consider that an honour, would you, Toby?' I remember he was stroking his beard and whenever he did that, it meant he was about to put someone firmly in their place. I was sitting in the corner, hoping they'd forget about me as it was past my bedtime. I recognised the danger signs and wanted to see where this would end. I was rooting for my father, of course. He went on to lecture Uncle Toby about Britain grabbing power in places where we weren't wanted. I think he even talked about brutalities against the natives. He asked my uncle if that was indeed something to be proud of. I remember Toby grinning smugly and looking at my mother. He fake-shook his head like this, like a disappointed teacher, and then he said: 'Felicity, I always said you married a liberal.'" Robert laughed.

"My father just smiled. I think he was quite proud of that."

Robert's father had not fought in the Great War; as a doctor he was exempt from conscription. But he was anything but exempt from the consequences of war. He worked in a convalescent centre near Felixstowe and treated the men who made it home. Robert said he called them 'the pulverised'. He said his father's heart gave out because it could no longer bear the weight of what the broken men told him over long days and endless nights.

I would have liked to have known Mr Stirling. I was not so keen, however, on meeting his wife.

I asked Robert if he thought his mother would like me. He'd laughed a little too brightly and pulled me into his arms, perhaps to prevent me from seeing his face.

"How could she not?" he said.

"Let me count the ways," I mumbled from the depths of his tweed-covered chest, my eyes anxiously peering ahead as the car swerved again.

Mrs Felicity Stirling née Pritchard was positioned at the top of the broad steps leading to the front door when we pulled up. Something about the way she stood, straight-backed with her hands folded demurely in front of her, rang false to me. It was as though she was consciously acting out the part of the elegant doyenne – recreating something she had seen at the pictures.

"She's wearing her pearls," Robert breathed as he stopped the car. "Heaven help us."

I was hardly a dream future daughter-in-law for that era. The fact that I had gone up to Oxford would have been extremely off-putting for some mothers. My origins, as we said then, were relatively humble. Educated, yes, but definitely not wealthy. Pretty but hardly stunning enough to justify an imbalanced match. I could tell, from the strained smile on Mrs Stirling's face, that I had already disappointed her and I hadn't even stepped out of the car.

"Robert, my darling," she gushed as he ran up the steps to her. "You look wonderful. I'm so thrilled you're here even if… well, the circumstances."

For a wild moment, I thought she was talking about me and I flushed. But then I remembered the war.

"Mrs Stirling, it is a great pleasure to meet you. Thank you so much for inviting me," I said as I climbed the stairs like a commoner approaching her Queen. I swear, Diane, I almost curtsied.

"Welcome, Lina. And you must call me Felicity, of course." She tittered gaily, tilting her head towards Robert whose face was stretched awkwardly between a grin and a grimace.

"Do come inside. You would hardly believe it is summer. I almost feel we should light a fire, although I cannot bring myself to ask Carter to do it. I'd feel like such a silly girl."

Despite my fears, Robert's mother was perfectly pleasant to me for the next few hours. She prattled and primped and flattered her son outrageously but if she occasionally took on Mrs Bennet-levels of absurdity, I spotted something harder, more calculating in her eyes when she thought I wasn't looking. She was a woman with a plan, a woman who had always had a plan. I concluded that she did not like me at all but on the brink of a war that even she could not control, she needed to focus on her son. Felicity Stirling was anything but the frivolous woman she pretended to be – I am sure that is what drew Robert's father to her – and she had no intention of estranging her only son before he went off to fight. Dislikeable people are never truly evil. We are all just trying to survive as best we can.

At dinner, Felicity leaned across the table to quiz me about my parents. I knew Robert had already furnished her with the basic details so I presumed the conversation was a not-so-subtle exercise in stating the obviousness of my inferiority.

"I imagine Oxford was quite the change for you, dear," she said. "Quite an achievement to go up to study literature." The unspoken "for a girl like you" hung in the air.

I flicked a glance at Robert. He raised his eyebrows in apology.

I turned a full smile on Felicity.

"I have my grandfather's genes, I believe. He was an editor on the local paper before the Great War and my mother says I got my love of words from him."

"You're too modest," Robert jumped in, no doubt to prevent his mother from making any snide comments about sensationalism in the press. "You don't just love words, you master them. I've read some of her essays, Mother, and they are excellent. Maybe you would like to read one yourself?"

"Of course, that would be delightful," Felicity said, clapping her hands with excitement. Or perhaps it was restrained fury at the realisation that her son really was in love.

"You must bring me a few the next time you come," she said.

There never was a next time. I was too busy during the war and whenever Robert got a few days leave, we hunkered down in London where I was living by then. Neither of us wanted to share our love with anyone else, not as long as there was a Doomsday clock ticking over us. Our time was too precious. We were too precious. Of course, Robert visited his mother once or twice but I had my own fretting parents to reassure so we did our home visits separately.

In 1944, Felicity Stirling succumbed to the cancer that had ravaged her spine and caused the excruciating back pain that explained the rigid posture I dismissed as so affected the first time I met her. I could not like the woman but I admired the way she loved her son unconditionally. In other words, more than I ever would, or could. I was glad she did not live to see what happened. It would have broken her heart. But perhaps if she had survived, Robert would not have taken his own life. Felicity Stirling would never have let her child kill himself. She would have shared his burden. She would not have dodged his need. The women of her generation, Charlotte's generation, were Amazons, a fact that we often forget because we focus on what they were not allowed to do, instead of on what they did. I have noticed, Diane, that as our lives have become easier over the decades, we have become softer and less able to cope. And so every technical and social advance seems to chip away at the best of us. Another irony of the human condition.

The next day, Robert enlisted. The flustered sergeant, who took his name and other details, could not say when exactly he would be required to leave for training and he seemed more put out by this than Robert.

"It's not like this whole mess crept up on us like a thief in the night," the sergeant said, shuffling his papers and repeatedly pushing his glasses up his sweating nose. "We all knew what we were doing when we said we'd bail out Poland if Hitler invaded it. That was March. Three months later and we still seem to be on the back foot. No dates for training yet, no locations. I swear I sometimes think the brass couldn't organise a piss-up in a brewery."

He shook his head dolefully.

Robert, who looked as though he was signing up for a week in Butlins, smiled broadly. He was fidgeting with his hat though and he had never been a man for idle movements.

"I suppose that's the downside of British phlegm," he said too brightly.

The sergeant didn't even smile.

"God help us when the fun really starts," he muttered.

When it was done, we walked down the steps outside the drab office. Wispy clouds scudded above our heads, pushed inland by the strong sea breeze like litter blowing down a blue street. Everything seemed disconcertingly normal. I felt cheated. My darling had just signed over his life and future to the army and here we were walking sedately down the steps, as though this Saturday would unfurl like all Saturdays ever.

I needed a bigger horizon. I needed to look over there to where it would all happen. That's where I wanted to say goodbye. Not on these steps and not in Felicity Stirling's house where she would smother my sorrow with her own. I wanted to say goodbye looking out at the sea that would separate us and then, one day, bring him back to me. I told you I was a silly romantic back then, Diane.

"Can we go for a walk on the pier?" I asked.

Standing at the end of the jetty, wind-whipped and glistening with sea-spray, we pushed into each other as we gazed out in the direction of Holland and France.

"I did always hope to travel in Europe," Robert said. "Although, I never thought I would be on a trip with half the young men in the country. I imagined sailing a barge alone, along the canals into Rotterdam, or wandering in grumpy Gallic solitude through Paris' Latin Quarter. Still, I suppose this trip is paid for and we'll likely cover more ground so that's something to consider."

I loved his irreverent, dry sense of humour, Diane. As to what he saw in me, I do not know. I can't say I believe in love at first sight but I don't know how else to explain how we ended up together. Robert's attributes were obvious but I never understood what brought him over to my table that day in the teahouse. I don't subscribe to the view that there is one true love for everyone, if we can but find that perfect match, but maybe there is something in the idea that some people are meant to come together. Call it chemistry, or Charlotte's kismet, or a kind of tragic magnetism.

"I can hardly bear the fact that you will be there without me," I said.

"I, on the other hand, am delighted that you will not be there," he replied and he was no longer smiling. He turned to me, brushed the hair from my face and took my two hands in his.

"I don't want you to see how I will be. All of us who go to fight will have to dig into the darkest parts of our souls to survive. We will do things we will be ashamed of, we will be weak and cowardly and brave and remorseless and broken and despairing and cravenly hopeful. Deep down, you know this. The poets couldn't gloss over it despite all their pretty words and you have seen what war did to your father. I will have to be utterly different over there and I need to know that you will be here, waiting for me to come back, waiting for the man I am now. That will keep me going. That will pull me back to sanity. I need you to be safe, to be here to guide me home. You will be my lighthouse."

He kissed me and our tears soothed our salt-seared lips. Seagulls wailed over our heads, pitting their puny bodies against the wind.

"I'm scared," I whispered. "The war will come here too this time. It won't be like before. Everyone knows we'll be bombed. How can I be your beacon if I'm also under attack?

Robert, I don't know what to do. I don't know how to do what we have to do to get through this."

"That just shows how smart you are," he whispered into my ear. "We should be scared. We will be scared but we will prevail. I don't know how, darling, but I do know that our story will not end here. We won't let it. We can't."

CHAPTER 9

The day war was declared set the tone for the next six years. Fear, expectation and farce. An entire nation glued to their wirelesses, listening to endless music on the BBC, everyone holding their breath. Then finally, the words that sealed our Fate. (Forgive me, Diane, I'm doing it again. Some of these tropes cannot be avoided.)

"This morning the British Ambassador in Berlin handed the German government a final note stating that unless we heard from them by 11 o'clock that they were prepared at once to withdraw their troops from Poland a state of war would exist between us. I have to tell you now that no such undertaking has been received, and that consequently this country is at war with Germany," Chamberlain said.

I was with my parents in their kitchen in St Albans. As Chamberlain went on to say we would be fighting against *"brute force, bad faith, injustice, oppression and persecution"*, Henry stood up and left the room. I watched him walk out to the garden, pick up his spade and begin digging in his vegetable patch. Charlotte gave a small sigh, rose and went to put the kettle on the stove. But her hands were trembling and she could not strike the match to light the gas. I took the pack off her and lit the ring.

"It's so very difficult to believe it can happen again," she said. Her eyes were huge in her haunted face. I hugged her. What could I say? By then, it was all so inevitable and so inexplicable at the same time.

We heard later that the air raid sirens went off in London just as Chamberlain was finishing his speech, sending people scurrying to the shelters. It must've seemed quite exciting that first time, although one person apparently died from a heart attack. The whole thing turned out to be a false alarm – a plane had been spotted over Maidstone in Kent but it was finally identified as French. We were all novices then. We would get better.

I signed up to the Women's Auxiliary Air Force in late October when I realised the only way to get through the days was to fill the hours with mind-numbing duty so that missing Robert would feel like a luxury. When I told Charlotte, her lips tightened but all she said was: "You realise that this is not a game, don't you Lina? You'll be in the armed forces. You'll have to obey orders. You'll have to drill and… and make your bed properly and whatever else it is they do. Peel potatoes and shine shoes, I suspect."

I pretended to be deeply offended but truth be told, I *was* worried and scared. I had enjoyed almost total freedom in Oxford and I was not at all sure I was military material. I feared I would not be strong enough, not fast enough, not obedient enough and my worries seemed to be confirmed by the secret knowledge that I chose the WAAF because I liked the uniform more than the others. I have always had a vain streak, my dear.

I tried to persuade Evelyn to come with me but she chose the Auxiliary Territorial Service instead.

"I'm not bloody peeling potatoes or pushing bits of paper around for the next however long," she told me. "They say women can join the ack-ack batteries now. If the Germans are going to threaten my life, I want to be able to do something real to stop them. They're saying London could be wiped out. Wiped out, Lina! Well, they'll have to do it over my dead body."

Her fighting words rang out like a phone in church in her girly bedroom with its rosebud-patterned bedspread, pink curtains and china dolls looking down at us from a shelf. Evelyn was always strong enough to bear her own contradictions. She seemed larger-than-life with her ginger hair, green eyes and loud laugh. She was a Daddy's girl but fiercely independent in all other aspects. She was patriotic but had no time for government meddling in our lives. I wondered how she would cope with being in the army.

"You'll go mad, Evelyn. You hate doing what you're told," I said.

"Talk about the kettle calling the pot black," she giggled. "I can do what I'm told when I think it's worth it. So can you. We'll be fine, Lina. And maybe it'll be fun. Look, I've checked it out. I just need to do the basic training, show some gumption in the exams and then push really hard to be assigned to the anti-aircraft mixed batteries. Of course, if I do badly in the exams, I could well end up cleaning latrines or cooking potatoes. But I won't be the only one suffering then. If they think the Germans are bad, just wait until they taste my cooking," she said, punching me playfully on the shoulder and laughing again with the full-throated chuckle that always made it seem like she was being in some way indecent.

I admired Evelyn's gusto. We knew this war would be fought mainly in the air and it stood to reason that those opposing the planes, both in the skies and on the ground, would be in permanent danger.

"Why don't you join with me?" she said.

"I can't. I promised Robert that I would stay behind a desk if at all possible. He says him risking his life is enough of a gamble. We'll be asking for too much luck if we deliberately put both of us in harm's way. He thinks if I keep my head down, the gods of war might find it in their hearts to spare him. He's a funny old thing."

Evelyn smiled. "He's right. There's two of you and one sacrifice is enough."

"Will you actually shoot at planes?" I asked.

"No, they won't let women do that. Not yet anyway,"

Evelyn said. "But who knows? If this damn thing goes on long enough, anything could happen. And you never know, maybe everyone else in the battery will get killed during an attack and I'll be allowed to get my hands on the guns."

I loved Evelyn like a sister and I was more upset than I cared to show that I would have to brave the WAAF on my own. But Evelyn would not be swayed, not even by my assertion that WAAFs were widely viewed as the classiest girls in the service.

"The ATS already has a rather fruity nickname," I told her. She nearly fell off the bed when I told her it was "Any time, Sergeant."

"That makes me even keener to join," she spluttered.

We spent the next hour thinking up lewd expressions for WAAFs, burying our sorrow at parting in vulgarity and bravado. We were learning fast: the war hadn't even properly started but we were already greasing and oiling our coping mechanisms. Over the next six years, vulgarity and gallows humour were among the few things that thrived in Britain.

A few weeks later, I travelled to London for a medical and after that I was sent to Cheshire for three weeks' training. It was everything you would expect: tedious, bureaucratic and frustrating. The saving grace was the friendly banter. Although I hate to say it, we did all feel we were in it together. That's a powerful sensation, as the government well knew. We slept in dorms, we drilled at dawn and we followed the rules, mostly. Afterwards, we were assigned our duties and on the basis of my university studies and, I suppose, early signs of my facility with words, I was sent to be a secretary at the Ministry of Information in London. It was a bizarre but useful start to my writing career. At the Ministry, I quickly learned that nothing could beat reality for sheer absurdity. This lesson has stood me in good stead.

I was lucky with my assignment; some WAAFs did became cooks and cleaners while others were assigned to the Accounts units, where their lives were governed by impenetrable and illogical form-fuckery, as I like to call it. We often forget the sheer, mind-numbing bureaucracy involved in killing so many people on a daily basis. We all know that the Germans kept meticulous, eventually damning records. It helpfully reinforces the common stereotype of Teutonic mania for order. But it was the same here. When I joined the WAAF, I got a glimpse into a sinisterly ludicrous system where the horror of state-sanctioned murder was distilled into tilting stacks of forms where everything, from staplers to engine parts, was given a number and a delivery code. The backroom banality of carnage was chilling. There were presumably similar forms with ridiculous code numbers for the dead, the dying, the brutalised and the irreparable. Today, I wonder what Robert's code number would have been? Or was he what they called NIV, or not in vocab. In non-form parlance, did they have no clue how to describe what happened to him?

The Ministry was the high temple of wartime absurdity and obfuscation. It was created to control the news and to keep morale high but it went about this task in the most ham-fisted way imaginable.

It managed to annoy the newspapers, the public and its own government. Thank God for Churchill. I think his speeches were sometimes the only thing holding the country together. Today they sound absurdly pompous, bombastic, even messianic. All that vaulting rhetoric with Biblical resonances. Thinking back on it, I wonder how we accepted that strident, know-it-all tone, but the truth is we needed a leader to tell us what to do in a terrifying world where everything seemed to be upside down.

At first, my duties were fundamentally secretarial: mostly typing up pamphlets, advice sheets and press releases. I must have pleased someone because after a few months, they let me draft a few of those releases. I suppose those were my first real articles, although thankfully my name was nowhere to be seen. I was told what to write, what to leave out and how long the piece should be. No argument was brooked. I was not expected to have an opinion. There was no place for free thinking, for verifying, for questioning. Loose lips sink ships and all that jazz. But I was happy enough. I enjoyed writing and whenever I could I snuck colourful adjectives into the text. Sometimes, I was even tasked with dreaming up quotes from *real soldiers* and *everyman families*. I began to realise the true power of words, that you could build worlds that even you, their creator, could believe in. This was a delightful discovery.

In early 1940, I was assigned to the Publicity Producers group, ostensibly still as a secretary but even the dimmest secretary stereotype could have seen straight away that most of the men had no clue what they were doing. Things improved slightly after Churchill took over from Chamberlain in May and the office was reordered. I was then assigned to the Home Publicity Emergency Committee. Today we might call it Nanny Comms. Our job was to help Chicken Licken figure out what to do now that the sky was falling in. I edited and typed up pamphlets on what to do during an air raid, how to black out your home and how to fight back in the event of an invasion. We had advice on rationing and the need to keep mum so that nothing one said could help moustachioed Foxy Loxy and his dastardly schemes. I have to admit, I did have some fun playing my part in the "war of nerves".

Here's an example of the gems we came up with: *Don't Listen to Scaremongers. You will always find scaremongers about. Just treat them as you would a smallpox case – move on quickly.*

Another of my personal favourites: *Don't Lose Your Head. There's nothing to be gained by going about with the corners of your mouth turned down and it has a bad effect on people whose nerves are not so good as yours. So even if a bomb falls in your street – which is unlikely – keep smiling.*

It is the "which is unlikely" that cracked me up then and still cracks me up now.

In fact, it was relatively easy to keep smiling through those early months. After years of fearful anticipation, the war started and everything seemed to stop. Not for men like Robert, who were already in France, but on the Home Front, the war was nothing more than an enforced period of restrictions and killjoy regulations. We called it the Bore War. All through that freezing January, when even the Thames was so bored it froze over and stopped moving, we plodded through our new duties, cold and hungry and hideously bored.

Evelyn wrote to me from near Hull, where she had been stationed early in the New Year.

Dear God, would it ever start already! Never have I been so cold and so stupid with boredom. Our Nissen huts were clearly designed for war in a desert, not in northern England. We heat bricks in the stove and put them in our beds but it barely puts a dent in the cold. I swear to you, Lina, I can't feel my fingers right now. And that's with gloves on, which explains the scrawl. Sorry. I hope you can decipher it. I'll pluck my own eyes out if I have to spend any more time staring at pictures of all those bloody German planes – Messerschmitt, Junker, Dornier, Heinkel and Focke this, that and the other. I just wish the bloody Fockers would come already. We are so rigid with idleness now that we've started playing pranks on each other. Last week, I pulled Sandra's bed into the yard and left it there. She was so mad when she came back from the parade ground. How I laughed but I'll have to watch my back now. You'd never know what she might do. You'd like her. She's phenomenally pretty, the boys turn into slack-jawed fish when she passes by, and she's very naughty too. We're in the same unit together and we work out the height and range of the incoming aircraft. Well, we would if they bothered to come. God, I wish it would start already. Write to me, Lina. Send me bright stories from London. I'll take anything to add some cheer to these endless days.

So I sent her long letters full of funny stories from 'the Ministry of Misinformation'. The ministry's very creation was based on deception. I found out later that planning started in 1935, but of course it could not be admitted. To have done so would have been to acknowledge the inevitability of war and in 1935 I do believe some of us still gave peace a chance.

So, in answer to that old chestnut: 'what did you do in the war, Mummy?' I can say this: I fabricated, I lied, I misled. I imagine you are smiling, Diane. A fitting start to a life of deception, you'll think. But remember dear, I was not yet lost. I still had ideals, I still had the man I loved, I still believed in an integral future that would extend the narrative arc of our lives. It pained me to collude in the lies being told to cover up the war, but I had signed up for this and I could see the merit of keeping morale up. And so, like a good soldier, I wrote despicably false press releases. For generals, I wrote speeches that depicted victory as a given, even as the bombs started to rain down on London and Hull and all the other cities. I even helped coin some of the more ridiculous slogans. You may have seen this one: *Make do and mend says Mrs Sew-and-Sew*. I had a hand in that. A colleague came up with this one: *We beat 'em before. We'll do it again*. I have to admit I felt a reluctant admiration for this statement's blatant refusal to take war seriously. The same stiff-upper-lip-and-head-in-the-sand mentality could be found in the posters exhorting us to be more can-do, more thrifty, more stoic. It was as though war was just a particularly tough mountain climbing expedition that anyone with a bit of gumption and an ounce of common sense could get through.

I laugh at some of those slogans now but it used to madden me so much, I would have to excuse myself from the office to stand shaking in the alley outside, desperately dragging on a cigarette, willing myself to calm down so that I could go back and do my job. Do My Duty. But there was actually merit in the madness: the Ministry could hardly tell the truth, especially as the skies darkened and the prospect of losing the war became increasingly likely through 1940 and 1941. If we had called a spade a spade, the whole nation would have run screaming off the nearest white cliffs. Morale had to be boosted because in the end, it was such a powerful force. Intangible, insubstantial and more potent than anything else in the dark days of the Blitz and after Dunkirk. Our biggest mistake was thinking we didn't need to boost morale when it was all over, when our men came back to a cold and hungry land.

CHAPTER 10

It is a glorious Sunday here in Lion-sur-Mer, Diane. I
have taken my writing out into the garden and I am sitting
recklessly in the full glare of the sun, listening to the muted
shouts and cries from the beach. It will be throbbing later
with parents and children and grandparents, wholesome
families with their pain buried deep. I may go and sit at
the gate and watch them. But I may not. Sometimes I
can lose myself in the happiness of others. I am content
to be an observer, to file little snippets of description or
conversation away in my brain for use later on in my work.
But sometimes, and increasingly, I feel like the little match
girl, looking in through the frosted window at the beautiful
people sitting down to their sumptuous holiday feast. Most
people my age must feel a similar isolation but my pain is
magnified by the fact that I had a family and I could not
hold it together. I was inside and I walked deliberately out
into the cold.

Sharpening my desire for solitude is the knowledge that
I do not plan any more books and so whatever I see is for
me alone. It feels odd to watch idly after so many years of
deliberate, calculated observation. I feel useless, bereft of
purpose. I also feel deliriously free.

I should address the issue of your name now. I imagine
you are furious that I have been calling you Diane throughout
this letter. But that is the name Robert and I gave you and

that is who you will always be to me. Please allow me this indulgence and if you cannot do it for me, do it for your father. I don't know when you chose to start using your middle name or why. You'll have had your reasons and who could blame you. That day in Brighton, the last words you yelled at me as you stomped up the beach were: "My name is Maria. I am not your Diane. She doesn't exist."

You were so utterly gorgeous, your hair whipping around your head, your arms outstretched, your feet planted firmly on the pebbles, girl-queen of all you surveyed. I have never seen a woman more fully embody the spirit of Diana, goddess of the hunt and the moon. I would have called you Diana but Robert preferred Diane. When you were born, he said you looked too gentle for Diana, but that's men for you: always underestimating us. I gave in to him because to be honest, I was so grateful he was showing interest. He had gone so far away by the time you were born. You pulled him back, for a while. You should know that. Maybe, if I had been stronger, we could have saved him together.

So I will continue to call you Diane here because we do what we must do. I don't dislike Maria – a name suggested by the nurse because we hadn't thought of one – but it cannot fit my memories of you, as few as they are. It is precisely because of this scarcity that I will do nothing to threaten their survival. All the things I imagined happening to you over the years happened to Diane. No matter that they were never real, these fantasies. They are all I have. I hope you can understand.

You might be wondering where I got my own unusual name. It's a sweet and sad story and one I reworked in *The Land Beyond*. I doubt you've read any of my books so let me tell you the original story here. Of course, you may not be curious at all right now but one day, you might wonder and I won't be around to tell you.

When Charlotte was a child, there was an Italian man who sold ice creams from a stall on Saturdays in St Albans. He had a white-and-brown spaniel called Lina who would sit at the front of the stall, as quiet as a mouse, her clear blue eyes tracking people as they passed by.

I'll let Charlotte tell you the rest, as she told me when I was about six years old. I had run home from school in floods of tears after a boy said my name was stupid and foreign. Charlotte pulled me onto her knees and brushed the damp hair from my cheeks.

"What a silly boy, Lina. Why don't I tell you how you got your name and then you can decide if it's stupid. Does that sound fair?"

I nodded, still gulping and hiccupping.

She told me the story of Mr Bianchi and his Lina.

"That dog was so sweet, just like you, Lina. But then a sad thing happened during the Great War. You know the war that Daddy fought in?"

I nodded. She had told me a little about this before although I didn't really understand the word 'war'. Even now, I don't think I do. It is too slippery a syllable to pin down.

"Everyone thought the Italians would be on the side of the Germans. In the end they weren't but it took them some months to say what they were going to do. Unfortunately, some people decided that Mr Bianchi was the enemy and they stopped buying ice cream from him. Some horrible people even wrote nasty things about him on his stall."

"What things, Charlotte?"

"Things like 'Go Home' or 'We don't like you'. It was such a shame. Mr Bianchi was such a gentle soul and he'd been living in St Albans for a very long time. He didn't have anywhere else to go. So he stayed and kept selling ice creams, though his big, toothy smile seemed to fade a little. One day, after I met your father, I took him to buy an ice cream from Mr Bianchi. When Daddy saw Lina, he bent down to pat her and she started licking his hand. He laughed and told Mr Bianchi that the dog was the best advertising he could ever have. We bought pistachio-flavoured ice creams and ate them as we walked around the park beside the Cathedral. Just like we did the other day."

"No, Charlotte. Not pistachio. I had lemon and you had vanilla and Daddy said he didn't want one."

"That's right," Charlotte said. "What a good memory you have. I don't seem to like pistachio any more. Isn't that odd? Anyway, the next thing that happened to Mr Bianchi was very sad. One day, when he was tidying up his stall, someone took Lina. One minute, she was there, snuffling along the street, as she did when Mr Bianchi was closing up, and the next minute she was gone. She wasn't a very big dog so I suppose it wasn't so difficult to grab her."

"Why? Why'd they take the pretty dog?"

"Because, Lina, sometimes people are frightened of things they don't understand and they try to destroy them to make that fear go away. And sometimes people are cruel. They just are. It's a sad thing to tell you but I want you to know the truth."

I nodded solemnly. I had learnt about cruelty that day at school. I was wiser now. It seemed right to nod like clever grown-ups did.

"They found little Lina in the river a few days later. Someone had put her in a sack with some heavy rocks and thrown her off the bridge just down where the park ends, not far from the Roman theatre. But eventually the sack had torn, the rocks had fallen out and the sack floated back to the surface. Mr Bianchi had tears in his eyes when he told me. The poor man kept saying: 'I just don't understand. Who could do that to my Lina?' I didn't know what to say and soon I was crying too. I'd loved Lina for years. She always licked my hand and if you gave her a treat, she would nuzzle right into your legs. All she ever wanted was to be loved. Even with everything that happened afterwards, all the horrible things in the war, I remember Lina's death as one of the most awful tragedies of that time."

Charlotte coughed and shook her head.

"When you were born and you looked up at me with your big blue eyes, you made me think of Lina. It wasn't just the colour and, of course, that has changed now anyway. It was the *way* you looked at me. I felt like you were offering me all your love and all your trust even though we had only just met."

"How? How had we just met?" I asked.

"Well, you'd just popped out of my tummy like all babies do."

I giggled. It was such a funny idea.

"As soon as I had that thought, I realised that Lina was the perfect name," Charlotte continued. "And it was also a way to remember a lovely man and his sweet dog and the importance of fighting back against silly people with silly ideas. Even as a baldy baby, you looked like the kind of girl who would know how to stand up for herself."

"I am, Charlotte. I'm going to box Terry's ears tomorrow for saying my name is stupid."

Charlotte laughed. "Maybe don't box his ears but tell him the story and see what happens. If he still says your name is stupid, you have my permission to box his ears."

"What happened to Mr Bianchi?"

"Poor Mr Bianchi," Charlotte said. "He left to go to Italy and nobody ever heard anything about him afterwards. It was a bad time to try to travel all that way because war was breaking out and I just can't imagine how he would have made it safely. But he couldn't stay, not after what we'd done."

So there you have it, Diane. I was named after a tragic dog and the death of an ideal. It could be worse.

Let's resume. We still have a long way to go.

At the Ministry, my direct boss was a man called Peterson. A north Londoner, he was shorter than me, which was handy as he seemed more interested in my breasts than in my face. A cynical, puffed-up fish of a man with fleshy lips and a way of explaining a task in a flat voice that made it quite clear he was being forced to elucidate because of the listener's inadequate intellect. I despised him but I was too polite to show it. Instead, I was reduced to shifting my chair every time he came to leer over my shoulder, ostensibly to look at my work but really to get an alternative view of my breasts. I tried wearing sweaters and jackets over my blouses but nothing worked so I told myself to grow up and resigned myself to being very much at his beck and call.

One day, I arrived at Senate House – a Soviet-style hulk of a building near Russell Square – in a frantic mess. I had been billeted in Swiss Cottage with a young mother and her two screechy daughters and one of the children had toothache and was up all night crying. I hadn't slept a wink until 5 a.m. and then missed my alarm. I rushed in, trying to shrug off my coat as I ran.

"Miss Rose, what time do you call this?" Peterson said, strolling up to me and ostentatiously pointing at his wristwatch.

I mumbled an apology but he was not going to let this opportunity pass him by.

"I knew this would happen. You girls want it all. You want in on the action, you complain about not being allowed to do more, not being allowed to run the country, heaven help us, but when push comes to shove, you spend so much time painting your faces and primping that you can't even make it to work on time."

"It won't happen again," I muttered. "I just didn't get much sleep, that's all."

"Not enough sleep? My dear, I do apologise. I had no idea you missed your beauty sleep. Good heavens. That really will not do. Would you like to have a nap on the sofa in my office? I'm sure our soldiers out there trying to stop Jerry from sweeping through Europe are also getting a bit of shut-eye, right now. Maybe a bath and a massage too."

I tried furiously to blink back the tears. I would not give this odious little man the pleasure of watching me cry.

"Her man is over there, Sir," came a voice from a nearby

desk. It was Keith Penrose, one of the senior writers. "I think you might leave it out now."

Penrose stood up and strode over to us, keeping his eyes firmly on Peterson's flushed face.

"Actually, I need Miss Rose's help on a document I'm drafting. I assume I can borrow her for a short while, sir?"

Peterson swallowed a retort and nodded but he threw me a vicious glance as I followed Penrose back to his desk.

"Thank you. You didn't need to do that. I don't care what he says," I said as I removed my hat. My eyes were still wet but my tone must have come out spikier than I intended because Penrose grimaced and said, "You're very welcome."

"Sorry, it's just I *am* very tired. Bloody screaming child kept me up all night. And I don't care what Peterson says, sleep deprivation is crippling."

Penrose nodded.

"I agree totally. I didn't sleep for nearly two weeks at Passchendaele and I found it quite annoying."

I looked sharply at him but his face was a picture of innocence. I burst out laughing.

Penrose, who must have been around 40, had a face that was so perfect in middle age it was impossible to imagine how he might have looked as a younger man. He was classically handsome – his hair was grey but thick, he had deep-set eyes and a long, slightly hooked nose. It was the kind of face you would want beside you when the balloon went up, I thought.

After that first rescue mission, he and I struck up what I suppose you might call a May-December friendship and though he ribbed me gently but relentlessly for my childish fits of impotent fury at the way the war was going and my strident impatience with the whole British establishment, I liked spending time with him. I suppose I was flattered that this worldly man wanted to be with a woman who was barely 20. We went to the theatre, we ate our lunch together in Russell Square and now and then we would meet on a rare day off to wander around London's parks. He was divorced and phlegmatic about it.

"Married too young," he said. "She was my childhood sweetheart but when I came back from the war, we were both different. We got married anyway because that's what one did but when she took up with another man and I demanded a divorce a few years later, I think we were both just incredibly relieved."

One mizzling day in March, we walked to the highest point in Hampstead Heath. You must know it well, Diane. Just above the East Heath. We tramped up from Parliament Hill Fields, past the sand pits where people were filling bags in preparation for the bombardment we were all dreading and simultaneously wishing would start so this appalling period of stasis could end.

"Made it," Penrose puffed as he turned around on the crest of the hill to look down on the city. "Not as young as I used to be. You, however, seem totally unfazed by that climb."

"We're tough in the WAAF," I grinned. "They put me through my paces at the camp in Cheshire. Strengthened all those muscles I didn't even know I had."

"I was pretty fit myself in 1917. Not any more," Penrose said, patting his stomach. "Peacetime is no good for middle-aged miseries like me."

We stood in silence, looking down at London and the barrage balloons hovering over the city like giant bees. Below us, an RAF crew was trying to raise a balloon, with little success. It flopped around the grass like an unbiddable, oversized pig. Birds sang around us as though they hoped their melodies could charm spring into life.

"I wonder what it will all look like when this is over," Penrose murmured. "The city looks so... substantial from here, as though nothing could change this skyline. But it doesn't take much, you know. When we left Passchendaele, it was like another planet. You couldn't relate it to any place on this earth or to anything we knew. Everything was gone. The trees, the villages, even the grass. Our capacity to destroy is staggering. It's as though, every few decades, we feel the need to subjugate the earth, to prove our dominance, to reduce everything to rubble and start again. One day we may go too far, I fear."

I didn't know what to say. I was watching five or six soldiers swarming around the ack-ack battery to our right and wondering how Evelyn was doing. Penrose followed my gaze.

"Sorry, how bloody tactless of me. Are you thinking of him?"

"No," I answered, surprised and embarrassed. I should have been, you might think, but sometimes it was too hard. I missed Robert with an ache that was physical. Sometimes it was like a dull pain in the pit of my stomach, sometimes I felt nauseous, and sometimes I felt his absence in the chronic fatigue that made me take to my bed at 6 p.m., not bothering with the blackout, knowing I would not rise until morning. I could not deal with the reality of his absence every moment and so sometimes I deliberately erased him from my mind. In the same way that you would take a pill for chronic back pain. It doesn't fix the cause but at least you can function for a few hours. I was self-medicating with conscious forgetfulness. I like to think I was being pragmatic rather than heartless but you may disagree and of course, there is danger inherent in any kind of self-medication. You always risk over-prescribing.

"I was actually thinking of my friend, Evelyn, who's up in Hull in one of those mixed batteries. She just wants it all to kick off."

"And your man, your fiancé I suppose we should call him? Have you heard from him?"

"I got a letter two weeks ago. No precise location but somewhere in France. He says they are having a sticky time of it. Don't tell anyone at the Ministry but he's not particularly optimistic. He thinks Holland will fall and then who knows."

Penrose – I never called him Keith, I think you can guess why – nodded.

"We always knew the Nazis were strong, we knew they were well-armed but we seem to have struggled with what that actually meant. Or maybe not. Maybe that's what drove all the appeasement. Chamberlain knew we weren't ready. He knew we couldn't possibly win. But here we are, so we'd better pull something out of the hat."

I started.

"That's more or less what Robert said in his letter," I said, huddling deeper into my coat as the wind whipped around our faces. "He wrote: We'd better have a plan now that we're in this. Not much sign of a plan here but heaven help us if someone doesn't have something up their sleeve back home."

"Do you remember all his letters by heart?" Penrose asked, smiling tightly.

"Yes. Is that silly? It's just because I have enough time to memorise every line before I get the next one. It's a kind of prayer, I suppose. No, more an enchantment. If I remember what he said, keep his voice alive in my head, then he'll stay alive out there. Mad, I know, but it seems to work for me."

"It doesn't sound mad at all," said Penrose quietly.

A few minutes later, he took off.

"Race you to the bottom. WAAF versus vet. Come on!"

And so we ran too fast down the too-steep hill until we could run no more and the skyline had gone.

CHAPTER 11

I did receive a poem in the post from Mrs Danton early on in the war but I never saw her again. Before I left England in 1949, I went to her house – a pilgrimage of sorts to the woman who had witnessed the start of our love story and knew my Robert before he became another. In my grief-griddled brain, Mrs Danton had become a larger-than-life oracle. With my parents and Robert gone, I needed a voice from the past to convince me that I was really alive and not just a figment of my own shattered imagination. I needed someone to tether me with testimony that it all really happened. And I had, after all, promised to tell her what I thought of her poem.

The house had not changed – Oxford was spared the bombing, some say, because Hitler wanted to claim the city as his capital when he invaded – but there was no reply when I rang the bell. A grey-haired lady tending roses across the street told me Mrs Danton had moved to Brighton during the war to be with her sister.

"She died in that dreadful raid that hit the Odeon cinema and killed all those children," she said, shaking her head. "1940 it was. Mrs Danton was not in the cinema but as I heard it, her sister lived on a nearby street and one of the bombs dropped by that German plane fell slap-bang on the house. I imagine poor Lizzie never knew what hit her. That's something, I suppose. No suffering. Best you could hope for, really. Mind you, I told her not to go to Brighton, many times, but she wouldn't listen. She said she wasn't leaving her sister to face it all alone. She was very kind was Lizzie Danton though she hid it well."

She turned back to her roses but then swung around to me, her clippers waggling just as Mrs Danton had shaken her finger at me that day we left for Felixstowe all those lifetimes ago.

"I remember you now. You were with that handsome lodger that Lizzie had before the war, weren't you?"

I nodded, tears prickling my eyes at this unexpected resurrection of my husband in the speech of a woman I hadn't known existed. How many more versions of Robert were out there? How many would I never know?

"I used to see you sneak out first thing. Oh, you were quick and quiet but I'm an early bird myself and I'd be watering my plants up there on my bedroom windowsill and I'd see you running down the lane, hair loose, face flushed, bold as brass."

She was nodding emphatically, the sheen of schadenfreude glazing her watery eyes. She pushed her glasses up her nose.

"Oh yes, nothing passes me by. Not on this street."

I couldn't speak but nor could I leave. This righteous busybody was my last link to Robert, to you, to the life I was about to abandon. We stared at each other over the garden wall until she muttered, "There you go," and headed back inside. She didn't ask what happened to Robert. The fact that I was alone told her all she needed to know.

I stood there a little longer, watching her yellow roses bobbing over the garden wall. Then, slowly and deliberately, I snapped every flower off and scattered the petals onto the pavement. Much later, alone in my hotel room in London, I buried my head in my hands and cried for us all again. I could still smell the fruity scent of the crushed petals on my fingers.

I found Mrs Danton's poem a few weeks ago when I was putting some papers in order at home. It is what it is but I thought you might like to have it. It will mean nothing to anyone else now.

A Fond Farewell

Too young they were
Life just a blur
Endless days of loving
They feared not shame
Nor death nor blame
Eternities of flesh
Bare feet running
Cheeks flushing
Infinities of stolen kisses
So young, so bold
Hands never cold
In secret places shushing
Her hand in his, deep is his stare
He sees more now than she can bear
She seeks his shoulder, she hides her face
Shame never saw them, but death does pace
And here, at last, their cheeks do blush
Red rose of love, red rose of death
These flowers of life bend from the knife.

I told you, amateur piffle. Still, it does bring a tear to my eye. I hate myself for such sentimentality but the truth is Mrs Danton's poem still moves me today.

The best thing about my job at the Ministry in London was that I could go and see my parents regularly. I didn't always manage to get a rail pass but sometimes I hitched a lift on army trucks heading to the bases north of London. I tried to go as often as I could. I was worried about how this new war would affect their fragile stability. Charlotte and Henry were only middle-aged but even before the war broke out, they seemed older than their years. I fretted about them as one might fret over elderly relatives.

Henry became increasingly withdrawn as it became clear that the unthinkable was going to happen again. It must have been agonising for him – each new strident exhortation to

119

prepare to defend the country must have felt like a knife twisting in his gut. He had done all he could to banish his memories of the Great War but a critical component of that deliberate amnesia must have been the conviction that such a thing could never happen again. The years of inexorable drift towards another conflict must have seemed like slow torture, and an indictment of his silence.

On one of my visits, in late 1939, Charlotte whispered that she had cancelled their subscription to the *Herts Advertiser* to try to spare Henry the daily drip-drip of grim news and stentorian edicts.

"At least this way, he can eat his breakfast in peace, without all those gloomy headlines, although I shudder to think what my father would've said if he'd seen me cancel the paper. Of course, Henry still knows what's going on. He listens to the wireless until he can bear it no longer and then he stomps off. Whenever he gets really worried, he heads out to the garden and spends hours weeding and pruning. Silver lining, I suppose. By the end of the war, we'll have prize-winning flowerbeds," she said, trying to smile.

"You know, he told me once that he loved gardening because he feels that in some way he's making up for all the damage done to the earth during the Great War. Of course I can only imagine, but they say parts of France were like a wasteland – not a blade of grass, not a tree left undamaged. Henry said it was almost the worst crime of all. He called it a savaging. No wonder he cannot bear to think about what lies ahead."

Henry was not alone. For many people of my parents' age, the prospect of another war was too awful to consider and so they simply refused to engage. They didn't sign up for evacuations, they didn't prepare bomb shelters and they didn't slaughter their pets in case of gas attacks or bombardment. They stuck their fingers in their ears and their heads in the sand. And until Christmas 1939, you might have thought they were the smart ones. In those first weeks, first months even, people at home in Britain could have been forgiven for thinking that it was all some kind of massive hoax or a Machiavellian publicity stunt to create a feeling of unity in the face of recession.

Charlotte, though, was not one to ignore reality however hard she worked to transform Henry's. In September, she joined the Land Army and was immediately assigned to pick potatoes on a farm near Redbourn.

"The farmer's two sons joined the RAF and left last week for training in Folkestone," she told me when I visited her after my WAAF training. "The main crop was ready so it was all hands on deck right away. I thought I was in good shape but it's very hard work. I think I'd prefer to drive the tractor rather than spend the whole day with my back bent. I've asked to be considered for tractor training and I think they might give it to me, what with me being so much older than most of the other girls. They must realise I'll be more use in the cab rather than puffing and panting in the trenches, as it were. So another silver lining: I might learn to drive."

She lifted her hands, turning them over to show me the calluses on her palms and her broken nails.

"It'll be easier on my hands as well. My goodness, if my mother could see these. She'd say I was letting myself down, no matter that there's no time between shifts to do much to fix all this damage. Some of the girls try but they're younger. They have the energy. And the motivation. I'm well past that now, thank goodness."

Charlotte could have sat out this second war but she would never shirk what she saw as her duty. I also believe she felt that this time she could play an active part rather than be forced to watch silently, passively from the sidelines as she had done in 1914. For all I know, she may have seen her new job as a kind of revenge on the Germans and on all those who had stolen her future. A thoroughly genteel revenge.

She seemed to enjoy her new outdoor life. It allowed her to channel all her buried angst and fear into physical labour rather than standing at the kitchen window, watching Henry pulling up weeds with a grim, cheerless determination. After joining the Land Army, she also cut down her drinking. I think she enjoyed spending time with young, relatively carefree women – girls my age who laughed and sang and curled their hair and worried about getting too sunburnt even as they worked hard and silently prayed for their brothers, fathers and lovers. Their gaiety took the edge off the daily terrifying tedium of living through another war.

Charlotte also relished her role as mother figure to this new generation. It was in her nature to want to protect them.

"I feel like God when Jesus asked him to take the cup. Remember, in the Garden of Gethsemane?" she said one day as we drank tea after her shift.

I shook my head. My parents had never properly introduced me to religion. By the time I came along whatever faith they once had was largely destroyed, although I often wondered if Charlotte played along with that too for Henry's sake. If he felt God had abandoned him, she perhaps nurtured an unspoken belief that a divine hand had brought Henry home. Both points of view are understandable. How could Henry believe in a merciful God after what he had seen? How could Charlotte not after her man made it home when so many didn't? Faith is so subjective. In any case, Henry's faith was always something of a social convenience while Charlotte was raised a Catholic. On her dressing table, she had a picture of her first communion – it shows a big-eyed, solemn nine-year-old, standing stiffly in a doily of a dress. That picture breaks my heart. I wish that little girl could have had a better life. Charlotte would have tut-tutted and said she had a fine life. We would both be right.

"Jesus asked his father to spare him the suffering that was coming," Charlotte went on. "Of course, God could not if mankind was to be saved but, as a father, he must have desperately wanted to. In the same way, I can't take this cup from my Land Girls but I can try to help them get through what's coming. I know I haven't got much to offer but just being with them seems to help. If nothing else, they can see I survived the last one. That cheers them up. After all, I'm nothing special. If I can survive, then anyone can."

"It won't be the same this time," I said, selfishly unable to spare her my fears. "Hitler is going to attack us and hard. Everyone says so. This time we won't be able to sit out the war at home. Everyone at the Ministry says we are going to have a bad time of it although Lord knows, that's not what we put on the posters."

Charlotte sighed.

"I know. I wanted to get one of those Anderson shelters to put in the garden but every time I try to discuss it with Henry, he shuts down completely. It would be useless in any case. There's no way I'd be able to get him underground again. He cannot abide small spaces. He says that being in the trenches was like being buried alive. He felt like a rat. He'll never go underground again. And I suppose we'd also have to tear up his flowers and vegetables to put the shelter down. You put them in the ground, right?"

"Half in, half out," I said. "I can send you an instruction leaflet."

Charlotte waved her hand dismissively.

"Henry would rather risk death than dig a hole for a shelter in his garden. We'll just have to cross our fingers and hope the wind blows the bombs some other way. Or we could try to run to the shelter at Fleetville but I can't see your father doing that either. And if he stays, I'll stay."

I wanted to hug her but she got up quickly, muttering, "Now, where did I put that yarn I wanted to give you."

Charlotte was on a mission to get me to knit for the soldiers. I drew the line at that. What was coming might prove to be the end of our world and I saw no need to knit while waiting for the apocalypse. I still have those balls of yarn in a bag in my attic – who's going to want khaki wool nowadays? Maybe I'll get a cat, just to have something to do with the wool. I wonder if you knit, Diane. I can't imagine you do but what do I know.

St Albans was bombed several times – near Clarence Park, off London Road and even our street, Hatfield Road – but the wind *was* always blowing the right way for my parents. Charlotte stayed with the Land Army throughout the war while my father continued to grow his vegetables and fruit. His own personal Dig for Victory crusade. He despised officialdom and never joined any volunteer force – Charlotte said he would rather die than wear a uniform again – but he often went out walking at night, wandering the blacked-out streets and lanes with a tiny torch clutched in his fist. If he stumbled on the aftermath of a bombing, he would help as much as he could. I wonder now if his withdrawal from society was not the result of fear or post-traumatic stress but instead constituted a deliberate rejection of the institutions and hierarchies that had reduced his generation to cannon fodder. I wish I could have asked him.

"Survival is so personal," Charlotte told me when I ranted to her about how dangerous it was for him to be out at night. "I think this is what Henry has to do. Maybe he's always been stronger than we knew. He's had the courage to survive, or he's at least felt obliged to go on. That's what took him to war in the first place: that sense of duty. But I don't think he will ever again believe in anything other than his own free will."

She paused.

"Maybe Henry has always been more free than we thought, though God knows, the price he paid was too much."

During all this time, Robert was racking up his own bill for the privilege of staying in the world.

He left England for France in late 1939, sailing from Southampton to Cherbourg to join the men digging trenches along the border between Belgium and France. Another irony: so much of war is construction destined for immediate destruction. I didn't see him again until after the evacuation from Dunkirk the following May. He was supposed to come home on leave in February but a week before I got a telegram to say he had fallen ill with a fever and would have to rejoin his regiment when he recovered. And all the while, the war spread.

Unlike the Great War, which stayed largely inside its trench boundaries, this new conflict was like mustard gas. It stole across the world, seeping under doors and into homes, poisoning life everywhere. During the Great War, British officers could leave the front in the morning, get on a train and stroll, dapper and dashing, into their Soho club for dinner. If the Great War introduced ordinary soldiers to a soul-destroying intimate knowledge of what man can do to man, it spared the rest of the population. Our second effort at chaos was much more egalitarian.

The long-awaited Dunkirk evacuation started on a Sunday. I was in Swiss Cottage with my landlady Michelle Perry, both of us hunched over my Marconi waiting for news of Operation Dynamo. Our heads were bent like fearful churchgoers, avoiding the gaze of a wrathful God. Every hushed breath was a silent prayer for a miracle.

For a while we held hands – Michelle's husband was also in France – and when it became clear that men were being saved, we hugged awkwardly before sitting down quickly to resume our vigil. Mercifully, her children – tumble-top girls of five and three – must have sensed the tension and spent most of the morning playing in the back garden. Every so often, Michelle, a sweet dough ball of a girl, jumped up as if she had just remembered her offspring and rushed into the garden to check what they were doing. I heard a few hasty reprimands, a subdued whining and then she was back, slipping into her chair like a guest in her own home.

"How will we know if *our* men made it?" she asked, her gentle eyes saucer-wide with the scale of what was happening.

"The army'll let us know, I'm sure. If we don't hear anything today, I can try to find out who we need to contact at work tomorrow," I said.

She looked crestfallen. I often forgot that much as I despised the morale-boosting twaddle we churned out at the Ministry, mindless cheer was the people's opium now. We had them well and truly hooked.

"But your Joe is sure to be fine," I said quickly. "Didn't you tell me he used to sail as a lad? Where was he from again? Somewhere on the coast, right?"

She nodded. "Cornwall."

"So this will be a piece of cake for him. He'll know what's going on, he'll get himself into a good position and before you know it, he'll be back here under your feet, mucking up the house and you'll be wishing they'd left him on the beach."

Her lips twitched but it was just the shadow of a smile.

"Be nice to have the bugger back for a while," she said. "Lord knows, he wasn't perfect and I had plenty to nag him about but all that doesn't seem important any more. I guess that's one good thing to come from all of this. You know what's what. And you know what's not."

"I should get you to write the Ministry's posters," I said. "You're a dab hand, Michelle."

She dared a tiny giggle but then we heard the familiar putter of a Post Office motorcycle coming down the street. Michelle gasped, blessed herself and bowed her head as the engine stuttered to a halt. I looked out the window and saw a spotty, red-haired teenager, his peaked cap askew and his face pinched with anxiety, squint at our door and then look at the plain white envelope in his hand. The telegram boy seemed to stare at that paper forever. But then the motor leapt into life again and the unlikely looking 'angel of death' pushed off. That day, the telegram was for somebody else. Michelle let out a sigh as deep as the earth, blessed herself again and left the room.

I heard from Robert five days later. He was calling from Dover and would be on a train to Reading in an hour. They were to take some rest there before moving on to a base somewhere further north. I didn't hesitate, to hell with the WAAF rules. I'd face the music later. Peterson was at lunch so I left a note on his desk, saying there was a family emergency and that I would try to be back in the morning. As I rushed down the corridor, I collided with Penrose. He put an arm around my waist to steady me and then hastily pulled it away. I didn't notice at the time but later, I remembered the awkward gesture. Memories can also have their roots in the future, Diane.

"Oh my God, I'm so sorry. I'm in such a hurry and... Robert is home. He got out of Dunkirk at last. I'm taking the next train to Reading but I've to go home and change and... I can't miss the train. I don't know how long he'll be there. He could..."

Penrose put a finger to my lips, the lightest of touches, a butterfly's kiss.

"Shush, it's fine. Go. I'll talk to Peterson and the others, square it all with them. Don't worry," he said. "Go."

One long look into his eyes and then I was on my way out the revolving door. As I turned, I caught a glimpse of him standing there, watching me. My lips still tingled from the barely-there pressure of his finger but it didn't matter. We were all experts in denial by then.

At home, after several frantic minutes of pulling clothes from the wardrobe, I decided to stay in my WAAF uniform. I slid my last pair of nylon stockings onto my legs and made up my face quickly but carefully – foundation, brown eyeshadow to complement my eyes and a bright red lipstick that Evelyn had sent me. I was so nervous it took me three attempts to get the lipstick right. Even as I primped, I scolded myself for focusing on such trivial things.

"You know nothing. Nothing," I told the flustered girl in the mirror even as I reworked my eyeliner with a shaking hand.

I was terrified Robert would have outgrown me, that we would have fallen out of sync. How could he still love me after what he'd been through? In terms of experiences, we had already spent a lifetime apart. Charlotte had managed to draw my father back and keep him safe with her but I was not my mother. Would I be strong enough? If I didn't measure up now, today, would that be it? We weren't married. There was nothing to tie him to me if I wasn't up to the task and I was so stupid and so inexperienced that I didn't even know what that task might be.

Robert was already seated in the teahouse when I got to Reading. I stopped for a moment in the doorway, paralysed by his solidity. He looked so real, so familiar. I raised my hands to my mouth and stifled a sob. I was so relieved. Here was the man I loved and half-feared I'd dreamed up. He was a little skinnier around the face maybe, but otherwise it was the Robert who'd been in my head all these months. I don't know what I expected. Some kind of Dracula-esque dishevelment, I suppose. I should have known that the worst injuries are those you cannot see.

A few seconds later, I was in his arms. We moved to a booth; neither of us wanted to let go.

"How long do we have?" I asked.

"I have to be back in the barracks by midnight and then we'll be shipped off to a base next week but I'll try to get leave to come and see you in London before we go anywhere else."

He pulled me closer, burying his face in my hair and breathing deeply.

"You smell so wonderful, my darling Gertrude. Good God, I feel alive again. I don't know if it's the bath, the shave, the food or you but it's like I've woken from a dreadfully long nightmare."

"It'd better be me, you scoundrel," I said, laughing through my tears but wanting to cry even more at the sight of his crooked smile.

"Of course, it's you. Always you."

He paused, looking around at the bleak, bland room where puny light bulbs were fighting a losing battle against the blackout gloom. There were only three other occupied tables but from the look on Robert's face, it could have been the Ritz.

"I can't quite believe it. It's inconceivable that all this is still here."

I wanted to hug him forever so that he would never need to feel like this again – especially not about something as unworthy as this down-at-heel teahouse. The impossibility of it made me feel nauseous.

He told me he'd been among the last soldiers to leave the beach. They'd been held up on their way to Dunkirk by streams of refugees and a ferocious air bombardment. They nearly missed the flotilla.

"A lot of lads were killed on the way. I don't know how to describe it, Lina. The whole thing is so surreal. It's like we don't have a language for this. How on earth can I make you understand? Especially here."

"Please try," I begged. "I want to understand, Robert. I really feel we need me to understand. If we're to get through this together, then you have to try to tell me."

You see, Diane, I did have good intentions then. I did want to share his burdens. It became so complicated later.

"Okay. Maybe if I try to tell you just one thing."

He took a breath.

"I'll have a go at describing the attacks on the way to Dunkirk. It happens like this: You hear the plane, you fling yourself into the nearest ditch or if you can't find one, you just hug the ground, pushing and pressing down with every muscle. It's like your body thinks that if you just try hard enough, you might sink out of sight. The bullets whine and the shells hiss and the noise is like nothing you've ever heard. Like a thousand damned souls screaming. The bullets whistle so close you feel like you're dying again and again. Even when they don't hit you, you think they have and you wait to die. And then it stops and you get up and you realise that you're standing there because Jimmy isn't. He's lying at your feet but it could just as easily have been the other way around. It would be just as meaningful and just as meaningless. I hadn't realised that before. How thoughtless it would all be. I assumed we'd be more… active. I thought we'd have some say in it but we don't. Nothing we do matters in the end. I hadn't realised how random it would all be. Silly of me, I suppose."

He shook his head as though he still could not grasp the concept.

I couldn't take my eyes off him as he talked, his words running faster and faster as his mind rewound. I feared that if I blinked, he might disappear. And then there was his voice. Robert always had a way of speaking that made his listener feel as though this was what they were born to do – to hear this handsome man with his measured speech delivered in a rich, deep voice. Now, his intensity had a raw edge that was even more mesmerising. I could no more stop listening than stop breathing.

"Somehow we got to the beach and then we had to wait again and they were still shelling us and firing at us and then I might've blacked out for a few hours. I was so hungry and so thirsty and it was so noisy with the planes coming over and strafing and bombing the sand and the sea. People were shouting orders and screaming prayers and cursing. I shut down. My brain couldn't take any more. I must've slept, right there in the hole we'd dug in the sand. The next thing I remember is running into the waves and flinging myself over the side of a small fishing boat. Two other lads climbed up after me. We fell onto the deck and then we just lay there. We couldn't do a thing. I didn't even say thank you to the captain. Big, bearded older man with a medal on his heavy jacket. Must've fought in the Great War. He'd the look of someone who'd seen it all before: he didn't even flinch when a shell landed right in front of us, showering us all with water and bits of whatever was in the water where it hit. I caught him looking at us a few times. He didn't look happy or sad. He didn't congratulate us or pat our backs or even smile. That's how I knew he'd seen war himself. He understood. I shut my eyes and blocked out the sound and the screams and the dead, dull noise the bullets make when they hit water. I've never felt so tired, Lina. I swear that if I'd have died then, I'm not sure I would've even noticed."

He tried to force a smile.

"Somehow the gloomy captain got us out of that mess and into the open sea. He transferred us onto a military ship and next thing I knew we were in Dover and people were cheering like we were heroes. And then they put us straight on a train for Reading. We got some strange looks I can tell you when we got off the train here. We hadn't even washed. A bunch of wide-eyed boys, blood stains on their shirts, wild hair, filthy from the mud and the sand and the sea. A lad next to me on the train had a piece of seaweed sticking out of his collar. When I pointed to it, he just took it out, looked at it for a long moment and then slowly put it in his mouth and began to chew. He was eating seaweed, Lina. Can you imagine?"

Later, we went to a nearby hotel and booked in for the night. I slipped the plain gold band I'd bought for such eventualities onto my left hand but the receptionist clearly couldn't have cared less. The hotel was too close to the train station for fusty morals to be a consideration by 1940.

We spent the rest of our time together in bed, rediscovering each other, mapping the changes that eight months of war and absence had wrought on our bodies. Robert was leaner, there were hollows under his ribs, his legs were hard-packed muscle all the way along. There was a new desperation to his lovemaking. He did not take his time. I suppose he thought someone had taken it already. I too felt under pressure. I wanted to get to the end so that I would know that I could still excite him. But then when he had come, all too soon, I felt as though I'd been cheated. To be more accurate, I felt as though *we'd* been cheated. This desperation, this frenzy, it

131

was not us. It was what the war had done to us. It was false, distorted. It made me want to cry.

"Sorry, I'm so sorry," Robert muttered as he fell back onto the pillows. He shook his head. "I've been dreaming about this moment for months. I wanted it to be perfect."

I stroked his hair but said nothing. This was no time for platitudes. It would be insulting to us both.

"I missed you so much, that's the thing," Robert said. "I just can't control it."

"It won't always be this way," I said. "*We* won't always be this way. We just have to see it out."

Robert sighed again and raised himself onto his elbow. He looked down at me, tracing his finger around my face, under my eyes, around my nose and across my cheekbones as though his touch was bringing me to life, as though he was my own Geppetto.

"I worry so much about you here. Anything could happen and I'm stuck over there, barely able to keep myself alive, never mind do anything at all to protect you. It's all wrong. They say we have to protect our women and children but then they take us away and make us fight in another country. Don't get me wrong, Lina. I understand the reasons. I know we have to beat Fascism. This is a fight worth fighting but sometimes I get so angry I can't breathe, or see, or move. I just have to sit, blind and furious, hoping that nothing will happen until the rage, or whatever it is, passes."

I pulled him down so that we lay face-to-face, staring into each other's eyes. I kissed him slowly. His lips curved under mine.

"I love you, my gorgeous Gertrude," he whispered.

We lay like that until it was time for him to go back to the barracks. I helped him dress, holding out his shirt and then turning him so that I could fasten the buttons.

"You don't have to do this. You can stay in bed," he said. "Fall asleep so that I can carry that image with me."

"No, I want to help," I replied. "You can easily call up a

picture of me sleeping. You were always the first awake in Oxford, remember? No, I want you to remember me helping you. Every time you button your shirt, know that I would do it for you a million times if I could. Feel my fingers. Here. And here. And here."

I started to tickle him, something he always hated, and he backed away, laughing as he tried to grab my hands.

I hate goodbyes and I will always try to lower the tone. Remember, Diane, I'd had nearly a year of learning how to smother any pain in fake cheer, vulgarity or profanity. We were all getting good at it. I couldn't help myself. If I was to say what I really thought as Robert prepared to leave, I would break both our hearts. And what good would that do. We were fighting for freedom and we were not yet free to feel, not free to love and certainly not free to give voice to our deepest fears. We censored ourselves so that we could stay alive. Loose lips could sink more than just ships.

I held it together until the door closed behind him. Then I cried for hours, tears of relief, and anger, and frustration. I slept fitfully, waking to find the world had not ended, I was still alive and I was expected back in London.

That is how the rest of the war passed for Robert and me; long, terrifying absences punctuated by brief, frantic, unsatisfactory reunions.

After Dunkirk, Robert was based in Aldershot for a few months but then he was sent overseas again, first to North Africa, later to Italy and then back for a few months before D-Day. I saw him twice in 1942, twice in 1943 and three or four times in 1944, before he left for France and the final push.

During those years, he grew leaner and harder. I watched him struggle to hold onto his hope, his humour and his belief that there could be anything beyond this war. We laughed about his inexplicable ability to endure every campaign without a scratch but eventually the joke wore thin and felt dangerous, as though we were daring the gods to do their worst. The other soldiers called him *The Untouchable* and, as the years went by, I did feel that Robert could be touched by less and less. He laughed less, he cried less, he was less thankful. Every lucky escape just condemned him to another day.

When his mother died in February 1944, he was granted compassionate leave to attend the funeral. We drove down to Felixstowe in my father's car. Robert took the wheel and barely said a word, except to ask me occasionally if I was cold or if I would like to have a nap. To be honest, I was afraid to sleep. Afraid of what this silent, sombre man might do if I didn't keep my eyes fixed firmly on his face or on the white-knuckled hands gripping the steering wheel. I finally understood what Charlotte was always looking for in Henry's face – early signs of a realisation that enough was enough.

Felicity Stirling was buried next to her husband in a gorse-studded cliff-top cemetery that seemed to be tilting towards the sea. Her brothers stood gaunt and grim in dark coats and hats under the low sky while Robert dropped a handful of earth onto her coffin. Nobody spoke apart from the vicar, whose words were torn from his lips by fierce winds before they could register with the small congregation. It was probably just as well. What could he say?

As we walked back to the car afterwards, Robert finally spoke.

"It's so odd to find death still has some dominion here. That we still have rites and prayers and ceremonies to mark the moment. But then I suppose Mother's death was different. There was time to prepare. She wrote to me a few weeks ago, telling me that she didn't have long. I didn't realise how short it would be though."

"Why didn't you tell me?" I said. "I could have gone to see her for you."

"She begged me not to tell anyone. I think she was embarrassed."

"Embarrassed? Why on earth would she be embarrassed?"

"Oh, you know Mother," Robert said and the flicker of a smile crossed his face. "She felt there was a certain lack of decorum in dying in such a trivial way during such difficult times. She was embarrassed by the banality of it. I honestly think she would have preferred to be killed during an air raid. She was a stickler for propriety. A time for everything and all that."

I laughed tentatively and he joined in and then we dissolved into hysterics, giggling and gasping until we were breathless and clinging to each other with tears running down our cheeks as the wind roared around us.

The rest of the day was devoted to the polite tedium that accompanies ordinary death. I did not get a chance to really talk to Robert again and the next day, he left soon after dawn to rejoin his unit. It was probably best as I had no idea how to help him through his sorrow. At some point, you become anaesthetised to grief. If only temporarily. I was also ashamed and shame is a great silencer.

My suffering during the war was nothing as compared to Robert's but it was not empirically nothing. I learned, unwillingly and with little grace, how to endure the endless waiting. During those years, like so many others, I lived for letters. As long as Robert's letters kept coming, I could wait in hope. Those little white envelopes that he always addressed to Lina 'Gertrude' Rose and decorated with a small sketch of a lighthouse on a pile of rocks. I read them hungrily, desperate to get to the signature at the end, that expansive 'R' and the crumbled scrawl that led to the dominant 't'. I would feel my shoulders relax, my breath return as I finished, at last truly believing that he was really alive, or at least had been alive when he wrote those lines. Those insubstantial pieces of paper were my lifeline even though the voice on the page became less and less familiar as the years passed. It was such a long war, Diane. So impossibly long.

CHAPTER 12

Today, it is raining. I feel invigorated sitting here, listening through the open windows to the steady pulse of drops hitting the bone-dry ground. I fancy I can see the flowers stretching a little higher, delighted with this unexpected bounty. There is a stone bird bath outside the window and now that it is full – I am afraid I neglected it since my arrival – dull chiffchaffs and sprightly blue tits are frolicking around, flapping their tiny wings and bobbing their heads like sages on steroids. I'm sitting here at the dining table, diluting my slight hangover with black coffee and wondering vaguely whether there is any point to this story I am telling you. Is this whole exercise just a brush to sweep the minutes along? They will pass anyway, without any help from me. They are passing faster and faster each day.

So much of life and art is silencing those pernicious internal voices that prate on about how futile all existence is, how pointless all effort. As a writer, I am an expert in the willing suspension of common sense. We all have to be but writers more than most. If we dared to acknowledge the fundamental pointlessness of our lives and of our work, the world would be a seething ball of fury or a place of utter stillness, devoid of art. There would be two choices: to rage or collapse. Through a monumental collective suspension of rationality, we do neither. We refuse the evidence because we yearn to survive.

Before I boarded the ferry to come here, I spent a day walking around some of my old haunts in London. I can't quite manage the trek to the top of Hampstead Heath these days – the spirit may be willing but my knees have other ideas – so instead I hobbled to the top of Primrose Hill. It's relatively easy if you come in from Swiss Cottage and take the gentle, meandering paths through the trees, the ones the serious walkers and joggers avoid. It was a cold, grey day but the top of the hill was still busy with tourists, all flapping, outstretched arms, flashing cameras and the gaiety that comes from having broken free from the chains of daily routine. I eased myself onto a bench, looking down at the zoo in Regent's Park and beyond to the jagged skyline of a city that once doubted its survival and now celebrates its continuance with an ever more frenzied rush to evolve, to push out and up.

Below me, the Snowdon Aviary spread its mesh-and-aluminium wings above the trees and the half-hidden sluggish canal with its grass-topped barges and tough city-slicker swans. I could hear the screeching of the Aviary's ibis, cranes and egrets. I saw their exotic silhouettes flitting back and forth behind the mesh. I have always loved the view from Primrose Hill, even during the war. I would sometimes sit on the hill and watch the German planes roar over the city, bombs head-over-heeling from their bellies like huge raindrops. It was such a colourful, somehow seductive, spectacle: the sun glinting on the windows and wings of the weaving, whirling planes; the yellow noses of the Messerschmitts, flak rippling across the sky like unfurled party streamers, barrage balloons burning and the criss-cross of brilliant white contrails, like piping on a blue birthday cake. Then later, oily smoke swallowing the sky above the docks; planes spinning down like so many flaming Icaruses; and the white pinpricks of incendiary bombs sparkling like stars that had tumbled to earth.

There was a terrifying, awesome beauty in the destruction.

I knew as I was watching that people were dying below me, cut down because they lost in the daily lottery that was life then, but I would have known that too if I had been hiding in the shelter in Michelle's backyard, my ears full of vaselined cotton wool. Watching the destruction play out in all its dreadful beauty from the top of Primrose Hill was more honest and less frightening than sitting in the dark, hearing directionless booms and thuds and truncated screams. Was it wrong to hold both awed admiration and fear in my heart? I am not the only one. Soldiers in the Great War marvelled at the stark beauty of skeletal trees rising above rigid waves of muddy ground that glowed red in the flash of flares and exploding shells. Very little of life is either/or.

You may be raising your eyebrows at my callousness. Hold your fury, Diane. Worse is to come. This is perhaps the hardest part of my story. And yet it is not the reason for everything. I can't believe that. But there is a voice that whispers, has always whispered: if I hadn't done what I did, if I hadn't let guilt poison my heart, would Robert still be here? I no longer have much to look forward to but the prospect of that voice falling silent one day soon is truly exciting. I yearn for it to stop.

The rain is still beating down. The elements will be of no help to me today, I fear. I can hardly pretend I need a walk to clear my mind. At my age, pneumonia would probably be the price of such folly. The weather will offer me no reprieve. There is no one to take this cup from me. I filled it and I must drink it and it is already five to midnight.

What can I tell you about my time in London during the Blitz that you will not have heard before, Diane? There are never any new stories, of course. We can only tell the old ones, reshaped and refracted through our own unique gaze. Like everyone else, I saw pulverised buildings, dead bodies and severed limbs. Dreadful at first, your stomach churns, you throw up and then within a week, or maybe two, it is no longer dreadful. Worse, it becomes tedious.

I ran to shelters at night, sometimes fleeing along dark streets with other faceless wraiths. Sometimes I decided that a warm bed was worth the risk, lying with the pillows over my head, my body curled up as though by making myself small I could escape the attention of those buzzing death machines in the sky. Sometimes, as I told you, I watched from Primrose Hill. But none of this is special. None of it is new. It was the same for everyone. The way our hearts raced and our palms grew sweaty as the sirens began to shriek; ash in our hair, in our eyes, in our throats; the stench from burst gas pipes; the dust that blocked out the sun; the smell of burning timber and burnt flesh; broken glass crunching like seashells under our feet; the mouldy air in the Anderson shelters; the stench of cordite from the anti-aircraft guns. But you will have read of all this before. I do not know how to make my story unique for you, how to make it stand out from what you already know.

That was always my dilemma as a journalist. Conflicts affect thousands of people but as soon as people become numbers, they lose their individuality, making it easier for us not to care. I used to feel a grumpy, unforgiveable impatience as I spoke to exhausted refugees huddled under leaky tarpaulins in ad-hoc camps and realised there was nothing new in what they were saying, nothing noteworthy enough to lift my story, to get me a place on the front page. Then later, when exhaustion held sleep at bay, I would remember the pleading, desperate faces and my hostile, self-centred reaction and I would cry, indulgent tears of helplessness and shame. I had a reputation for being a hardened war reporter, a woman who could stomach anything, but really it is not the stomach one has to worry about, is it?

I have no desire to make you cry with my stories of the Blitz. That is not my goal. Or perhaps I am worried that my stories would not move you at all. Why should you care? I mention the Blitz only to remind you that we were all living in a rarefied world where death was ever present and life all the more precious and reckless for it. I am, consciously and cynically, preparing you for what comes next.

One evening in March 1943 – the Blitz was over but there was still the odd bombing raid – I had an early dinner with Penrose in a small restaurant on England's Lane and then we headed towards Primrose Hill. I was giggly and lightheaded from the stomach-stripping red wine. Penrose was in a particularly ironic mood, telling tales from absurdist planning meetings at the Ministry.

"Peterson, of course, was furious. He slammed the table with one of his pudgy fists and roared: 'Will someone give me one bloody good piece of news that we can illustrate with a pretty girl and stick on a bleeding poster before this country dissolves in its own self-pity!' Well, I say roared but it was more like a strangled squeal, really."

I laughed so hard I stumbled. Penrose's arm shot out and then his hand stayed below my elbow.

"You're always stopping me from falling over," I said with unforgiveable inattention.

He was silent for a moment and I blushed as I realised that I had pushed a door I had sworn would remain shut.

Before I could laugh it off, he said quietly, "That I am. I'll be here whenever you need me, Lina. You know that."

"Let's go to the top of the hill," I said quickly, pulling away from him and rushing up the path. "Come on, it's perfectly safe. It'll be light for at least another hour."

In the wan rays of the setting sun, the city looked more insubstantial than ever, as though its roofless homes and gutted ruins might be pulled up and away by the rose-tinted flying whales dotting the sky.

"It looks like a mirage," I said. "Too fragile to stand up to everything that has been thrown at it."

"It's not over yet," Penrose said. "Every time our lads bomb Berlin or any other German city, Hitler will send the Luftwaffe back. The Blitz might be over and London might still be standing but there's a long way to go. I've even heard rumours that Hitler has a super weapon up his sleeve. Some kind of rocket that'll be a hundred times worse than anything we've seen so far."

Suddenly, I felt exhausted as though I'd hit a wall. Maybe it was the run up the hill. Maybe it was Penrose's words, the thought of the fear we had yet to experience after four long years of holding our breath and expecting the worst. I was in front of Penrose and, overcome by it all, I allowed myself to lean back for a second. I swear that's all I did, Diane. I merely moved my weight to the back of my feet and let myself tilt backwards. The slightest of shifts in a world where everything was moving so fast, and yet it was enough. His arms came around my waist and I didn't move.

"Anyway, enough of that whingeing, as Peterson would say. Let's jolly ourselves up," he said, as though what was happening was of no consequence. But he didn't let go and he didn't step back.

"Tell me where you would most like to go in the world, if you could go anywhere. Let's turn our frowns upside down."

"Oh, I don't know. You go first," I said. I knew I should move away. I should break his hold but I was so comfortable in his arms. I had not realised until that very moment how desperate I was to feel a heart beating alongside mine.

"Very well. I've an uncle, Uncle Percy, he's in his 70s now and he's been living in Kenya for the last 20 years. Has a little farm for himself in a place called Nyeri. Since I was a boy, he has sent me the most wonderful letters. I swear to you, Lina, I can smell the heat and the eucalyptus trees when I open the envelopes. He writes of safaris and horse riding and hunting and fishing and the birds and the waterbuck coming onto his land and it sounds so idyllic. Sometimes he sends me pressed flowers, jacaranda blossoms and those gorgeous frangipani blooms. I imagine he must live in a kind of Eden. That is where I plan to go. I won't stay here when this is over. I've made up my mind. It's time to get out of Europe."

He edged sideways and his lips brushed my ear.

"It's a dream, I know. But I'm entitled to dream, aren't I? Aren't you?"

I could make any number of excuses, Diane. I was bone-tired after four years of war. I was hungry for physical contact. It had been months since I had seen Robert, who was now somewhere in the deserts of North Africa. I was only 23. I was not yet married. I was scared and exhausted and life seemed so, so short. In a world full of death and hate, surely every kind of love was permissible. Shouldn't we take love whenever it presented itself? More than that, it was surely my duty as a proud British citizen to encourage cheer wherever I found it. We were being told: *Freedom is in peril. Defend it with all your might*. This was a kind of freedom too, was it not?

You will certainly mock me, Diane, but I was not alone. Illegitimate births shot up between 1939 and 1942 and the same for sexually transmitted diseases. Crime statistics also rocketed higher during the Blitz, although you do not hear about that very often. It did not, and still does not, suit the sanitised, heroic narratives we spun out of that trauma.

What do you make of my efforts to excuse what I did, Diane? Don't worry. Whatever you are thinking, I've thought it all before. There is no criticism you can throw at me that I have not levelled at myself. Because in the end, everything I have said was true for everyone and while there was infidelity, there was also its opposite. Loyalty is only proven in the testing and I failed.

Penrose pulled me closer, entwining my hands in his. He started to kiss my neck, sending shivers down my spine. I kept my eyes on the skyline and refused to think. I had done too much of that: thinking about rationing, about blackout curtains, about where to shelter, about how many bombs must fall before I would be hit, about how to calculate the odds of Robert's survival, about whether the war could ever, ever end. I was worn out by my merry-go-round thoughts.

As the sun sank to our right, it broke through the clouds

that had shielded us all day, gilding London's shattered spires and broken towers so they looked like they belonged to a fabled, lost city. I could hear birds trilling the end of the day, shouts from the men swarming over the anti-aircraft battery below and the soft sound of traffic hissing around the edges of the park. We were out of time, out of place, up on our hill. Penrose turned me around and we kissed, slowly at first, both of us hesitant but then when I didn't pull away, his lips grew more urgent and I found a matching desire in mine.

"Come home with me, Lina. Please."

I could have ended it then. A kiss is not so bad, not in wartime. But I didn't. I went home with Penrose, both of us silent and tense as we ran through the park, caught a bus and then walked the short distance from the stop to his home in Marylebone. He lived on a street of tall, austere houses, all sparkling windows and boxed geraniums apart from the last one, which looked like a giant toddler had taken a hammer to it. The front wall of the top two floors was missing. I could see a crumpled bed and a dresser, still covered in squat tubs of cream for skin that no longer needed them.

"A close call," I said as we walked past. I was relieved to have something other than what we were doing to talk about. The blasted home on that graceful street stood like an abomination. A rotten tooth in an otherwise pristine mouth.

He nodded.

"They were lucky. An elderly couple, the Prescotts. They died in each other's arms. A direct hit."

We walked on.

"Is this yours?" I asked as he climbed wide steps to a black door.

"My sister's," he said. "She's been evacuated with her children. Her husband is fighting in Africa, I can't remember where right now. Anyway, I don't want to think about all that," he said, pulling me inside and slamming the door.

"Tonight, the war stays outside. Okay?"

I had a vague impression of a large, airy lounge and then

we were upstairs, in the bedroom and he'd pulled the blackout curtains and we were just two faceless people making silent, slightly sorrowful love in a darkened room on a broken street.

"Are you okay?" he asked me afterwards.

"It's a little late for that," I replied.

"I know. I just… I mean, you shouldn't feel bad, you know. You're not married. And who's to say…" His voice trailed off.

"I hardly think Robert is being besieged by nubile young women in whatever desert he's stuck in, if that's what you mean," I replied, more caustically than I had intended. I knew I shouldn't be angry with Penrose. This was not his fault. It was not my fault. There was no fault. But I still felt dreadful. I still feel dreadful, Diane, if you can believe me.

I remember the exact date. It was March 3rd. I remember it because of what I learned later. While Penrose and I were making love, 173 men, women and children were suffocating to death on the narrow rain-slicked steps of the Bethnal Green tube station. It was the worst civilian disaster of the war and for two days, not a word of it leaked out. They hushed it up because it was too horrible to bear, even for people who had learned to cope with so much. And then there was also blame to be apportioned. People knew the entrance was unsafe. They had been told this. Official neglect was not a story the authorities wanted told, not when we were all supposed to be pulling together.

Apparently, a woman holding a baby fell at the bottom of the steps, a man fell over her and then all along the stairs above, people started to fall. At the same time, they said, an anti-aircraft battery opened up across the street, trying out a new system, which blasted 60 rockets into the air simultaneously. Nobody had heard the terrifying sound before so the people at the entrance panicked and surged forward. They didn't know someone had fallen down. The people already in the tube didn't know anything was happening on the steps above them. In just seconds, scores

144

of people were piled upon each other, parents crushing the breath out of their children even as they tried to save them, bodies turning mauve as the air was sucked out of them. After two days, the news made it into the papers but the location was not given and nor was the death toll.

To me, that incident embodied the essence of that war. Pointless deaths, fear, horror beyond enduring, secrecy and lies told to keep spirits up. You might think my transgression would pale in comparison. You'd be wrong. In my mind, what happened at Bethnal Green magnified what we had done at 17 Marylebone Lane. It amplified my feelings of shame. Irrational, I know, but I can only tell you what I felt and still feel. I have not the wit to break down the complex chemical and electrical signals that caused my brain to twin these two completely separate events. Unless we decide it was my conscience. I do have one, Diane, although I will be the first to admit that I have muted it as much as possible over the years. But as I age, I find its power is increasing even, or perhaps especially, as my rational mind's supremacy wanes. I have too much time on my hands now and it appears my somewhat enforced idleness has breathed life into my moribund moral sense. I suppose that is why I am writing to you as well.

I do not believe Robert ever found out about our affair, for want of a better term, and I do hate the corporate banality of that word. But that is not the point. I knew, and in the end what my relationship with Penrose told me about myself was damaging enough: I was weak, faithless, fickle and needy. It was all true but I did also love Penrose, in a fashion. I loved his solidity, the fact of his survival, his immediacy. These qualities may seem superficial to you, Diane, but you were not there. You did not experience life on the edge of oblivion as we did. What would you do if you thought… No, that is not accurate… If you truly believed, with good reason, that you could die tomorrow. Would your love for Paul survive *that* test? It is, of course, an impossible question. You might well

145

say your love would but you will never know. It doesn't take much, Diane. That is what we all forget. Until it is too late.

Robert came home again in July after the Germans had surrendered in Tunisia. He was nut-brown and weary but, more than that, he didn't know where he was headed next and he didn't seem to care. Even being, as General Alexander said, 'masters of the North African shores' seemed to mean nothing to him.

"It's just another rung on a ladder to who knows where," he said. "We're climbing but there's no end in sight. And we don't even know where the ladder goes. Maybe we'll all end up in heaven. What do you think, Lina?"

We were lying on the bed in my room in Swiss Cottage, our arms wrapped around each other, too tired to do anything else. Michelle had taken the children to her mother's for the weekend and we were blissfully alone. Such solitude was a rarity during the war. We were constantly forced to be with others, either fighting or pulling together or keeping calm or cheering each other up. War had forced us Brits to be gregarious and social. No wonder we were exhausted all the time.

Robert spent most of his week's leave sleeping or dozing fitfully, his arms jerking, his face twisting, his mouth forming words that I could never make out. I watched him from my side of the bed, scared to touch him in case I would startle him, trying to convince myself that we were still together even if sometimes it felt like I was looking at a stranger, trying to stifle the guilt I felt over my affair with Penrose, telling myself that I would end it and knowing that I did not have the strength to do so, not while the war continued, not while Robert's life was not his own or mine.

What else can I tell you of those years? We tried to survive. We tried to stay human. I loved two men. It was my salvation and my undoing.

Chapter 13

Robert's last leave before D-Day came in May 1944. We were all primed for the invasion. The south of England was thronged with American GIs, French, Canadians, men from all over the world. Overpaid, overfed, oversexed and over here. Unspoken was the most important word: Overlord. No one could visit the coast, there were fake camps and dummy ships and trains full of troops heading hither and thither as we all waited for the attack on Fortress Europe.

At the Ministry, there was a palpable air of excitement and a melodramatic sense of secrecy. Peterson prowled between our desks, shushing any talk as though the walls might have German ears. I knew Robert was taking part. He was due to report for duty in a southern town that had been taken over by the army. The residents were told to leave their homes and given vague assurances of compensation. We were all too far gone by then to care about compensation. For what? Our homes, our loved ones, the endless minutes spent in fear and trepidation when we should have been laughing, sulking or worrying about which shade of lipstick made our teeth look whiter? You cannot compensate for a cataclysm.

A few days before Robert was due to rejoin his unit, one of my Ministry colleagues, a wisp of a WAAF called Sarah whose deep-set eyes were prone to well up at the slightest provocation since her fiancé drowned at Dunkirk, invited us out to dinner in Portobello to celebrate her birthday.

"I wasn't going to do anything," she said. "I mean, the bloody bombing seems to have started again and it's not even a very important birthday. Twenty-four isn't much of a number but then I thought, what if it's the last birthday I get? You just can't know. What if I die next week and I didn't even bother to celebrate that last birthday. That would be so sad I couldn't bear it."

Her eyes were glistening and she flicked her fingers around her face, pretending to straighten her thick fringe as she brushed tears off her lashes. We were on a cigarette break and I was only half-listening. I was worrying about whether I should get Robert a gift before he left. I wanted to believe that something given in love could somehow carry him through the next few months but I also worried that he might read it as a sign that I believed his luck was running out. That was our problem in 1944, Diane. Those of us who had survived so far. We were sure it was only a matter of time. Our luck was on a two-track race with the war.

"Don't be daft," I said as Sarah's words registered. "If you die, it'll be sad anyway whether you celebrated or not. And of course you'll have another birthday. Lots of birthdays. We must be getting to the end now. All we have to do is hang on. Maybe a few more months. Everyone is saying Hitler is running out of options. Look at what we've done to his cities. And we've driven them out of North Africa. It can't be much longer now."

"Maybe," Sarah said. She shook her head.

"Anyway, you'll come? With Robert?"

I said I would although part of me was reluctant to share the final precious hours of his leave. But maybe we could do with some company. All too often, we locked ourselves away. That intensity could be suffocating. A night out would help us see each other differently, as a normal couple with normal fears and normal desires.

Robert must have felt the same.

"Let's do it," he said when I arrived home and told him. "I

want to go out. I want to drink and eat and forget everything. I want it to be how it was before. We need to seize the moment because you never know."

I must've looked concerned because he lifted my chin and gave me a long look.

"Don't worry, darling. I'm not saying goodbye. We're just going out."

He suddenly slammed his hands onto the table, rattling the cups and making me jump.

"God, I just want to live a life that isn't so bloody dramatic all the time," he breathed.

So off we went to Portobello, fumbling our way through the dark with our torches. We had both tied white handkerchiefs around our necks so that we wouldn't bump into other people. I joked that this was the only surrender Churchill would ever accept – surrender to the demands of the dark.

The restaurant was small and muggy with flickering candles reflected in varnished dark tables and a jazz band playing on a raised platform in one corner. The menu was classic wartime haute cuisine – a bland pie made with some kind of Spam, stodgy green pease pudding and baked potatoes that seemed to have been plucked from the ground before they were fully grown. But there was red and white wine and even a little champagne. Sarah had brought her sister Denise, who was home on leave from Egypt where she was serving as a WAAF administrator, but she had also invited almost the whole team from the Ministry. I hadn't realised Penrose would be there.

I never had any contact with him when Robert was home on leave. Even in the office, we steered clear of each other by mutual unspoken agreement. It was an untenable situation but we never spoke of 'what next' either. Robert and Penrose had met once or twice – it could not be avoided as Robert had insisted on meeting the people I worked with, saying it would help him picture me in my London reality when he was far away. The two men seemed to like each other, which did not surprise me. They were similar in many ways. You're wondering perhaps how I dealt with the guilt, Diane, when Robert was home. I wish I could say it was terribly complicated but it wasn't. I simply ignored it. I lived in the moment, each moment separate from the next. When I was with Robert, I did not allow myself to think of Penrose and vice versa. It sounds callous and maybe it was but we were living in the cruellest of times. My deceptions bothered me but only as much as a headache might trouble a person whose skin is on fire.

When we walked into the restaurant, Sarah stood up and waved us over.

"Lina, Lina, come and sit here," she cried. "How lovely to see you, Robert. You look wonderful. Shove up, boys. Robert gets the comfy chair. No, don't sulk. He just does."

Normally, Sarah was the quietest person in any crowd, and certainly not one to stir up resentments, but her flushed cheeks and glittering eyes suggested she had started celebrating early, if celebrating is the right word.

Penrose was sitting at the other end of the long table, sipping a glass of red wine. His face was in shadow so that I could not read his expression. He leaned into the light to give me the briefest of smiles. He'd had time to prepare at least.

Robert slipped into the chair nearest Sarah. I sat opposite him, next to Denise.

"Hello darling," Sarah said, bending towards Robert and hiccupping loudly. She burst out laughing and pretended to hide her face against Robert's chest. He raised his eyebrows and smiled at me, feigning apology. I rolled my eyes and found myself grinning back, pathetically delighted by this normal nonsense. Sarah deserved Robert's company tonight. And he could probably do with her adoration too. We could have been normal people in that moment.

I dared another glance at Penrose. He lifted his glass to me and smiled again. It was a sad smile, Diane, but ours was just one tiny tragedy.

We ordered the food just to get it out of the way and then we drank quickly and very deliberately, as was our habit. Soon our laughter was too loud, our arms waved around too wildly, a bottle smashed on the floor, napkins were flung across the table. We were just children really, apart from Penrose who maintained a dignified otherness at the end of the table, like an indulgent but watchful parent.

"So you're in the WAAF too?" Denise asked, leaning closer. She looked like Sarah except that where Sarah's features were soft and childlike, hers had a harder edge. Her skin was tanned and she had an angry red scar on the left side of her neck.

"Yes, for my sins," I said. "Sarah says you've been in Egypt for a year. What are you doing there?"

"Oh, you know, pushing endless bits of paper from pillar to post," she said. "And partying in Cairo, singing in the mess, the usual."

"We all have to do our bit," I said, tipsily raising my glass.

"Oh yes," she said. "That's the rallying cry: We're all in it together. Of course, it's utter rot. I'm having a wonderful war, apart from one unfortunate incident with an overfriendly piece of shrapnel."

She pointed to her neck.

"It looks worse than it is. I was lucky. But take poor Sarah. She's lost her man and who knows if she'll ever recover, while I've had more men than I can count. And look at us here now, all having a jolly good night, while somewhere someone is stuck in a hole, wondering if he'll ever taste wine again."

"It's a funny old war, alright," I said, looking down the table at Penrose.

"Do you think it will be over soon?" she said. "I mean, really over?"

"I don't know," I said. "I guess it all depends on how things go in France when we finally get over there."

"Is your man going?"

For a moment, because of where I was looking, I thought she was talking about Penrose, who was chatting to one of the young chaps from the Ministry. The boy, who ran our messages, a skinny, big-eared lad of about 16, was hanging on his every word. With a start, I realised Denise was talking about Robert, whose flushed face was close to Sarah's as they sang along with the band.

"Yes, he leaves for the south the day after tomorrow."

"Are you scared?"

I giggled. The wine was taking its toll and really, what a question.

"No, I'm over the moon that he'll be able to give Jerry what for," I said, making my eyes as big as I could and drumming the words on the tabletop. Denise burst out laughing.

"I'm sorry, what a stupid question. What a bloody ridiculous question. Oh my, oh my. The wine has clearly gone to my head. Hopefully, it'll stay there because it'll strip my stomach if it gets anywhere near it."

I took a cigarette from my pack and offered it to Denise. She took it, placed it between her lips and I flicked my lighter. The flame ignited and at the very same moment, air raid sirens began to wail, as though I had called them forth by striking the flint.

"Bugger," Denise said, the cigarette falling from her lips. She fumbled to pick it up. "I was hoping we'd get away with it tonight. For Sarah's sake."

She stood up but Sarah rose to her feet and shouted her down.

"Denise, where are you going? Don't leave. It's probably just a false alarm again. Let's stay and have another drink and if it keeps going, we can leave then. What do you think, boys and girls? Shall we stay?"

There was something mesmerising about Sarah at that moment, stumbling slightly and sloshing wine over the top of her glass and yet a symbol par excellence of the defiance that was supposed to carry us through. Penrose was standing too.

"Come on, Sarah," he said. "I think we should go to the shelter. They've been doing a lot of damage these last weeks. Let's not chance it. Come on, old girl. We can take some wine with us if you like."

"No, I'm not going."

Sarah fell heavily into her seat.

"I refuse to spend my birthday evening in a damp, disgusting hole with a bunch of strangers, singing and pretending to be cheerful. Not again."

A few of the other guests in the restaurant cheered. Penrose sighed, put down his glass and started to move towards Sarah.

That's when the bomb that had been falling on us forever finally found us. A noise beyond description, dull and loud as though all our screams had been distilled into one roar, a flash of light and a rush of air, in and out, like a giant's hot, dusty breath.

When I came to, I could not understand where I was. My ears were ringing, my eyes were watering and I could taste metal in the back of my throat. I could see clouds of smoke, wafting almost lazily above me. Flames were crackling somewhere, lighting the underside of the smoke clouds that seemed to be drifting across a starry sky. I realised it *was* the sky. The roof was gone. As my hearing returned, I heard the silver sound of tinkling glass, the creaking of wood, and then cries, small and strangled and very far away.

"Lina, Lina!"

Hands were on my shoulders, pulling. I wanted to tell them to stop. I was quite happy in my strangely whistling, dust-filled world, gazing up at stars that shouldn't have been there. I wanted nothing else right then. I suppose part of me knew what was coming and I wanted to put it off as long as I could, even when it was clear there was no changing what had happened. Robert finally managed to pull me out from under the table legs and other bits of rubble that had exploded onto me when the bomb rearranged our world. We stood swaying together.

"Come on, we have to get out. Those fires could spread and then the gas... Come on, Lina. Please try to walk, darling."

I looked into his face. He had a cut on his cheek and his hair was covered with dust and plaster but otherwise, he seemed unhurt.

"You are untouchable," I breathed groggily.

"And you, my darling. And you. Together we are doubly untouchable. I told you when this started, our story cannot end. Not like this."

I leaned into him, becoming aware of other shapes rising from the ground, of the bells of fire engines ringing, the crunch of wheels in the street, which seemed to have drifted into the restaurant. The front wall, the façade that made us believe we were stepping out of the war for a few hours, was gone. I could smell gas and mud, the sharp stench of cordite and the bitter ferrous smell of blood. Survivors were switching on their torches. For a moment, I thought I was staring at the stars again but this time, they were all around me.

"Where are the others?" I asked Robert as he tried to steer me outside. "Where's Sarah?"

"I'll go back and find them. I promise. I just need to get you out of here so the rescue people can have a look at you, make sure you're okay."

I couldn't move. I kept looking frantically around me but it was as though some important connection between my eyes and my brain had been sundered. Remember what I said about the inadequacy of our measurements of time, Diane? How could one possibly fathom that such radical change could take place in just one second? We struggle when the sun gives way to rain, fussing for our umbrellas, buttoning our coats, grappling with the new reality even though the looming clouds had told us what was coming. When the car stalls, we try to get to grips with our new status as stationary on the hard shoulder. But eventually we adapt because that is what we do. My brain recalibrated and I started to understand the roofless, formless reality before me.

154

Sarah was lying on the floor. But something was not quite right. It was Sarah, yes. She was on the floor, which was odd but yes, it was definitely her, on the floor. But her body ended at the red hem of her lilac dress. It could not be, my brain said. It is, it is what I am showing you, my eyes replied.

Sarah's legs were gone. I squinted but the image didn't change. Denise was on her knees now. She had seen Sarah too and was trying to crawl towards her but all that used to be the restaurant was on the floor and blocking her way. Denise was screaming Sarah's name. I wanted to tell her that Sarah could not hear. She was clearly dead, my brain now said. My mouth would not move. I saw the big-eared boy stumble past me, eyes blinking sticky blood from a deep wound on his head.

"I think I'll go home now," he muttered as he went past. "Time to go home, sonny boy. Time to go to bed, Timmy."

Robert was still trying to drag me out.

"Can you see Penrose?" I said.

"No, but he's probably out already," Robert said. "Look, there are people in the street now. I remember those men, you see, those ones there, they were at a table in the corner. He's probably out there somewhere with them. Look at them, Lina. Let's go and let the rescue services do their work. We can tell them about Penrose."

But I still couldn't move. Suddenly, light washed over us. Firemen had arrived and had set up a floodlight. It made things so much worse. At one table, a couple sat bolt upright, frozen forever in that moment before their world ended.

My eyes followed one fireman as he moved closer to us. He fell to his knees and I saw his mouth open as if he was going to shout something but he closed it again, too quickly. I knew it was Penrose. We all had a sixth sense for tragedy by then. Or maybe it was just that we always expected the worst and inevitably sometimes we were right and then we remembered the foreboding we had felt and invested it with a false significance. It gave us a sense of control, I suppose.

I broke from Robert's arms and stumbled across to the fireman, falling on my knees beside him.

"A friend of yours?" he asked.

I nodded, then realised he couldn't see me in this dark corner and said slowly, "Yes."

That too was a lie though.

The fireman shone his light on Penrose's face.

His eyes were open and his mouth gaped darkly as if death had taken his breath mid-shout. There was blood pooling under his hair. I put my hand in it before I realised. I was looking at his chest, where a jagged piece of metal was softly steaming. The fireman ran his light over the rest of Penrose's body, slowly, respectfully. I became aware of Robert standing behind me but there was no need to dissemble. I had no untoward grief to show. I was numb. I could have been looking at anyone.

"He won't have felt a thing, darlin'. I fancy he was gone as soon as that metal hit him. With the shock 'n all, he likely never knew what happened," the fireman said.

I nodded again. I felt Robert's hand on my shoulder.

"Thank you," I said. "I doubt it's true but it's nice of you to say so."

I got up then and let Robert lead me into the street.

Two days later, Robert was gone too. And as we waited for the invasion, I lost my mind for a little while but there were so many of us walking around with minds and hearts and other pieces missing that nobody really noticed.

Penrose was swiftly buried in the City of London cemetery in Manor Park, alongside Sarah and the other people who died that night. I went to his funeral with some colleagues from the Ministry. We stood at the back, an awkward group of official doom-fighters brought face-to-face with the reality of a war we had reduced to snappy, saccharine mottos.

CHAPTER 14

Sometimes, Diane, I try to imagine where you are reading these letters, if indeed you are reading them. This exercise requires a double-dose of what my literature professor used to call the willing suspension of disbelief. Maybe you have a special routine. Perhaps you read my letters over breakfast. Or maybe you read them late at night in your bed. Do you discuss them with Paul or keep them for yourself? Perhaps you take the pale yellow envelopes to your favourite café before you go to work. Maybe you don't work any more. Do other people run the gallery now that you've done the hard work of putting it on the map? Oh yes, I have followed your career, darling. I am a very British stalker. Very polite, very unassuming and very passive-aggressive. You never even knew I was there, did you?

I visited the gallery once. It must have been five or six years ago. I pretended to myself that I might as well pop in as I happened to be in the neighbourhood. Of course, there was no other reason for me to be on that street in Mayfair. Nothing other than an old woman's penchant for poking her nose into things that are none of her business. Fooling myself again.

I love the name: Silent Poetry. You are a clever girl. I had to look it up when I got home. I'm afraid I hardly remember what was on the walls. I was so nervous and I know so little about art anyway despite my experience with wartime posters. I have a vague memory of vibrant colours, strong asymmetrical shapes. There were also twisted, disturbing sculptures, little wooden nightmares, on plinths in the centre of the room. I liked those.

I approached a slender, austerely pretty brunette with the most beautiful knee-high leather boots. She was behind the desk but she could have been one of the exhibits. Boots On The Ground, perhaps.

"Hello, could I speak to Diane Spencer please?"

She raised her perfect eyebrows.

"Do you mean Maria Spencer? The owner?" she asked.

I ignored her tone. I've been hearing it a lot since I hit old age; a mixture of annoyance and slightly contemptuous pity. I just nodded.

"She's out this afternoon, I'm afraid. Can I take a message for her?"

I said no. I was already regretting my fake spontaneity. I left as hastily as a 70-year-old woman can, feeling her eyes on my back as I tottered out. She probably feared I might stumble into the sculptures or careen into one of the pictures. She was not entirely wrong to be concerned.

It was February, a depressing nowhere month, neither winter nor spring. It was cold and the skies were low and leaden. I'd had a bout of pneumonia over Christmas and I suppose I was feeling feeble and lonely and that drove me to seek you out. My only excuse for such appalling behaviour is that rational thought becomes more and more of a luxury as we age, Diane. Increasingly, I find I am ruled by my emotions. This susceptibility angers me. I thought I had turned my back on those bastards long ago.

Now we come to the bitter heart of this story, Diane, but I'm afraid I can't tell you everything yet. You will have guessed already that something definitive, maybe something dreadful, happened to Robert when he came to France as part of the D-Day invasion. Why else would I be here? But, you see,

I didn't find out what it was until many years later in the most unlikely of places – a noisy bar in the heart of Saigon in 1963. If you are to understand why things unravelled the way they did, I have to keep this information to myself for now. You must see things through my eyes. It is the only way we can get to the truth, or at least to my truth. We can never get to Robert's now. He took it with him. You'd better hope I don't do the same and drop dead before I get to the end of this missive. I like to think of this, my last work, as a kind of Scheherazade safety net for my increasingly precarious existence. But it's all in my head. It always is.

My reticence to fill you in does not just lie in some kind of professional allegiance to a linear narrative, however. I have never set much store by that. I am being sneaky, as all novelists must be. I have to keep you turning the pages. That is always the greatest challenge: to weave a spell so powerful that it withstands all of life's other distractions. We structure deviously, we hoard information, we use sleight of hand, we manipulate. I've done all of this in my books and this time, I have something even more potent to add to the mix. You cannot skip ahead because there is nothing to skip ahead to. You will have to keep opening these yellow envelopes if you want to know the whole truth. I will have to keep filling them. I hope we both do.

Robert fought his way into France from the beach here at Lion-sur-Mer. He pushed inland with the other Brits, Americans, Canadians, French, the terrified, the clueless, the courageous and the cowardly.

As 'our finest generation' moved forward, inch by painful inch, war's dominance over the continent shrank, and village by village, town by town, city by city, the end came. Peace arrived like a gentle mist, wispy and insubstantial at first but swelling slowly until you realised it was everywhere and you wondered why you hadn't noticed its presence before.

At the time, I knew very little about where Robert was or what he was doing. He had stopped sending letters. We were beyond letters. We no longer had the energy to give voice to our hopes, our fears and our dreams. We were all hoarding our words for the day we would be able to spill them out, face-to-face, all the words that had been smothered for six long years by other implacable noises. We knew it was coming but we no longer dared to believe in the obvious. Besides, the imminent end of the war did nothing to lessen our fear of the imminence of death. Someone has to be the last to die.

Then, in May 1945, it did stop. Just like that, as though some magnificent muscle-bound hero had finally managed to slam the lid back on the box of buzzing horrors that had burst open in 1939.

I was lying in bed in Swiss Cottage, staring at the ceiling and wondering if I would ever feel something other than weary, when Michelle knocked on the door. She opened it a few inches and popped her head around. Her face was ashen.

"It's over. They just said so on the wireless. Germany has surrendered in France. It's really the end."

We didn't cheer or laugh. Had I been religious, I might have fallen to my knees but as I was not, silence was the only respectful response. We were saved, delivered finally from ourselves.

Michelle stepped into the room, loose-limbed and wide-eyed as though she was sleepwalking. I beckoned her over to the bed. She sat awkwardly and then I pulled her down beside me and we lay there, arms around each other, crying into each other's necks, as the room grew dark. Outside raucous cheers vaulted from house to house, from our street to the next and on and on, maybe to wherever Robert was spending his night. We could hear singing and shouting and all the indistinct high-pitched caterwauling that marks a public celebration.

"If he'd just hung on for a few more months," Michelle said. She was no longer crying but the deepest sobs would have been easier to hear than the desolation in her voice.

Her Joe had been killed in what came to be called the

Battle of the Bulge. I have to say, Diane, I cannot bear how we have trivialised this term to mean little more than the willpower needed not to eat too many biscuits. I find the misuse of the language of war deeply offensive. It ages me, I know, but I don't give a damn. I am outraged when I see the words 'battle' and 'frontline', 'taking flak' and 'in the trenches' in financial news today. Some things should be sacredly singular.

Michelle eventually fell asleep in my arms. When I woke in the morning, she was gone. It was officially VE day and we were all expected to celebrate.

I didn't want to be with anyone I knew but neither did I want to be alone. I wanted to mark the day anonymously, free of the weight of love and regret. There was no point going to work as a public holiday had been declared. I wondered idly if I would ever need to go into the Ministry again. Our part of the war was over, even if men, women and children were still dying in sweaty, unfamiliar foreign lands, each last breath creating a universal sigh that would eventually end in an almighty mushroom-shaped exhalation that would silence the guns, all at once, at least for a while. From inside my room, I heard London rejoice – wild cheers echoing among ruined houses, laughter exploding, machine-bursts of song and under it all, the honking of thousands of horns. I went outside and started walking.

My memories of the rest of that day have a dreamlike quality because reality felt like a dream. How could it be that the war was over? Six years ago we had lost our grip on reality, then the new altered state became normal and now we were being asked to believe that something that seemed so immutable could end. At the stroke of a pen. If that could really be true, then why did it take so long?

I wouldn't have believed it if I'd stayed inside but all the shops were decked in red-white-and-blue banners and yards of bunting. I wondered if they'd had the bunting ready. For how long? Days, months or years? People were hugging each other and smiling and crying and shaking their heads. I was wearing my WAAF uniform and I had to keep stopping to be kissed, by men and women, soldiers and civilians. Dogs wore tricolour rosettes and barked at everyone, bewildered by the crowds fizzing along usually quiet streets. There was a giddiness in the air and I fancied I could see it hazing over the city as I looked down from the top of Primrose Hill. But then I thought of Penrose and how he had loved that skyline. I thought of Michelle, sitting at home in her tiny house, realising that the war was over and that I would leave and that then she would be on her own with two fatherless girls and that that would be her life until the end of her time. I thought of Sarah, rosy and drunk and about to die, and all the other people who had 'bravely given their lives' by being in the wrong place at the wrong time. I retched and ran to the trees at the side and threw up until there was nothing left inside and tears were streaming down my face.

"Alright, love? Having a bit of a turn there, are we? Need a little help?"

A wild-haired young man with bulging eyes was leaning against a nearby tree and smoking in the way one does when one has drunk all night. His soldier's uniform bore the marks of the night's carousing, peacetime battle scars.

"I'm fine," I gasped, wiping the tears from my cheeks. "I think I just threw up the war. It's just… too bloody much."

He laughed, a gentle chuckle that aged him.

"Too right," he said. "Here."

He held out a hip flask.

"Take a swig of that. They used to give us rum over there, before the big ones, and if it was good enough for that madness, it's good enough for this."

I took a swig.

"What's your name, doll?"

"Lina."

"What's that short for then?"

"Nothing. It's just short for all that is me, I suppose."

He laughed again, motioned for the hip flask and took a generous mouthful.

"You're a smart one. Well, Lina-short-for-nothing, let's go. I've a feeling you've had a rough time of it these past years. God knows, I have. I reckon we've earned this party."

I hesitated. Could I bear to be with anyone today? Could I bear to be on the streets, celebrating as though something good had happened instead of something bad just not happening? Could I be with this man when I still didn't know where Robert was, or when he'd be back or how? Could I bear not to be?

"What's your name?" I asked, stalling.

"Tommy," he said, laughing. "I'm the original Tommy. Who else would you want to spend today with, right?"

I laughed and there it was, gurgling up from some deep well inside, a rush of relief and hope and love for the world that was so strong it nearly made me gag again. It really was over.

I reached for the hip flask.

"Give me that," I said "I hope you have a refill."

"You'll have to catch me first," he said. "Let's see what a dinky, little WAAF like yourself can do when the chips are down."

He sprinted off down the hill, holding the hip flask aloft and whooping with every stumbling step. A bunch of girls and boys saw him and suddenly they were all running after Tommy, whooping and stumbling and falling and rolling. I ran too, all the way down the hill, faster and faster until I felt like I must definitely fall on my face and I didn't care at all because it felt so good to just feel afraid of falling.

After that, we walked through Regent's Park and Marylebone and Mayfair until we got to Buckingham Palace where we joined thousands of people chanting, "We want the king, we want the king." People in their best hats and suits and soldiers in uniform and children with victory-clean faces and celebratory curls. Everywhere I went, people cheered me and

I tried to hold onto the idea that they were only cheering my uniform. I did not want to be cheered. I did not deserve to be cheered. All I had done was not die. That's all any of us could claim. But my anger subsided because in the end, we were all happy for a good reason.

There were too many people to count. We were pressed up against each other with barely room to move our arms. I wondered where we would have put those who had died if they had been luckier. We were so many here and each one of us must have had three or four or more ghosts dancing above our heads, cheering and crying because they were happy for us but sad they could no longer fit into this crowd.

When the King and Queen and their daughters came onto the balcony, it was as though we'd learned nothing. We roared like animals, earth-belly creatures seeing the light for the first time. Then out came Churchill, his hand flashing the victory sign, as bald and stooped and fierce as ever. Another giant roar. I couldn't help myself, I joined in, feeling as cheap and stupid as I ever had but unable to defy the primeval urge to salute these tiny, powerful deities on their altar in the sky. After that the day seemed to spin faster and faster into the night. Thinking back, I can only summon flashes of unrelated images, blurred and indistinct. Faces swimming out of a background gloom, glittering eyes and wide smiles and bared teeth. But there are other faces too: wide-eyed and confused, tear-stained and haunted. I think one of those faces might be mine.

I remember sailors and their girls dancing in the fountain at Trafalgar Square and a couple kissing improbably at the top of a lamppost. I was so worried she would drop her handbag. I was swept into a conga line somewhere near the Strand, feeling stupid and then stupidly happy, kicking my legs and grabbing someone's waist and losing my grip and then running forward, bent double with laughter. I was kissed by soldiers and sailors and Wrens and WAAFs and ATS and policemen. It was crazy and so very unBritish but at some point, I realised I desperately needed to be kissed and to kiss back. I saw young men pulling down advertising hoardings to make bonfires, I saw children waving Union Jacks in the ruins of bombed-out buildings, I saw exhausted men and women, sitting on the pavement, leaning into each other, eyes closed, fast asleep in the middle of the maelstrom. They looked like children as all people do when they sleep. They looked like they might never wake up, lucky things. What a time to fall asleep. If they slept long enough, might these youthful Rip van Winkles forget everything we had seen?

I lost Tommy after we saw Churchill at Buckingham Palace. He'd been a real gent, shielding me from the worst jostling of the crowd, keeping me topped up with rum or vodka or whatever he managed to get his hands on. The best thing was that he never asked who or when or why. I was just Lina and he was just Tommy and on this day, that was enough. The unbridled euphoria could only be borne if we did not speak of the war. We had to play at being born again on May 8th, newly hatched fledglings with no past and no definite future, just this moment. Many years later, I stumbled across a news report from that day. The authoritative voice of the male presenter ended his narration with these words: "We are living in the midst of many great events. We know that in the days when war seems remote and far away, these will be historic pictures. They will tell another generation how England celebrated Victory in Europe Day."

I hope I have given you another perspective, Diane. I hope it is more nuanced than that news report with its rousing tunes and irrepressible sense of triumph, with its inexplicable description of our war as "many great events".

CHAPTER 15

I was demobbed in September, travelling back to my training camp in Cheshire to hand in my uniform and receive my release papers, railway warrants and clothing coupons. A middle-aged man with empty eyes and a limp grip shook my hand and said, bizarrely, "Thank you for coming". I almost said, "Thank you for having me." The supper party was over.

With hindsight, I should have seen that *my* war was just beginning. I should have remembered Charlotte and Henry but I was unable to hold myself apart from the universal tidal wave of relief. We needed to believe in a happily ever after, if only for a short while.

Outside the barracks' gates, girls hugged and cried and stood around as if unsure where to go next. Many had fallen out of touch with the families they would now return to, older and wiser and less biddable. It was such an odd thing to expect – that we would just go back home. After all we had done, and some of these girls had been posted overseas or had flown planes around Britain, we were now expected to slot back into our pre-war roles, as if nothing had happened. It says a lot about society that they expected us to do that. It says more about us that we mostly did just what they expected.

In a way, it was just a more extreme version of what every woman does today. We, or rather you, because I cannot count myself among these ladies, give birth, nurture the baby and then you are expected to leap into your high heels, get back to work and say not one word. They say women are good at multi-tasking. No wonder. We are required to have multiple personalities just to be what we want to be and to do what we have fought to be allowed to do. Each version of ourselves – mother, carer, careerist, sex toy – can and must take on a unique role and we must be all at the same time. My case is different, of course. I jettisoned several of those roles in 1947.

Let me try to explain why.

After I was demobbed, I went home to St Albans to wait for Robert. Charlotte and Henry were a little gaunter, more inclined to pensive silences and uncharacteristically skittish despite the outbreak of peace. We all felt a bit lost in those first weeks and this was their second rebirth. They were, however, delighted to have me home and we settled quickly into a kind of inert routine, waiting for our lives to begin again.

On a bright October day, we decided to go for a walk on Nomansland Common. It had been an unusually mild autumn, although gales would flare a week later, sweeping the laggard leaves off the trees and speckling the ground with thin branches as though the trees were creating their own confetti to welcome 'our brave men' home.

I still did not know when Robert would return. I knew he was on his way, retracing those costly steps through the shattered lands of Belgium and France, but I was beginning to lose faith that he would ever reach St Albans. I was Penelope, waiting for Odysseus and I feared he had found Calypso. As the weeks went by, the euphoria of VE Day faded, forcing me back into the arms of my nemeses: patience and forbearance. I had struggled with these brutal masters even when there was a war raging. I found it almost impossible to bear their strictures now that peace had been declared. I wanted my real life to start. I needed it to begin so that I could be reborn, free from fear and the original sin of my affair. The longer Robert stayed away, the more I feared that I could still face the ultimate retribution for my infidelity. His return would constitute a kind of absolution, I thought.

Charlotte and I walked together, arms linked. Henry was ahead, swiping at grass heads with the ebony cane he had taken to carrying. The sun was warm on our necks, blackberries winked darkly from the bushes and the leaves crackled under our feet. Out here, you could pretend nothing had happened. Squirrels still scampered up the trees, flinging themselves brazenly from branch to branch; shy blackbirds still loitered in the dank shadows; the wind still nuzzled the dying wild flowers and the wispy grasses; the conkers were still falling. Nature had seen us do our worst and had shrugged her shoulders. Out here, she felt indestructible. But we were fooling ourselves. Nature was putting on a show. She too had been mortally wounded by our war.

We were all aware of the Rubicon we had crossed in August when the Enola Gay dropped her noxious load onto Hiroshima. For the first time, we saw that we could obliterate the very essence of life, and end time. It is a sublime irony that the plane was named after the pilot's mother – a giver of life – and the bomb dubbed "Little Boy". And they say writers are fantasists. We are all, every day, guilty of linguistic hypocrisy. Collateral damage, casualties, carpet bombing. We sanitise what we dare not visualise.

"This feels almost indecent, all this busy, busy life," Charlotte said as we walked. "As though nothing has changed. I suppose Nature never changes, no matter what we do."

"Everything has changed," I said, chewing a stem of grass as I used to do when I was a child. "We've shown we can and will visit total destruction on the world. What we've done can never be undone, it can never be unseen. Even if and when the grass eventually grows again in those Japanese cities, even if and when all those bones are cleared in Germany and Poland, what we did will stand unchanged. The permanence here, nature's permanence, is a chimera. It will only last as long as we let it. I always thought nature would outlast us. I thought that was a given. It seems I was wrong."

We had reached our bench. It was at the top of a small hill, facing north towards Wheathampstead. Henry was already sitting on the right-hand side as he had done since I was a child. I took my place between my parents and we looked down at the fields and woods unfurling before us like a textured rug.

"I never thought I would live in the countryside," Henry said. "If I ever thought about it, I assumed I'd always be a Londoner. But I suppose I didn't do that much thinking about the future before the war. The Great War, I mean."

"You're to the manor born now," I said, patting his knee. "Mr Allotment, with your vegetables and flowers. You must spend more time in Wellington boots than in shoes these days."

He smiled with his mouth.

"I wonder why we make life so hard for ourselves," he went on. "If you had told me then that I would see the things I've seen and that I would survive and build a life with this wonderful woman..." He reached across me to grasp Charlotte's hand, " ... I wouldn't have believed you. But then if you'd have said that there was more, that my daughter would have to live through the same and that we would all have to rebuild again, I think I wouldn't have bothered going through it all in the first place."

I felt Charlotte squeeze his hand on my lap. I put both my hands around theirs. We sat in silence for a few moments, looking across the bleached fields as though we might decipher some answers in the patterns of the dried stalks, if only we looked hard enough.

"I thought nothing could be worse than the Great War," Henry said. "What we did to each other, what we let each other do, what we inflicted on ourselves and on the land, on the earth. It was unthinkable. And then it wasn't."

I sneaked a look. His face was weary but his voice carried a note of surprise that was heartbreakingly fresh and young.

He seemed somewhat perplexed to find himself speaking, bemused by his new need to give voice to thoughts long muted. It was as though the end of this second war had finally broken the spell that kept him silent all these years. After all, it had been proven definitively that not speaking of evil yielded no dividends.

"After the Great War, we reshaped our sense of ourselves with what we'd learned and we were frightened of what we'd become but we thought that was it. We couldn't be any worse, and in any case, it would never happen again. But now we see there was another level."

He turned to us and his face was raw. I fought the urge to turn away. I had seen the same flayed look on Robert's face when he woke, screaming and panting, from his nightmares.

"I've seen the reports from the camps in Germany and Poland; I've seen the pictures. Everyone has now. What really scares me is that we still ask, how this could happen? I remember thinking the same thing when I was running across no man's land and watching men fall all around me, cut to bits, screaming, bleeding and dying in the most horrible ways. I thought, how could this happen? How could it happen to us? So I have to ask myself now, where does this all end? How much savagery can we bear? How much savagery can we commit? The lampshades made of human skin, the living skeletons, the teeth, the bloody horror of it all, the sheer enormity."

He stopped as though he was finding it hard to breathe. He pulled his cigarette pack from his breast pocket, lit up with trembling hands and then offered the pack to me. Charlotte disapproved and out of the corner of my eye, I saw her lips tighten but I lit one anyway. Surely, there could be no place for etiquette or niceties after what we had seen. Of course, horror is soon forgotten and these things always sneak back.

Henry spoke again.

"Everyone says 'never again, never again'. But when something like this happens, and if the world doesn't end, then it happens again. Because each time we chip away at our humanity and you can't stick those pieces back. If we don't say 'stop' at the time, we can't say 'never again' because the next time it will be even harder to say 'stop'."

Henry was right, of course. Look what we have done since 1945, Diane. Korea, Vietnam, Iraq, Bosnia, Rwanda, just to name a few. War is like a bushfire. You stamp it out again and again but when your back is turned, it flares into life. Maybe, as a species, we are destined to be at war. Maybe peace is the anomaly. I wish I could dream up a better theory but my poor imagination can only do so much. There is only so much evidence one can deny.

A few weeks later, I was walking down St Peter's Street, heading into town to buy some flour and eggs for Charlotte, who wanted to make a cake. It was raining heavily but I stopped at the war memorial as I usually did to read a few more of the 600-plus names of those who died in the Great War. It had become something of a ritual, a way to acknowledge those who had to die so that we could live. I usually sat on one of the benches in the memorial garden, but, because it was wet, I stood under my umbrella, gazing up at the Portland stone cross. I was not keen on the religious symbol – I found it distasteful in its evocation of more cruelty – but I had made my peace with it, deciding to focus on its decorative qualities, the eternal circle linking the four branches.

I had reached the Gs. Garment, Gates, Gathard, Gazeley. I mouthed the names silently. It was the closest I ever came to praying. I wondered where they would carve the names of the new dead. Could the architect have imagined more space would be needed? The plinth was full but there was more stone around the base. So maybe he had come to the same conclusion as Henry.

I got to the end of the Gs and as I turned to leave, I saw a man walking stoop-shouldered up the path on the other side of the road. He was wearing an ill-fitting brown suit, a

Fedora sat low on his brow and he carried a large duffel bag. It was his strange halting gait that caught my attention. He walked fast and then slow, as though he was in two minds about where he was going. He passed by and it was only when I saw him from behind that I realised it was Robert. It was the stretch of his back and the length of his legs and the swell of desire and delight and despair that sent me dashing across the street, shouting his name. He stopped and turned just in time for me to throw myself into his chest, holding onto his shoulders as my discarded umbrella twirled like a child's spinning top on the rain-slicked path.

"Are you here? Is it you?" I sobbed.

I had waited so long for this moment that would mark the end and the beginning and all I felt as I clung onto him was the most incredible sorrow. I could not stop crying. I held his face in my cold hands and stared at eyes that seemed darker, cheeks that were hollow, the new lines around his mouth, the undamaged whole that was the same and yet so different. He kissed me hard, pulled my hands away and buried his face in my neck.

"It's over," he said, breathing heavily. "It is really, finally over, my darling."

I think we both knew even then that he was lying.

CHAPTER 16

We got married in December at the town hall in St Albans. It was a blustery day and I wore the same dress Charlotte had worn to marry Henry. It was a drop-waist, shift-style affair made of silk and lace. I dyed it turquoise. Robert always liked me in blue. He said it made me look like a mermaid. Charlotte and I joked that the dress was our 'war's-over-let's-wed' gown. There were few flowers to be had but Henry went to Nomansland at the crack of dawn and came back with a spiky bouquet of holly, ferns, rose hip branches and two hardy dog roses. Robert wore the same brown suit he had come home in with a sprig of holly in his buttonhole.

We tried so hard to wring every last drop of joy out of the day. That we succeeded at all was down to Evelyn, with her smutty jokes and indecent laugh, and our other witness, a soldier friend of Robert's whose wide-cheeked, ruddy face and stocky body led me to assume that he was a man of the soil, a farmhand who mucked out stables and rubbed down horses, perhaps. Age had made me no better at judging the book by its cover. I got Douglas Bennington as wrong as I had Robert the first time we met. He was landed gentry and had travelled from the family's estate near Bedford for our wedding. Robert had told me very little about him, beyond insisting that I would love him, so I did not know what to expect when he strode up to us as we huddled awkwardly on the steps in front of the town hall.

"Douglas Bennington," he said, shaking my hand firmly. "So you're the one that got Robert through the war. On behalf of all of us, thank you. You got him through and he got us through. We knew he was untouchable for a reason. And it certainly wasn't on his own merit."

He gave Robert a hug, thumping him vigorously on the back.

"Congratulations, old boy. You deserve this. Once more into battle, eh?"

When he had been introduced to my somewhat over-whelmed parents, Douglas clapped his hands briskly and said: "Well, we're not getting any younger out here. What say we go in and do what clearly has to be done?"

After the short ceremony, and before heading off to celebrate in a squat pub hunkered in a corner of Verulamium Park, the photographer made us pose in front of the Cathedral's giant West Door despite our protestations.

"We're not believers," I said hotly.

"Not believers in what?" he said, rushing over to me and gently edging me closer to Robert. "Beauty? Because that's what this is. A beautiful wooden door. Nothing more and nothing less. Now smile, darling!"

I've enclosed that photo with this letter, Diane. I would like you to have it so please don't reject it. We made a good-looking couple, didn't we? I like the photo even though it is a little blurry because we are smiling at each other. There is a natural quality to it, unlike most wedding snaps. The fact that it is ever so slightly out of focus reflects the way I felt that day. It was all so unreal. A whimsy as flimsy as my blue dress. My affair with Penrose still hung over me like cloud. I could not believe I deserved this happiness. Even with Robert back in St Albans, in my arms, I was still terrified there would be a price to pay. Not to say I feared anything as crass as a tearful confession or rage-filled discovery. Penrose was dead and whatever we had together had died with him. No, I dreaded some kind of oblique retribution, a punishment that would creep up on me, on us, when I least expected it. I wish I had been wrong.

Everyone cheered when we entered the pub and the landlord gave us our first drinks on the house. I got delightfully drunk, not just on the ale but on the sheer relief of having got through the day. Douglas regaled us with war stories – the acceptable kind: all joking Tommies, stubborn and foolish commanders and lucky escapes. Robert smiled and drank and nodded happily and even sang a ribald soldier's song that had the pub cheering and Charlotte blushing. He held my hand as we sat together and it would have been as perfect as one could expect in 1945 were it not for how hard he squeezed my fingers. It was a desperate grip and so I tightened my own hand on his, placing my thumb on the throbbing pulse in his wrist. Every beat rang like an explosion.

"Are you alright?" I whispered.

"I can't believe this is happening," he said. "It feels like a dream. I think I'm afraid I'll wake up and you'll all be gone and I'll be back there."

He bent to kiss my hand. I pinched his arm.

"See, it's definitely not a dream. We are here. This is happening," I said firmly, as much for myself as for Robert. "We just need to hold on to each other. Then there will be no danger of waking up somewhere else, alone."

Later, I went to sit by Evelyn, who was sipping her vodka-and-orange and smoking with the languor of a femme fatale.

"You look happy," I said.

"I *am* happy. Or at least not sad. That's it, today I am not sad and that's as good as being happy," she said, smiling broadly and then shaking her head.

"Bugger, sorry. It's your wedding day. You're marrying the love of your life. I'm ecstatic, of course. So sorry, my darling. I've been a little down recently."

"Do you miss it?" I asked.

"The ATS? No. A little. Oh Lord, maybe a lot. I just don't know what to do with myself now. I went to London the other day and I walked from the Strand to the East End, down to the Thames and back again to the Mall. It broke my heart, Lina. Everything torn up and smashed. Puddles and ripped cables and blasted homes. I hadn't realised how bad it was. When I was in the battery, I didn't see the damage much. It was all about getting the plane in our sights and calculating the numbers. We cheered when we got one but deep down we must have known it was just one. We must have known the others got through but we tried not to think about it. You know I went into Hull once, in 1943. It made me so sad I didn't go again. I couldn't bear it. To see what happened when we missed. If you thought about it, you'd never hit another plane. You'd be too paralysed with nerves."

She sighed and dragged on her cigarette. Her big green eyes were moist but she blinked ferociously until they were clear again.

"I suppose I'll have to try to find work as a secretary now. They'll still want women to type up their letters. The men won't do that no matter how much unemployment there is. It just feels like such a comedown. I miss the excitement and I miss feeling useful. It's a terrible thing to say when so many died, but that's the truth. What about you? What will you do, Lina?"

"I have no plans," I said, realising with a jolt that this was the brutal truth. I had not thought beyond getting Robert back. It might seem ridiculous today when we school our children to imagine their future careers from the earliest age, but we hadn't even discussed jobs or how we would earn a living. I suppose we thought we had earned our living already. We were still staying with my parents, still struggling to repair the rips the war had torn in our lives. That was enough for the time being.

"I suppose we'll look for our own house," I said. "Robert has money from his mother. She left him her home but he doesn't want us to live there. He's happy to stay around here where at least we have some family. I imagine he could get work in a law firm. Maybe he could even finish his studies somehow. I don't know, Evelyn. It makes me tired just thinking about it. It seems too much to ask us to start again."

Evelyn had a funny look on her face. Amused, almost indulgent. Somewhere in my fuzzy head, I realised how insensitive I was being, moaning about my future life with the man I loved. What casual cruelty. In our post-war world, you had to be careful not to be too happy, too cheerful or too hopeful. But you also had to avoid being too sad, too ungrateful or too surly. There was always a worse story. There was so much pain and anguish in the air; it was as though we had to learn how to breathe again, in and out, very carefully.

"What about you, Evelyn? Will you be settling down? Surely, some of those men in the mixed batteries must have fancied you?"

"Oh my darling girl, you are so delightfully naïve," Evelyn said and her indecent laugh made heads turn in our direction. "Of course, I did have admirers but… how can I put this without shocking you? I am not exclusively interested in men and to be honest, I lost my heart to a woman when I was up there."

I took a deep slug of my beer.

"Don't look so horrified, Lina. I'm bisexual, not a Nazi. It's perfectly acceptable now, or if it's not it jolly well should be. As if our sexuality could matter after everything that's happened."

She shook her head but I knew her too well. Her ostentatious defiance was as much to silence her own doubts and her own fears.

"I don't know what to say," I said, slurring a little. "Is it congratulations?"

Evelyn guffawed.

"Maybe, just maybe it bloody well is," she said. "And before you ask, Robert has nothing to fear. You're like a sister to me, Lina. If the war aphrodisia didn't send us rushing into bed together, then trust me nothing will. No, I fell for a girl, a tough, bird-like Mancunian called Sandra. I think I wrote to you about her, about how I pulled her bed into the yard one time? Well, she got me back for that, with bells on. She only stole my bra and hoisted it onto a flagpole in the yard. God knows how she got it up there because I had to get a whole team of airmen to get it down. She thought she was the bee's knees after that. We worked as a pair for months, operating the height-and-range finder. So many nights shivering, trying to stay warm as we waited for the sirens. Then one night she was asked to work the searchlights because the girl who usually did it was sick. Bloody food poisoning and no wonder given the gloop they served us in the NAAFI. Sandra said yes, even though everyone knew that the searchlight teams were the most vulnerable. The whole job was designed to give away their position. Anyway, I saw the plane come in. It was a Messerschmitt and it was escorting the bombers. I knew it would fire on Sandra's lights but there was nothing I could do. I tried to get a reading for it so the girl beside me could calculate the range and then we could pass it on to the gunners but there wasn't enough time. The plane strafed Sandra's little trench and the light went out. A sprinkling of sparks and gone. Just like snuffing out a candle. I actually saw the pilot; he came so low. He didn't look like much. Just a black helmet, buggy goggles and a mouth that was fixed and hard and, I thought, cruel. I suppose all pilots, whichever side they are on, look cruel if you're looking up at them from the ground. Sandra was killed by a piece of metal that sheared off the lamp. It cut her throat, clean from side to side. I don't think she would've felt much pain. But who knows. She died alone. I was the first to reach her and she'd already gone. She didn't look anguished or anything, thank God. Just a little surprised. As if she'd been caught out by a prank that she knew was going to get her into trouble."

Evelyn stubbed out her cigarette and then looked at me with eyes that had been washed hard and clean a long time ago.

"Funny thing is, even though nothing ever happened

between us, not even a kiss, I think Sandra might have been the love of my life. Do you think that's possible, Lina?"

I shrugged. I was too drunk now to trust myself to speak.

"I suppose it doesn't matter because we'll never know. That's what makes me saddest, you know. The fact that I'll never know. I'll always wonder and I've a feeling that won't be good for me."

She waggled her nearly empty glass at me.

"I see spinsterhood beckoning, Lina."

She drained the drink. "I'm getting another. You?"

I shook my head gently. It seemed too heavy all of a sudden.

"I think I should go, Evelyn. Can you get Robert for me?"

She smiled and sashayed across to the bar where Robert looked like he was propping up Douglas, who had broken another of my stereotypical assumptions by getting atrociously drunk on just three beers, despite his girth.

Robert came over and sat down, putting his arm around my shoulder.

"Evelyn has just told me the saddest story," I slurred. "So terribly, dreadfully sad. I don't know what to do with it."

He pushed my hair off my face.

"Do you want to tell me? Or shall we wait until the morning? There's always plenty of time for sorrow, Lina. Let's not rush it. Not today."

I nodded and let my head slump onto his shoulder.

"I think it's time for you to lie down now," he said. "I know I said be happy but you might be a little bit *too* merry now."

He winked and I giggled and just like that, we were the same people we'd been in Oxford. Before. The spell lasted all the way to the hotel where we were to spend our wedding night, and all through our lovemaking, which was newly tender and slow as though we had all the time in the world. And even though we didn't, we also did because that night we made you and despite what happened later, you and yours have pulled Robert and me into the future, despite our best efforts.

CHAPTER 17

The day you were born, August 28, 1946, a tempest blew through St Albans and whistling, raucous gusts of wind frayed the rain into spray. One could read something into that but it would be as vapid as guessing your destiny from the position of the stars at the hour of your birth. I sneer but one of my secret vices is my daily scan of the horoscopes. I have no loyalty to any particular astrologer – I will read them wherever I find them, the more obscure the better. I always read mine first, then Robert's, even now, and then yours. Gemini, Leo and Virgo. It is an utter waste of time but it amuses me to try to fathom the meaning of platitudes masquerading as enigmas. I feel a ridiculous sense of achievement when I link a particularly vague phrase – *a challenge awaits* – to something that is really happening. I checked the stars today in the local newspaper. Apparently, I must fight against those who seek to control me while you will find happiness in the mundane. As with everything, horoscopes sound better in French. I hope you do find happiness, be it in the mundane or the extraordinary, today and every day, my dear.

To say I was ill-prepared for giving birth would be a gross understatement. I had no idea even though I had devoured Grantly Dick-Read's *Revelation of Childbirth*, hoping for just that. His emphasis on allowing the mother to do what she needed to ease the pain did not exactly allay my anxiety. Charlotte had told me in her typically serene way that there was no point in her describing the pain as it would be beyond imagining. I had laughed at the time, believing she was joking. She did not contradict my mirth, which was a bit cheeky.

Robert was not allowed to be with me. I had wanted him to stay, telling him only half in jest that whatever happened it could not be worse than what he had seen during the war. He did not seem convinced but help was at hand.

"We don't hold with such new-fangled notions," the brutally efficient midwife told us. I opened my mouth to disagree but she fixed me with a furious glare and I thought better of it. This woman would be shepherding me through whatever was coming. I wanted her to love me like a daughter. I thought I detected a somewhat indecent lightness in Robert's step as he trotted off to the waiting room after kissing me goodbye and rather shamefacedly wishing me luck.

They let Charlotte stay. She glanced enviously at Robert's retreating back.

"Charlotte!" I hissed.

"Sorry, darling," she said. "It's just not very pleasant and I've never liked the sight of blood. But don't worry. I'm here for you. This is what mothers must do. After all, I brought you into the world. It's my job to stand beside you."

You may find it hard to believe but her words have rung in my head all these years, Diane. I was never Charlotte's equal and I suppose I must conclude that I had a different interpretation of a mother's duty. I believed I must let you live. Sometimes standing too close can be stifling.

Your birth was what birth is. There were no epidurals then but I had gas and air, although to be honest I wasn't quite sure how to use it and nobody else seemed to be any the wiser. The best I can say is that it took the edge off. Possibly.

After panting and cursing for what seemed an eternity, you squirmed your way into the world. You were squashed and slime-covered and pug-dog ugly and I needed to hold you in my arms immediately. I watched breathlessly, sweat

181

still dripping into my eyes, as they wiped you down, counted your fingers and toes and did whatever checks they had to do. Then you were on my chest and although Charlotte was crying and I was whimpering, everything seemed to have gone silent, like a forest awaiting a fire. The midwife and nurse stood by the bed, all of us gazing at this tiny being whose very existence seemed a blatant act of defiance against the death that had ruled us for so long.

Another cliché I fear but I fell headlong in love with you. I threw myself into this new obsession, arms outstretched, feet peddling me into the void. I was ecstatic and terrified and so eager to get to know you. And yet I was already also in mourning. With a clarity that was divine and awful, I glimpsed the true tyranny of time. As you grew, I would age. Our Fates were linked in a vicious circle of growth and decay. I felt dizzy with the knowledge. I looked at Charlotte for reassurance. She leaned over the bed, put her hands on my cheeks and said, "Now, you know. Beyond imagining."

She left quietly and a few minutes later Robert burst in and I watched him fall in love too. For an hour, before they took you away to be properly cleaned, we huddled together on the hospital bed, a completed trinity. It was the happiest hour of my life. We were all and all was us. You, Robert and I. The closest I have ever come to experiencing such otherworldly calm again has been on those few occasions when I thought my time was up and there was nothing I could do. Like once on a plane high over northern Africa when we hit an air pocket and dropped 100 feet in a matter of seconds. Everyone was screaming and crying but I felt the most preternatural calm. It's not that I am particularly brave. Quite the opposite. It seems that when fear hits its peak, my body and brain shut down, transporting me to a state I can only describe as bliss. That is why I don't fear death now, my dear. My fear has peaked. Death now is so terrifyingly close that the thought of it spins me into the kind of calm that only perfect happiness and perfect fear can produce.

A month before you were born, we moved into a two-bedroom house we had bought in Folly Lane. It had a rose-covered, red-brick front and a little garden with a mature apple tree and a small wooden shed. After we brought you back, it felt for a while as though we were playing house, performing our new roles like self-conscious actors. During that time, we were beyond happy. We were living off Robert's inheritance, you were sleeping relatively well and although I was constantly tired, I felt as though I was doing what I had been born to do. I was completely absorbed by sleeping patterns and feeding schedules, nappy rash and laundry. Temporary hormone-driven insanity, I'm sure, but there can be a pure delight in managing these things if you do not fight their dominion.

Today, as we demand the right to do everything, all the time, we sometimes forget that pure domesticity can have its attractions. Or maybe it is less the tasks and more the single-minded focus. I have found similar joy in writing. It is the pure release of losing oneself in another or others.

Robert and I were planets to your sun. You were our talisman, the living proof that beauty and grace were still possible after the horror of Hiroshima and Nagasaki and the concentration camps. You were a delightful surprise, the kind that seems inevitable after the fact. We had never spoken of having a child. There was no point during the war, and then you were here. I doubt we would ever have talked about it explicitly. We would have felt it was in poor taste. How could we, who had already been gifted so much, expect another blessing? Your birth, your health, your indisputable presence reassured us that life was not a zero-sum game. We didn't have to lose because once upon a time, we had won. It seems obvious now but we had to relearn these truths.

There were, of course, signs that our idyll might not last forever. As the weeks went by, it became increasingly clear that Robert was tormented by something but I did not dare probe any deeper. You have to understand, Diane.

We didn't have words to describe how we felt. There was no talk of PTSD then. With no vocabulary, how could we expect to understand? We knew soldiers struggled because even those of us who never saw battle were struggling to readjust to peacetime. Once again, our leaders demanded the impossible; change, forget about the war, as you were. But the war had pulverised our norms: men-turned-soldiers were encouraged and badgered and shamed into ditching decades of so-called civilisation to become killers and executioners and destroyers. Then they were supposed to shrug off the new rules along with their battledress jackets. It was a ridiculous idea and there were no feel-good posters to guide them or us in this impossible endeavour.

Robert started to disappear. At first he would go for an hour or so, and only every now and then. Then his absences became longer and grew more frequent. When he came back, he seemed unsure of where he had been. I wondered if he just did not want to tell me.

"Walking," he would say.

"Where?"

"I don't know. Here and there, all around. I don't really pay attention. I just like to be moving."

You will no doubt wonder why I didn't see this for what it was – a clear indication that the man I loved was losing his grip. All I can say is that I was lulled into a false sense of security by the dull quietude of our lives, Diane. When Robert first began to wander off, I assumed he just needed a break from our near-total domesticity. I had darker thoughts too but my own behaviour with Penrose removed my right to give them space. When he went to bed early, complaining of a headache, I didn't remark on it because I too wanted to sleep and I too had daily headaches. When he fell silent in the evening, his eyes glazed and empty, I told myself it was new father fatigue. I didn't press him on what he was feeling because I was so eager to forget what we had been through. I assumed he felt the same and so I decided to draw a veil over those years. That meant turning a blind eye to Robert's obvious struggle to rebuild himself. I could have asked him more, pressed him to talk of his feelings but I had no desire to look back. Knowing what I know now, I realise we were both tongue-tied by guilt.

In January 1947, one of the coldest winters ever, the plates we were spinning began to fall off their poles. Snow covered the ground and the washed-out sky hung low and mournful over our heads. Electricity was cut and animals froze to death in the fields. You were struck by colic and our freezing house was filled with your plaintive cries, all day and all through the long, bitter nights.

I had no idea what to do. We tried all the medicines available in the poorly stocked chemist. Charlotte spent hours walking you around the living room while I tried to sleep, the pillow pressed over my ears, my eyes screwed shut so tightly that my temples hurt. Robert started leaving the house more often and for longer. I slipped into a kind of depression. I was either lethargic or furious. At times, I scared myself with the strength of my hatred for you. It is unpleasant to write and, I'm sure, unpleasant to read but it is the truth. Some days, I loathed you, Diane. Your crying was a form of torture and I was terrified that I would do anything to make it stop. We know so much more today about post-natal depression and although I am reluctant to give myself an out with a handy label, I do think I was suffering from something more than the blues.

Of course, we had no real understanding of depression then either. We would have said I needed to cheer up, buck up and turn that frown upside down. I didn't know how to describe what I felt, much less what to do to silence the screaming that echoed all day in my head, a counterpoint to your wailing. I felt trapped by the cold, by the post-war economic hardship and by my own apathy. I began to see you as my jailer and the guilt was excruciating. I would start crying from frustration at my inability to comfort you and then I would be filled with self-pity and then I would cry for Penrose, and for Robert, and for all of us, and finally I would cry hot tears of shame. Saint Augustine was wrong, Diane. Repentant tears do not wash out the stains of guilt. They just wet your face.

One breath-freezing, bitter day, I pushed your pram into St Albans, slipping and sliding on the icy pavements, beyond caring whether I fell. I could no longer bear to be in the house where your cries seemed to pierce the walls and colour the air with a suffocating sadness that I feared would haunt the rooms forever. You were still crying but it was manageable outside; your wailing was muffled by other snow-smothered sounds.

As we walked past a teahouse on the high street, I saw Robert sitting in a corner, hunched over a newspaper, his head in his hands, his hair wild. I stopped stock-still, hurt and humiliated and angry. He had left us to come and sit alone here. What gave him the right to opt out? I pushed awkwardly through the door, creating a commotion as I rammed the pram ahead of me. You started screaming.

I saw Robert look up and flush.

I stormed over, lifted you out of the pram and stood over Robert, rocking you on my shoulder. It was all I could do not to scream and swear like a fishwife.

"So you're here?" I said in a low, strangled voice.

He looked faintly amused. It infuriated me.

"And so are you, it seems," he said. "Why don't you sit down, Lina? Let me get you a cup of tea."

I wanted to refuse but I also wanted to sit and I craved a hot drink.

I slumped, defeated by my own body and weak will, into the chair opposite him.

"Why are you here?" I asked, breathless and tearful. You had stopped crying, Diane, but I was afraid to raise you from my shoulder in case you were sleeping.

"I don't know. I just couldn't be in the house any more.

I feel like I'm losing my bearings there. It's starting to seem... not real. *I'm* starting to feel not real. Does that make sense?"

The waitress came and we remained silent until my cup of tea was steaming in front of me. Emboldened by the prospect of a hot drink, I risked lifting you off my shoulder and laid you in the pram. For a mad moment, I wanted to rush from table to table, urgently whispering that nobody could speak because my child was asleep. "Stir that sugar quietly, don't touch the sides," I would hiss. I hallucinated a lot in your first year, Diane. I imagine most mothers do.

I sat down again, gingerly, afraid to disturb the air around you.

"Are you tired of being with us?" I said, hating my sullenly beseeching tone.

"Don't be crazy," he said and then added hastily. "Sorry, I didn't mean that. I didn't mean crazy. I just meant unreasonable. No, not unreasonable just... Damn."

I flushed. He had called me crazy one night when he found me lying on the floor in your room, curled into a ball, fists hunched over my ears as you hollered. We had a furious, muted row, our muttered insults gyring around each other like miniature storms. I whispered that he was walking himself out of our lives, leaving me to carry all the burdens alone. He said I had no idea what he was dealing with, that sometimes he was afraid to leave me alone with you and that I no longer laughed. We slept apart that night for the first time in our married life. It was a fatal decision because afterwards, it became the way we dealt with arguments. We distanced ourselves from each other. Once you do that, Diane, you have broken the covenant. You are saying, "I cannot help you, I do not want to help you and I can live with not helping you." It is that last part that is so damning and yet so prosaic. The things that tear us apart always are.

In the teahouse, I was too tired to fight.

"What's in the news?" I said.

He squinted at the paper on the table. He seemed bemused to find it there.

"Nothing much, nothing interesting. You know, even the paper is smaller now. There are fewer pages. It's because of the cold weather. They've had to cut fuel supplies because they can't get the coal to the power stations. The RAF has been dropping food to some of the cut-off villages and they say they used flamethrowers to clear some of the drifts in Dorset. Can you imagine it? They're saying it's the worst snow this century," he said.

"I feel like we are wearing that word out. Worst war, another worst war, worst unemployment, worst snowfall," I said. "Is there never to be another best? Are we the worst generation? Are we being punished?"

"If we are, it's fair and just," Robert said, shaking his head. "After what we did and what we allowed to happen, maybe we don't deserve happiness, never mind the best."

Looking back, Diane, I realise that was when I failed. That was the exact moment when I should have pushed him to talk. But I didn't ask the question. I didn't say "what do you mean?" or "what did you do?" because I didn't recognise the turning point, and maybe also because I didn't want to know the answer. It was an unconscionable act of cowardice. It was *the* unconscionable act of cowardice that was to govern the rest of my life.

The silence grew. He stared at me for a while. I avoided his eyes. He finally looked down again at his paper and turned the page.

"There's a report here about the Nuremberg trials," he said. "They're trying the Nazi doctors now. The details are horrible. It's almost enough to make you believe again that what we did was right. Of course, these people had to be defeated. They were the face of pure evil. What they did to the poor people in those camps… it defies belief."

I too had read the stories, secretly, sneaking newspapers home in my handbag and reading the articles in the bathroom because I was afraid of upsetting Robert. Such a silly, girlish deception.

"But I wonder, was it as simple as good versus evil?" he went on. "Even knowing what we know now. When I think what it took to defeat the Nazis, I wonder. I'm not just talking about lives. It's the principles we squandered, the lines we crossed, the destruction we meted out, the future we locked ourselves into – all because we told ourselves, or were told, that it was the only way to end the horror. Were we right? Maybe we should be on trial too."

He paused and ruffled his hair with his hand, as though the action could somehow release the answer from wherever it was hiding. I said nothing.

"I just can't get my head around it, Lina. I was able to put up with all of it, most of it, until the very end because I believed in the cause. I like to think of myself as educated but perhaps I was blindly following an ideal that was simply not true, that we adopted to make it all bearable. To ensure our own individual survival, every one of us. I don't know how to measure if what we did was ultimately worth it. Or whether it was ultimately forgivable. Even if it was, who on earth should we seek forgiveness from now?"

I took his hands in mine.

"We have to forgive ourselves, Robert. We have to move on. You cannot look back, darling. None of us can. There are no answers there, only questions. If you just repeat the questions, you'll go mad. The questions can do no good now."

He smiled sadly.

"The problem is I can't go forward until I have the answers, Lina. It's like I need to know that what we did was justified. Because if it wasn't, we're just killers. As bad as the Gestapo, as bad as the Nazis. How can we go forward if our entire self-knowledge is built on a lie? I saw things, Lina. I did things. It is not enough to have survived. It is maybe too much."

I opened my mouth but never got to say what I was going

to because at that moment, Diane, you started crying. I bent to pick you up and when I turned back to the table, Robert was signalling for the bill.

"Anyway," he said after he paid and was folding the paper to put in his pocket, "I mainly bought this to look for a job. We can't live off my mother's money forever. I need to do something else."

We walked home together through the snow, shuffling like old people, our faces too cold to speak. There was, in any case, nothing to say. I was not going to ask him what he had seen or what he had done. Those of us who were still alive in 1947 were all guilty of surviving. That fact alone was enough to deal with without having to rake over the embers and dig up the bones. That is what I thought then. That is why, even if you had not cried at that moment, I was going to shut Robert down, pull the brakes on his train of thought. I was too young and too stupid and too self-obsessed to realise that he was looking to confess his sins to the one person he believed would still love him. I failed Robert that day and he did not bring up the subject again in the few months that remained to him.

CHAPTER 18

On Wednesday, September 10th that same year, I woke to find myself alone in our bed. Robert must have left already even though it was still early and I could hear no noise coming from your room next-door. I lay there, watching dust motes dance through the golden rays piercing our thin curtains, revelling in the fact that I felt rested and relaxed. Your colic had begun to ease around March and you had grown into a bubbly, capricious one-year-old with a mop of golden curls bouncing above a pair of fierce eyes. As your tummy settled and I gradually caught up on my lost sleep, my despondency lifted. That's all it took. It seems absurd but it's the truth: the worst winter of the 20th century came to an end and my child's stomach settled and I reclaimed my identity and my sanity.

I was not entirely cured, of course. I still felt on edge and every crying bout sent me into a panicked spin, terrified that the colic was back. There was also Robert. It was clear that whatever was goading him was not letting up. In April, he started working at a law firm in Watford. Despite not having finished his degree, he was allowed to research cases and offer advice. I hoped this new venture would reignite the spark that had been extinguished by the war. I thought naively that being out of the house, mixing again with other men and becoming involved in the humdrum legal affairs of our corner of Hertfordshire would ground him. But if anything, he became more distant, less engaged. I don't know how he behaved at work. I never met any of his colleagues. I can imagine why. The light-hearted, funny student who swept me off my feet in Oxford had quietly slipped away, leaving a shell of a man with only a passing interest in the world in which he found himself. He was not often a jolly companion.

The depression that tore your father apart was not a typical mental illness, as we might understand it today. It was contextual rather than chemical. The whole nation was suffering from a version of it as the 40s rolled on with the rationing and shortages and the physical reminders that war had changed everything forever. You mustn't worry about a genetic predisposition for depression, Diane. It only just occurred to me last night that I might be frightening you with this story. A depressed father and a cruel mother. What a family legacy. But don't worry. I believe in nurture over nature every time. And in any case, what happened to us did not come from within.

I finally roused myself and went downstairs. I put the kettle on the stove and then I heard you gurgling. I remember smiling as I looked up at the ceiling, imagining you on the other side, arranging your teddies into a line as you did each morning before we brought them downstairs for breakfast.

I made tea and went to get you. As I turned to the stairs, an envelope on the hall table caught my eye. I was sure it hadn't been there the night before. It was yellow and there was a drawing of a lighthouse on the front. But there was no light shining from the lantern room and the sky around it was black.

For a terrible moment, I wondered frantically if I had dreamt the end of the war. But no, this was real tea in my mug. I was in our house, in Folly Lane. I could still hear you gurgling, louder now, demanding attention. I picked up the letter. A single word: *Lina*.

I sat on the bottom stair, the letter clutched in my hand. What was this? Had he left me? I slid my shaking finger under the fold and pulled out a postcard. I saw the back first. On it, Robert had written:

I have come to the borders of sleep,
The unfathomable deep
Forest where all must lose
Their way, however straight,
Or winding, soon or late;
They cannot choose.

On the other side, there was a black-and-white aerial view of a town dominated by a magnificent church topped by an ornate spire. I had never seen the place before and had to turn the card over again to see if there were any clues. The photo was of Caen in 1929. Why would Robert have left this to me? I knew he had fought around Caen and that the town had been heavily bombed after D Day but I still couldn't fathom the meaning. But the words from Edward Thomas' *Lights Out* had left me trembling with fear. I knew how the poem ended and now I mouthed the final lines:

Its silence I hear and obey
That I may lose my way
And myself.

Your gurgling had turned into impatient cries so popping the card into the pocket of my dress, I ran up the stairs, grabbed you from your cot, threw a coat on you and raced downstairs to get the pram. I half-walked, half-ran to my parents' house. I didn't know where else to go. I was filled with the deepest sense of foreboding, more terrifying even than the endless, suffocating anxiety I had felt all those years when Robert was fighting abroad.

By the time I got to Hatfield Road, tears were streaming down my face and my breath was coming in childish gasps. You stared at me from the pram, eyes like blue pools under your white bonnet. I kept repeating: "It'll be okay, darling. It'll be okay" but it was a pointless mantra. There was a heavy stillness in the air that spoke of an unbearable absence.

Charlotte opened the door as I ran up the path.

"My God, Lina, what's happened?"

I fell into her arms, sobbing like a child. I couldn't speak. I just took the postcard out of my pocket and gave it to her. She looked at it, took the pram into the hallway, picked you up and led the way into the kitchen.

When you were in your high chair, demolishing a biscuit, she sat down at the kitchen table and read the postcard.

"Is this his own poem?" she asked.

I shook my head.

"And Caen? Why Caen?"

"I don't know. I don't know, Charlotte, but he fought around there after D-Day. He never talked much about it though. I don't know what this means."

To my eternal shame, Diane, I was already trying to absolve myself in Charlotte's eyes. It is true that Robert did not talk much about Caen but it is also true that I did not ask him to. Robert opened the door several times, like that day in the teahouse, but he could not force me to enter. I had to want to and instead I turned away. I knew this even as I crafted my excuse. The start of my lifelong effort to deny my own responsibility for my tragedies, you might say.

Charlotte rose from the table.

"I'm going to ask Henry to call the law firm in Watford to see if Robert is at work. That is the first step and if he is there, that's fine and you can ask him about the postcard this evening when he comes home. I'm sure he'll have an explanation. It might not make sense to you but these men have to live by different rules when they come back. You must realise that."

She left the kitchen and it was just you and me, Diane. I wiped your face and sticky hands and I whispered, "What will we do, you and I? What will we do if he is gone?"

I remember you laughed loudly and I tried to smile.

The thing about imagining the worst is that it is always a tiny bit cathartic. Even as you practise despair, you know, in that tiny section of your brain that holds itself apart from the general panic, that you may be wrong. That part of the brain observes your meltdown with a quiet, slightly supercilious smile, insisting *sotto voce* that this not real. All the chaos is the fault of the imagination, that childish mischief-maker that regrettably, it says, can never be tamed. So although I was terrified, I did not fully believe what I told myself must be.

Henry came into the kitchen and sat beside me. Robert was not at work. He had not, in fact, been in work since the previous Friday. He had called in sick on Monday and they had assumed he was still under the weather.

"But he was out at work, all this week. He left in the morning and came back in the evening. He said everything was fine. He said the office was still a little chilly but that they were going to fix the broken window soon," I said. Charlotte had been staring out the window. Now she came and sat beside me, putting her arm around my shoulder. I turned to her. She must have some answers.

"If he wasn't at work, where was he?"

Henry and Charlotte looked at each other and then Charlotte said I should lie down and rest while Henry went into town to see if he could find out any more.

"Maybe I should go home," I said. "Maybe he is there now. It might all be a terrible misunderstanding. Maybe he told me something and I forgot. I do that sometimes, especially when I'm tired."

"I'll go and check," Charlotte said. "I'll take Diane. She'll enjoy the walk and you can lie down for an hour. By the time you wake up again, I'm sure we'll know more or he'll have turned up somewhere and we'll all feel silly for having made such a fuss."

I didn't want to lie down but I did as I was told because I knew they could only do what needed to be done if I

195

promised to stay in one place. As I heaved myself up the stairs, I heard Charlotte and Henry whispering urgently in the kitchen.

"The lads from the rescue services might help," she was saying. "Ask them where he might have gone. They'll know the kinds of places people go."

In the end it was one of Henry's acquaintances from his nights as an unofficial air raid warden who found your father, Diane. His body was lying in a copse of fir trees high on Dunstable Downs. Apparently the silent grove with its carpet of pine needles and slender burbling stream had witnessed these desperate departures before. When I woke from my nap to find Charlotte sitting on the bed beside me, with Henry staring out the window behind her, I knew Robert was gone.

"Where was he?" I said without sitting up. The certainty sat like a boulder on my chest. I could hardly breathe.

"On Dunstable Downs. I'm so sorry, Lina. So, so sorry. We didn't know. We didn't see. *We* should have been able to see it."

She started crying, long, breathless gasps. Henry stood rigid at the window. He didn't turn around. I hadn't yet thought of you, Diane. I could only deal with what was in front of me and inside of me.

"How did he get there? Did he go on the bus?"

It was an absurd question and an unbearable idea. I closed my eyes.

Charlotte sobbed.

"I don't know, darling. We don't know."

I asked for more details. I needed to know everything. Too late this hunger, I know.

In a tight, hard voice, Henry told me that Robert shot himself with a Mauser, a pistol used by German soldiers. He shot himself in the head. They were taking his body to the morgue at the hospital. Henry would go later to identify it.

My head reeled and I thought I would throw up. I gagged and Charlotte rushed out to get a bowl. But the horror twisting my guts was not something that could be voided. Not then and not ever.

Where did he get the gun and why did he keep it? Did he always plan to do this, I wondered. What did that mean for us? If he was always going to do this – and why else would he keep the gun – then why did we even try to make a life together? Why did he come back to me? The answer to that last question was terrible because it implied that there was something I could have done to prevent this from happening. Yes, he kept the pistol, perhaps with the idea that one day he might need it to silence the voices in his head. But his return, our marriage and your birth told me he'd hoped he would not have to.

I could have stopped this, I thought. I should have. I began to shake. I felt I might fall to pieces, like a wall crumbling to dust. My body could not bear the strain. I started to moan.

"I'll never know, Charlotte. I'll never know what I could have done. He told me our story would not end. How could he say that and then leave me? I won't be able to go on without him. I just won't."

Charlotte pulled me into her arms, rocking me against her chest like a baby.

"You will go on, darling, because you have to. Because you have Diane and because you have us. We will all go on. Whatever reasons Robert had, they were his reasons and his alone. You have Diane to think of. Don't lose sight of that."

I cannot remember much of the following weeks. I was heavily sedated most of the time. I heard the doctor once, as I drifted back to oblivion, say, "I'd recommend continuing with the pills, Mrs Rose. We don't want her doing something foolish." What a funny way to describe what I might do, I thought.

I went to the funeral, of course. Or the shell that was my body did. I was allowed to see him before they closed the casket. They had bandaged his head. The bandage also went around his jaw. He did not look like Robert. He looked like a wax replica. I bent to kiss him but I could not bring myself to do it and so I just touched his cheek. I don't know what I was feeling. I was drugged and exhausted and I know I should have felt something profound but I didn't.

You didn't come to the funeral. It was not the done thing then and Charlotte insisted you stay away. If that was wrong, I apologise on her behalf. She meant no harm. You would not have remembered it anyway. But maybe there is something more subtle than visual memories. A sense of belonging or a sense of certainty, perhaps. You must be the judge of that.

Robert was buried in Hatfield Road Cemetery on the right-hand side of the stone cross war memorial. Someone must have lied to get permission for a suicide to be laid to rest there. I was not privy to these deceptions at the time. I was incapable of dealing with any of the details. Charlotte and Henry handled everything and took care of you. Evelyn came to stay and helped them. I was lost for weeks. I woke and rose and ate and sat and slept but I was never entirely present. I had switched off.

One day, in early October, I woke to find you by the side of the bed. You had just begun to walk – I think you took your first steps before Robert died but I do find it difficult to remember precisely. Robert's suicide rippled forwards and backwards, distorting time so that remembering precise dates for that period is difficult, even today when the past is more real to me than the present.

You pulled yourself up on the mattress, puffing and panting and giggling. Triumphant, you snuggled into the space he had left and put your arms out towards me. I stared at you for a long moment and I saw it. Robert's face. It was in your smile and the unflinching look in your blue eyes. I couldn't bear that gaze and so I pulled you into my arms, burying your head in my chest. Your giggles ran through me like an electric current. As we lay there, I begged for the strength to see you for who you were. I begged for selflessness and blindness and for fortitude and forgetfulness. In time, my wishes might have been granted by whoever grants such things. But there was not enough time.

Later that month, Charlotte and Henry died in the freak train crash I told you about and after that, I decided that the only way to survive was to start again. If I wanted to succeed, I would have to be alone, untouchable. I could take no baggage. I could not afford to care.

Rebirth, rather than suicide, turned out to be my foolishness, to paraphrase that doctor. I did not have the single-minded strength necessary to kill myself. I was too selfish. Ultimately I did not want to die. I wanted to live. There it is. I knew that to live I had to go far away from St Albans and I had to go alone. If I stayed, I would die a slow death, eaten away from the inside by guilt and memories and regrets. Only by rejecting every element of my existence could I hope to survive. When I emerged from the spasm of grief caused by my parents' deaths, I was cold and clear-eyed and very calculating. I had crossed a line.

The only person who knew about my decision to give you up was Evelyn, and she was furious. She came to stay again after my parents were killed. I wonder if you harbour any fleeting memories of her – she took care of you during those first weeks after the train crash. I wonder if sometimes you smell her perfume – always Chanel No 5 – and wonder why it comforts you. Do you gravitate towards redheads? Maybe you sometimes turn in the street as a throaty, saucy laugh cuts through the hubbub and wonder why it snags on your ears. Maybe the same thing happens with the elements of me that you had time to absorb. But you might have banished those.

"If you give up this child, you will never forgive yourself, Lina," Evelyn said. She was sitting on the sofa, wound tight like a spring. I could tell she was trying to rein in her fury, to tamp it down because I was grieving. But her hands were shaking and her fingernails were buried in her palms.

"I will never forgive myself anyway," I said.

"What are you talking about? What Robert did has nothing

to do with you. You must know that. That was the war, Lina. How can you not see that after all we know? Robert was killed by the war. Don't add to that tragedy by creating another one."

"You don't understand, Evelyn. How could you? Only I know the degree of my responsibility. I *am* guilty. I wasn't faithful to Robert when he was away and so when he came back…"

"Stop right there," she said, leaping to her feet. She grabbed her handbag from the table, took out her cigarettes and lit one. She breathed out deeply, closed her eyes and then walked over to sit beside me. She took my hands in hers.

"Lina, it doesn't matter. Can't you get that through your head? Whatever supposed treachery you are beating yourself up over, do you think it can stand against what Robert endured? Are you really that arrogant?"

She tried to smile but I knew what I knew.

"I didn't listen to him, Evelyn. I couldn't. I didn't want to talk about the war at all. I was afraid of what I might say. I let him down and now everything is poisoned and I just can't do it. I can't be this person any more."

"You don't think Diane deserves her mother, however flawed?"

"I don't think I can be her mother, Evelyn. Every time I look at her, I see him and I remember what I did and didn't do and that is too much for a person to bear. I'm sorry but I've made up my mind. Please tell me you can understand. Please say you can forgive me."

She got up and put her cigarette out in the ashtray over the mantelpiece. Slowly, deliberately she picked up a vase of lilies – flowers sent by some well-wisher to cheer me up after my parents' deaths. She took the vase in both hands and then slowly and deliberately flung it across the room. It smashed against the wall, scattering pieces of porcelain onto the wooden floor and the cream rug. I heard you cry out in your cot upstairs.

"I'm sorry," Evelyn whispered. 'But you make me so angry, Lina. If you're blind to what you have, I cannot make you see it. If you are too… selfish or scared or I don't know what to take care of that child, that must be your decision. But don't bloody expect me to forgive you. And no, I don't understand you either."

She walked out and I didn't hear from her again for many years. I found out later that she left shortly afterwards for Asia. For all her wise words, she too wanted to run away, she too was seeking a rebirth. Was what I did that different?

Has any of this helped you understand why I gave you up, Diane? Does any of it make sense? What else can I say? I was 27. I had lived a lifetime already and I did not know what to do with all of that. I thought I was doing the right thing. I knew I could not be the mother you needed. I was crippled by grief and guilt and I might have survived one of those but I could not survive both. I had to eradicate them. I could only do that by eradicating everything that reminded me of who I had been, who I was.

After I handed you over to the lady from the adoption agency, I walked slowly up the stairs of our haunted house, sat on the bed, put a pillow over my face and screamed and screamed until I was breathless and exhausted and utterly, intoxicatingly empty. Lina Stirling was gone.

CHAPTER 19

Today, I am writing on the beach, Diane. I don't usually like being around strangers but for some reason, I felt like stepping back in. At home, I have hardly any real friends left, but because of my daily walks through the woods around the golf course, I am on nodding terms with a number of other, mostly elderly, refugees from the world. Occasionally, we exchange a few words about the weather. These amuse-bouche conversations leave me feeling pathetically grateful. I wonder too much about these people on the periphery of my life. Where does the lady with the purple-tinted grey hair go after she finishes her energetic run around the links? What drives her to jog for hours each morning? Is she running away or running towards something? What is the young man in the dark hoodie thinking as he walks hunch-shouldered with his scowling pug? Why isn't he in work? Where is his smile? I get enough material for a thousand books from one week of step-stepping carefully on my old lady's feet through the muddy woods or around Verulamium Park and up to the Cathedral. It's probably a good thing that my swollen and twisted fingers can no longer keep pace with my imagination. Who needs another book from me? Surely I have said enough.

The sand is warm under my outstretched legs. I am sitting beside the seawall, below the promenade where people are strolling loose-limbed and eating ice creams. I need the wall's support for my back and I prefer to know there is no one behind me. Years of frontline journalism have given me an irrational fear of what cannot be seen. Behind you, in the dead zone, is where the fighter will be lining up his sights on your back. That is where the RPG will come from. That is where the rebel soldier will be unsheathing his knife ready to creep up on you. There is nothing I fear more than footsteps behind me. This fear is more acute than ever now as I realise I cannot outrun anyone. And so I have taken to regularly glancing over my shoulder as I walk. At my age, that's not as easy as it sounds because I have to stop and turn my whole body. Even paranoia becomes trickier with age.

For Robert, the danger zone always seemed to be up ahead, over the hill, in the trees. I used to catch him scanning the horizon, any horizon, his eyes flitting from side-to-side, assessing the dangers concealed in the rolling hills of Hertfordshire, among the trees of Nomansland or on a busy high street. I once asked him what he was looking for. "Answers," he said, with a sad smile. "But they are so well hidden."

I've brought a thermos of white wine to the beach to keep me going. These wonderful contraptions work just as well on cold drinks as on hot ones and I threw in a few ice-cubes to be sure. It feels deliciously naughty to be drinking wine out of a shallow plastic cup in the middle of the day. Such little tricks please me. They salve my sense of indignity at being such a lonely-old-lady cliché.

In front of me, there is a French family. The parents are in their 40s, but French 40s so she has a trim waist, immaculately tanned legs and a bare face that lacks the laughter wrinkles that snare the features of other nationalities. She is wearing a bright yellow bikini and her toenails are also painted yellow. He has grey hair, a firm stomach and strong legs. If anything lets him down, it is just the slight wobble of fat on his underarms. He is reading a paper. It looks like *Le Monde*. Heavy material for such a sunny, frivolous day. A blonde-haired teenage girl is stretched out gloriously on her own towel. She is with them but apart. She stares resolutely at the sea, I assume; I cannot see her eyes behind her oversized sunglasses. A much younger boy, maybe six or seven, is building sandcastles. They seem happy but it's hard to tell. There is little interaction; each is enjoying the beach in their own way. Every now and then, the mother tilts her head towards the daughter. She looks as though she wants to say something but she doesn't. Every now and then, the boy looks hopefully at his father. He looks as though he wants to say something but he doesn't. There is nothing obviously wrong here but everything could be wrong. We are always on the fault line between the commonplace and catastrophe.

Once upon a time, I would have jotted down some notes about this family, describing their languid ease, their clothes, their features. I would've noted down snippets of dialogue – my French is quite up to the task. I might even have sketched them. I would have taken their essence and distilled it through my own and then I would have had a sentence, then two, then a paragraph. I would head home, put the pages in the black-and-white box I call my magpie emporium and a few months later, I would find that this unremarkable family had muscled their way into my mind, demanding a rebirth, insisting I bring to life the secret desires and yearnings that only I, the omniscient writer, had been able to see.

Today, though, this family is safe. I no longer play God with everyone's lives. I will not create a tight-lipped conversation between the suspicious wife, the philandering husband and the truculent teenager, who has just found out she is pregnant. I will let them be, let them live their own private dramas, unexploited.

I published my last book six years ago in 1991. Technically, it was a novella. That had not been my intention but I was already finding it increasingly difficult to summon the faith and blind ambition needed to build new worlds in my head and recreate them on paper. My imagination was not at fault but my concentration was no longer up to the task. A chronic case of self-doubt, I suppose. As my physical relevance faded, I was starting to question the relevance of my work. Not what I had done, you understand, but whether there was any point in doing more.

I wonder if you read that novella, *The Starfish and the Pearl*? Critics were harsh: they said my pseudo fairy tale rang hollow, that it lacked depth and was – this hurt the most but it also made me laugh – ill-conceived. The book was a metaphor for my short relationship with you. I am the starfish because they too can survive when a part of their body is removed. You are the pearl. I wrote the book in a kind of frenzy over two months. It was certainly a work of indulgence. I gave it the ending we never had.

After I gave you up for adoption at the end of 1947, I threw myself into creating a new life. I had given up my past and lost my stake in the future and so I resolved to live exclusively in the present. I did what I wanted when I wanted. I had no fear of consequences because I had no fear of pain. I was utterly liberated.

I moved to London, took a room in a creaking, leaking boarding house in Kensington and dropped Robert's surname. I partied too long, and drank too much and smoked too heavily and slept with sad men who had come home from the war to find they no longer loved their wives, with dangerous men who had never really come back and never would, and with suave men who had had a 'good war'. I slept with any man who wanted me until, eventually, I realised that the money I had got from selling our house and my parents' home was running out far too quickly even for someone with my limited interest in the long term.

One cold morning in February 1948, I woke early in a stranger's apartment in the City. I had only the fuzziest idea of the identity of the man sprawled jelly-belly down on the bed beside me, and less interest in finding out. I dressed in the dark, picked up my shoes and tiptoed out, my head throbbing and my blood still pulsing with toxins.

I made my way around St Paul's Cathedral, treading

carefully on the wet cobblestones. The church rose above me but I did not care to raise my eyes. St Paul's had become too iconic an image, representing what they were calling the spirit of the Blitz, a kind of fantasy stoicism I neither remembered nor wished to commemorate.

I wandered down Fleet Street, smoking a cigarette and wondering idly where I might go to begin the cycle anew in the evening. To be honest, I was exhausted, worn out trying to maintain the hedonism I had adopted as my new religion. A woman in a blue coat came towards me, pushing a wailing pram. The baby's cries cut through the fug of booze and smoke and the shield of deliberate unfeeling that I carried with me everywhere. The woman stopped and leaned into the pram to adjust the covers and to stroke her keening child's cheek. She was haggard in the way only new mothers can be, her face all pallid flesh, dark shadows and loose lines. Then she smiled down at the child and she was transformed. I remembered the superhuman energy it took to create that look of love when all you wanted to do was lie down, close your eyes and go to sleep. A vivid memory of your face creasing up as you began to cry ambushed me.

I stumbled off the kerb and onto the road. A car honked furiously as I dashed to the other side, my heels listing under the weight of my self-induced panic. I mustn't allow myself to be caught unawares, I thought angrily. Usually, I steered clear of families, babies and especially mothers. I would see them coming from a distance and change course immediately. My London was the London of the childless – I avoided parks with playgrounds, streets with toy stores, doctors' surgeries and churches. Part of my rebirth involved reshaping my world and deliberately Pied-Pipering the children away. You have to remember, Diane. I was engaged in a battle to survive and the biggest threat came from within.

As I stepped up onto the pavement, I turned to wave apologetically at the cars I had dodged and I clattered into a short man. As he pulled his face out of my chest, I realised I was looking down at Peterson and he was looking where he had always looked. A few seconds later, after he'd raised his eyes, he gasped, "Lina, Lina Rose. Fancy bumping into you here?"

For a few seconds, I just gawped like a tongue-tied teenager. I felt as though worlds were colliding around me, that I might fall down whatever magic portal had deposited this human anamnesis before me.

"Sorry, goodness this is so bizarre," I said. "I'm afraid I wasn't looking where I was going. Are you alright?"

He smiled broadly, those fleshy lips curling back from his teeth.

"Of course, of course. But how wonderful to see you. What a coincidence. What are you doing here? I thought you were in St Albans. I heard about your husband... and your parents. I'm so sorry."

I stifled a gasp.

"How did you hear?"

I was genuinely perplexed. I had thought the tragedies of 1947 were mine alone. I had felt so isolated during those awful months that I could barely believe that others were aware of what had happened. It seemed somehow indecent. These were *my* traumas.

"I work for the *Gazette*," he said, licking his lips as he used to do when he was particularly proud of something. "We hear a lot of things from our colleagues at local papers up and down the country. After it all stopped, I decided that I might as well use my wartime skills on civvy street and so when the Ministry shut down, I applied for a job and now I'm one of the home editors. I didn't really know what else to do. No other skills to speak of. The money's not great but I can't complain, not with all the men looking for jobs."

There was a new humility about him as though peace had punctured the mini-dictator syndrome that the Ministry had allowed to flourish. Peterson, like everyone else, had had to bounce back into shape. We were a nation of contractions and constrictions after the war.

"Can I buy you a cup of tea? Or coffee?" he said quickly. "Listen, I know we had our differences before but it's so bloody nice to see someone who lived it too, someone who knew the others, who understands. I don't feel like I can talk to anyone else about what we did. Sounds so trivial, you know, with everyone coming back with half their limbs, or horrible wounds, or worse. Can you spare half an hour? There's a place just near the office, not too bad."

I said yes. I said yes to everything then. My days were an endless search for oblivion through mindless interaction with people I didn't care too much about. I didn't care that he was already focusing on my chest again. I didn't care that I had disliked him intensely when I worked at the Ministry. I was perfectly content to have a cup of tea with him. It was just another way to kill some more of my endless time.

When he asked me, surprisingly delicately, about Robert and my parents, I said: "If you don't mind, I'd rather not talk about those things."

I was ever the deceiver, Diane, and grief is a great enabler. I could hide my sins under a cloak of stoic sorrow and no one would be any the wiser.

"Of course. I'm sorry. How insensitive of me," he gabbled. "It's just you find some people do want to talk about it all. They say it can help. But of course, that doesn't hold true for everyone. Women are different too."

He hadn't changed entirely.

We talked a little about Sarah's birthday and what happened that night.

"I always thought Penrose would make it," he said, shaking his head. "He seemed somehow indestructible, having been through the Great War and all that. But I guess that's the thing. There's no accounting for luck."

I stirred my tea, avoiding his eyes.

"I'm sorry. I know you were friends. And with Sarah."

I looked up sharply but I saw no guile.

"You might be surprised to know that I was supposed to

come along to the restaurant too that night. I know you all hated me but Sarah was always too kind. I decided to have a little nap before getting ready – couldn't sleep with all the sirens the night before – and next thing I knew it was midnight. I didn't find out what had happened until I got to the Ministry the next morning. I knew, of course, there'd been some hits across town but I never guessed. Makes you think, doesn't it."

"I try to think as little as possible," I said in the too-bright voice I had adopted for the new me. "Thinking doesn't change anything. It's not going to bring them back and you just end up going round and round in circles. To my mind, thinking is terribly overrated."

He laughed and I realised I'd rarely heard him laugh during all the time I worked with him. It was a surprisingly robust sound.

"So if you are not thinking, what are you doing these days?" he said.

"Nothing," I said. "It's not ideal but I haven't found anything that suits yet. I have a high threshold, I guess."

"You were always good at writing. Maybe you could come and work for us. I could put in a word."

I looked at him over my teacup. I had despised this man and I had always thought the feeling was mutual. Apart from his fondness for my breasts, obviously.

"I thought you had a rather low opinion of working women?" I said.

He laughed again.

"I thought a lot of things before the war. I was wrong about almost as many. I thought the world would change when we won, that peace would be the answer. But look at us now. Our allies are our enemies. The world is more fractured than ever and our dead are still dead."

I gawped. I had never heard him speak like this. He took a sip of tea.

"You know, we all kept ourselves to ourselves at the Ministry. Keep it under your hat and all that. But the real reason we stayed mum, I think now, was that no one wanted to spread pain. Everyone was hurting. Why add to what others were feeling with your own tragedy? My brother was killed in 1941. Twenty-six years old. Eight years younger than me and fit as a fiddle. He held that over me – the fact that his lungs were stronger than mine. I was always sick, always wheezing. He said I was a weakling. I said his healthy lungs just made him louder not smarter. I don't know why they decided my lungs made me unfit for the military. After all, they're not going to stop the bullets or bombs, strong lungs, are they? After Jim's death, I hated everyone. Especially myself and everyone else who was huddled here when they were all over there, fighting our battles. I thought we were all cowards. I knew I was. Because my brother was right all along. He *was* smarter, faster and braver. When he died, I thought it should've been me. Who'd miss me? He was married, had a little boy, two years old. They killed the wrong brother."

I didn't say anything. By 1948, we had already used up all our words of sympathy.

"I'm not the same man now as I was at the Ministry, Lina. How's that for a statement of the obvious. You could put it on a poster."

He smiled.

"None of us are the same. So you needn't worry that I'll bellow at you like I used to if you come to the *Gazette*. At least, say you'll think about it?"

I didn't need to think about it. I knew I couldn't go on partying forever. The oblivion was too ephemeral. I needed something stronger to take me out of myself. Work might be just the ticket. Apart from my facility with words, I also liked the idea of continuing in my grandfather's footsteps along the route that Charlotte briefly trod during her war.

"I will. I have. I think it's a great idea. I need a job and I do like writing, as you say," I said, feeling a shiver of excitement despite myself.

"We could go to the office now if you like? Meet a few people?" Peterson said eagerly, waving to the waitress for the bill. "I can't promise you anything but I'm sure you'll charm the socks off them all."

I held up my hand.

"Not looking like this, I won't. I haven't been home yet, I stink of alcohol and I must look a state. No. Give me your number and I'll call you tomorrow. If I meet anyone now, they'll have me cleaning toilets or making tea and I warn you, I have no interest in *that* kind of work."

I started at the *Gazette* two weeks later. At first I covered London society, producing frothy pieces about parties and engagements, fashion and weddings. But as you can imagine, Diane, I swiftly tired of this and started pushing for more exciting beats. I began to court the foreign editor, Thomas McNeish, a razor-sharp, unflappable Scot with a sad look that made him seem older than his 35 years. I pestered him so much that eventually, whenever I sidled up to him, he would shake his head sadly and mouth 'No' before I could even get a word out. We soon had a well-rehearsed double-act where I would ask him to send me abroad and he would retort that I had to prove my worth first. Then he would suggest a mind-numbingly boring story about city council politics or repairs to the damaged and decrepit sewers that he felt should be covered. I would do whatever he suggested with my eye on the prize because deep down I knew that I could never be truly free while I stayed in England. I had to get out.

You probably think I was already much too free, having given you up and buggered off to London. It is true, to a point. But no matter how hard I worked, or how much I drank, or how many men I slept with, or what little thinking I did, I could not escape my memories, not in 1940s England where bombed-out buildings, broken pavements and piles of rubble were lurking like women with prams around every corner, in case we dared forget.

Try to put yourself in my shoes, darling. I had already done the hardest part. I had given you up. This agonising sacrifice would prove pointless if I did not take the next step and break free of my physical limits too. I worried that if I did not leave, I might eventually want you back. And even if I could get you back, how would I ever explain what I had done, to you or to anyone? What I had done could not be undone. It must not be undone.

One autumn day in 1949, I brought Thomas a cup of tea with my usual side of entreaties.

"Tea, Thomas? Any chance of a post abroad?"

I was already holding out the cup, anticipating his usual reply: "Just give me the tea, Lina."

But he pulled off his glasses, cocked his head to one side and said: "What about Paris? Would you go to France for us, Lina?"

Three months later, I was on the international sleeper train as it pulled out of Victoria station and rumbled its way through a London made soft and shapeless by thick mist. For one sentimental moment, I let myself wonder where you might be; I imagined a cheeky three-year-old with flushed cheeks being tucked into bed. You would sleep quickly because for you nothing was changing this night. You would not know your mother was leaving. You would not know that another chapter was closing. I let self-pity wash over me, knowing full well I had no right to this emotion but unable to stop the tears.

This then was the conclusion to our story. The story that Robert had promised would never end that day on the Felixstowe pier. As the train picked up speed, the houses flashed by and the smoke sped backwards and I felt all of my life falling away in a blur of bricks and fences, poky gardens, small hopes and smaller dreams. I was shedding my skin, but it is not as painless as one might hope, Diane.

CHAPTER 20

I fell over today on my way to post my latest letter to you, Diane. It was not a serious fall – grazed knees and gravel-pocked hands – but it shook me nonetheless. I've shrunk a little since I hit 70, or maybe it is just the curvature of my spine, the result of spending most of my life hunched over a typewriter. My new proximity to the ground has not, however, lessened my fear of falling. It's never how far you fall but how hard.

I had taken my usual short-cut through the park when my feet seemed to stumble over each other and the next thing I knew, I was sprawled on the ground, peering bat-like at my glasses, which had fallen off and lay on the path a few inches from my face. I lay there for a few seconds, trying to catch my breath, that breath that seems more elusive and precious each day. I hauled myself up and then a neon-clad woman came bouncing past and stopped to ask if I was all right. I said yes, appalled by my quavering voice and the tears that were welling in my eyes. I felt horribly exposed, like an old lady with her slip showing beneath a frumpy A-line skirt. Everything about the flushed, vibrant woman in front of me, jogging on the spot even as she spoke, emphasised my frailty. I could no more imagine exercising to prolong my life than I could imagine saving for a rainy day. The rain is falling on me already. I tried to tell her I was on my way to the post office but I couldn't remember the French for 'to go'. She smiled sympathetically and said, in heavily accented English, "You are visiting? A tourist?"

I nodded mutely, still trying to dredge up the wayward verb from wherever it had gone. How ridiculous, I thought. I speak excellent French. Maybe the fall had shaken me more than I thought. But we can't always believe our own lies and mine are becoming less convincing by the day.

The young lady helped me to a bench and then sped off, hair like a pendulum ticking down her life despite her efforts to outrun its heartless swing.

Generally, I relish my twice-weekly walks to the post office. I go early when the bronzed denizens of beach and bar are still safely snoozing in their borrowed beds. I am not jealous of their vitality, but some days I can't see the beauty for its transience and I find that heartbreaking.

It is an established truth that you become invisible as you age, especially if you are a woman, but less well known is the fact that sometimes one craves that invisibility. We may seem grumpy, dotty and out-of-touch but we have not lost all our faculties. We recognise our irrelevance but it can still hurt to see the truth revealed so brutally in eyes that look right through our shrinking, shrivelling selves. Sometimes, it's easier to just avoid those eyes.

I post my letters to you on Wednesdays and Fridays. That is why the Wednesday missives are heavier. I spend most of the weekend at the typewriter but if I'm honest, I waste a lot of that time staring into space. This epistolary effort has brought all my people to life again and sometimes they are too real to be confined to the page. What I write here is just the tip of the memory iceberg, Diane. There is so much more below the waterline and it demands my attention before I can focus on what I want you to see above the surface. I must relive it all before I can choose what to recreate. It is exhausting but this is what I have always done and there is a comfort in the familiarity of the task. Who knows how long these frozen monoliths of memory will survive?

I cannot lie, Diane; I enjoyed my years in Paris. I found I could reinvent myself wholly. Everything was different – the food, the landscape, the people and the language. I had learned French at school and I worked hard to improve it when I arrived, taking lessons from a slit-eyed, elderly lady who would hiss angrily whenever I failed to meet her exacting standards. I made friends and lied to them about my past. Or rather I told them nothing, maintaining an impenetrable air of mystery that was, I liked to believe, both bewildering and beguiling. I was appalled and delighted at how easy it was to create who I wanted to be using just words. It was another step along the road that eventually led me to fiction.

Paris in the early 50s was a city riven by poverty and angst: it thrilled and repulsed me. I wandered along the Seine for hours, marvelling at intact churches and monuments. My wide-eyed appreciation sat side-by-side with revulsion at the price the French had paid, although I could understand the drive to preserve such beauty. We had cheered news of the French Résistance from London and now I found the physical evidence of the flip side of that bravery – collaboration – hard to bear. And yet, the truth is, as always, more complex – apparently in 1944, Hitler gave the order to destroy Paris but General Von Choltitz had fallen in love with the city and could not comply. Paris was saved, in the end, not just because some French collaborated, but simply because it was too beautiful to destroy. I can only imagine how this tainted beauty made Parisians feel. Perhaps they didn't notice, particularly those who had never walked, mouths agape, down London's bombed-out streets. Maybe Parisians could not see the shadow of capitulation flitting across their city's undamaged façades, but we Londoners could not ignore it.

Despite all of this, it was uplifting and invigorating to live in a city that bore so few scars. Especially for one who was trying to erase all traces of her own wounds. I threw myself into my work, determined to excel. What had started as a means to get through endless days grew into a fervent ambition to succeed. Survivor's guilt? Perhaps I felt my life had been spared from the cataclysm of war because I was destined to 'do something great'. I doubt if I formulated the thought as concretely or as cheesily as that but I cannot be sure such feelings were not spurring me on. Going deeper, this idea might have been all the stronger because my survival was such a calculated act: I felt duty-bound to make my life count. I could not simply wait for my destiny to be revealed. If I had played God once, then I must continue in the role I had chosen.

It was an exciting time to be a journalist and exhilarating to be a woman in this field. We were still relatively few in number and during my first months in Paris, I stuck mostly to relatively anodyne social and cultural stories – the *Gazette's* editor still struggled to believe that women could understand, much less write about, politics or economics. But our voices were growing in authority and soon I submitted my first articles on France's efforts to spur greater European economic integration, the fledgling nationalist movement in Algeria and Communist protests. I must have done something right because nobody ever questioned my gradually expanding remit despite the fact that I never shied from proclaiming my opinions in my articles. I have never had much time for what Martha Gellhorn called 'that objectivity shit'. I could not separate my feelings from my journalism and so I quickly established a reputation as a so-called passionate reporter. It was not entirely positive as a description but it was better than hysterical or, heaven forfend, emotional.

For years, women's emotions were used as yet another reason not to employ us as journalists but by the 1950s, passion and enthusiasm were no longer seen exclusively as negative qualities. Journalism was changing. I was, for once, in the right place at the right time.

In June 1950, war broke out on the Korean peninsula and by July, the US was involved and Britain was sending troops as part of a UN force. I badgered Thomas McNeish to let me go. He was, at first, agog at my temerity, if such a calm man could ever be described as 'agog'. His tone certainly tightened a notch or two, the equivalent of a raging tantrum in a lesser man.

"I sent you to Paris, Lina. I've put your stories on the news pages. I've let you write about pretty much whatever pleases you. And you're still not happy?"

"I don't think that's the right question," I hollered down the crackling phone line. "Am I good? If not, you're doing me a rotten favour by letting me work for the *Gazette* and you should be ashamed of yourself. If I am, send me to Korea."

"It's an ugly conflict, Lina. No place for a woman," he said.

"Thomas, are you really saying that to me? I lived through the Blitz, you silly man. I think I can cope with an ugly conflict, don't you? Or do you think we women were somewhere else during the war? Kept safe in pretty gilded boxes tucked away in rose-covered bowers, were we?"

"Now you are being ridiculous, Lina. That was utterly different. You were not on the frontline. You were not reporting. You'd be deliberately looking for trouble if you went to Korea. And anyway, reporting on a war is different from living a war. I'm just not sure you'd be able for it," he said.

"You're too late with that logic, Thomas. Women have been reporting from frontlines since the last century. Don't make me list them. You won't be able to pay the phone bill if I do!"

In fact, I had to make several phone calls and even travel to London to stalk poor McNeish in person and speak directly to the newspaper's owners – a pair of whiskered men in their 60s who allowed me into the meeting but were only prepared to hear McNeish speak. My efforts paid off. In August 1950, I arrived in Korea to bear my witness to what was in effect the first hot salvo of the Cold War.

Incredibly, the Korean conflict has almost been forgotten

today. It became a mere footnote to the televised, mythologised war in Vietnam. It was as though a line had been drawn through time and Korea was placed indisputably in the past, while Vietnam became the symbol of a more complex, morally dubious modern warfare. But for those of us who were there, the Korean War looked like a stepping-stone to another global conflict, a direct link between the horrors of the recent past and a potentially devastating future conflagration. Coming just five years after the end of the Second World War, we genuinely feared that this could be the next one. It was hard not to see a direct line when they were even using the same comedians, people like Bob Hope, to entertain the US troops as they had done during the Second World War. And our old preacher-politician Churchill was back, rhetoric unleashed, to warn again that the stakes were high. "Once again," he intoned, "America and Britain find themselves associated in a noble cause. When bad men combine, good must associate." You can see why we were nervous, Diane.

As more and more countries were drawn in – albeit under the banner of the UN – we prayed that reason would prevail and the war would stay on that little spit of land far from our still-traumatised homes. We knew that for many leaders this was the red line across which Communism could not pass. They saw the war as a battle for the souls of the future, for a way of life. That absolutism, that existential angst reminded me of the 1930s and that is partly why I had to go. I could not bear to sit in Europe, waiting and worrying. I needed to see with my own eyes whether the end to the last war would really start the next global conflict. We had made that mistake with the vengeful Treaty of Versailles. We made it again with the division of Korea. We even risked repeating our greatest mistake – there were whispers from very early on that the US might be driven to use an atomic bomb in Korea. Some say Clement Atlee talked Truman down. In any case, it created a feverish atmosphere for those of us for whom the past was still all too present. Truman was one of us, for sure.

Two months after I left Korea, when he fired General Douglas MacArthur for his gung-ho insubordination, Truman said the aim was always to prevent conflict spreading. "So far we have prevented World War Three," he said. In some ways that is all we did then and all we have been doing since. I wonder how long we have to keep preventing it, Diane? All the best, most enduring stories contain the rule of three – three characters, three temptations or three tests. Must this not also be the case with the human story – surely the greatest tale ever told? Does this strike you as absurd? Perhaps but somewhere deep inside, I believe this and I am glad that I will not be around for the conclusion of this particular triptych.

I had another more personal reason for wanting to go to Korea. I had, to some degree, made my peace with Robert's suicide but it was a false armistice. I did my damnedest not to think about it but curiosity could not be so easily dismissed. I yearned to experience something of what he had endured. I did not presume I would find all the answers in Korea but I dared to hope for some kind of revelation, that I might then bury in the deep hollow of my brain where I had hidden the act itself.

The Korean War was a nightmare to cover. I stayed for six months – long, tedious days waiting for permission to travel to the battlefields while trying not to catch the eyes of irate US generals, who did not want to see any journalists, much less female ones, buzzing around their troops. Shortly after I arrived, US soldiers recaptured the port of Inchon, took Seoul and pushed past the 38th towards Pyongyang, their furthest incursion into the north. I covered the advance, finding champagne bottles still on the bar of the Russian commissar's building in Pyongyang. These bubble-filled sentries stood under a portrait of Stalin who seemed to be glaring balefully down at the evidence of his allies' sudden reversal of good fortune. He needn't have worried: barely six weeks later,

Pyongyang had been retaken by the Chinese, who probably found the same bottles of champagne to welcome them. I left with the American troops just hours before the city was retaken, watching in bemused horror as the retreating soldiers set fire to petrol dumps and stores, hoping to delay the Chinese advance. It was a ping-pong war, Diane, but the truly dreadful fighting was mercifully short. It was more or less over by the time I left in February 1951 and peace talks were soon to begin.

What did I learn from my first real war assignment? I learned that I was what people call brave but this was simply because I did not fear death as much as I should. I learned that peeing on the side of the road is nothing. I learned that drinking water from rice paddies is not good for your stomach. I learned that appropriate clothing is critical for an army's success as I watched US soldiers shiver on their push to the Yalu River. I learned that lying to please a leader never ends well and that if intelligence officers had dared to tell MacArthur the truth – that the Chinese were already in the country as he pushed his forces north – many lives might have been spared. I learned that 'home by Christmas' is never something you want to hear. I learned that what I was doing was what I was born to do. That raises a lot of uncomfortable questions for us both, I know. But it is the truth.

And what did I learn about Robert? I glimpsed his war-scalded features again in the exhausted faces of too-young soldiers. I heard echoes of his dry wit in the banter that filled the mess tents at night. I remembered the torment of his nightmares when I woke, sweating and tear-stained but with no arms to hold me. I understood more but I knew it was not enough. As I said before, Diane, war is personal. And I was still not a fighter and that made all the difference.

Have you seen the monument to the Korean War in Washington? Imagine; I don't know if you have ever been to Washington DC. It seems such an irrelevant gap in my knowledge and yet our whole story is encapsulated in that lacuna. How can I feel any connection when I know so little about you? That's a mystery for smarter minds to ponder, I think.

I read a newspaper article about the monument when it was dedicated a couple of years ago. The steel statues of the platoon on patrol gave me goosebumps. Anxious, tense faces, waterproof ponchos stretched over backpacks, uncertain steps and the last soldier looking over his shoulder, face haggard, mouth slightly agape, as if about to say something. In my opinion, the memorial captures the paradox of war perfectly – ordinary people asked to do extraordinary things. The fact that the figures patrol in a manicured park of disciplined trees adds to the feeling of displacement. The whole thing embodies that sense of being in a parallel universe where all the rules have changed and the ground is no longer necessarily stable under your feet.

After my stint in Korea, I returned to Paris, where I remained based until 1963. I spent my 30s working feverishly while friends got married and settled down. I had no desire to do either. I relished my role as the eccentric, educated single woman, who could balance a dinner table and regale the other guests with fantastical tales from foreign lands. I was, in many ways, in my element. It was me, but not me, and yet more me than I had ever been.

I continued to travel: to Algeria to cover the nationalist rebellion that would eventually threaten the destruction of the French Republic; to Hungary for the 1956 revolt and several times to Berlin. In 1953, I covered the trial in Bordeaux of 25 ex-SS men and 11 Frenchmen accused of the 1944 Oradour massacre when an entire village was wiped out in retaliation for the kidnapping of an SS officer. Men were shot in the legs and then burned to death while women and children were locked in a church that was then set on fire. Anyone who tried to escape was gunned down. I thought I was ready to hear the testimonies but my notes were so smudged by teardrops that I sometimes had difficulty reading them. It brought it all back.

Some days I could hear Robert's anguished voice rising from the corners of the courthouse, asking me again if what *we* did was justified by what *they* did. At night, I lay gasping for breath in my narrow hotel bed, overcome with fresh terror as I remembered the completeness of our collective fall.

The key witness, the only woman to escape the blazing church, was so ill she could not take the stand and the judges had to cluster around her chair to hear her frail voice whisper that she had come out from the "crematory oven". My stories from that trial pulse with a desperate, futile anger. I was partly frustrated with myself, with my inability to find the right words to persuade the world that these voices were a warning for the future, not simply an indictment of some distant past that belonged solely to 'the monsters'.

But my time in France was not all doom-and-gloom: despite my refusal to be stereotyped as a 'women's issues' correspondent, I was not above covering the frippery that was the film festival in Cannes, or indeed the marriage of Grace Kelly to Prince Rainier of Monaco. We are none of us perfect and in any case, glamour and gore are rarely mutually exclusive. Quite the opposite, in fact.

In May 1955, Evelyn finally came to visit me. We had not seen each other since I gave you up and I had heard little from her although I received two or three faded postcards from India, which were sent to the *Gazette* in London, undoubtedly after she had seen my byline. She never wrote personal messages on the cards – just a few lines from Indian philosophers she had come across along the way. I took the postcards to mean that I was not forgiven but that I had not been cast out entirely.

I enclose one of those enigmatic cards. I love the picture because it is so Evelyn – two pink elephants covered in silks and jewels rearing at each other. She told me the picture was meant to represent our feud.

"Bizarre, melodramatic and absurd," she said dryly.

On the back of the postcard, she had written: *Happiness*

is your nature. It is not wrong to desire it. What is wrong is seeking it outside when it is inside.

I now know that those lines were from Ramana Maharshi, a Hindu holy man who retreated to the mountains after a near-death experience aged 16. He became something of a guru, attracting big-eyed, gullible followers to his hillside retreat. One of the many philosophies he advocated was self-enquiry as a way to banish ignorance. Forgive me, I am simplifying here, but essentially the idea was to concentrate the attention on the source of the self, the fountain of all thought. I may be maligning the great man but I understood the quote to mean that Evelyn still thought I was being selfish and blind to the consequences of my own actions.

When I asked her, she nodded but said only: "If the cap fits, my dear."

When she wrote to say she was coming to Paris, I was relieved that she had found a way to live with my decision but I was also nervous. I had become so comfortable in my new identity and I feared that if I opened the portal by meeting someone from my past, I could be sucked back. I had worked so hard to forget it all, to forget you. It was the most enormous act of deliberate delusion. I blanked you from my mind and if at times you came to me in my dreams, warm arms around my neck, laughter in my ear, I cast those images off as you would a nightmare. Like Henry after the war, I gave you no oxygen and so you could not survive.

On Evelyn's first evening, we walked from my apartment in the Marais towards the Jardin des Tuileries, picking our way through the traffic and skirting any awkward subjects with equal care. I kept up a breathless patter, filling any silences with titbits of history, gossip and throwaway observations about the landmarks we passed.

When we were finally seated on the terrace of a café in the shadow of the Louvre museum, our cigarettes lit and beaded glasses of rosé blushing in front of us, there was no way to stall any longer.

"I'm so delighted you came. I did so hope we could still be friends," I said.

"Of course, we are still friends, Lina," Evelyn sighed. She had aged noticeably since I last saw her. The Indian sun had taken its toll and the death of her beloved father just a few months before had etched the wrinkles even deeper. But the fresh lines and new patina of sorrow somehow enhanced her beauty, giving her an otherworldly air.

"But don't take that to mean that I feel any better about what you did. I still believe it was wrong and it bothers me enormously that you will only see that for yourself when it is too late. There is nothing I can do now. You've made your bed, Lina. It just makes me so mad that you refuse to accept the obvious."

I tried to smile. I spoke to reassure her and maybe to reassure myself.

"It's not that I don't understand but I believe I did the right thing, the only thing, Evelyn. Don't you see that I am happy or as close to happy as one can reasonably expect? Can't you see that I've made a success of it all? I would be dead now if I hadn't left. And who knows, maybe she would be too. I couldn't be a proper mother then, Evelyn. I did this for her too."

Evelyn's lips bent in a wry smile.

"You were always very good at excusing your actions," she said. "It's not your most endearing quality, I have to say, Lina. Still, I do understand how terrible everything must have seemed then. I just…"

She paused. I couldn't see her eyes behind her sunglasses.

"I'm 36, Lina. I will never have a child and while I never thought I wanted one, I now feel a little shook by this reality. Oh, I'm sure it's just my biological clock ticking and there's nothing I can do about that, not given my preferences. But this sadness or whatever it is makes it even harder for me to understand why you gave her up. But that's not even my main concern. I'm just so worried that this whole thing is waiting to explode in your future, like one of those bloody bombs they keep finding underground in London. I don't want to be the one holding your hand when you realise years from now that you gave up the one thing that made life worth living. Because I care about you too much."

"Don't worry," I said, trying to keep my voice neutral although every word she said was screaming its echo in my brain. "I did the right thing," I repeated.

"Ah, but Lina, what you are forgetting is that it was not just your decision to make," she said quietly, taking off her glasses as the sun dipped below the buildings opposite. "Have you realised that yet? And if you think my questions are uncomfortable, and I can see in your face that you do, what will hers be like? Because you might have to answer to her one day."

She looked at me for a long moment and then waved the waiter over and ordered another bottle of rosé. We didn't speak of you again during that visit. But her words echoed through the years and probably played their own part in driving me to seek you out a decade later in Brighton.

When I said goodbye to Evelyn a week later at the train station, things were almost back to normal between us.

"I'm so relieved to see that your efforts to reinvent yourself have spared some of the Lina I loved," she said, hugging me hard. "I promise never to bring up your decision again, unless *you* want to. I've done my duty as a friend – I've told you what I think and that will not change. I'm going to take a leaf from your book and move on."

She smiled, too brightly.

"After all, I have my own problems to deal with. I've got to find a job, for heaven's sake. At my age. In England, which as far as I can tell is as petty-minded and smug as it ever was. So damn grey and so damn full of smog. And still marked by those bloody bomb craters, even now. And we have teenagers to contend with and those horrible jeans everyone insists on wearing. Do you know they are even going to introduce new laws on drinking and driving? Apparently, successfully completing a tongue-twister and walking in a straight line is no longer bloody good enough. Oh Lord Lina, I am really going to miss India. Maybe I'll head back there sooner than we think."

She tossed her cigarette to the ground and climbed the steps into the carriage.

"*Au revoir*, Lina," she said, delivering an ironic salute before she disappeared.

I will be forever grateful to that woman, Diane. She knew the worst of me and yet she never cast me off. One must never underestimate how difficult it can be to stay friends with someone. The effort is all in the act of loving.

I stayed in Paris for another eight years. I had my share of flings but there was no one of any note. Pretty men and cheating men and earnest men. They all fell short or made me fall short and neither outcome was acceptable for any length of time. A rather sad résumé of my 30s but I was happy enough with my lot.

I would have to leave Europe to find love again. But that was still some way down my road, if you can pardon the ludicrous literary notion that we are travelling down a well-defined route towards an actual destination. Before I could find love again, I had another war to cover and a secret to discover.

Chapter 21

I arrived in Saigon in September 1961 and it was in that city, later that year, that I discovered the secret that had tormented Robert. I never expected to find my dead husband's ghost roaming that sweaty, edgy town. I believed I had made my peace with what he had done. I had assumed my role in it, I had paid the price, and I had forgiven us both for our failures to believe enough in each other. But there is always more forgiveness to bestow. There is always room to understand more, if you can bear it.

When I got to Vietnam, the US was preparing to jump to the next level of engagement. A big push by the Viet Cong to take Phuoc Vinh had convinced the US to send more advisors and President Kennedy had swung his full support behind South Vietnam's leader, President Diem. By the end of 1961, there were over 3,000 US military personnel, still euphemistically called advisors, in the country and we knew it was only a matter of time before there were more boots on the ground.

The Communist insurgency had taken control of large parts of the southern countryside, leading the US to adopt its so-called strategic hamlet programme, which sought to create secure villages that would be safe from guerrilla attack or infiltration. The programme was not a success but we were not yet in a morass. It was still just a mess in 1961 but already many observers were saying the war would last a long time and there would be no good ending, even if Diem had been dubbed "the Winston Churchill of Asia" by Vice President Johnson.

I was among the first wave of journalists to show any sustained interest in Vietnam. The war was not yet a guaranteed headline-grabber but I had persuaded McNeish that it would be in our interest to get an early view from the ground rather than wait for all hell to break loose, as we knew it would. The military coup against Diem in 1960 had piqued news editors' interest, not least because of the massacre of hundreds of civilians, including a group who charged the presidential palace walls at the urging of one of the coup leaders. My strongest argument was that whatever was going on over there was not yet a full-blown war and so I should be perfectly safe. I had followed France's doomed war against the Viet Minh rebels through the late 40s and early 50s and so I felt something of an armchair expert. I'm sure McNeish was as sceptical as I was about my baseless, uninformed assertions, but sometimes everyone needs just the merest hint of plausible deniability.

Because of my early arrival, I avoided the worst of the US military restrictions on journalists – the five o'clock follies and all that nonsense came much later. By and large, we were free to cover what we wanted, although travel outside the main cities was dangerous. I spent most of my six months in and around Saigon, talking to residents and politicians and trying to determine how far down the rabbit hole this war would take us. Some of those articles were reprinted in *Beyond the Battle,* which my publisher decided to issue after my second novel was released in a bid, I suppose, to give my fiction a ring of authority and to build a new following among non-fiction readers. I agreed with the idea at the time but when the book came out, I blushed as I read these examples of 'my early work'. The rage and naiveté on display in my articles are both uplifting and mortifying. I still believed then that knowledge could be a deterrent; I believed the pen could sheath the sword.

Vietnam was something of a reporting watershed for me. I was 41 and, in some ways, already a relic: a print journalist in an increasingly visual world. I brought a camera with me but I was never very good at taking pictures. I found the lens drew attention to my presence in a way that a notebook never did. I felt conspicuous, which made me uncomfortable, and you could see that anxiety in my badly framed, unstable pictures. Taking photographs seemed like such an intimate intrusion. I felt like I was stealing people's souls. I was hardly the best person for this new world of televised, access-all-quarters news.

I was also beginning to feel my years. I feared I came across as matronly, a somewhat quaint and ridiculous figure among the long-haired, lithe and youthful reporters. Don't get me wrong. Like you I've been blessed with strong bones and my skin has always worn the years lightly. Despite my aversion to exercise, I was still trim. I dressed well. It wasn't my physical appearance that aged me so much as a kind of heaviness, a fatigue that stared out at me from the mirror every morning. Looking back, I think I was already casting off my mooring ropes, ready to drift in a different direction.

One blissfully cool evening in November, I wandered down to the bar at the Continental Palace hotel, where I was staying with most of the other early-bird journalists. I had spent the day driving around the countryside with an interpreter, trying to gather material for a piece on government efforts to build civil defence forces in vulnerable villages. After bumping around the potholed roads, trying to sweet-talk angry, silent villagers and slipping knee-deep into filthy water while crossing a rice paddy, I just wanted to sit in a corner with a cold 33 beer and let the traffic fumes and motorcycle honking anaesthetise me. I was staring vacantly into the busy street when a tall, gangly, balding man, carrying a raincoat over his arm and an umbrella, came up to my table and said in a London accent that had had its edges polished off: "Are you Lina Rose of the *Gazette*?"

I nodded, annoyed that he had punctured my empty reverie but not that surprised to be so easily identified. There weren't that many women reporters on the ground yet and I had been in the country long enough for people to know how and where to find me of an evening. Saigon was like one of those decorative snuffboxes they used in the 18th century – glittering, ornate, smelly on the inside and very small. Nowhere to hide in a snuffbox.

"Wonderful. May I join you for a moment? My name is George Wallis and I'm from the British embassy."

He held out a large, knobbly hand. After a beat, I shook it and gestured to the chair.

"Be my guest. It's a free country, for now anyway."

He laughed nervously, draped his coat over the back of the chair and sat, fumbling awkwardly with his huge black umbrella until he finally propped it against his chair.

"Can I order you another beer?"

I nodded and stubbed out my cigarette, not taking my eyes from his twitching, sweaty face.

"But I have to warn you," I said. "If you've come to wheedle information out of me, you're barking up the wrong tree. You'll have to read my reports in the *Gazette*, like everyone else. I have no intention of becoming friends with anyone from the embassy, thank you."

The blush that fired his cheeks and forehead made me wonder just how desperate the Foreign Office was if this was the calibre of operative they were sending to war zones. The umbrella slid onto the floor. Jumping forward to catch it, he knocked the table, sending my empty bottle crashing to the floor.

I relented a little. He might be a Waughesque bumbler but his eyes were kind and like me, he was no teenager. Maybe he too was feeling displaced in this young man's war.

"Sorry to be so blunt," I said. "It's just that in my experience there is no such thing as a free beer. If you're offering me a drink, which is gratefully received by the way,

230

I feel obliged to tell you, from the outset, that I intend to drink your beer and give you nothing in return. I hope you understand."

His blush deepened, he shook his head with a wry smile and signalled to the waiter for two beers.

"Am I that transparent?" he said when the waiter had brought our order.

"I'm afraid so," I answered, lifting my bottle towards him. "Cheers."

We drank in silence for a short while but I couldn't keep it up. I was tired, my usual prickliness had been deflated by the tough day and I hoped a little conversation in English would silence the frightened voices of the people I had interviewed, which were still echoing in my head.

"Have you been in Saigon long?" I asked.

He leaned forward too eagerly.

"Since the beginning of the year. Feels like forever. I came over from Malaya. I'd been there for a couple of years."

"Where are you from originally? I think I hear London though you're doing a good job of disguising it."

He smiled.

"Yes, I was born in the East End, round Leyton way. Haven't spent much time there since I was a boy though. I signed up at 21 just as the war started and then afterwards, I came back and everything was so dreadful that I just turned around and took myself off straightaway. I went to India first, travelled a bit and then ended up getting a job at the High Commission just after partition. It was pretty messy but good for my career, as it turns out. I've been on the circuit since. Not quite sure what I'm supposed to be doing here but I think that's quite a normal feeling for British diplomats these days, what with the Empire shrinking and the Cold War and all of this."

He waved his hand around the bar that had filled up with beefy, loud GIs, hollow-eyed hacks and shiny-haired, doll-like Vietnamese girls.

He asked me a few questions about myself. I gave him

my edited highlights – born in St Albans, spent the war at the Ministry of Information, natural segue into journalism, Paris, Korea. I had it down pat by then. He didn't push for extra details. People of my generation rarely did. We knew that those hide-all façades were there for a reason – to spare blushes on both sides of the wall.

"I know you can't tell me what the British are doing with the Americans – we all know you've got a hand in the strategic hamlets programme..."

I paused, just in case, but he held up his hands and would only smile. Maybe not so Waughesque after all, I thought, smiling back in spite of myself.

"As you know, we Brits are not *directly* involved in this particular shindig and long may that continue," he said.

The emphasis was most definitely his. It was well known at that time that the British supported the US policy and I wondered if George might be involved in the oddly-named BRIAM, an advisory group that had been set up a few months before and that some said was a cover for British military training of US and Vietnamese soldiers, using techniques developed during the 1950s in the Malayan emergency, or liberation war, depending on which side you were on. George didn't look the type but then Hitler looked like a dandy, Churchill like a doddery uncle and Stalin like a jolly wrinkled grandfather, so you never know.

"Okay, so what do you think of the boys fighting here? Does it remind you of yourself?"

I must've been a little merry to ask such an odd question. Drunk, dehydrated and disoriented and probably also desperate for a kindred soul who could see this war as I did. Someone who saw life as I did. Another survivor.

He took a moment to answer.

"No. And yes. The fighting here is so different from what I experienced. I never fought in this part of the world. It was all on the Western Front for me and a little bit in North Africa. So, this doesn't feel at all familiar. But then, if you talk to the GIs, and sometimes I do, it's all there, all the same. You see them confused, scared and unsure. You can tell they're overwhelmed, just as we were. Then it's the morality of it all. No one ever asks a soldier how he feels about the rights and wrongs. You can't really. You can't ask because then he'd have to answer and then he'd have to think and if he did that he wouldn't be able to fight and after all, that's what he has to do. So yes, I guess some things never change. The human condition and its conditioning."

He drained his beer and started to gather his belongings.

"I know you don't want to give me any information. I respect that," he said. "But would you like to meet up now and then, for a drink and a chat? It's just that there are so few of us in this town. Don't you think we Brits need to stick together a little? If only so we can make fun of the Yanks?"

I smiled and said yes. I've always found it useful to know people in embassies, even if their main interests are usually self-serving if not downright selfish. The same could be said for most of us journalists. Besides, there was something delightful in how out-of-place George seemed to be, despite his on-paper experience. He was like a student who excels at all subjects but who might still need help figuring out how to cross a busy road. I wondered if his apparent ineptitude and social awkwardness might be a mask that served him well but I detected a real vulnerability there too. A rawness that none of the young reporters had but that I recognised.

George and I became friends, or perhaps more accurately we were occasional drinking buddies. It was he who told me, quite by accident, what really pushed Robert over the edge into the unfathomable deep.

It was a few weeks after our first meeting and we were sitting in an outdoor bar on a street near my hotel, trying to make ourselves heard above the drone of chainsaws being used to tear down majestic hardwood trees at the bottom of the busy road. We didn't know it then but the authorities believed the streets were too narrow for the military vehicles that would soon pour in. They were already preparing for the inevitable next phase. In the end, war is so predictable: once the engine ignites, the whole thing moves forward relentlessly. Even as we sat there that evening, plans to poison many more of Vietnam's trees were being hatched in dim, panelled rooms far, far away, where shrewd politicians were preparing to cover their tracks with misleading words, like *defoliant*, *pacify* and *body count*. War murders meaning, Diane. That is why truth is always the first casualty.

George seemed melancholy, less chatty than usual, though the whining of the saws was making it difficult to hold any kind of conversation.

Finally, the day's light began to fade, the workers packed up their tools and the mouth-watering smell of marinated pork being grilled enveloped the street.

"Are you okay, George? You seem very quiet this evening?" I said.

"Sorry," he said. "I *am* feeling a little down. I get like this sometimes but usually I can shake it off fairly quickly. I suppose you'd call it an attack of the blues. This time it's lasting longer though. I don't know what it is. Something about the air here right now, the smell of the flowers, or maybe it's the war, the way it's all going. Bloody hell, maybe it's just the damn sound of those chainsaws."

He sipped his beer. A skinny, big-eyed boy with blue shorts and red flip-flops leaned over the railing between our table and the street, holding out a bunch of pink peach flowers. I waved him away but George held up one hand to me while he rummaged in his pocket for change. The boy's delighted smile seemed to hang in the air like the Cheshire Cat's grin long after his whippet-thin body had disappeared.

George held the bouquet out to me.

"Pretty bedraggled I'm afraid but they'll brighten up your room for a few hours, at least until the petals fall off."

I hesitated.

"Don't worry," he smiled, taking out a white handkerchief

and running it over his sweating head. "I'm not making a pass, or whatever it is those damned Yanks say. I just thought the flowers looked pretty and the boy looked hungry and you probably haven't had any flowers for a while so I knew you wouldn't reject this bunch, poor as it is."

"That's very cheeky of you. Maybe my hotel room is a rhapsody of flowers," I said.

"If that was the case, I doubt you'd be here having a drink with an old fogey like me."

I tilted my head to him. "Good point."

"They look a bit like pink poppies," he said. "I bloody hate poppies."

We laughed together but his mirth was joyless – a birthday cake without a candle.

"Ah sod it! I'm going to tell you what's eating me, bugger the security protocols. They took us on a trip the other day, to see one of the villages the guerrillas attacked. Or so they say. No one left to confirm whether or not that's the truth. And don't ask who took us, or where it was, or anything else, Lina, because you know I can't tell you."

I shut my mouth and wished I had my notebook discreetly on my lap. If George was about to dump news on me, I'd better hope my memory was up to the task. So far though, there was no exclusive here. We knew villages were being bombed or burned. This was nothing new, nothing that would distract my readers from their cornflakes, as McNeish would say.

"Anyway, I was walking around the huts – you know what it's like: charred floors, crumbling half-walls and the smell of death everywhere. No bodies though. They never let the foreigners see the bodies. Not that they were particularly discreet. The ditch where they threw them was right there at the edge of the clearing. They hadn't even bothered to rake over the earth."

He stopped, lit a cigarette, picked up the flowers, smelled them and put them down again.

"It was a shoe that did it. A black canvas shoe half-buried in the earth. You could tell the foot inside it was small, but not necessarily a child's. Not here. But before, in France, it would have been a child's. It *was* a child's, dammit. It brought it all back. The smells, the terrifying silence, the burnt, black trees. I was in Caen again, the day after we bombed the place to smithereens."

I sat up straight. Caen, the town with the church on Robert's last postcard.

"You were in Caen? When?"

"After D-Day. We landed at Lion-sur-Mer on Sword Beach and our first job was supposed to be to take Caen, to stop the Germans from pushing up to the coast."

"My husband landed at Lion-sur-Mer."

George shook his head.

"He was probably in a different unit. I don't remember anyone called Rose. I'm sure I would've. He would've been mercilessly ribbed for that name," he said, trying to smile.

"No, I don't use his name, not since he died. He was Robert Stirling. But the other boys called him—"

"The Untouchable?" George's eyes drilled into me. "You're the girl he talked about all that time. The one who was working in London. The one he thought..." He paused, shook his head and rubbed his hand over his sweating pate.

"Jesus Christ. Robert. But..."

His wide brow furrowed. I tensed. I knew what was coming next and I took a deep breath. I was clear about what I was going to say but even all these years later, my sanitised version of the truth could still hurt. Like I said, war strips words of their meaning and after Robert died, I too was guilty of euphemism. I couldn't keep pulling off the bandage. You do understand, Diane. Don't you?

"He died after the war, didn't he?"

I nodded.

"Yes, he died in 1947. We weren't married that long. It was very sad."

"I heard he killed himself. Is that it? I remember I bumped into someone from the battalion and he told me. He said it was the only way Robert could possibly go. Nothing else could hurt him."

I said nothing and so he continued.

"You know, we used to fight over who would get to stand beside him when the balloon went up. We knew he'd make it so being next to him seemed the safest bet."

"I suppose it was until it wasn't," I said.

George looked mortified.

"I'm so sorry. Good God, I wasn't thinking. It's none of my business. None whatsoever. Damn, this whole day has been one monstrous fuck-up after another."

I said nothing but not because I was exploiting his confusion. I was lost in my memories. I hadn't thought of that nickname, The Untouchable, for years. To be honest, I hadn't thought that much about Robert himself for several years. It's unforgiveable but most things we are forced to do to survive are unpardonable.

George's face was in shadow now. Night had come suddenly as it always did in Saigon. I decided to ignore his question. My confirmation of Robert's suicide was not necessary.

"Did you fight in Caen together?" I asked.

"Yes, although I don't think I would describe it as fighting. Nor would Robert. It was the one time he was not untouchable. But then again, no one who saw what happened could remain untouched. Even then, even after all those years of war."

"Tell me."

He shook his head.

"Long time ago. Nobody needs to go over that again."

"Please. *I* need to know."

Chapter 22

This, Diane, is George's account of what happened in Caen. It is as accurate as it was on the night he told me. I have not forgotten one word. I can still hear him telling the story in a flat monotone that was more distressing than any emotional rant could have been. I took a few notes that evening in Saigon but I didn't really need to. You don't ever forget a revelation like this.

I need to stop using words like 'ever'. You'd think I'd know better by now.

I will let George tell you the story because it is his to tell.

I made sure I was right beside Robert in the front of the ship as we came into the beach. It wasn't just his reputation, the way he'd survived all the battles and campaigns without a scratch. It was something about the way he was as well, something about his face. He always managed to look calm. There was a little smile he'd give you just before the off, like this, with his eyebrows raised. Like he was laughing at it all. Like it was all a bad joke, a childish lark. You knew he didn't believe it, he wasn't one of the empty-headed ones who enjoyed the fighting, saw it as some kind of macho game. Robert was smart and that's why his smile, calm and a little world-weary, helped us all more than he could know. If you ask me, that smile was why we all wanted to be beside him. That and the fact that we'd seen him help other lads out when things got tough before. He was truly brave and for those of us who spent the war wondering about our own courage, he gave us something to believe in. He gave me the smile as the bullets pinged around us, just before they opened the ramp at the front. Then we were up, queuing like good Englishmen to get off. I remember there was quite a swell and I could hear a bagpipe playing somewhere. It was surreal. Just before I jumped into the water, Robert straightened the spade in my pack, thumped me on the shoulder and pointed to a landing craft running alongside us, where soldiers were trying to get their bikes down almost vertical ramps into the choppy sea.

"Thanks be to Christ, they didn't give us bikes as well, like those poor lads over there," he said as he pushed past me.

"Good luck, Georgie. Stay right behind me and do what I do."

After we got off the beach, we were supposed to secure Caen to stop the Germans from getting to the coast. We knew there were Panzer divisions around and we'd heard the stories of what Hitler's youth troops, the Hitlerjugend, were doing to captured paratroopers. True or false, it didn't matter. It got our blood up. We were fired up for the fight. We'd been told that this was it, this was where we were going to win the war. And we wanted that end; we wanted it so very badly by then. So yes, you might say we were itching for a fight. And then we'd all come over from Blighty, we'd seen the damage that'd been done to our cities and our towns so there was a desire for revenge too. And the fighting in Normandy was brutal – dashing across open cornfields or tiptoeing down those lanes with their high hedges, not being able to see the enemy but knowing he was there. It was enough to break the strongest spirit. So there we were: tens of thousands of angry, vengeful, tired young men who just wanted to be done with it all. Against us, some of Hitler's most fanatical fighters. It was never going to be pretty but what happened in Caen was beyond awful.

The town had been bombed as part of the invasion but it wasn't enough. We still couldn't break through and so we held back. It was July before we went at it properly. I remember the day the Lancasters and Halifax bombers came over. I was standing with Robert on a hill outside the town. You've never seen anything like it, Lina. Wave after wave of bombers, dropping their loads like confetti at a wedding. We watched the bombs float down, then the flowers of smoke bursting all over the town. We'd been told the people had been ordered to evacuate and we believed it but still. It was terrible to stand there and watch the city get hammered like that. It was brutal and sickening, the air was vibrating with the shockwaves and the ground was shaking under our feet.

That night our guns opened up on Caen. Hour after hour of shells whining and crashing and exploding until none of us could bear it any more. It was as though the machines had taken over the earth and were hell bent on destroying it. Metal and noise and smoke and flames – that's what I remember. Treads and tracks branding the ground. We'd sold our souls to get the machines on our side and now they'd become our masters. That's what I thought.

Robert and I were with some other chaps in a barn a few miles away but we couldn't sleep. The dead themselves wouldn't have been able to sleep through that. So we went back up to the hill and watched the flames devour the town until the smoke burned our eyes so much we had to go back.

I remember Robert said: "Will they ever be able to forgive us when they come back and see what we have done to their home? I know we say this is the only way, but what will they think? Is this any different to what the Germans did to our towns and cities?"

He took his helmet off and held it in front of him, like he was in church. Or at a funeral. I felt odd looking at him like that but I did the same. He didn't say anything else for a while. The shells didn't leave much space for talking. They filled every moment.

"Can peace be worth this?" he said eventually. "Is this really the only way or is this the only way we can imagine?"

I remember his face flashing like a beacon in the light of the explosions, white eyes and teeth like holes in the night. It was the first time I doubted his survival. And I suppose by extension my own. I was suddenly very scared.

"This is who we are now," he said. "We can never be other than what we have done here."

The next day, we walked into Caen together. I say walked but that's not right. Every road was knee-deep in rubble. Wood, bricks, chunks of plaster, torn curtains and sheets, smashed furniture, toys, splintered branches from felled trees and broken cartwheels. Houses gutted, churches pulverised. Like sandcastles smashed by children. And the smell. Death on our lips so that we didn't even dare lick them to quench our thirst. Death in our throats so we didn't even want to breathe in case it would get into our lungs. What would you do with death in your lungs? There were bodies everywhere, some out in the open, some in shallow graves, others we could only smell. On one side of the road, someone had tried to bury a child. There was a doll sitting underneath a cross made from two bits of branch. The doll was wearing a green bonnet. She'd yellow hair and was sitting quite daintily on the pile of earth. Only thing was they hadn't managed to dig deep enough – the soil was hard by then, parched and dry. One shoe, a black canvas shoe, like the one I saw today, was poking out of the grave. I could see the tiny shin too. Socks all rumpled like kids' socks always are. And the doll there like a guardian angel. Only not even angels could save the people of Caen.

The only sound was the creaking and whining of the tanks blasting a way through the rubble ahead of us and the dull thud of shells falling away to the north where we were still trying to drive the Germans out. And the odd gunshot because there were still snipers around, taking potshots at us.

We ran between the broken buildings, hunkering down low. As ever, Robert was in front of me, racing across the street, leaping over piles of rubble, glancing quickly behind *him every few minutes to make sure I was there. You have to understand how important his concern was, Lina. We all felt dispensable by then. To have someone pay attention to your life, as well as to their own, it felt like a mother's kiss. It really did. Every now and then, bullets pinged into the masonry around us. We tried to get a line on the snipers and the tanks blasted away in the direction from which the shots were fired but those deadly, single shots kept coming. I saw the soldier in front of Robert fall as he stepped around a corner. He didn't shout out, his death was silent, just an intake of breath, a space left in the heart of the noise. Robert rushed forward, grabbed the man's arms and lugged him into the shelter of a crumbling wall. I couldn't tell who the fallen man was. I didn't want to know. He was probably gone. Time enough to count the dead later and what good would knowing do anyway? I hunkered behind my own bit of smashed wall and watched Robert bend over the body, ear to lips and then the slight dip in his shoulders that meant the man was dead. I saw Robert close his eyes and rise. He stood for a moment, tall and exposed, facing the direction the bullet had come from. I will never forget that sight. I wanted to shout at him, to tell him to stop mucking around and get the hell down but the cry died in my throat. I felt like standing up myself. What if we all, on both sides, just stood up and let our arms drop to our sides and just looked at each other? What if? Robert did that for us. He made us believe that things could change and that was maybe the only thing that kept us going sometimes.*

A few streets later, we came to a cobbled square. The ruins of a church rose over the eastern side. The steeple looked like it had been cut down the middle with a knife. The body of the church had taken a direct hit. You could look straight through the windows to the street on the other side. Few of us were believers by then, but even so, the sight of a bombed-out church always made us pause. A few of the lads crossed themselves as they went past. Something flashed in the corner of my eye, a splash of colour. It was a little boy, couldn't have been more than four or maybe five. I've never had children so I could be wrong and by then, a lot of the French children in that area were small for their age because of how hungry they'd been for so many years. He was wearing a red wool jumper. That's what caught my eye. He was hunched low beside the church wall but he straightened up when he saw us. Robert took his hand from his rifle and waved. The boy waved back and then he dashed towards us, arms pumping, little legs vaulting over the piles of rubble. And then he stopped. We heard the shot a second later and a second later than that, an unguished cry. Something between a sob and a scream but it didn't come from the boy. It came from Robert. The boy was a few yards from us. His eyes had widened under his dirty brown hair, the smile was still half on his face but it was going rigid already. His cheeks were dirty and there was a single tear track on the flushed, mud-streaked skin. Robert got to him and caught him before he fell. I whipped around, whirling like a crazy man, trying to see where the shot had come from. Dust sprang up around Robert's feet as he sprinted back with the boy in his arms. We ran towards a café and smashed through the splintered wooden door. Robert laid the boy on the floor as I crouched by the glassless window. I could hear Robert whispering behind me. "Come on, come on, little man. Not like this. Not after all you've been through. Come on."

I couldn't bear to turn around, I didn't want to see another death but I couldn't leave Robert to handle it, not after all he'd done for me. I crept from the window and put my hand on Robert's shaking shoulder. I could see the boy was dead. His face was grey now. He'd taken the bullet right in the chest. Blood was pooling under him. I was glad we hadn't turned him over.

"Robert, we should go. This is over. There's nothing you can do."

I held out his helmet to him.

"I don't know why I waved," he moaned. "What's wrong with me? Why did I do it, George?"

He looked up at me and his eyes were red and the boy's blood was on his cheek and his lips were trembling.

"I did this, George. I did this."

He closed his eyes for a minute. I thought he was going to collapse. I'd seen it before. Men falling to the ground, legs crumpling under them when whatever it was that kept them upright just ran out. Some never got up. I'd never thought it would happen to Robert.

"This is it, George. This is why I'm untouchable. It's blood on my hands, deaths on my conscience. Every fucking scrape I come through means someone else has taken my bullet, my shell, my death. Why the hell should I survive? What makes me special?"

He stood up and ran to the door. I tried to grab his arm, he shook it off and then he was outside, walking bareheaded, without his rifle, straight across the street, screaming something at the sky. I got to the door. I wanted to follow him but I couldn't. My feet wouldn't cross the threshold. I knew the sniper was still out there, invisible, playing God from on high. A bullet pinged past my ear. I ducked back into the café. When I dared to look out again, Robert was still striding across the square, towards a half-demolished four-storey building on the other side. The sniper had to be at one of the blackened windows. Bullets were pinging into the ground around Robert but he kept going. I was terrified. The sniper would adjust his aim, it was only a matter of seconds before Robert would drop. I could not tear my eyes away. Death was usually instantaneous so Robert's walk across that square was something of a miracle. And then, the hollowed out shell where the sniper was hiding disappeared in a dull detonation of smoke and dust. One minute it was there and then my ears were ringing, Robert had stopped and the square was filled with dust. When it cleared, I saw that the top three storeys of the building were gone. Just like that. The tank crew had scored a direct hit. For a moment, everything stopped. There was total silence. I ran towards Robert but stopped a few feet behind him. He was still staring at the building. His arms hung empty at his sides. A captain ran towards us.

"What the devil do you think you're doing? You want to get killed? 'Cos you know you don't have to try that bloody hard here."

He was shaking with fury.

"Turn around soldier when I speak to you."

Robert turned around slowly. I wish to this day I hadn't seen his face. There was nothing there. It was so empty. So hard.

"Go get your helmet and your rifle, you idiot," the captain bellowed. "You pull something like that again and I'll shoot you myself. Still, you smoked him out for us, I suppose. I'll give you that."

He looked up to where the building had been just seconds before and shook his head.

"C'mon, lad. Pull yourself together now. We've still got a lot to do."

He smiled at Robert but he might as well have smiled at a statue for all the reaction he got.

As Robert was walking back to pick up his rifle and helmet, a small woman with wild hair rushed past him into the café.

"Il est oú? Il est oú, mon fils?"

We heard her shrieking when she got inside.

"Christophe, mon ange! Non, pas Christophe! Ils t'ont fait quoi, mon ange?"

Robert stepped towards the door, paused for a second and then went in, picked up his rifle from the floor and walked away. He didn't look back and he never wore his crooked smile again, not even on the day the war ended. Caen was the breaking of him, I think. It nearly broke me too. It would've if I'd been the one to wave at the boy. I nearly did. I so nearly did but Robert was always two steps ahead of me.

***

So, there you have it, Diane. That was the cancer that ate away at your father's heart until he could bear it no more. It is a tale soaked in tears. George wept as he told it and I wept as I heard it that night and I have cried again now in the retelling of it to you. It is a story so terrible it transcends time to ring its hopelessness through the ages.

This was the secret that Robert struggled to tell and that I could not help him carry because of my own guilt over Penrose. My shame made me fearful and fear displaced compassion. They say fear can unify but I don't believe that. Fear diminishes us. It diminished me and it diminished the sniper who shot at Robert with a child nearby. It diminished us all when we bombed cities and towns and villages so that we could win a war that had mechanised fear, turning us all into killing machines. For Robert and I, guilt and fear overpowered our love. We both paid the price. And you, my darling. You too paid a heavy price.

Chapter 23

After I left Vietnam, I lost touch with George. I genuinely liked him, even before he told me Robert's last story, but I was never very good at staying in contact once people were out of my line of sight. Perhaps after giving you up, I had to cultivate an extreme level of detachment to be able to go on. That may sound like another of my self-serving excuses but I do believe there is something to it, even if it cannot offer total exoneration. Out of sight had to be out of mind. Otherwise *I* would have been out of *my* mind. Evelyn was the exception. Our friendship was immutable because she always knew the true me.

I found it hard to sustain the relationships I developed after I started living my lie. I had lost too many loved ones already and although I carried on because I could not face the alternative, when it came to meeting new people I felt a bone-deep fatigue. If the price of love is grief, it was a price I had decided was too high. Or was it something else? A lacuna at the heart of my personality? I don't think we'll ever really know.

I returned to Paris in April 1962 and with McNeish's blessing took a month off. I told him I needed to recharge my batteries but really I needed to grieve. It was as though I had lost Robert all over again. I needed to revisit his death in the light of what George had told me.

I rented a cottage in the Drôme and I drove myself south into a land where still-brown lavender bushes contoured the dips and rises of vast fields and where cool rivers cut through deep gorges. I passed through sleepy red-roofed villages where old men cycled high bicycles down silent streets, offering an illusion of stasis and permanence. My one-bedroom bungalow with its unfenced front lawn was at the end of a rutted lane in a pine and cypress forest. You could go this far and no further. I revelled in the solitude, walking up and down the hills until I couldn't take another step and couldn't tell if it was sweat on my face or tears. Each night I drank a bottle of wine, sitting on the veranda, watching bats trace secrets onto the darkening sky and listening to the cicadas, the lowing of the cows and the odd car juddering along roads I could not see. I don't know that I found peace or salvation or answers but I did what I needed to do: I stayed alive in the present. I drowned my pain each night and then I sweated out what was left as I trudged for miles under the prickling, punishing heat, now and then stopping to lie down and scream into the fragrant ground as unbending, uncaring fir trees looked on. I forced myself to relive every moment, every glance and every word of those last weeks with Robert, remembering it all through the prism of what I now knew. It was utterly pointless and utterly unavoidable. Nothing could change what had happened but I owed it to Robert to stare directly into the sun. When I returned to Paris, I was scorched, inside and out.

For the next few months, I threw myself into my work. I became a recognised voice, my opinions lauded or loathed but always provoking a reaction. I relished the freedom I had to choose my stories, set my own lines and argue my points of view. I watched Europe split into two, travelling to Berlin to write about people trying to escape from the east over the 'wall of shame'. I was there when a young man was shot in the pelvis as he tried to flee and then left to bleed to death for an hour as the East German police looked on. The West German police could only throw him bandages as he lay writhing under the barbed wire, his bloodied hand marking the sand with desperate ciphers. The needless waste of that young life made me shake with fury.

In late 1962, I held my breath as we teetered towards a nuclear Armageddon because of a missile site on an island half a world away. It should have come as no surprise. We had opened that box nearly two decades before and although we did it in the name of peace, one would have to be a fool to believe one can force the evil one creates to do one's bidding forever. Henry had known that. We all knew we had crossed a line in 1945 but we tried to forget about it when the war ended because otherwise we would have to acknowledge the price not just of the war but also of the peace.

I watched the US slide ever deeper into a moral and military quagmire in Vietnam and I thought about going back but I knew this was a war for a new generation. I would not be able to capture what it meant, as a good journalist should. So I became one of the watchers of this televised conflict and I was forced to recognise that in this new world, my place was less secure. Editors used to say they didn't need photographs when I reported because my descriptions were so vivid but this praise was no longer relevant because the pictures were always there and now they moved too.

I was also becoming less ambitious. Whatever hunger or fear used to drive me to see what had to be seen firsthand was waning. As my truth-telling impulse diminished so too did my empathy. One would probably call it compassion fatigue now, although I did not recognise it as such. I assumed I was becoming grumpier and more heartless because I was getting older. I groused, mostly to myself for I was not entirely stupid, about how similar all crises were. Refugees were refugees wherever they ended up; their plight was always the same; their faces were always the same, the very words they used lacked originality. I realise now I was burnt-out.

I decided I needed a break; I yearned to get away from what I saw as the West's destructive impulses, its wars and scandals and unremitting harshness. I wanted to find my own Shangri-La and I picked Africa, in an uncharacteristically sentimental act of loyalty to Penrose. I recalled how he had talked so excitedly about his plans to visit his uncle in Kenya after the war. I knew so little about the continent myself, having only ever been to Algeria, so Penrose's enthusiastic descriptions seemed a good place to start.

I can't say I never thought of Penrose after his death but I tried very hard to forget him. Our time together was so short, so surreal and so inseparable from the unlife that was the war. It would have been absurd, given all of that, to wonder 'what if'. A meritless dream, like wishing for clouds made of candyfloss. And in any case, I had forced myself to bury his memory when Robert came back. We were already living on a cliff edge and I knew thoughts of Penrose could push us over. In the end, I was more like Charlotte than I imagined. I had a will of steel too and who is to say that I did not also use it for the greater good.

But 20 years on, I felt a move to Kenya could offer both an escape and a fitting tribute to a wonderful man who passed as most wonderful men do: silently, barely ruffling the air around him.

The *Gazette* did not have an African correspondent at that time, relying instead on the news wires for any information it thought its readers needed. But as the Cold War split the world into us and them, and African states began to shake off the shackles of colonialism, McNeish was open to the idea of a permanent correspondent to track these changes. I suspect he also sensed my ennui and he was always a loyal man. He was grateful for what I had done, proud of what I had become and he wanted to keep me on board. Making the case for Nairobi was easy: I pretended, once again, to be running towards something rather than running away.

After the Mau Mau rebellion, the state of emergency, the horror of the detention camps, the torture and the murders, it was clear that independence for Kenya was a given. I wanted to be there to witness it. I felt, somewhat arrogantly I know, that I deserved a good news story. I assumed I could find one in Africa. It's hard to believe now that I could have been so naïve.

I arrived in Nairobi in February 1963 and at the end of the year, I covered the country's independence and met the man who would teach me to love again. What gluttony! To seize another chance at love after all I had done. What can I say, Diane? These are the cards I was dealt. I may have stacked the deck a little but it was not all my doing. I was granted, or I granted myself, a second chance at life and now I found another love. It seemed too much and indeed it was. Do not despair though, Diane. The delayed punishment now coming my way is both delightfully vindictive and wonderfully apt.

I loved Kenya. For a time, I thought I would live out the rest of my days there. I realise I will come across as a ludicrously dewy-eyed white tourist but I can't help it. I was captivated by the colours, the heat, the chaos and noise of the street markets, the depth of the inky night skies with their freckling of stars, the unbounded sweep of the savannahs and the ponderous grandeur of herds of elephants trudging through low scrub. I felt truly alive for the first time in decades.

I thrilled to a certain loucheness I found in Nairobi, a refusal of consequences. Or maybe I am remaking a city, and indeed a country, in my own image. That would not be beyond me. By the time I got to Kenya, I no longer believed in consequences. I refused them their due. Maybe there was nothing quintessentially louche in the clammy heat, the long, hot nights, the intoxicating air after early afternoon downpours. Maybe it was all me. Me, me, me. Kenya was what I wanted it to be. What I needed it to be.

I rented a low bungalow in Muthaiga, not far from the diplomats' residences and the notorious but now rather seedy Muthaiga Country Club. I hired a driver, a heavyset man from the Luo tribe called Norbert. He wore a black leather jacket in all weather and had a thrilling disregard for any and all driving regulations. At best, he regarded the rules of the road as guidance for other less skilled individuals. At worst, they were challenges.

I dived into the job, rediscovering the enthusiasm that had propelled me to Korea and Vietnam. Kenya was at a crossroads and the potential thrilled me. I had seen too much of countries laboriously rebuilding after war or blindly wandering down the path to conflict again. I needed hope and I found it in 1963 in Nairobi.

I reported from the slums of the capital, from the Indian Ocean coast around Mombasa where monkeys chattered in the palm trees and dhows glided lazily beyond the reefs, and from the sprawling farms of British settlers who couldn't believe the natives were actually going to take over. These men and women reminded me of Neville Chamberlain: they too supposed that their stubborn refusal to believe in the inevitable could change the course of history. Children with their hands over their eyes, convinced that no one could see them. I pitied them and I despised them. I realise now that I was too harsh. Their views had been forged in battle – they had lived in fear of being hacked to death and had seen neighbours and children murdered. I should have recognised the anger that fuelled their refusal to accept the obvious. But I wanted to forget those feelings. I wanted a good news story for once.

However, I could not totally ignore the other side and there is always another side. We had all heard whispers of the torture of Kikuyu men, women and children in the detention camps set up during the state of emergency, although details and numbers were disputed. They are still being disputed today. There is no doubt that during the 1950s Kenya was often a violent, brutal place for its own people, particularly the Kikuyu tribe, but by the time I arrived, the price of freedom had mostly been paid. The labour pains had reached a climax and a new life was ready to be born. Of course, there was excruciating poverty and need and it was there if you wanted to see it but if you didn't want to, it was easily avoided. Especially around Muthaiga. You've probably heard stories of the orgies and drug-fuelled parties that allegedly took place at the club, Diane? I can't say I ever saw anything too terrible – things had quietened down considerably since the heady 1920s and the murder of the Earl of Erroll. On the few occasions I went to the club, the misdemeanours I witnessed were disappointingly tame: a few people staggering around in a drunken stupor, the odd semi-naked couple running across the lawn and the occasional fist-fight, sometimes over a woman. But it was no Sodom and Gomorrah by 1963.

Independence was declared on December 12th. I stood near the dais in Uhuru Park in the centre of the city as the Duke of Edinburgh handed over the articles of independence to Jomo Kenyatta, who wore his customary fez-like hat and held his traditional fly whisk throughout the ceremony. At midnight, the Union Jack was lowered and the red-black-green-and-white flag of Kenya was raised. People danced and cried and sang and fireworks exploded overhead and there was something beautiful and pure about this birth of a nation despite the bizarre, unsettling juxtaposition of British pomp and African pageantry. Even a hardened hack like myself couldn't help but feel uplifted. I do, however, remember feeling concerned when I was told that the red in the flag signified the blood spilled to achieve freedom. I never did trust gains made through the shedding of blood. Blood meant sacrifice and in my experience, sacrifice never went unpunished.

I had been frantically busy for weeks, writing about the prospects for Africa's newest country, interviewing settlers and slum dwellers and politicians. And despite my emotional response on the day itself, my articles were characteristically prescient. I *did* raise the spectre of corruption, of tribalism, of a cronyism encouraged for decades by British rule. Today, I read of Kenya and it does not cheer me at all to find that I was right. All the potential that I pretended I could believe in on that December day was illusory. We British had already done too much damage. The baby never had a chance, some might say.

The day before independence, I was invited to Government House in Nairobi for what was billed as an informal farewell to the British. The Duke was there, this time in a lounge suit, alongside an array of finely dressed members of the Kenyan and white elite. I wandered around the parched garden, feeling ridiculous in my white dress and straw hat and stumbling like a drunk in the high heels I had bought especially for the occasion. I almost never wore dresses by then. One of the greatest things to come out of our war, to my mind, was the fact that women could wear trousers always and everywhere. I had embraced the trend with a passion and I was annoyed that I had to conform to such outdated British convention in such an exotic location.

I tottered to the edge of the garden and leaned gratefully against a palm tree. Looking around at the crowd, I wondered if any of the smug-looking guests had been in the Mau Mau and had taken the legendary oath to drive out the white settlers. I tried to guess which demure British wives had slept with loaded revolvers under their pillows as their husbands patrolled Nairobi's streets during the state of emergency. I was thoroughly enjoying my fantasies until a tall man with a lean fox-like face stopped beside me. His fair hair was thinning on top and there were deep lines etched around his mouth, like a pair of parentheses. His eyes were a startling slate-grey and there was something infinitely capable about his sinewy frame. In his crumpled cream suit and brown loafers, he looked as uncomfortable as I felt. He glanced at my notebook.

"I suppose you're one of those hailing the dawn of a bright new era," he said.

I tried to place his accent. The words were perfectly correct but the clipped way he uttered them was definitely not English, or South African, my second choice for a white man at such a grand do.

"Well, isn't it?" I replied, slightly stung by his dismissive tone.

"A new era, yes. But not necessarily a bright one. But I suppose I must not spoil the party."

He fell silent, morosely sipping his drink and running a hand through his limp hair as he surveyed the guests in their suits, summer dresses and colourful kangas. I felt unreasonably annoyed that he was raining on this admittedly elitist parade. It was one thing to harbour my own doubts but I didn't want to hear them voiced by someone else on this day. I thought about moving away from the palm tree's precious shade. I had enough quotes already for the piece I planned to write and I did not feel up to engaging in conversation with another white doomsayer. I had heard enough of their arguments and while I agreed with some of their concerns, I wanted to postpone my natural cynicism for another 24 hours.

"Who do you write for?" he asked.

When I told him, he shook his head.

"Never heard of it but I do not read very often."

"A man of the soil? Brawn over brain?" I said tartly.

"Nothing is wrong with that," he replied slowly. "Humans have been writing forever and I cannot see what good it has done."

Despite myself, I laughed. His tone was so disparaging and he looked so very cross that I couldn't help myself.

"Go on, then. What's *your* prediction for Kenya's future? You seem to consider yourself a bit of an expert," I said.

He turned to me, seemingly surprised by my mirth but too uncertain of the reason to join in. Definitely not a native English speaker, I thought.

"It will be the same as before. Except this time the blacks will be in charge. This time, they will keep the others under. They will do the stealing and the oppressing and the looting. It will be the same as everywhere else. This... This kind of... What is that English word I love, yes, farce... This kind of farce makes me feel sick. So many people, all with blood on their hands, all puffed up like peacocks, all this entitlement but no sense of responsibility."

He pulled a handkerchief from his jacket pocket and mopped his brow.

"Things will be the same because people are the same, whatever the place, whatever the colour of their skin."

"My goodness, you're not very optimistic, are you?"

He turned and fixed his penetrating eyes on me. I blushed and it had been years since I did that. I felt naked before him as though he could read the darkest recesses of my mind.

"And you *are* optimistic? You must not be very good at your job if so," he said.

"You're very blunt," I said, feeling my cheeks redden even more. "And annoyingly judgmental, if you don't mind me saying so. You know nothing about me. How dare you jump to conclusions."

"And yet that is what you did just now," he said. "You judged me. Brawn over brain, you said. And just because I do not read your magazine."

"Newspaper," I said hotly.

"Fine, so newspaper. There is no difference. My point is there are not only two ways to be. One can know things without reading them in newspapers or books or magazines. One does not have to be ignorant just because one doesn't read all the day. But I imagine that does not suit the way you see the world. It is funny to me how you British are. So rigid, so inflexible in your ideas and often very, very wrong."

He finished his drink, burped demurely and bowed his head.

"Anyway, we shall see, I suppose. We shall see what happens."

He started to walk away but I grabbed his arm, alarmed and excited by my own passion.

"You are very sure in your assumptions about the British. Let me at least know where you are from so that I can make my own snap judgments."

"I am from the Netherlands. But I am not representative of all the Dutch. Obviously. Since I am here."

He laughed then, a rough, barking sound.

"And so, I should imagine you may not be representative of all the British. Since you too are here. I apologise for my assumptions. I may have been wrong about your countrymen."

"But not about me? Is that what you mean?"

He stepped backwards and then with a bizarrely ostentatious wave of his hand, he disappeared back into the crowd.

It was a long time since I had felt so angry and so offended and so very alive.

Chapter 24

A few weeks later, on a sweltering January day, I was sitting outside a popular roadside bar halfway between Nairobi and Naivasha. I'd been to interview some settlers around the lake and I was eager to get back to my peaceful, jacaranda-shaded home where I hoped to turn the scribbled fragments in my spiral notebook into something thoughtful about the future of the nation. But Norbert was hungry and I knew better than to force the man to drive on an empty stomach. While he ate at a roadside kiosk, I went into the bar for a beer. I was sitting outside, doodling in my notebook and wondering whether I should travel to neighbouring Uganda to see how independence was working out there, when I heard a plane approaching. There was a flat strip of grass to my right and I'd been told that white settlers sometimes flew in from the surrounding farms for a drink at the bar before sundown. It had sounded too exotic to be true so I was eager to spot one of these mythical everyday pilots. Remember, Diane, flying was still quite a rarity then. I straightened up excitedly as the small, twin-engine plane touched down and then gasped as it skidded slightly on the parched, brown grass. It taxied to a halt and a man hopped easily from the cockpit. The sun was behind him so all I could tell was that he was very tall. He strode towards the terrace where I was sitting in the corner, hopped over the small wooden fence and walked straight to the bar. I resisted the urge to turn around.

"Stijn, man! *Karibu*. Cutting it a bit fine if you want to be home by dark?" the barman said loudly.

"Not going home this time, my man. Heading to Nairobi. I was a little thirsty there and I thought I'd stop off at my favourite watering hole."

The barman's reply was drowned out as a hyena screeched somewhere in the dusky scrubland stretching between the bar and the eggshell blue hills floating on the horizon.

I could bear it no longer. I twisted around in my seat just as the lanky man at the bar turned. We stared at each other for a long moment and then he did it again. The ostentatious wave with a flourish of his long fingers. He walked over, gestured to the empty chair beside me and sat, plonking his beer down so hard that the rickety table shook.

"Did you enjoy the rest of the party?" he said.

"I did. It got steadily better, in fact," I said. "I managed to find quite a lot of optimistic people, some of whom weren't English and others who were not even necessarily well-read."

He grunted but his lips were twitching.

"So what are you doing here?"

I told him about my reporting trip. He asked who I had spoken to and laughed loud and long when I told him that I did not feel comfortable discussing my sources with a stranger. I blushed again. This blunt Dutch man with his unsettling eyes really knew how to irritate me and yet a part of me was thoroughly enjoying the conversation.

He caught me looking at his plane.

"Do you fly?" he asked.

I burst out laughing.

"What a question. Do many people say yes?"

"Around here they do," he said. "And anyway, I am trying not to make assumptions since you took it so badly last time."

I bowed my head in acknowledgment.

"No, or rather I fly in planes flown by other people."

"Would you like to fly in mine? Flown by me?"

I looked again at the plane. Here on the ground, it seemed fragile and ungainly.

"I can't say your landing just now filled me with confidence," I said, stalling. I did want so very badly to fly with him and I couldn't understand why.

"I hit a tiny bump," he said coolly. "This is not asphalt, you know. I can say I have never crashed, not even a little bit. Why don't you come with me to Nairobi now and you can see for yourself. Before you make, what did you call it, yes, a snap judgment."

"Maybe," I said. "But I think you should tell me your name first. You can tell a lot from a man's name, you know."

"My name is Stijn, Stijn van der Berg. In English, I would be Stijn of the mountains."

He seemed endearingly pleased with his immediate translation.

"Lina Rose," I said, stretching out my hand. His hand was warm, the palm rough and hard like the skin of an animal.

"I don't know what that would be in Dutch."

"Lina Roos," he said swiftly. I liked the way it sounded.

And so, Diane, I took off in that tiny plane with a man who annoyed me and thrilled me and was the living embodiment of everything I thought I was not. Norbert was not best pleased to be told he would have to drive back alone. He stood, hands on hips, at the bar and glared in turn at the plane and then at Stijn.

"Mama, I am not sure it is safe. You know, these planes, you cannot trust them. Many, many people have died in these planes. I think it is better for you to come in the car with me."

I calmed him as best I could, told him to leave the car at my house when he arrived and promised I would see him in the morning. He left, shaking his head and muttering under his breath. As he crossed the yard, I saw him stop to share his dissatisfaction with the security guards slumped on low stools under a giant mango tree. His arms windmilled, his head bobbed, his listeners laughed. They were probably right, I thought, turning back to the bar, where Stijn was settling his bill.

I hovered behind him uncertainly, exasperated by the barman's frankly curious gaze. They exchanged some low words in Swahili and that annoyed me even more. I didn't want to come across as a star-struck child but neither did I want to be seen as some kind of latter-day Idina Sackville, a man-eating, hedonistic socialite with no regard for custom and convention. Maybe this was a bad idea. I could probably still catch Norbert before he left. I turned away. The sun was sinking to the horizon, dragging the heat out of the air and spreading a rose-tinted light across the land.

I felt a hand on my elbow.

"Let's go. We don't have too much time and the light is so beautiful now. We must make the most of it."

I knew he was right.

Stijn helped me into the cockpit where I perched nervously beside him as he flicked switches, muttering all the while in Dutch.

"Wear these," he said, handing me some ear protectors. I felt safer once I put them on and the world disappeared behind a wall of silence.

It was all I could do to prevent myself from gripping his arm as we bumped down the short runway and into the sky. I had flown on helicopters in Korea and in Vietnam but I had never trusted my life to a single almost-stranger in such an intimate space. I stared straight ahead, willing the plane higher, even stretching my torso and neck as if I could physically lift us up. At first, I didn't dare to look out of the window but when I did, Diane, I was enraptured. As we flew out over the Rift Valley, the ground fell away so that even the clouds were below us. It was breathtaking. The sweep of the green and brown plains with Mount Longonot rising like an omen above the mango and papaya trees.

"I can take you up Longonot if you like. You can walk around the top, or even sit and read if you prefer."

His voice was crackly, absurdly intimate in my covered ears. It felt like a kiss.

The setting sun cast a red flush over the tiny houses, tinting the clouds below us. We were flying in a glorious red-and-orange bubble above what one could only too easily believe was the birthplace of mankind. There was something primeval about the soft tree lines, the jagged mountain edges, the huge scale of what was unfolding below. I was aware my mouth was gaping open but I could not hide my joy. I did not want to. I finally turned to Stijn and spoke through the microphone.

"You can do this any time you want?"

He nodded curtly but his eyes were warm.

"You may just be the luckiest man alive," I said.

He smiled.

"Maybe."

All too soon, the buildings of Nairobi rose ahead of us; squat and solid and smothered in a red haze. We flew over Nairobi National Park and I squealed when I saw zebras and Thomson gazelles running below. Stijn smiled and dipped the plane abruptly so that we were gliding just above the animals. We soared up again and I caught a glimpse of giraffes ambling contentedly among the trees.

"We shouldn't scare them too much," his voice said in my ear. "I shouldn't have gone so low but you looked so excited. I thought it would be fine just this once."

As his words echoed in my head, I realised I couldn't possibly bear it if this was "just this once". Suspended thousands of feet in the air above a scrubland spotted with wild animals in a tiny two-engine Cessna with a man I barely knew, I felt safer than I had in years. Completely secure and intoxicatingly free. As we glided in to land at Wilson Airport, I sat as if in a trance. I looked down at my hands, clasped tightly in my lap. I lifted one, or someone who was now in charge of my body did, and I placed it for the tiniest moment on Stijn's hand. He didn't look at me but he smiled a long, slow smile.

"I'm glad you have enjoyed the tour," he whispered

straight into the most open part of my brain. His voice lit a fuse and I closed my eyes for a second to enjoy the colours exploding inside my brain.

Stijn did take me walking to the top of Mount Longonot. He took me boating on Lake Naivasha, where we got as close as we dared to the submerged hippos, whose comical foreheads and bulbous eyes belied how dangerous they were. I flew with him many, many times, mostly from Nairobi to the flower farm he owned on the northern banks of Lake Naivasha. I eventually learned to relax in the air, to be less spellbound, but those journeys over central Kenya always filled me with wonder.

At first our friendship was platonic. We enjoyed spending time together but we were in no rush. Stijn had been married before to a Dutch woman who found life on a struggling flower farm in Kenya was less than she had imagined in ways she couldn't have foreseen. She had returned to Holland after the war but their daughter Else had joined Stijn when she turned 18 and now aged 20 acted as the de facto lady of the house. She was a tall, capable young woman with her father's grey eyes and her mother's dark hair. She spoke perfect English and Swahili and like her father, she made me feel as though nothing bad could ever happen while she was around. She had a preternatural calm and something of that calm reminded me of Charlotte.

Did Else remind me of you? Truth to tell, she couldn't, Diane. I didn't know who you were by then. I could not imagine you as a nearly grown woman, just a little younger than Else. And besides, I did not then think of Else as a daughter. She was more of a friend, despite the age gap. She was wise beyond her years and I was still immature in many ways and so we made a good pair.

I never told Stijn about you, Diane. I said I had been married and that my husband had died after the war. I talked about my time at the Ministry and what I had done afterwards but never in any great detail. It suited us both that way. Stijn liked to say he was a simple man who just wanted to live in the present. He said there was so much to see and feel and hear and experience in a single day that there was no time to indulge in the past. I don't think he managed to live solely by that mantra. I do believe there was more going on than simple sensation when he fell silent as we sat on the veranda in the evening, listening to the birds calling and watching the bats darting in and out of the eaves. But I respected his decision to try to live totally in the present. It was, after all, simply a purer, less tainted form of what I had tried to do since the war.

Through 1964, I spent many weekends on the farm Stijn had named Ol Mlima, or the Mountain. I went riding with Stijn, we hiked around Lake Naivasha and we spent hours inspecting new blooms in his greenhouses. Else sometimes joined us but seemed to know instinctively when we should be alone. She was, and is, in the purest sense, a lovely person.

One day, we were in the greenhouse when Stijn picked a rose and held it out to me. I raised it to my nose and sniffed.

"Beautiful. And I love the colours. I've not seen this mixture of red and yellow before."

"I hope not," Stijn said. His usually dour face split into a wide smile.

"I made it. Or no, that is not correct. I designed it. Is that better?"

"You made it?" I said. "You know, that makes you a god, Stijn."

"It makes me a foolish man," he said. "I'm calling it 'Lina'."

I didn't know what to say. We had been growing steadily closer and I think we both knew we were progressing along a path that would lead to something more. I was becoming increasingly attracted to Stijn. The face I had first deemed ugly I now found strong, vibrant and reassuring. I longed to run my fingers over those lines by his mouth and feel his sharp eyes on my body. I was increasingly captivated by lips I had once dismissed as thin but now realised were exquisitely shaped. I wanted to feel those capable arms around me.

I was falling in love but I was in no rush. Isn't that strange,

Diane? That my sense of urgency diminished as I aged. You'd think it would be the other way around. I suppose there was a delicious comfort in the certainty of knowing that what was going to be was definitely going to be. A kind of luxurious foreplay, I suppose.

But in that greenhouse on that damp October day, as he stood before me, telling me that the rose I held was called Lina, I knew the time had come. I stepped towards him, fancying I would give him a gentle kiss on the lips but he met me halfway and pulled me hungrily towards him. We kissed like teenagers, abandoning all restraint. It was shocking and inevitable. And that was it. We were together.

I quit my job a month later and moved to Stijn's farm. McNeish was disappointed but he was retiring himself in a few months and he wished me the best in a voice that rang with determination and quiet desperation.

"You said it's a flower farm?" McNeish said. "I can't quite imagine you as lady of the manor, Lina."

"It's not like that at all," I laughed. "I won't be dressing in chiffon and drinking gin at 11 a.m.. Well, not every day, I'm sure. I might write. I feel I could write something else here. There is enough space for that, enough space to create another world, or maybe even worlds. It's quiet and slow and I can hear myself think for the first time in years, Thomas. And what's more I'm not afraid to listen. Does that make sense?"

"Maybe," he said. "I have to say, I'm a little frightened of the listening myself. I've been doing this for so long, I don't know what else is in my head. If you take away the news, the global crises, the deadlines, the angles, I wonder if there will be anything else. I suppose I'll find out soon enough."

"Maybe *you'll* write a book," I said. He laughed.

McNeish might well have had a book in him. They say we all do but he would have had the skill and the discipline to get it out. He never had a chance though. He was dead by the end of that year. They said it was a heart attack but I wonder if it was the strain of listening.

Chapter 25

Stijn and I grew into each other like trees that over time become conjoined, the bark abrading until two merge into one. It wasn't always a smooth progression. Our arguments became legendary among the staff at Ol Mlima; as soon as my voice started rising, piercing the bungalow's thin walls, our housekeeper Mary and houseboy Joshua would hurry away to the back kitchen. They would take the wireless with them and turn it up loud so that in my memory, our rows always play to a soundtrack of Kenyan gospel songs. The only person who seemed unperturbed was Else. She could sit calmly in a wicker chair, reading her book or knitting, as our rage crashed around her. Or to be more accurate, while *my* rage crashed around her. Stijn was not given to sustained outbursts, which wound me up even more. He would start off strong, yelling back at me with his clipped, too-perfect sentences, but eventually, he would run out of steam, answering my tirades with a grunt, or a raised eyebrow or a one-line sarcastic dismissal. He made me furious and I drove him mad with what he called "your talking and talking and your needing and needing". He had me down pat.

Having eschewed love or even strong attachments for so many years, I threw myself into this relationship as though I had to feel everything as intensely as possible to make up for all the things I had buried for so long. As I was no longer working, Stijn became my sole focus, the source of all my emotions and the receptacle for all the fallout. He struggled with that. He too was having to adjust after years of being alone, answerable to no one.

One day, I exploded after he told me he was leaving for three days to visit flower farms in the west around Lake Kisumu. It must have been sometime in April 1965, just at the start of the rainy season.

"When are you leaving?"

"Now. Well, in the next 10 minutes or so. Why are you looking at me like that?"

He appeared genuinely bewildered.

"You're going to leave for three days, just like that, without asking me if I am okay with it, okay with being here on my own?"

"Of course," he said, a touch of irritation creeping into his voice. "Anyway, you will not be alone. Else will be here and all the staff. Why are you so annoyed?"

"Because you should ask me first, you fool."

"Why?"

"Because it is common courtesy. You can't just wander off without even asking. Maybe I had other plans?"

"What other plans? You don't do anything."

He didn't say it in a biting way. His tone was totally neutral. It was the matter-of-factness of it that drove me wild.

"What exactly is *that* supposed to mean?"

"What it means, of course. You do not have a job, Else manages the staff, I do the flowers, so you do nothing. Or am I wrong?"

It gives me no pleasure to admit that at that point, I threw the book I was holding at his head, turned on my heel and stomped out of the room. He didn't come after me – that was not Stijn's way – and a little while later, I heard the car sputter into life to take him to the airfield at the other side of the farm.

After a few hours of sulking on my bed, I realised that he was absolutely right, as usual. Stijn was maddeningly clear-sighted although like all of us, he was not immune to blind spots when it came to his own character. But on this occasion, I had to admit he was correct. I was doing nothing. I wrote the odd piece of journalism when asked to, commentary mostly. Despite waxing lyrical to McNeish about writing something else, I still hadn't taken the plunge into fiction. I wandered around the farm with Else. I followed Stijn into the greenhouses to check the roses and keep him company. I read voraciously. I tried painting but found I had no talent. Mary taught me to prepare a few Kenyan dishes – stodgy ugali, spicy githeri and the green sludge they called sukuma wiki that Stijn adored. But that was it. I was in truth doing very, very little. That was probably why we were sparking off each other like flints. I was almost always the instigator. Perhaps I was just bored, I realised with some surprise.

I climbed out from under the mosquito net and went downstairs to the room Stijn had given me as an office but which I had never used. I unearthed my typewriter from under a pile of invoices for bulbs and carried it out to the veranda. I called Joshua and asked him to bring me some chai and then I fed a blank page into the roller and sat back, fingers poised. Two hours later I was still sitting there, fingers still poised, having drunk two teapots of tea and having written precisely nothing.

Else wandered out, bronzed and capable in knee-length shorts and a crisp white shirt.

"So, he got under your skin again?" she said with a smile, flopping down into a chair. "You mustn't pay too much attention to what he says. He doesn't mean to be judgmental. He just says what he sees and he never thinks how this might affect the person he is talking too."

"I know, Else. But as is too often the case, he was right. I do nothing. I've done nothing in all the time I've been here. And that's no good."

"Maybe you needed to do nothing for a while," she said, helping herself to some tea. "Maybe you did too much and now you need to rest."

For a second, I thought about confiding in her. I could tell her everything and I knew that she would listen without judgment. But I held myself back. Else didn't ask for my problems. She didn't deserve the burden.

"What are you trying to do now?" she asked.

"I thought, with typical arrogance, that I might start writing a book. But it turns out you need ideas as well as a sulky disposition and an immature desire to prove yourself," I said, laughing.

"Well, if the words are not coming, why don't we go for a walk instead? I'm going down to the waterhole to clear my head. I've been looking over the books all morning and it's made me tense and nervous. My father has no patience for book-keeping and it really shows."

She went inside to get the rifle she always carried when travelling beyond the edge of the farm, then we pulled on Wellington boots and headed down the front lawn. The rains had cleared and although the ground was soggy and the drains running high and noisy, the sun was already turning the water to steam, giving everything an ethereal quality. Else pushed open the gate in the fence that divided Stijn's reclaimed patch from the surrounding bush and we followed the track that led through the knee-high scratchy grass, spiky euphorbia and umbrella acacia trees to the waterhole, about a mile away.

For a while we walked in silence. That was the thing with Else and Stijn. They never demanded conversation for its own sake. I must admit I found it by turn exhilarating and frustrating, depending on my mood. Sometimes their comfortable calm could weigh heavy on someone like me. Sometimes after an evening on the veranda together, I would get to bed and realise I had been talking almost exclusively to myself. I had mistaken their smiles for interventions. It made me feel silly and very secure at the same time.

"Do you plan to stay here forever, doing your father's books?" I asked.

"Maybe. I don't really like to make plans," Else said, her

eyes sweeping the horizon as we talked. There should be no elephants around but one couldn't rule out the possibility of a cheetah or leopard deciding to wander into the area to hunt. Our askari, or guards, tended to keep an eye on such things and alert us when there were new dangers but there always had to be a first sighting.

"I love it here. I tried Holland and that wasn't so good. I will stay here as long as he will have me, I suppose. I don't want to be anywhere else and I am quite happy to help with the flowers."

"What about your mother? What does she think?"

"My mother has her own life now. She has married again, she has a fine house in The Hague. She is happy and I am happy for her. But I don't want to live her life any more."

Else spoke without rancour or bitterness or any negative emotion that I could discern. I shook my head in wonder.

"You do not think this is good?" she asked, turning to me.

"No, I think it is great. You seem to have a very mature relationship with your parents."

"I don't really see them as parents. Not any more. They are just very nice people that I like to spend time with. Was it not the same for you with your parents?"

I tried to answer as honestly and briefly as I could – I was still being circumspect even then, Diane. Somewhat to my surprise, I concluded that I had always seen them first and foremost as parents. I felt a little guilty.

"Although, I never called my mother anything other than 'Charlotte'," I added. "I never knew why. It was just our way."

"I like it," Else said. "It seems better than defining our parents by their roles. Better to allow them to be their own people, their real selves. Maybe if we all called our parents by their names, we would have better relationships because there would not be all the expectations that come with the job descriptions."

"Perhaps," I said. "So, do you see Stijn as a man first and your father second?"

"I think so now. I hope so," she said, turning her grey eyes on me. "I like to think I feel for him as I do because of who he is and not just because of what he did for me, as my father."

"That's ambitious," I said. "I wonder if it is possible as a parent to ever see your child as anything other than your child?"

"You'll have to ask my father when he comes back. It'll give you something to talk about to break the ice after your argument," she said, smiling again.

We had reached the scraggy bluff overlooking the waterhole. We sat in the grass and as the sun began to set, we watched as zebras, gazelles and baboons came to drink, filling the damp, heavy air with their whinnies and cries and soothing my soul so that when I came back to the house, I wrote the opening pages of *Under the Canopy* in just over an hour. If you have read the book, you will now realise that I lifted some lines straight from that conversation with Else. I thrilled to the notion that we could somehow step outside our designated roles by rejecting the associated nomenclature. It was not just because Else's idea – that we could be more than our relationships – offered a justification for, or at least a mitigation of, my own actions. It was the dizzying freedom implicit in the concept. Sitting at that waterhole, watching zebras tiptoe delicately to the edge as baboons hooted around them, I felt as though everything had turned out all right. It was as though I had been given permission to enjoy my life. Or rather to finally acknowledge that I *was* enjoying my life, despite my guilt over what I had done. This slender, dark-haired Dutch girl with her frank eyes and singsong voice seemed to be saying it was okay.

When Stijn came back, I didn't ask him if he would always only see Else as his child. We would never have that kind of discussion and that was fine. Instead, I apologised and told him, shyly, that I had started to write a book.

"That is very good," he said. "That is what you were meant to do. And I think you know that too."

Those words, and his many encouraging comments afterwards, kept me going as I slowly pieced together that first novel. I wrote with abandon and deleted with equal fervour, with no thought of publication, just because it was the something to do that I had always been meant to do. I never completely recaptured that feeling of weightlessness in my subsequent novels. That is to be expected, I suppose. One's first book is always written out of a kind of delirious excitement, a child-like wonder at the magic and your role as magician. All the books that come after are burdened by the fear that comes with producing something, anything to order.

Despite Stijn's assertion that I was fulfilling my destiny, a question nagged at me, tugging at my brain so that I found myself writing ever more furiously, and if I am honest, ever more brilliantly just to silence it. Was I meant to do this to the detriment of all else? Did I have to abandon you in order to be able to fulfil my destiny as a writer? Even as I tried to quash the question, I heard an answer ring loud in the dark corners of my brain: Yes, this is what had to happen and you'd better make damn sure you succeed after paying so high a price.

I tried to tell Stijn how I felt, obliquely without giving too much away. I needed to voice what I was beginning to realise was the question at the very heart of my existence.

One evening, we were sitting on the veranda and the air was heavy with the promise of rain, the way you can sometimes feel a row brewing before a single word has been said. I had given Stijn my latest chapters and he was reading them silently as I paced up and down, swatting at mosquitoes, lighting more coils and generally making a nuisance of myself. I had to force myself not to look at his face as he rustled through the pages. That way madness lay. I couldn't quite bring myself to go inside and leave him in peace but neither did I want to inadvertently catch any twitch of the lips or raising of eyebrows that might puncture the fragile self-confidence that is the only thing that separates a writer from a dreamer.

Finally, out of the corner of my eye, I saw him look up and remove his glasses.

"It is good. I like it. Maybe a bit too wordy at first but it gets better as you go along. Well done, Lina."

My heart sank. Of course, one never hears the praise, however much one tries to be mature and balanced and receptive. I only heard "wordy". I stomped to the wicker sofa beside his chair and collapsed onto it, covering my face with my hands and moaning, "I knew it was rubbish. I knew it."

When I removed my hands, Stijn was grinning at me. He swung his lanky frame onto the sofa, took my hands in his and turned what I called his grey headlamps full-beam onto me.

"Even for you, Lina, this is ridiculous. I said it was good. I made a small critic, is that what you call it?"

"Criticism," I said. "And no criticism can ever be small. I knew it, I knew I was out of my depth."

"You are not out of your depth. But you are learning to swim and you can only try to improve. That is all I was saying."

"You don't understand," I cried, pulling my hands away. I was worn out after a sleepless night, tormented by mosquitoes and buzzing self-doubt, and I had struggled all day with writing what I hoped would be the climax of the book. Of course, it wasn't. If I remember correctly, I scrapped that whole section a few weeks later. I was also quite drunk having decided at around 4 o'clock that a gin and tonic might oil whatever jammed synapses were holding up my creative process. Stijn, as ever, was right in the path of this toxic current.

"I have to be good at this," I yelled. "There is nothing else. I thought being a good journalist was enough but I didn't change anything really. It didn't matter. Not in the grand scheme of things. So, this is my last chance."

"Lina, you are making no sense. Your last chance at what? And why last? Are you planning to leave, to go somewhere else? Are you dying?"

"No, you fool," I said, standing up and pacing and hating myself for pacing like a classic hysterical woman. It was as though I couldn't even live without being clichéd, much less write without using clichés.

"You don't understand. You don't understand what it has taken to get here, to get to this moment, to be on the cusp of doing something that might, just might, justify everything else. If I am meant to do this but I am still not good enough to stand apart, where does that leave me? What does that say about the life I have lived, the people who had to die so that I could go on, the people I lost, the sacrifices that I and everyone else made so that this life could be what I wanted it to be?"

Stijn said nothing. He always let me vent and not just because he knew I would anyway, with or without interruptions. I believe he also kept quiet because he wanted to really listen, to fully understand what I was trying to say. He was that rare creature who does not need to be talking or doing to know that he exists. He never needed an audience to prove to himself who he was.

"You know, Lina, everyone who survived the war lived because others died. That is the nature of life. But it is the nature of life even in peacetime. You miss a plane and someone dies in the seat that would have been yours. You leave the house earlier than usual and the car that was travelling too fast smashes into someone else. It does not mean that your life is more valuable or that those who died were less valuable. It does not mean that you have to do something wonderful. It may be difficult to accept but there is no meaning of that kind. These are just things that happen. Death is just a thing that happens, like having blue eyes or finding a coin in the road."

I almost told him then, Diane. That was the moment to tell this strong man that I had had a daughter, as he had, but that I had abandoned her because I believed there was no other way, because I didn't have a partner to whom I could have passed the burden for however long it took me to pull myself together and rediscover the maternal love that society demanded of me. But I didn't tell him, Diane. I didn't have the courage of my convictions, if indeed we can truly believe that my conviction was that I had had no choice. I suppose we must conclude from all I have written here that I have never been as sure of my innocence as I pretended at the start of this letter. Maybe I am not as free-thinking as I believed. Maybe I always knew what I did was wrong. A sin against motherhood, against you, against a society that could not survive if all women behaved as I did.

In truth, Diane, I have never been able to disentangle my own reckoning from the reckoning of society. I have tried; I have faked nonchalance, I have run away, I have reinvented myself, but in the end I have never managed to quash those voices that said, and still say, that I did wrong.

At that moment, on the veranda in Kenya, I didn't believe that Stijn could manage it either. And as the years went by, it became harder and harder to run the risk that he would not understand, that he would not forgive. To tell him would be to become another in his eyes – a mother, worse, an absent mother. He might doubt my capacity for love. I could not bear the thought.

And so that day and all the days that followed, I stayed silent. I hid my biggest secret from the man I loved and we were happy. We created a life for ourselves there in the Kenyan bush. Might it have been otherwise if our meeting in Brighton had ended differently, Diane? Perhaps. But these are the parallel tracks that run alongside our lives, the paths we didn't take. Maybe there is another Lina – a quieter, calmer, less successful, more rounded Lina – walking along one of those paths. If so, I wish her well. In all honesty though, I still don't believe I could travel beside her.

Chapter 26

It is time to revisit our meeting in Brighton, Diane. It is the only shared memory we have as I can't imagine you still remember those months we spent together at the beginning of our story. Do you? I wish you were here beside me to answer my questions directly. I have not heard from you so I assume that means I failed to convince you to come and see me. I did not win you over, despite my lauded writing skills. Was it the emotion you found wanting? Never mind. The moment has passed. I always suspected this would be a monologue. Here is my side of the Brighton meeting,. For this part of the manuscript, you will be my editor. I hope you have your red pen at the ready.

Why did I decide to seek you out in 1967? I had built a new life for myself in Kenya. The book was coming along nicely. I was becoming happier with what I had written and more than that, I knew, despite my doubts and my regular ranting to Stijn, that I would finish it. Publication was still a dream but I suppose the thought was there.

In the end, it was this sense of fulfilment, of contentment, that spurred me to get your address and telephone number from the adoption agency and to return to England to see you. The agency told me very little, stressing that you might not want to see me and that that was your prerogative. I detected a note of disapproval in the brief letter they sent me. I imagined a stern-faced woman with tight curls and tighter lips angrily typing and commenting about women who wanted to have their cake and eat it too.

Something else was driving me. Else. I was growing closer to her and increasingly, unforgivably, I found myself searching her face for signs of the child I had given up. One day, we were eating sandwiches on the roof of Stijn's Land Rover in the Aberdare National Park, keeping our eyes peeled for elephants and buffalo. Else was giggling at one of Stijn's jokes, her hair was escaping in tendrils from the bun at the back of her head and the hot weather had brought out the freckles across the bridge of her nose. As I looked from Stijn to his daughter, I realised that I was in love with both of them. I was in love with an 'us' as I had been with Robert when I believed that together we were more than ourselves, that we were indestructible. I felt my throat constrict. I coughed loudly and they both looked anxiously at me. I waved away their concern, grabbing Stijn's bottle of Tusker beer and gulping deeply. I looked again at Else. I found myself wondering if your hair had darkened, if you had freckles, if you ever laughed with such abandon that your mouth fell open. I knew what I had to do. Before I could fall in love any further, I had to try to see you. You had to be real to me so that I could not easily replace you with another woman.

I flew into Heathrow in mid-May and stayed at a hotel near the airport. I wasn't sure if you would agree to see me and I didn't know what I would do if you refused. I could go to St Albans and visit the graves of my dead, I could travel into London, or I could turn on my heel and return to Kenya. All I really wanted was to see you. I couldn't think beyond that and as I wandered around the terminal, trying to find my way to the taxi rank, I realised I was not sure if I dared venture any further into a country that had changed so much since I left it almost two decades before. My life in Kenya still had a nebulous quality. I worried that if I ventured too far I wouldn't be able to find my way back to the wardrobe and the door that had magically opened to offer me a new life of sunshine, flowers and Stijn.

Later in the hotel, my hands shook as I dialled your number. It rang three times. Do you remember? Who did you think it was? Were you expecting another call? I closed my eyes as I waited. Surely, there would be an immediate connection. Surely an image of you would flash before my eyes. Wasn't that what blood was for?

You answered and I felt a rush of the most debilitating shame twinned with a gut-wrenching joy. I squeezed my eyes shut tighter and saw your face when I gave you away. I sat down heavily on the bed. I would have hung up but it would have required superhuman strength to prise my white fingers from the phone.

"Hello?" Your voice was testier now, hurried. I had put you out already.

Do you remember what I said, Diane? I can't. I remember silences I think I begged. You agreed but you were reluctant. I felt like you were saying yes to get me off the phone, out of your life again. But I was too grateful to worry about my dignity.

Two days later, I waited in front of the Odeon on the seafront at Brighton. I didn't think you would come. I was wearing a red rose in my buttonhole. I had brought it all the way from Ol Mlima because I knew I would need to suggest something when you asked how you would recognise me. I thought one of Stijn's roses would be a good omen. It was, of course, a loaded choice.

I was looking the other way when someone said: "Lina?"

I wish I could say I recognised you straight away. That would be a lie. Later, I found myself in your terse laugh, I saw Robert in your eyes and around your lips and chin, but in that moment, as you stood an arm's length from me, you were just a stranger, someone who could have asked me for the time and who I might have remembered later because of your clear unflinching gaze and the strong lines of your young face.

We did not hug. We stood looking at each other. I suppose I will never know now what you were thinking. I can tell you what I thought. I thought, My God, she is so beautiful. She is alive. She is fine. She grew up. What is she thinking, my God, what is she thinking?

After some awkward small talk – how was my hotel, did I like Kenya, how long was I staying, were you enjoying art school – we walked across the path and stumbled our way over the pebbles and onto the thin ledge of sand by the sea. It felt good to be doing something together. The noise of the pebbles underfoot, the wind in our ears and the waves rushing to shore filled the awkward silences. We walked along by the water for a while, you setting the pace, always a few steps ahead so that I struggled to keep up with your retreating back. I kept opening my mouth to speak but the words died on my lips. We were never going to relive two lives in a few hours, I reasoned, and in the end, we did not have even that much time.

You stopped and stared out to sea. I stood by your side, noting silently that you were a few inches taller than me. At one point, a strand of your hair slid across my cheek. It was the first and only time our bodies touched that day.

"Why?" you said. Actually, I thought you said "I". I waited for more but I could barely hear you above the waves. I leaned in. You shuffled away.

"What?"

"Why? Why did you come now?"

"I don't know. I wanted to see you. I needed to see you. I thought it was time. I thought it was time for both of us."

I am sorry, Diane. It was such a terrible answer. My failure to express myself clearly that day is another reason why I had to write this long, long letter to you. I was too overwhelmed by your presence to be able to think clearly. How to put into words what I could barely explain to myself? I couldn't tell you about Else without telling you about Stijn and I could not do that on an empty, cold beach near a spray-peppered pier, the very sight of which catapulted me back to that day on the pier in Felixstowe with Robert.

"Okay. You needed to see me and now you've seen me. Is that enough to assuage whatever guilt or longing or long-delayed maternal instinct you're feeling?"

I flinched at your tone. Your eyes were hard on my face.

"You have your father's eyes."

I blurted it out without thinking.

"No, these are my eyes, in my face. I am not yours or my father's. You do not have a right to label any part of me."

You started walking again.

"I don't know how much they told you about us," I said as I struggled to keep up, my feet feeling leaden and old on the wet sand. "They said you wanted to know at 18 and they gave you our names and where we were from. I don't know whether they gave you much other information."

I thought you nodded. I rushed on, my words falling over each other in their haste to leap out and hold you back. I knew I was losing you.

"So I am Lina, Lina Rose. Your father was Robert Stirling and he... well, he killed himself after the war, after you were born. We lived in St Albans. I gave you up because... "

You turned around then.

"Yes?"

"Because I thought it was the only way I could survive. I thought it was the only way that *we* could survive. I wasn't able to care for you. Robert died and my parents soon afterwards and... I was broken."

"But you were able to head off and make quite the career for yourself? Oh yes, I've looked you up in the archives at the library. You are quite the celebrity, Mother. Or should I call you Lina? Which name do you *need* most?"

I bit my lip to hold back the tears. I hadn't expected hugs and flowers but I wasn't prepared for this either. It was stupid of me. How could I not have foreseen that you would feel as furious as I did when Robert died? More furious, in fact, because I had not died. I left. And to add insult to injury, I had not only survived, I had thrived.

"I don't *need* any name. You don't have to call me anything. We don't have to ever meet again if you don't want to. I just wanted to give you the opportunity to meet. In case *you* needed it."

I still wasn't saying what I wanted to say. I stamped my foot in frustration, the way I do now when the words on the page do not do what I thought they would do, what I told them to do.

Do you remember what you said then, Diane? I imagine you do. It is not an easy thing for either of us to forget.

"I don't need any opportunities from you. I wish you'd piss off and leave me alone. You've had a look, I'm fine, I've grown up, no thanks to you, and there you go. You can head off again now, conscience soothed and do whatever the hell it is you do wherever the hell you want to do it. Yes, I looked you up and yes, I wanted to know who my real parents were, but it was nothing more than idle curiosity, Lina. I feel no connection to you. Why should I? You gave me up. You're just a middle-aged, sun-wrinkled woman standing in the wind on a beach I don't even like. You could be anyone. That's what you wanted, I imagine. And whatever guilt that drove you here, rest assured. I don't need it. I don't need your guilt, I don't need your interest and I don't want you in my life. Okay?"

"I'm so sorry," I said, crying now. "I wish I could—"

"What? Turn back time? But do you really? Don't you really want to leave time as it was but nonetheless find yourself here as you are now with a more obliging, grateful daughter? I suppose you wanted me to hug you and cry on your shoulder. You'd have had a ready-made daughter and I'd have had another Mum and life would go on, broader and better than before? Isn't that what you really want? Well, I'm afraid that is not on offer here today, Lina."

You stomped off up the beach, stumbling and slipping

on the pebbles. I wanted to run after you, to hold you in my arms.

"Diane! Wait, Diane!" I started after you and that's when you yelled back: "My name is Maria. I am not your Diane. She doesn't exist."

Nine months inside me, a birth, 14 months together, 30 minutes on a beach, a lifetime of wondering and now this long letter. Is it enough? Or is our connection too tenuous to bear the weight of my expectations, the weight of this letter, my last and best work? Diane, I was wrong. I was mistaken. I was weak. But I was also right and correct and strong. I have parallel universes inside me. We all do, I suppose. It is how we survive. We do what we must to survive. Can one be guilty if one didn't have a choice? I hear that question echo through the ages, through me and Robert and Henry and you, yes you, Diane. Are you guilty for closing your heart to me? I will say no. I will absolve us all here because I truly believe that we are compelled by events beyond our control to do the things we do to build the lives we need.

I left England the next day, flying back to Kenya in a daze. I believed I would never see you again and the knowledge punctured me. But it also liberated me. I had seen you, you were fine, you had grown up and you were making your own choices. I had not destroyed your life for I had seen you so wonderfully, incandescently alive. I was devastated and vindicated and I have never been able to reconcile these feelings. I returned to Ol Mlima, I worked on my book, I fell deeper in love with Stijn, I grew closer to Else, I started to dye my greying hair, I worried about my expanding waist, I endured the menopause and I continued to thrive, my darling. I am sorry.

That would probably have been the end of my story but for one persistent mosquito and the bite I received while writing on our veranda one evening in March, 1973. A few days later, Stijn flew to the coast to visit some of his suppliers. He was also going to spend a few nights with some Dutch friends in

Watamu before flying back. He left on Wednesday, March 13th. I already felt a little off and my brain seemed fuzzy but I put it down to too many hours at the typewriter and too many glasses of gin the night before. By the next day, my bones were aching, my head was pounding and I could feel a fever drilling down to the very core of me. I knew it was malaria. Else put me to bed and sent one of the guards to buy quinine in the pharmacy in Naivasha. It took him three hours to make the trip and by the time he got back, I was almost delirious. I took the quinine but instead of getting better, I got worse. My body was wracked by chills and then scalded by fever, over and over again, the same malicious cycle until I felt as though I would actually quite like to die.

On the 15th, Else found a doctor who could come to the farm. He was a retired army medic from Somerset, a gruff man with an extravagant moustache who came with no instruments, no time and no bedside manner.

"Well, I can't see why you had to call me at all," he scolded Else as she stood by the bed. He had taken my temperature, looked in my eyes and ears and asked me to lift my arms and move my head from side to side. I was shaking with the cold, but sweat was still pouring off me. At least, the delirium that came with the fever had lifted for a while. I could concentrate fully on what he was saying.

"It's perfectly clear that she has cerebral malaria. You need to get her to a hospital and you need to do it now. Any fool could have told you that."

I tried to raise myself from the pillows so I could tell the old curmudgeon not to speak to Else like that. I could see that she was biting her lip to hold back the tears. I felt dreadful for having put her in such a position, disdained by a pickled geriatric who had spent too much time telling too many people what to do.

And that is why I said what I did. No good deed ever goes unpunished, Diane. That is the thing to remember.

"Don't be so rude. She's doing her best. Please Else, try

to get hold of your father. He can come back and take care of me. If he comes tonight, he can take me to Nairobi tomorrow. I don't want you to have to worry about it. Call him and I can explain everything to him."

The doctor harrumphed and muttered something about the dangers of delaying but I had no desire to humour his arrogance.

"I'll explain to Stijn when you call him. He can talk to me and then he'll come and we'll go to Nairobi in the morning. Okay?"

Else nodded, the doctor left and everything was not okay.

Twenty minutes later, I fell into a fever and when I woke up, Else had called Stijn, he was on his way and I had set in motion a chain of events that would change my life again. That afternoon, the oppressive heat that had been building above our heads, pushing the acacia trees and the euphorbia deeper into the ground, cracked, sending shards of lightning and thunderbolts shooting across the bush. I drifted in and out of consciousness, alternately shivering and sweating, straining in my more lucid moments to hear a plane flying overhead, or a car on the gravel drive. By mid-afternoon, rain was pounding on the corrugated iron roof. The noise killed all thought, drumming me deeper into delirium so that my dreams were full of marauding hooves, strangers hammering at locked doors and armies storming down hills. And bombs, of course. Bombs squealing as they fell as though they too were horrified by what they were doing.

When I woke up hours later, I was alone, exhausted but free from fever. I felt as though I'd been vigorously washed and wrung out by ladies with beefy arms and hardened faces, the tight-faced women who sat on doorsteps on Hatfield Road when I was a child. I sat up, my head spinning. Then, I heard it: an absolute silence. The rainstorm had subsided but it was more than that. I could hear my own breathing; I could hear my own heart.

I hauled myself out of bed and pulled myself along until I

found my feet again and could reach the door. I headed down the corridor, peeking into Else's room as I passed. It was empty. I continued down the corridor and heard something. The slightest of sounds, barely a movement of the air around me, but I heard it. I got to the rain-dimmed living room and wondered why Joshua had not lit the lamps, why the grate was empty. Something moved on the veranda and I pulled back the French doors. The air was rich and wet and full of false promise. The clouds had broken and the setting sun had turned the fresh puddles into mirrors. Grasshoppers were clicking, somewhere an animal brayed and heavy drops were still falling from the sloping roof. Under the familiar sounds of a rain-drenched land, I heard Else sobbing quietly. She was on a chair in the corner and the rainwater had pooled at her feet so that for a moment I thought she was sitting in a puddle of her own tears. She had pulled up her legs and placed her arms on top and her head on top of that. It was as though she was trying to make herself as small as possible. But it didn't matter. Bad news, Fate, destiny, call it what you will, it had already found her.

Sobbing and gulping for air, she told me what had happened as the sun set in a blaze of red-and-gold so that it seemed like all that colour bleeding into the bush was coming from our pain. Stijn was dead, she said. The police had been. They'd found the plane in the foothills of Mount Kenya. He must have been blown off course, they said. Or he'd deviated from the route to avoid the storm, they said. He might not have known how bad it was, they said. Especially if he set off in a hurry, without making all the required final checks, they said. Else spoke in a flat voice. I knew that sound.

I comforted her as best I could. Mary came silently, placing a tray with a teapot and two cups on the table. She had already adjusted. We were two now and there would be no need for three cups any more. Mary brought me a blanket to wrap around my shoulders and her brow creased as she whispered that we should perhaps move inside. But Else and

I stayed where we were, squeezed into the same wicker chair, arms locked around each other, until the sun had gone and the moon rose, proving that the world would continue even without Stijn in it.

They brought his body home the next day. Mary and Joshua lined up with the rest of the staff as the flatbed truck with the plain pine coffin lashed onto the back struggled through the deep puddles gouged into the gravel driveway. It was raining again, the sky was low, squeezing the light out of the air so that all around us the land seemed quelled and colourless. Stijn's friend and business partner Wilhelm, a gruff giant of a man adored by both Else and Stijn, jumped out of the driver's seat and took off his broad-brimmed hat as he came across to where Else and I were waiting on the veranda. He shook my hand solemnly and then Else threw herself into his arms.

I heard him whisper to her in Dutch, the same words over and over. There was no one to comfort me, not this time. I longed to feel Charlotte's arms around me, more than I ever had since her death. But I knew with excruciating clarity that there would never more be any arms to hold me. That's when I broke down, startling Else and Wilhelm with my sudden sobbing. Else stumbled over to me and tried to pull me into an embrace, but I couldn't bear it. I walked away, out into the rain, up to the truck, caring not that everyone's eyes were on me, all watching as I placed my hand on the box and whispered: "I'm sorry, so very sorry, Stijn."

If I hadn't sat out on the veranda that night to write, if I hadn't fallen ill, if I hadn't urged Else to call him, to summon him home. As I bent over the coffin, my forehead on the wooden lid, I tried to remember what our last words to each other were. He'd kissed me softly on the lips as he walked through the kitchen. I think he said, "See you later", but it could have been "Goodbye". I couldn't remember if he'd used my name. Did I tell him I loved him? Sometimes I did but I couldn't remember now. Stijn rarely said those words and never as a goodbye. It was simply not in his nature.

Later, Wilhem told us that no one was quite sure how Stijn drifted off course, although they suspected the plane might have been hit by lightning and that that affected the controls. I insisted on seeing the body. Else declined.

"I do not need to see his body, Lina. If you are happy to do it, please go ahead but then close the coffin on him. I do not need to see him now to remember him. I have all the memories I need. What is in that box is nothing more than a shell. I do not want that to be how I remember him. I do not need to go there to say goodbye. I am going to go to the waterhole to say goodbye to him in my own way."

She left with Wilhelm. As ever, she carried her rifle and she did not take the arm he offered, instead walking ahead of him, her long legs propelling her across the lawn so that he was forced to run to keep up. I hoped he would be able to catch her but Else could be stubborn. Like her father, she cherished her independence. She needed space as he had done. That was why they were here, on the banks of a giant lake in a wilderness so vast, it made the flower farm seem like a misplaced English front garden.

I headed back into the house, shivering as the malaria pulsed the last of its deadly load through my blood. The staff had carried the coffin into the dining room and surrounded it with tall glass vases filled with birds of paradise from the garden and roses from the greenhouses. They must have been preparing all day. A few elderly Samburu women were clustered in a corner, singing. When I came in, they rose to their feet and shuffled out, moving together like a single being. They did not look at me directly, understanding no doubt that my grief needed no witnesses. Their crooning and keening was meant to fill the house and perhaps to distract me from the screaming inside my head. I had never understood this tradition before. I did now.

The staff had taken the lid off the coffin. Stijn's hands were bandaged and there was an unreal sheen to his face. His features seemed to have melted at the edges so that in death, he looked older. He looked dead. It was also because of that damned suit. Someone – I did not know who – had dressed him in the cream suit he was wearing when we first met in Nairobi. It was his one suit and all the years we were together, he only wore it a handful of times for weddings, meetings with government ministers and, of course, funerals. He cared nothing for the tradition of wearing black. He said he couldn't think of anything less meaningful and that was that. He didn't expand.

As I stood looking at him, I realised how much I was going to miss his unflinching certainty, the terse one-liners that tested my patience but also made me feel that the world might actually make sense. My legs felt weak, my heart was racing and tears were flowing down my cheeks. I went to one of the vases, pulled out a Lina rose and laid it on top of his bandaged hands.

"*Safari njema*," I said. "Travel well, Stijn. I thought we would be together until the end. Such a stupid idea, especially for me, but I did really think that."

Chapter 27

We buried Stijn under a whistling thorn tree on a hill at the edge of the farm. I continued writing my book at his graveside, sitting in the tree's shade at a small wooden table that Joshua carried from the house for me. I didn't know what else to do, Diane. So for two months, I sat by his side, typing and talking and finding solace in the silence that would forever more be his answer to all of my questions. It was a rich silence: grasses rustling, the plaintive whistle of the wind passing through the black gourd-like thorns above me, the shrieking of a fish eagle swerving over the lake. Stijn's silence was the crackling quiet of the bush. His strength found its reflection in the power of the sun. The sight of animals lolloping to the waterhole below reminded me of his slow smile as he raised binoculars to his eyes.

There on that hill, I rebuilt myself and prepared for another life. I didn't realise it at the time but with every word I typed, I was saying goodbye to Stijn, Kenya and Africa. Every chapter, every sentence, every change and every edit was leading me to another place. I finished *Under the Canopy* and immediately started *The Ultimatum*. I still had no specific plan to publish anything. I just knew that I needed to be writing. I must write all the time.

Else and Wilhelm grew closer and a month or so later, he moved into the farmhouse. They never made me feel anything less than welcome but I knew it was time to go. I booked my flight back to England in late May. Else drove me to Nairobi to spend my last night in a hotel in the centre of town. It was a subdued, strangely awkward farewell – a last meal in a too-bright restaurant with bland food and canned music designed to make tourists feel at home. We sat in a corner and found little to say. After so many years together and the shock of Stijn's death, there was too much between us and so we said nothing of consequence. But really, who does have consequential conversations at such moments? It can only happen in fiction when the author eschews authenticity in favour of the deeper, more meaningful truths that we rarely manage to voice in the real world. Yet another reason to love fiction, Diane: it elevates the mundane to the extraordinary by pretending that we all manage to say what should be said at critical moments.

We discussed where I might live in St Albans, my hopes that I would keep writing and my tentative plans to seek an agent. Else told me she would try to keep the farm going, with Wilhelm's help. The flower business had been hit hard by the global recession but she thought they could hang on.

"It's not just loyalty to my father. That would be futile. He is no longer here so pretending to do something for him would be foolish," she said. The tremor in her voice belied her words but of course, one can hold both pragmatism and a kind of idealistic love in the same heart.

She promised to come and visit and I believe she meant it and I meant it when I said that would be wonderful. But seated in that half-empty restaurant under a lumbering fan with twitchy-eyed waiters poised to grab our plates as soon as we paused eating, it was hard to imagine either of us in St Albans. Our mutual promises shone too bright under the fluorescent lights, like puddle mirages on a straight hot road.

We drove to the airport early in the morning, speeding through streets where the sun's scalpel carved slivers of light into the night's shade. Men, women and children walked in tidy lines on either side of the highway. In the rising sun's rays, they were faceless, austerely beautiful silhouettes, like the polished ebony statues sold in craft markets. Sometimes, we can be more than we are and we don't even know it.

"I won't come in, if you don't mind," Else said as we drew up outside the terminal. "Now, it is time to say our goodbyes. Otherwise, we will end up wishing our last minutes together away. We will be uncomfortable and then we will be grateful to be alone and that would not be true to how we feel."

We parked and a porter grabbed my two suitcases and typewriter. He looked on impassively, the straps loose in his hands, the bags limp on the pavement, as we hugged, letting all the emotion of the last weeks finally break free in the most absurdly public place. Maybe we needed the eyes of others to allow us to let down our guards without falling to pieces.

"He really did love you," Else whispered.

"Oh darling, you don't have to tell me," I said. "I know that. I always knew that."

"And I loved you too. I love you now," she said. "But I understand why you are going. If it were not for Wilhelm and the farm, I might do the same. I would look for a new world where he had never been."

I tried to smile.

"You don't have to leave, Else. You are already in the world without him and you are still standing. It will be painful but you have your life here. He would not want you to go. But I must leave because I do need a new world. Stijn was my life and this was his world. Without him, I feel like a boat cut loose on a foreign sea."

I stepped away and the porter shouldered my bags with an ostentatious grunt. I almost smiled. He was earning his tip even though my bags were so light I could have carried them myself. I hadn't taken much. Everything Stijn and I bought together belonged at Ol Mlima. How could it be otherwise?

"Do you think it was our fault? Did we do this by calling him back?"

Else was clutching my sleeve. She had been working up to

this question – it was in the bags under her eyes and the new lines that had etched themselves into her forehead. With a jolt, I realised she wasn't a girl any more. In that moment, the 10 years I had spent in a kind of happy daze in Kenya caught up with me. Else was no longer a girl, I was beyond middle age and Stijn was gone. His death would be a permanent epilogue to this part of my life. It really was over.

Else was waiting for an answer. She might be a woman now but she needed me to be the adult, to banish this bogeyman and I was ready. I had asked myself the same question many times: in the still, terrifying hours before dawn, in the oppressive silence before drifting into oblivion in my empty bed and as I walked around the waterhole, my hand reaching for one that was no longer there.

"Who do you think was responsible for me meeting Stijn at that garden party?" I said. "Was it my fault for stopping to rest by that tree or his for pausing to talk to me? Why did he go to the coast? Was it his fault or the suppliers in Mombasa who invited him down? Did he need a break from me, from us? Was he bored and if so, who was to blame for that? Why did I choose to come to Kenya after Paris? Can we place the blame for all of this at my editor's door? After all, he approved my request to move. We could. He's dead. He won't mind. But if we are to be honest, Else, and you know Stijn would have wanted us to be truthful, we must acknowledge that we can no more assign blame for what has happened than we can decide who makes the rain fall. In the end, there can be no pure reckoning, no accurate appraisal of what we have done and what we have failed to do. Since we cannot know for sure, it is better not to speculate. Trust me on this, my dear. This is not my first time on this particular merry-go-round."

I stroked her hair and turned to go but she still looked confused. I tried again. I had to remember she was new to this game.

'I don't know why Stijn died, Else. However, since things

cannot be different now, since nothing we do or say or think can change what has happened, we cannot indulge in guilt or regret. They diminish us because they make more of life than it is and that makes less of us and of what we endure. His death was one of the things that happen. No more, no less. Like finding a coin on the road. That is all, no matter how much we want to believe in something else."

I left then, knowing I had not really managed to banish her doubts. She might carry them to her grave. Some truths we each have to discover for ourselves.

It took me a while to find my feet in St Albans. I hid in a hotel for a week, barely leaving my room, sleeping and crying and watching television. It was a kind of hibernation and although I was not reborn, I did not die. Again. A few weeks later, I bought the house I now live in. It's near the centre of St Albans, a few streets behind the medieval clock tower. I did look at some properties on Folly Lane but everything had changed so much. In the end, I decided that it made no sense to park myself on a road that bore no resemblance to the street where we had lived. Proximity would only have increased my sense of displacement.

In those first months, as I told you earlier, I was lost, unable to find my feet in this town that had known another me. I could not truly imagine that I might have the energy to start again. To be honest, I doubted I had enough time to try. Stijn's death brought mortality knocking at my door. I believed I was on borrowed time. I am of that generation, Diane. We still think 50 marks old age. We are not wrong but where we fail is in our inability to understand that there is so much old age to be lived now. I told you about walking my way back into a kind of sanity and through all those lost months, I never stopped writing. It was my saving grace. I edited *Under the Canopy*, completed my first draft of *The Ultimatum*, wrote short stories and poems. I tamed my despair and my loneliness by refusing to live in this world, by seeking other shores and inventing my own certainties. Eventually, I realised my writing was more than just therapy, more than just a hobby. It was good. Ambition rescued me again.

I found an agent and then a publisher and from there, I was able to construct another Lina Rose, the woman the world believes I am still and the woman they will mourn when I die. I am pleased: she is my finest creation and if she lacks my faults, we share her writerly virtues. She is witty and erudite. She is arrogant and supercilious, but that is permissible because she is a literary heavyweight and art can excuse anything. Lina scorns the festival circuit but will occasionally write a thoughtful piece on a modern literary trend for the broadsheets. She uses the same photo for all of her dust jackets. It is shamefully outdated now – more sleight of hand – but glamour sells and it is one of my favourites.

Stijn took the picture on Lake Naivasha in 1965, I think. I am in a rowing boat, squinting slightly into the sun. My hair is up in a loose bun and tendrils frame my face. I am neither young nor beautiful but I cut a striking figure with the water and bush behind me and the sun lighting my face, smoothing the wrinkles. Most of my readers will know that I am older now but I was that woman too and she is the one who decided to write. That Lina was the one who discovered, as Stijn said, that she was born to write.

I wrote steadily for nearly 20 years. I then stopped after I published *The Starfish and the Pearl* in 1991. After addressing our relationship, however obliquely, I found I had no more stories to tell. For the past six years, I have produced very little beyond filler pieces for newspapers' book sections; some reviews of books that seem increasingly bound to disappoint me, and a handful of short stories that I freely admit are trinkets, all sparkle and sass but with very little substance. It's not that I suffered from writer's block. I never felt frustrated. It was more like a natural winding down, a diminution of desire. I turned 70 and I felt increasingly outpaced by the world. I still do. This is the only story I could imagine writing.

You may wonder what I have been doing since 1991. What could an old lady like me, a woman who rejected all the codes and conventions, be doing in the winter of her life? I wish I could tell you I have been living in painful solitude. There would be some relief for you there, perhaps. If I could tell you that I've been lonely for years, that my success meant nothing in the dark of the night, would that make you happy? It is the worst kind of hypothetical question because I have not been alone. Lonely, yes, sometimes, but not alone. I should have been. I know.

What I am going to tell you now, Diane, will hurt, perhaps more than everything else. I know I promised the truth and what I have told you here is the truth. It is just not the whole truth. I needed to keep some secrets until now. I was playing a high-stakes game and unfortunately I lost. You did not come. But I knew the odds and I knew the risks and in the end, I expected to lose.

I told you I was not dying and that is true, insofar as I can tell. But death is not the only thing to fear. I forgot that as I patted myself on the back for ageing so very productively, for seizing the winter of my life by the neck and forcing it to yield to the talent I was born to display.

Remember I said I craved oblivion. Be careful what you wish for, Diane.

I am losing myself. Soon, very soon now, I will not know who I am, what I did or what I failed to do. I will remember none of the stories I have told you in this long, long letter. My ghosts are already fading. It turns out their immortality depends on the living. We are their keepers. Without us, they die again too. I trust I have saved some souls by bequeathing my ghosts to you.

I didn't expect it to be like this. I expected to die, to vanish. At one time, I craved the end. What I didn't plan for is this living death. It is perhaps my due. But it does seem a little harsh, my darling.

A little harsh and bitterly just. I will finally forget all the things I hid for so long. It is, in the end, the only way I can forgive myself. Forget to forgive, that is my Fate. The only absolution I can offer myself comes at the price of losing my mind.

You remember I spoke before about parallel universes, those galaxies where our other possible lives run along on the tracks we did not choose. It is a handy way to come to terms with what is about to happen to me. I will be here but not here. I will be me but not me. I wonder if somewhere the real Lina will live on, wandering down another path, while this one falls down the holes that gape like ravens' jaws inside my own brain.

If you decide to come now, at this 11th hour, I will likely not recognise you. I didn't write these words just a week ago. The temporal gap between us has been an illusion. I have been sneaky until the last, I'm afraid, but this deception was born of love, I hope. I had to do it this way to prove to myself that I was really doing this for you and for you alone. Or at least, mostly for you because there is no such thing as pure altruism. I simply can't believe in it.

You were always behind the curve, darling. It was the only way. If you had come when you got that first letter, in June, I would have still been here but I am nearly gone now. Or at least the woman who wrote these letters is no longer running the show.

What you have been reading is history and I, dear Diane, am also history. When I concocted this plan in the long, dark days of January at home in St Albans, I did intend to send the letters each week, as I said I was doing at the start of this exercise, but my Alzheimer's had other plans. I started to deteriorate faster than expected. I had been told this was a risk. I was given a list of the symptoms, the warning signs they call them, although I cannot see the point of a warning if there is nothing that can be done. My prognosis was initially good, although some of the long-haired young doctor's upbeat analysis was probably a result of his belief that I had already lived a good life and that every day was a blessing. I forgave him his chirpiness because I liked the way his green glass earring flashed at me while he talked. He too will have to learn that a long life is never long enough while a short one is always too long.

Just before I came here to this cottage on the beach, I could feel myself losing my grip on reality. Everyday words were disappearing. I stumbled and bumped into furniture that hadn't moved in years. I struggled with simple concepts. I forgot appointments. I could not remember how to use the television and I got lost walking home from the corner shop. It is a terrible thing to watch the world slipping away, to feel yourself drifting from the shore and to know that there is nothing, absolutely nothing, you can do to get back.

I realised I had to change my plans. I arrived here in April, not June, and in writing this in the way I have, I have bent time so that what you think is the present is in fact the past. This voice you hear in your head, my voice, has already probably been silenced by a disease named after a German psychiatrist who died of heart failure during the Great War and who probably never realised how his name would become a byword for the worst kind of living death. As confusion sought to take a firmer hold of my faculties, I wrote faster, furiously, sometimes all night in those first weeks here. I did not send you the first letter immediately because I was concerned that I might not be allowed to finish, that this story would be half-told, unresolved. What is a story without resolution? It is simply chaos, a tale with no end and no beginning; in short, a life. I refuse to leave such a mess behind. I will have my literary reckoning. I insist on my right to sculpt the sands of my long life.

In those early weeks here, some days were worse than others. Some days the memories came but the words did not. Some days I could not write for crying.

As the present faded, the past became more real to me. As though I was being allowed to say a final goodbye, allowed to take a last long look at the stage before the curtain came down. I wrote like a woman possessed and I suppose that is what I will be soon. I will be possessed by another Lina, an emptier, quieter, perhaps even a happier one. I cannot call her my creation though. She is not the work of Brahma but of Shiva.

I need to move fast now, to write more than ever before and yet, for the first time in my life, the deadline is not motivating me the way it should. Or rather it is not motivation I lack but the means to turn that drive into typed pages. The words are there, lurking in the corners of the sun-filled lounge or up in the branches of the trees outside. I can see their silhouettes on the periphery of my vision. But they do not come willingly any more and it takes me so very long to catch them.

By the time you read this, the dementia will likely have taken over, flooding my brain with waves of confusion so that even on my best days, I will be constrained to hop anxiously between islands of lucidity. I know what is coming but finally I am ready. I have finished my story. This is the last letter and all the others have been placed in addressed and numbered envelopes so that my helper knows which one to send when. You will look now and you will see the tiny numbers written in red pen in the left-hand corner. Did you wonder why they were there? Maybe you thought it was to help you organise the letters. I wish that was why. It would have been a nice idea.

As I write this, it is the 12th of June. I cannot guess what date it is for you. Already our worlds have diverged. I'm on that parallel path, Diane, and there is another fork in the road, very soon. Today, it has taken me five hours to get these lines down. I can no longer use the typewriter. I simply cannot make sense of it. The positioning of the letters has no logic and I forget what I am supposed to do to make it work. It looks familiar and sometimes I remember to place my fingers on the keys but then, I wonder 'what next'? So I have had some help and this, my dear, is the last revelation.

Else is here with me. In fact, Else has been my companion now for several years, ever since she left Kenya in 1990. Her life was upended when a pick-up truck speeding from Meru to Nairobi with a cargo of the narcotic plant miraa hit a pothole, swerved across the two-lane road and slammed into Wilhelm's car. She buried him beside Stijn on the hill overlooking the waterhole. She tried to keep the farm going but she could not face down powerful rivals from Kenya's ruling elite, who knew they could force her out. When she left, she came to St Albans – her mother was already dead and the years she'd spent in Africa meant she had no other close family. Wilhelm's parents – ageing and isolated on a flat farm in Friesland – only met Else once and they had never understood their son's decision to live in Kenya. They didn't so much cut him out of their lives as simply forget about him. When she turned up on my doorstep, she said: "You are the only one now who knows who I was, who can talk to me about them all. I think we must stay together for a while."

She heaved her bag into the hall and after her came her beautiful son, Lucas, Stijn's grandson. He was seven then and today a long-limbed giraffe of a teenager sits outside the window here. He is on one of the loungers, reading *Under the Canopy*. I tried to warn him that it might not be his cup of tea but he just gave me one of the slow smiles that break his solemn face in two and reminds me so much of Stijn that I often have to turn away too brusquely. I am sure he thinks I'm very odd.

For the last seven years, I have, somewhat inexplicably, built a new life with this new family. I did not deserve the laughter, the shouts, the sound of glasses breaking, the thunderous feet on the stairs, the rows over the television and the squeals of delight. Else will surely continue living in my house in St Albans when I am gone. I wrote a will last year and left the house to her and Lucas. I think you will agree that she needs it more than any of us but she is uncomfortable with this. She says you will think that she deliberately usurped you. She insists on believing this despite having read these letters alongside you.

At first, this proofreading was just another chore I dumped on her. I begged her to do it because I was already worried that my mind might have wandered off while I was writing, without me noticing. But she says she has enjoyed the story. Enjoyed is not quite the right word. She has been gripped by it, by us. But despite this, she is still concerned about how you will react to the news that she and her son have become my family. After everything she has done for me, I think she should speak to you directly now.

So here is Else. She sits beside me at the typewriter, as she has done for weeks, turning my words into a story. I will let her talk and type for herself now. I will ask her to say the words out loud as I do. I like to hear the calm voice that has answered my querulous calls all these long months. She still has a slight accent but after all her years on the flower farm, it is more Kenyan than Dutch. She is blushing now. I should let her speak for herself.

Hello Diane, or Maria if you prefer,
I do not have much to say except to invite you to come and stay with us in St Albans whenever you want. You must bring your children. We would love to see them, Lucas and Lina and I.

I cannot imagine how you will feel to know that I have been living with your mother but please understand that there was no intention on my part to take your place. I did not even know you existed when I arrived. If I had known, maybe I would have stayed away but that is in the past and irrelevant. Lina gave me a refuge when I needed it. I was lost and she let me come into her home and she welcomed me and my son. Now, I hope I am helping her as she crosses into a new place.

When I found out that Lina had a daughter, I was shocked and pained for you and her. I did make judgments. Lina is smiling as I say this. She remembers my questions. They were

299

hard, maybe even harsh. I am a mother too, Diane, and I could not imagine giving up my son. But having read Lina's story, even typing some of it myself, I have more understanding. I would not say I can forgive what she did. It is not my place to forgive. All I know is that she loves you as much as is possible given the way your lives have been. You do not have to love her back, of course. You do not have to forgive her and you do not need me to tell you that. But as one mother to another on behalf of the woman who has been something of a mother to us both, I do wish you would come and see her and us. If nothing else, we could be friends, sisters of different mothers and different fathers. Lina will be different but then we are all, every day, different. I would like to meet you. I have loved Lina and she has loved me and she has loved you and beyond all else, that means something.

You are welcome whenever you would like.

Are you angry that I asked Else to speak directly to you, Diane? I was torn. I do not want to force you to come and see me but neither do I want my departure to burden you with guilt. If you would like to come, that would be wonderful. If not, know that I suspect I too would have stayed away if the boot were on the other foot. In a sense, I have left it too late anyway. You might wonder what is the point if I am no longer fully present. But I am trying so hard to be selfless here, Diane. You can imagine that it does not come easy to me. I want to do the right thing for you. I don't want to leave any marks on you when I go. I do believe, fervently, that you will like Else because how could you not? If I can gift you a friend with my passing, I will have done something right at last. I will have given you love, instead of grief, as the price of love.

In the end, and not to be too Pollyanna-like because it goes against my nature, but this death in life is very civilised. One gets a little time to prepare before the lights go out. And while saying goodbye is unbearable, the alternative is not much better. As silver linings go, it is imperfect but comforting nonetheless.

I am struggling a little now. It has been a long day and I am forgetting the things I wanted to tell you. What have I forgotten, Else? Nothing? Yes, I remember. I am writing to Diane. Diane is my daughter. I am Lina. This is France. Else makes me repeat these phrases whenever my mind starts to wander.

I am about to be reborn again. I suppose I should consider myself lucky. I get a reincarnation of sorts in this life. How many can say that? I will still be here, I will still be able to look out this window and enjoy the sparrows flapping and frolicking in the birdbath. I will sit on my chair at the end of the garden and listen to the waves whisper secrets to the sand. Then, when I go home to St Albans, I will wake in the morning and if I do not know quite where I am or who I am, I will pull back the curtains and watch the orange-red sun rise above the rooftops like a promise. To experience these things must surely be to remain human. I can be more than the sum of my memories, I hope.

I must confess I did have a different ending in mind when I first arrived here. I thought I might finally have the courage to join Robert, and my parents, and Penrose and all the others who did not have my luck, if you can call it that. The symmetry appealed to me: I could end it all here where it all began, near the beach where Robert landed and the town where he lost his soul. I imagined I might buy some pills and take a last walk into the countryside, wending my way along the lanes where their ghosts still roam, until I found a place where I too could sit and rest and cross over. I must admit that despite my avowed hatred of euphemistic words, I imagined this as a somewhat painless passing. In the end, you kept me here. You and Else and Lucas. And this story. Or perhaps it is just because I am, as I have always been, a coward. You may persist in that belief but it cannot be the whole truth because surely my continued existence is proof of some degree of courage, even if it is only the courage needed to do nothing? In the end, I have resolved to accept my punishment, to embrace my Fate, Diane.

***

I must sleep soon and then we will see what the morning brings. The dawning of a new era. I was being honest, Diane, when I said I did not need your forgiveness, even if I desire it deeply. It will be of no use to the woman I will be soon. She will not remember why. I did not write this to excuse my behaviour, her behaviour. I wrote it to record what happened so that when you decide you want to know, you will have this account.

So this is my story and your story and I give it to you out of love and with some regrets. There are always regrets. No one believes that French singer. Her name escapes me but you'll know who I mean.

I hope you'll always know now what I mean and what I meant. Even when I don't remember myself. I do regret that I will not be able to answer your questions, if you have any. This was not deliberate. I wasn't afraid of your judgment, I don't think. Now I will never know and that too must be accepted even if the thought hurts so much that I long for the coming oblivion because I simply cannot bear this uncertainty any more.

There is a pretty boy standing at the window. Else is waving him in. She whispers that he is Lucas. Of course, I know Lucas. I know Else. Diane is my daughter. I am Lina. This is France. I am staring at a new blank page.

Acknowledgements

My deepest thanks to Tom Chalmers, Lauren Parsons and the team at Legend Press for believing in me yet again. I am especially grateful to Lauren for her excellent editing and guidance.

As ever, thank you to my parents, Máirtín and Máire, for all their support and love. Thank you to Martina, Gearóidín, Máirtín, Esther, Máirín and Antaine for the craic and the kindness. Thank you to all my extended family and friends for their constant encouragement.

This book is dedicated to Lucy and Rachel, two wonderful young women who inspire me every day. Thank you, girls, for putting up again with a very distracted mother. And to David, without whom none of this would be possible.

COME VISIT US AT

WWW.LEGENDPRESS.CO.UK

FOLLOW US

@LEGEND_PRESS